PRAISE FOR UNCONVENTIONAL LOVE

"A beautiful collection that captures love in its purest, most rudimentary form."

—R Lynn Hanks
(Author of *Gamma Raids*)

"A beautiful representation of love in its many forms from parents and children to the families we forge for ourselves, this anthology expertly captures the depth and complexities of love."

— Amber Torro
(Author of *Umbra*)

"Unconventional Love is an exceptional collection of poetry and short stories that bring together a wide variety of characters and all the ways they love. Not only is it eye-opening to other's perspectives of love, but it's also comforting to know one isn't alone in the way they understand this often complicated and misunderstood emotion and state of being."

—Effie Joe Stock
(Author of *Son of the Prophet* and *Human Scars on Planet Skin*)

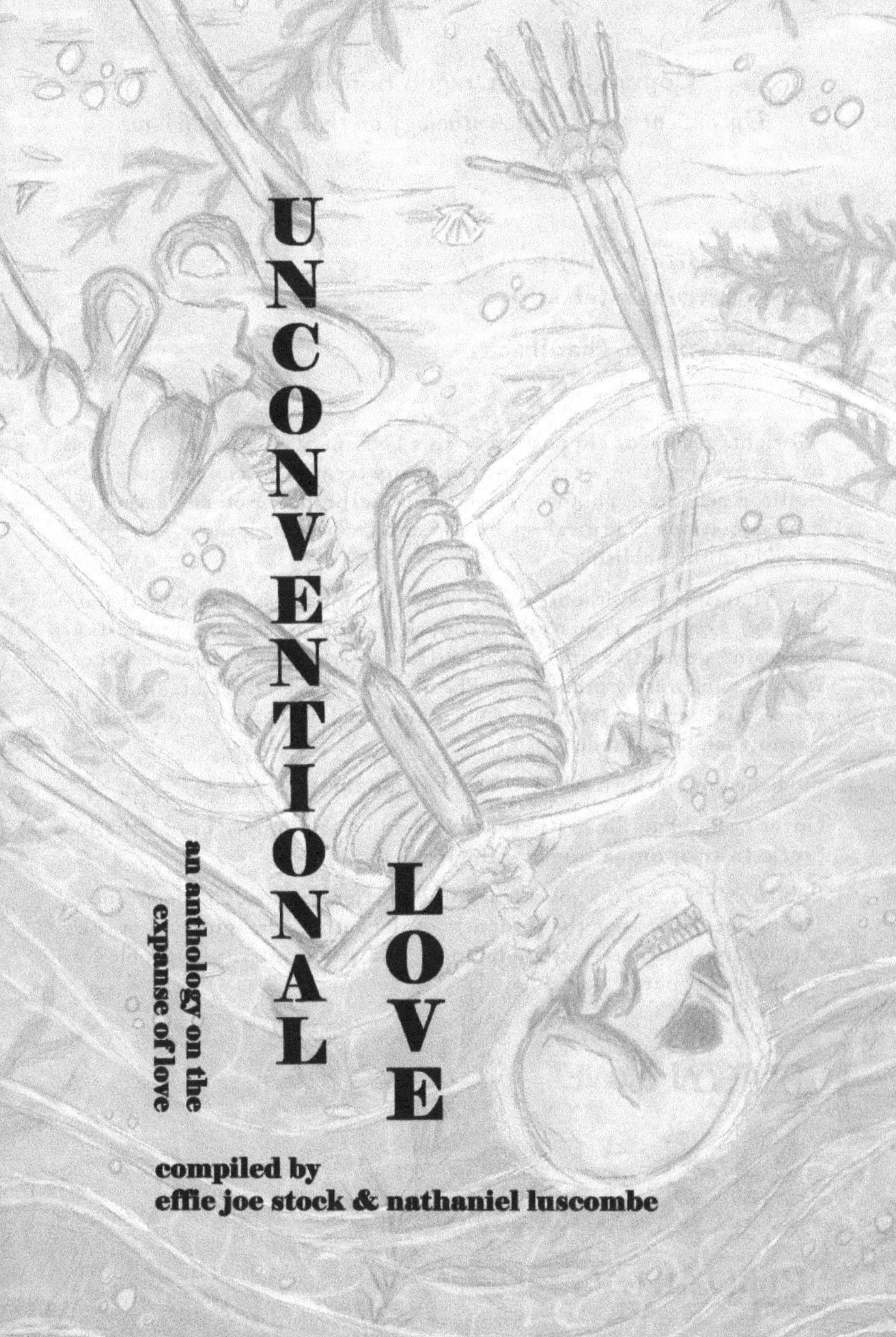

UNCONVENTIONAL
LOVE
an anthology on the
expanse of love
compiled by
effie joe stock & nathaniel luscombe

Copyright 2025 Dragon Bone Publishing
Unconventional Love: Anthology on the Expanse of Love

ISBN:

978-1-962337-23-6 (paperback)

978-1-962337-24-3 (ebook)

978-1-962337-25-0 (hardback)

Published in Hackett, AR, USA by Dragon Bone Publishing™ 2025.

Cover design and illustrations are created by and copyright of Effie Joe Stock. Interior formatting by Effie Joe Stock.

Publisher's Note: This novel is a work of fiction. Names, characters, places, and incidents are either products of the author's imagination or used fictitiously. All characters are fictional, and any similarity to people living or dead is purely coincidental.

To my mother who taught me so many ways to love,
And to the gentle souls I've met in the world
Who taught me all the rest.

TRIGGER WARNINGS:

Written in the Stars: Attempted SA, Homophobia
Nebulous: Mention of Suicide
Who You Could've Been: Implied Suicide
A Curse of Spines: SA, Suicidal Ideation

CONTENTS

Anthology on the Expanse of Love

UNCONVENTIONAL LOVE

Featuring Works By

Abigail Hawthorne / Abrigail Julian / Aisling Revell / Ava Lauren Grayson / Bethany H. Watson / Brett Salter / Cassandra Hamm / Charleigh Frederick / Darby S. Fisher / Effie Joe Stock / Honora Quinn / Jacob Kelley / Jenni Sauer / Jessica Erdmann / Jess Autiero / Judy Liu / June Elliott / K. Helmet / K. R. Yauger / Katie Fitzgerald / Kara Siert / Katherine Kempf / Kit Aldridge / Lexie Kauffman / Lorelei R. Jensen / Marion Cedar / Michaela Bush / Michelle Bulsiewicz / Myka Silber / Nathaniel Luscombe / R.C. Lloyd / Rhyker Dye / Seren J.H. Wolfe / Tristan Durant

PART ONE

Thicker than Water

/THE WOMAN YOU WERE / ARE / BECOMING /

Effie Joe Stock

Dedicated to the Greatest Woman I know

You **sounded like** Celtic Women, Enya, Andrea Bocelli / playing on CDs in a gifted stereo / CDs *you* bought at concerts / bought during the life *you* lived and the woman *you* were before *me* /

You smelled of chicken and dumplings, of sloppy joes, and chili and cornbread / drifting out from a kitchen not quite fully renovated / recipes *you* learned years ago from the life *you* lived and the people *you* knew before *me* /

You felt like butterfly kisses, and practiced fingers wrestling curls into **my** pin-straight hair / (remember that time *we* were going to the Nutcracker, and *you* dropped the iron on **my** eye?) / and gentle smacks the first time *you* asked if **I** wanted a "hurts donut" / silly little jokes, and skills, and dances *you* learned and picked up long before *you* knew **me** /

You overflowed with stories / of barrel racing, and sheep

showing, and tap dancing, and *your* dream of being an opera singer / stories *you* told **me** / to help **me** learn who *you* were before *you* met **me** /

I was a choice / *you* always made sure I knew / a dream *you* had of a little girl with curly dark hair / (it turned blonde so fast but that just meant **I** looked like *you* when *you* were that age) / but was giving up so much of *yourself* a choice? / did *you* know the sacrifices *you'd* make for **me**? / for **us**? /

One day it was *you* / the next it was **us** / one day *you* spoke of *your* own stories and dreams / the next, *you'd* given them up to make room and time to listen to **mine** instead /

Now **we're** deep long talks in a feed shed, and a silly slappy handshake **we** learned from a game **we've** never played / **we** smell like hay and essential oils / (neither of **us** like perfume much) / and wear matching crystals **we've** gather from little shops **we** ducked into to prolong the time **we** spent with each other /

We sound like old chick flicks during the day / (**I** still swear **we'll** go out like Thelma and Louise) / and wild Viking songs in the night / dancing around a fire / holding each **other's** hands / feeling each **other's** heartbeats /

We taste of greasy fast food fries / another excuse to spend more time **together** / (they're never quite salty enough for either of **us**) / or home-cooked meals **we** made **together** half-asleep and much too late in the night /

We're the embodiment of friends / family / soulmates / entwined by **our** souls / memories of **our** love stretching back eons / (do *you* think **we** love each other like this in every universe / life / timeline? / **I** believe **we** do) /

You are everything to **me** / am **I** everything to *you*? /

Twenty-two years have almost passed / eight thousand thirty days / each one spent chipping away little pieces of *you* / pieces sacrificed to make more and more of **me** / pieces **I** gathered to build **myself** from / hoping to evolve into even just a reflection of the woman **you** were / are / becoming /

Now **I** hope the time has come / for a little less of **me** / and a little more of *you* / for a day to dawn when *you* can find that woman again / the woman *you* were before *you* met **me** / so someday **I** can meet the incredible woman *you* were / are / becoming / who gave everything / time / music / belongings / love / to become the woman *you* are today / the woman **I** so proudly call / *Mother* /

THESE ROOTS WILL TEAR ME APART
Nathaniel Luscombe

i feel the need to put down roots
and plant myself in one place.
i've been aching to bloom,
to find my piece of earth
and cling to it.
though i'm still young,
i know what i want
just not where i'm meant to be.
i'm held in place by my family,
large and loud and loving.
i could never leave them behind,
but can i really stay here forever?
it's hard, not being rooted by location
but by the people around me.
i'm rooted in their hearts,
their souls, their very presence,
my roots stretching in every direction
as we all begin to drift.

i feel the need to put down more roots
because the ones i have
are likely to tear me apart.

BELYN BELOVED
Kara Siert

Maia had traded, bartered, and traveled to the ends of Queen Marguerite's kingdom in her quest to craft the perfect mobile. Dragonstone for strength, mermaid's tears for empathy, and fairy-glass for love, all dangling from a branch of delicately carved wood. A gnomish cradle, a blanket of elf's-spun wool, and birthing garments sewn by the finest artisans ... Maia had spent months preparing for the arrival of her son. But after he had come, and her body had healed, Maia realized nothing could have prepared her for this.

Beneath the ornate mobile, Belyn was screaming again. Perhaps he had been screaming for hours. His face had grown red, tears staining his fine silk clothing. At first, the sound had bothered her, but now Maia hardly heard him.

Chasing goblins from the kingdom's borders, slaying rabid beasts rampaging through villages, and defending the helpless from bandits ... Maia had done it all. She had worn the queen's badge on her tunic with pride—a blue heart shimmering on her breast—a sign she was a protector, a leader. But now, it seemed, she was nothing at all.

In the corner, Maia's shield rested against the wall, untouched. Out of habit, she had kept her sword and daggers sharpened, but they had not tasted blood in months. Her bow and arrow hung on the wall—her only companions as she had gazed into Belyn's cradle.

"He's alive!" the village physician had said. "That's what matters."

Yes, he was alive, and Maia thanked the gods every morning and evening. She had heard the wails of the bereaved when she arrived too late, when she was called to protect a village only to find monsters and bandits had found it first. Maia knew she was gods-blessed to have a child still living. Yet why did she not feel it?

After three moon cycles of the same empty feelings, Maia had ventured back to her mother's home. "Did you love me?" Maia asked. "When I was born."

"Love you?" her mother repeated. "I loved you when you came home from the queensguard with that great big sword upon your back, and I knew we'd eat that winter. I loved you then and not a moment sooner."

"But—" Maia began.

"Is this about the boy?" her mother asked. "Mai, what's love got to do with it? The boy can attend her majesty's academy. He'll have a good life. You can't make yourself love someone, so don't bother."

Belyn screamed loudly enough to pierce the fog in Maia's head. He was reaching for her, hands scrabbling at the air, yet she felt nothing except an urge to turn over in her bed and ignore him. *You're meant to love him,* Maia told herself. *You're his mother.*

She forced herself to rise, throwing off the blankets and walking barefoot across the stone floor. One of the maids had brought her goat's milk and a small pot with a spout. Maia cradled Belyn in her arms, watching him suck the jug empty.

"Hold him close to you," the midwife had said. "Let him look into your eyes." Surely when Belyn looked at Maia, he did not see love. He must see bloodshot eyes, mussed brown hair, and a scarred face but not love. The midwife had told Maia how to birth, feed, and swaddle him, but what use were any of those other matters when love, the most important part of all, was missing from her heart?

Thank the gods, Belyn had finally quieted. But Maia didn't even feel a sense of relief. She felt ... nothing. Nothing at all.

You can't make yourself love someone. But what if there was a way? What if Maia *could* make herself love Belyn?

There had been rumors of a woman in Oldtown. Earlier, when Maia had left her quarters and gone down to the dining hall, she'd heard some of the guardswomen murmuring. Perhaps they were only simple rumors, but Maia was not someone to sit about and wait.

Maia wrapped a piece of linen behind her back and around her shoulders. Then she held Belyn to her chest, enveloping him in blue fabric, and fastening him to her body. Maia had buckled her sheath, checked for hidden daggers, and slung her quiver and bow over her shoulder before realizing what she had done. She was not on duty, but arming herself felt as natural as pulling her unruly hair up into a bun, slipping into her woolen shift, or saying her evening prayers.

Maia made her way out of the barracks, through the courtyard, and into the humid summer air. She pulled up the hood of her cloak to shield her face from the sun and lost herself in the meandering streets until the crowds, houses, and merchants dwindled to rundown huts and unkempt dwellings.

Maia stopped at a small shack. Someone had splashed bright red paint across the faded exterior, marking the inhabitant as dangerous, and ripped away the door. Magic was not forbidden in Queen Marguerite's kingdom, but it was rare to find a true practitioner, and most were treated with suspicion. Maia hesitated for a moment; then she stooped and entered.

A small fire pit smoked away in the center of the room, and bunches of herbs and flowers hung from the ceiling. Between the many shelves of bottles and potions, Maia nearly missed the small woman stooped over in the corner.

"Well, you're a brave one," the witch said, blue eyes shining out from a wrinkled face. "Aren't you afraid I'll eat 'im?"

Maia shook her head. "I don't believe in the old superstitions."

The woman sniffed. "Well, what is it, girl? You wish to have another? Fertility potions, I have those a plenty." She gestured towards a shelf of labeled bottles. "A spoonful each day, and you'll be pregnant again within the year. Two spoonfuls for twins, three for triplets. Or perhaps you're looking for something to make you slimmer. I have those too–"

"No," Maia said. "I ... I need something else. Something to ... make me love him."

"Ah." The woman turned away. "I've got nothing of the sort, child. Pray to the gods, that's all I can say."

"Surely you have something," Maia said. She grappled with her coin purse, spilling gold tokens across the table. "Please. The midwife's no help nor the physician either. I'm desperate."

The woman shook her head. "Love potions are as mythical as witches who eat children, I'm 'fraid. Believe me, if I could grow affection in a bottle, I'd be rich. But I can't, and I'm not."

Rage coursed through Maia's veins, as hot as her campfire on a winter's night. "No!" she cried, slamming the table with her fist. The coins rattled onto the floor, and she met the witch's gaze with her own. "You know magic. You *must* help me."

The woman let out a dry laugh. "The magic is gone, girl. Witches haven't had it for centuries. Unless you can find a dragon, you're out of luck."

Belyn awoke, letting out a scream, his hands clenched into fists. Gods, there had to be *something* she could do. "A dragon?" Maia asked, hollering to be heard. She bounced Belyn as she'd been taught, but still she felt empty. "They exist?"

"O' course they do." A glint entered the witch's eye. "There's one up in Lost Forest, blue with white horns."

Maia frowned. Lost Forest was technically part of the queendom, but it was ill-explored and laden with bandits and beasts.

"It's said the last of the magic dwells there," the witch said, "but you'd be hard-pressed to find anything there without a map."

Ah. The witch only wished to sell her wares. Perhaps she was not a witch at all, only a woman who mixed herbs and told tales. There was no magic, no dragons, and certainly no map of Lost Forest. Maia gathered up her coins, feeling foolish.

"I'll give it to you," the witch said. "A gift for a gift."

"And I suppose you wish for coins," Maia said.

The witch laughed. "If I'd wanted gold, child, I would've sold you a potion."

"I have nothing else to offer," Maia said.

"Yes, you do." The witch pointed at Maia's quiver. "I want that."

"My arrows?" Maia glanced around the hut, searching for a bow. "Take my coin and buy yourself a quiver full. You don't need mine." She had trimmed and bound the arrows herself while Belyn had grown within her. They were *her* arrows, fine weapons—not to be traded away to a charlatan who would not even know how to use them.

"Your arrows and your quiver," the witch said, holding up a worn piece of leather. Maia could see faint drawings etched into the surface.

She's lying to you. There are no more dragons.

Yet Maia had heard rumors in her travels, crossing paths with beasthunters. Killing a dragon was forbidden, but occasionally a hunter might find tracks or sight one flying in the distance. Maia had thought those were little more than hearsay or tall tales ... But there were some who said the same about witches.

They're only arrows. You can make more. And your quiver ... it can be replaced.

"Let me see." Maia snatched the leather from the witch. Lost Forest had only been partially charted; in her mind, Maia compared this map to another she had seen. The landmarks, paths, and trees were as she remembered. At the end of the trail, she saw the symbol of a cave and a depiction of a sleeping dragon.

What am I doing? Surely this was a fool's quest. And yet she could not spend another day in her room, alone with Belyn and her own traitorous thoughts. "Fine." Maia pulled the quiver from her shoulder and laid it on the table. "But if this map leads me to nowhere ..." She glared at the witch.

The old woman made a shooing motion. "Go on with you."

Maia was accustomed to traveling by horseback, but usually she carried only her weapons. Now she felt like an itinerant merchant as she made her way through town gathering supplies. She had rented a donkey, and it plodded along beside her. Belyn was still wrapped under her cloak, and they had one last stop before departure.

Maia heard and smelled the goats long before their pens came into view. A small boy perched inside, fending off three animals who had cornered him. One seemed to have chewed through his tunic. "Hullo there!" the boy called and, seeing her queen's badge, offered a mock salute.

"I'd like to borrow a milk goat," Maia said. "I'll be traveling down to Lost Forest and back. I can pay now and then again upon my return."

"Lost Forest?" The boy's brow furrowed. "We've only three goats at the moment ... a bear took two the other night. And you're asking for the *whole* goat. That's ..." He began to count quietly under his breath. "... fifteen, sixteen jugs of milk a day we aren't selling. For who knows how many days." He raised an eyebrow. "*If* you return."

Maia bit back a curse. She was not about to be held up by a goat, of all things, and she was not in the mood to barter. "How much?" she asked.

"Ten tokens," the boy said.

"Ten!" Gods, the child was robbing her. "That's ridiculous, even for–"

"I'd be willing to trade for your bow," the boy said.

Maia reached back instinctively, touching the curved weapon. While not her first bow, this weapon had vanquished many foes. She remembered the day she had bought it, one of her first purchases as a queensguard.

"You're short of arrows anyway," the boy pointed out. "With your bow, I could take down the next bear that comes after my goats."

It's just a bow, Maia told herself. It was standard fare, not worth ten tokens; she'd only kept it out of foolish sentimentality. Every moment's delay was sunlight stolen from her journey. She handed him the bow, her fingers lingering over the yew wood for a moment. "You'd best shoot straight."

The boy offered another salute, accompanied by a smile that seemed too large for his face. "Go on with you, Miss! And see you bring my goat back in one piece."

The trees towered overhead, limbs reaching ever upwards in a constant struggle for sunlight. Moss and ivy hung across the branches like draped fabric while ferns and saplings found refuge beside fallen trunks. Maia even spotted a few suntrap flowers. Their blooms formed small glowing orbs, enticing any insects foolish enough to venture inside. She bent down and uprooted a few, placing them in the donkey's saddlebags. They would serve as additional light once she made camp.

When Maia stopped to feed Belyn, she swore there had

been two green eyes, peering at her through the underbrush. But when she blinked, the apparition disappeared. The fortnight of slow travel must've made her uneasy.

Courage, Maia. You have braved much worse than this. The map showed a cave, deep within the forest, surrounded by boulders and jagged rocks. *Once you find the dragon, all will be well.*

By the time Maia reached the river, watered her animals, and started a fire, her eyes were nearly closing. In the last light of dusk, she set up tripwires and a few small traps around her camp. Then she unpacked her bedding and blankets, laid Belyn beside her, and tried to sleep.

A snap of a twig, and Maia's hand had closed around her sword's hilt. Instinctively, she clutched Belyn to her chest. Her eyes studied the darkness around her, searching for any hint of movement. Nothing.

After several long minutes, Maia loosened her hold. She laid her sword nearby and forced her body to relax. Rest came for Belyn, but not for her. She stared at his tiny body nestled beside her own. *He trusts me, but he shouldn't.* Maia reached out a finger, touching the boy's arm. Nothing, still nothing.

As she packed up her camp the next morning, Maia spotted large pawprints in the underbrush. Three toes with long claws. She hoped to the gods that whatever animal had stalked her had no taste for human flesh.

The second day passed, a haze of tree trunks, soft leaves, and the constant buzz of insects. The heat clung to Maia's skin, and Belyn's body next to hers felt even warmer than usual. He screamed half of the afternoon before falling into an exhausted sleep. Every few hours, she stopped to milk the goat and feed Belyn; in a way, Maia mused, this was not so different from her life in the barracks.

During her pregnancy, Maia's work had been reduced to simple guard duty, everyday the same monotony, the same nothingness. When Maia had left to birth Belyn, her senior matron had suggested changing roles once more. "Transfer to the clerk's office," she'd said. "You're nearing thirty, Maia. Your days of adventuring would've come to an end sooner or later; settle down and raise the boy."

Maia couldn't imagine sitting at a cramped table every-day, filling out paperwork. Clerk duty was what happened to guardswomen who were injured or lived long enough to grow gray hairs. She'd be a queensguard in title only; there would be no need for her weapons or skills.

As night fell, the temperature dropped to an unbearable chill, and Maia was glad for Belyn's warmth against her. *What am I doing?* she wondered. Perhaps it would be best to pack up her goods, return to the city, fall asleep in her own bed, and forget about witches and dragons and love. In a few years, Belyn would be old enough to attend the academy; surely she could suffer a few years of clerk's duty and then return to adventuring. It was who she was; it was what she did best.

Maia's fingers wandered to her bare neck. Some women wore tokens, signs of affection from their lovers. Belyn's father had left her no necklace, only promises of a future that could never come to pass. His token had been the child she had been left to raise, a baby that did not even bear his like-ness. *How can I learn to love*, Maia wondered, *when I have never known love myself?*

"Excuse me, miss."

Maia jumped and turned towards the sound, one hand grasping her sword. "Stay back," she warned. But instead of a beast or a bandit, Maia saw only an elven child dressed in the simple robes of a priestess acolyte, her thin arms bare to the cold. Maia lowered her blade but did not release the hilt. "Who are you? Come closer."

The girl stepped into the firelight, sandals shuffling through the underbrush. "I–I saw your suntrap flowers; bandits don't use those. And then I noticed your Queen's badge and knew you could help me." She shivered. "I need something to make into firewood. I was given an ax"—the child held up a small hatchet—"but the tree branches are too high, up and the underbrush too wet to start a fire."

"I passed Skies Temple three days ago!" Maia cried. "Did you come all this way alone? Stay here for the night and warm yourself."

"Thank you," the girl said, "but I'm to spend the night in Lost Forest alone if we're to receive the dragon's blessings."

Maia bit back a sigh. Such a task seemed too dangerous for a child, but she held out a small bundle of kindling. "This should do."

The priestess bit her lip. "If it's not too much trouble ... I'm meant to chop it myself. With the ax. To signify strength." Her eyes flickered to the blue-and-white shield resting beside Maia's bedroll.

"You wish to chop up my queensguard shield to light a fire to the gods?" Maia asked. She thought, by saying the words aloud, the priestess might realize the foolishness of her request, but she simply nodded.

Maia noticed the goosebumps on the girl's arms. Her thin gown may've been embroidered with symbols, but it did little to protect her from the chill. It would be a dishonor to Maia's badge to leave a child to freeze, and she supposed there could be worse ways to destroy a shield. "Are you allowed a torch?" she asked. "It will make starting the fire much easier."

"There's no need," the girl said. "The gods will light my way just as they led me to you."

Maia handed the child her shield, and the girl tucked it under her arm, barely able to carry it. She grinned, the wide smile spreading across her entire face. "Gods be with you," she said, "and go on with you."

After her departure, Maia realized what the girl had said. The priestess had been seeking the *dragon's blessings*. Perhaps Maia was not the only soul in Lost Forest searching for a dragon. The thought made her feel less alone. She drifted off to sleep, holding Belyn a little closer.

According to the map, Maia should have reached the dragon's cave by now, but she saw no sign of boulders or any change in topography. The animals were all worn, and Maia felt the same. Only Belyn seemed unbothered, sleeping against her chest.

Give it one more day, Maia thought. *Then we'll all go home.* As she stopped to feed Belyn, Maia heard footsteps padding across the ground. But a hundred noises echoed throughout the forest, from beasts or her own imagination, so Maia paid little mind.

It was not until the sunlight caught a glint of metal peeking out from behind a tree that Maia whirled around. Two daggers flew from her belt, one slamming into the tree trunk and the other disappearing into the underbrush. Maia's fingers had closed on her sword hilt when she saw drawn bows all around her. A dozen faces met her gaze, unshaven and unwashed, with hard mouths and harder eyes.

Maia stifled a curse. Gods, she should've turned back long ago. To face twelve bandits alone, with her sword and shield, she could manage. But she was not only protecting herself. Belyn squirmed, as if sensing Maia's unease. *Breathe with me. In and out, in and out.*

Maia turned slowly, surveying her surroundings. She had no daggers left, no bow or arrows, and no shield. Thank the gods for her sword. "I mean you no harm," Maia said. "I seek the dragon of this forest. I've no quarrel with you."

A dwarf stepped forward, his bone-ax still drawn. "No quarrel and yet here you are, trespassing in our domain." Maia noticed leaves and vines threaded through his hair and beard. These were not bandits; they were forest folk who worshiped the trees. Perhaps they could be reasoned with.

"Take the donkey," a gnome ordered, "and the goat too. We'll have stew tonight."

"No!" Maia cried. "I seek the dragon's wisdom. I have harmed no tree here nor broken any branch."

"Perhaps we'll let you go, then," another forest dweller said. "But only if you promise to turn 'round and go back the way you've come."

The offer was better than Maia had hoped for, but still she hesitated.

"She's an outsider," another argued. "I say we take the animals and leave her."

"There's kindling on that donkey. How do we know it's not one of our trees?"

"Wait!" A human stepped forward, sheathing his sword. "Look at her chest. She's got a blue badge."

A few of the folk drew back. One lowered his bow.

"She's a queensguard. We've no fight with Marguerite."

"So long as she don't send her women here!"

"Didn't you hear? The girl's on a pilgrimage. She seeks the dragon!"

The man who had noticed Maia's badge raised a hand for silence. "Give us your sword, and you may pass. Blades are forbidden in the forest."

"My sword?" Maia's fingers tightened around the hilt. Her weapon had slept beside her since she had joined the guard. She knew how it felt, how it moved—it was part of her. To be without it ...

"An offering of metal to the trees," the man explained. "Or ..." He shrugged. "Keep your blade, and we'll escort you to the forest border."

Gods be blessed, she could go home! Her barracks, her life in the queensguard ... her room with the gnomish cradle, the spinning mobile ... the emptiness, the nothingness, her failure screaming at her from every wall. *You're meant to love him. You're his mother.* She had come so far. Could she truly turn back now?

"Will I find her?" Maia asked. "Will I find the dragon?"

"Not if you turn back," the forestman said. Something about his face seemed familiar, the crinkling at the corners of his eyes.

Maia glanced down at Belyn. He had quieted, but a fisted hand reached out for the unknown. He deserved this. He deserved a mother who could love him. He deserved more than her emptiness, her nothingness. She could not return to the queensguard until she repaired this. Until she repaired herself.

Maia held out her sword.

The man took it gently from her as if it were his friend, too. "Go on with you," he said. "The dragon is up ahead."

It felt wrong, walking without her sword. Her body seemed strangely light, as if she were missing an appendage. Her quiver no longer rustled on her back, and she could not feel the assurance of hidden daggers pressed against her leg and side. Instead, there was only Belyn. He stirred, letting out the tiniest squeak. Maia laid a hand on his head, touching his soft hair.

As she passed through the circle of forest folk, the trees seemed to fall away. Instead, rocks and boulders led to a cave with a wide mouth. The air felt dry instead of humid, and the forest floor became sand, crunching beneath her boots.

Maia crept forward. How did one approach a dragon? Priestesses knelt to worship the gods, and forest folk danced to praise the trees. But no one had ever taught Maia how to greet a dragon.

"Hello?" she called out. Her voice echoed through the cave, bouncing against the emptiness. "I ... I come seeking your wisdom, O great dragon." She bowed quickly.

Nothing moved at first, and Maia wondered if she were speaking to no one. Then two green eyes blinked at her through the darkness, and Maia caught a glimpse of pearl white and dull blue. A long, scaled muzzle and a reptilian foot with three toes emerged from the shadows.

"Well, you're a brave one," a soft voice said. The dragon's tones sent vibrations through the ground. "What have you to offer me, child?"

"I—" Maia looked around her. She doubted the dragon would want her paltry coin, borrowed milk goat, or worn horse.

"Never mind that," the dragon said. A claw reached out, curved talons moving towards Maia's chest.

At first, she thought the dragon meant to snatch Belyn, and she closed her arms around him and pulled away. But instead, the dragon's claws snagged on Maia's blue badge, the fabric she had worn into battle, the symbol that had saved her from the forest folk, and the sign of everything she was ... a protector, a leader—compassionate, brave, and strong. The dragon took everything Maia was and pulled it away, threads ripping and snapping, the blue badge gone in an instant.

"This will do," the dragon said. "May I have this?"

"I—" Maia choked on the words. She was a queensguard. Without her badge, who was she?

"Will you teach me?" Maia asked. "Can you tell me the secret? I want to love him. More ... more than anything." More than bow and arrows, her shield, her daggers, her sword, her badge ... More than being Maia of the Queensguard, she simply wished to love him. She would become Maia the Clerk and sit at a desk writing scrolls for the rest of her life if it meant she could love him. Anything to replace the empty nothingness in her chest with the ability to feel again. With the ability to love.

The dragon laughed.

The sound sent tremors through the ground, and Belyn awoke. He let out a loud cry, tears pooling in his eyes. Maia tried to quiet him, bouncing him with gentle movements. *Belyn, please ... it's all right.*

"Silly girl," the dragon said. But it was not the voice of the forest dragon any longer but the withered voice of a witch. Maia looked up to see the old woman in front of her, laughing, her eyes crinkling in the corners.

"You!" Maia cried. "What have you done? Where's the dragon?"

"Silly girl," the witch said again. "Didn't I tell you there's no potion for love?"

Maia felt rage bubbling up in her stomach. She had not traveled through Lost Forest and traded away all of her weapons to be mocked by a witch. "What have you done with the dragon? Give her back!"

"A mother is someone who leads," the witch said, "who finds a way when others find none." Before Maia could reply, the witch's face was replaced by the wide smile and laughing eyes of the goat boy.

"A mother is someone who protects," he said. "I wished to keep my goats safe from harm. You wish to keep Belyn safe."

"How did you—" Maia stopped short as the boy's wide smile turned into that of the priestess, and the girl stood before her now, a small campfire burning beside her.

"A mother is compassionate," she said. "You gave me your shield so I could be warm. May the gods reward you."

The crinkled eyes of the witch returned, but instead of the old woman, Maia saw the forestman who had taken her sword. "A mother is brave," he said. "You faced us with courage and did not turn back when given the chance."

Then the dragon stood before Maia, her green eyes bright

with laughter and her mouth stretching into what Maia could only describe as a wide smile. "Silly girl," the dragon said. "You do not need to learn *how* to love. You already know."

"But—" Maia frowned.

"You did not need to prove your love to me," the dragon said. "You needed to prove it to *yourself*." She smiled, and in that moment Maia saw the witch, goat boy, priestess, and forestman all in one. "I have lived many lives," the dragon said. "I am the stars burning in the sky, and I am the peasant boy watching his goats. I am the trees the forestmen praise, and I am the simple witch selling her wares. I am the gods of the earth, and I am the lowly priestess who worships them."

The scenery faded around them, the sand beneath Maia's feet becoming an earthy forest floor. "I can be anyone I wish, and yet I always return to this." The dragon moved aside, and in the back of the cave, Maia caught a glimpse of two eggs. "Of the thousand lives I've lived and roles I've claimed, being a mother is the one I always return to." The dragon turned towards her nest, her blue tail flicking in the darkness. "Now," she said, "go on with you."

As Maia made her way back through the trees, she felt Belyn squirming against her chest. They had many days' journey ahead of them, and Maia was tempted to push forward. Instead, she stopped, set the animals loose to graze, and sat down on a fallen tree. These moments with Belyn would be short. Her travels could wait.

The sunlight filtered through the branches above, and the insects sang their evening melodies. Maia unwrapped the blanket and nestled Belyn into the crook of her arm. His dark eyes blinked up at her, and as she looked down at him, Maia noticed the gentle curls in his hair, the flush in his soft cheeks, and the way his tiny fingers reached for hers.

"Hello," she whispered. "I'm Maia ... your mother."

FATHERS AND DAUGHTER
Jenni Sauer

Soulmates aren't just for lovers
Twin flames/missing halves
Two sides of the same coin
Can come in so many forms
Friends/ allies /rivals /enemies

Or sometimes they're the way
A daughter is born to challenge her father
In ways her mother never could
No one butts heads with a man
Quite like a daughter finding her voice

OF DAWN
Katherine Kempf

As if navigation wasn't hard enough, she had the weather to deal with now, too.

Ice crusted her eyelashes. Her eyes were the only part of her face exposed as she leaned into the wind roaring across the tundra. She knew she should be grateful the storm would cover her tracks, but it made blinking hurt. She was an anthropologist, for *Zorya's* sake. She was supposed to still be in St. Petersburg, or at the very least, Svalbard, preparing humanity for what was coming. But the *Ásatrúar* – the true believers – had seen to that.

She focused on the compass, trying to hold it steady as tears leaked from her eyes, freezing on her cheeks mid fall. Her friends had, at least, tried to prepare her. But how does someone who spent their life hunched over books in dusty lecture halls prepare to survive in a frozen wasteland on their own? She was almost grateful for the internment camps and the lessons they'd taught her. She pocketed the compass and shoved her gloved hands into her armpits for warmth.

Under different circumstances, it would have been harder to ignore the grumbling in her belly or the ache of her muscles, but she'd been at the camps long enough that neither of those bothered her as much as the dropping temperature.

She distracted herself with what she knew to be true; that she was currently trudging through a tame prelude to the ice age the next generations would inherit. That Nina would not remember the face of her own mother. That by this time to-morrow, she would either be dead or free.

It would only waste precious warmth to adjust her parka, so she simply pursed her parched lips under the snow-encrusted face wrap and trudged onwards, orienting herself to the iced-over tributary on her right that she was supposed to follow to its source. That's what he'd said: that the *izba* would be at the spring.

As the grey of the snowstorm faded to the black of night, she heard the howling of a wolf harmonize with the icy trickle of the water. The running water was a good sign. It meant she was close to her quarry.

Sure enough, two dozen hopeful steps later she could make out the swinging glow of a lantern hung in a distant window. A singular light penetrating the tempestuous night.

Her heart pounded with the promise of a fire and hot meal, pushing new blood into her tired legs. She stumbled in her haste and caught herself on a snowbank, gloves pressing handprints into the snow. Nothing to worry about, the wind and snow would take care of it. Her scent was another matter entirely. A wolf howled, again. Closer, this time.

She pushed up, wading through the snow until she made it to the steps. Her legs gave out at the top. Sinking to her knees, she lifted a fist and pounded on the wooden door. She leaned her cheek against the weathered wood and tried again, pounding over and over as she caught her breath.

Abruptly, the door opened and she tumbled into the

house.

"*Mokosh,* protect us!" A woman's voice swore to the earth-mother, but a bearded man's face stared down at her. "Shut the door, Yuri!" the woman's voice spoke again over the ferocious clacking of knitting needles. The man obeyed the command, pushing it closed with great force against the wind.

Yelena pulled back her face covering and pushed the icy hood from her head, copper curls spilling out, the faintest streaks of white starting to glimmer in her hair. She was still self-conscious about that. Late as it had begun for her in life, it had started in the camps. And Nina would see.

Yuri offered her a muscled, leather-worn hand. She accepted.

"What's your name?" he asked, stroking his beard with one hand and pulling her to her feet with the other.

"Yelena," she replied and felt how coarse her voice was. She cleared her throat and tried again. "Yelena," she said again, this time stronger.

"Nice to meet you," Yuri replied, his weathered face smiling. "This is Oksana." He said. The knitting needles clicked harder.

"Don't tell her our names!" the woman hissed.

"You already told her mine, Ksenia." Yuri's voice was soft and Oksana scowled. "My wife," Yuri added.

"Nice to meet you both." Yelena tried to sound stronger than she felt as she peeled back her frozen layers. Yuri took them from her arms and hung them by the fire to dry. "Dmitri said I won't have long here, before I have to move on."

He nodded and Oksana's needles clicked impatiently. "Even less, thanks to the storm," the gruff man admitted.

"But enough time to rest."

"And he'll be there to meet me?"

"They should all be there, as far as I know," Yuri replied.

"All?" Her nerves shot through her stomach. "At the Research Center?" She bit her lip, hardly willing to believe it. Yuri nodded again and moved towards the fire, to a pot of simmering soup.

"Something hot to eat while you warm up?" he asked and Yelena's stomach growled.

"Yes, please." She replied sheepishly. He ladled a meager portion into a small, hand-carved bowl.

She was prepared to curl up like a cat by the fire, but Yuri went to the table, pulled a chair out and patted a sheep hide draped over the back.

"Thank you." She sat down and he handed her the bowl. Oksana's needles were clicking so fast she could start a second fire.

"Don't mind her. She's just wary of the danger that comes with, you know, helping people escape." He pulled an unmarked bottle out from an ornately carved cabinet. Yelena bit her lip, guilt settling in her throat like a knot.

"Do you do it often?" she asked, nerves still tight on her jugular. Yuri shrugged.

"Every few months or so, when they manage to get someone else out from the camps."

"Always someone important." Oksana added, with a critical eyebrow raised.

"Ksenia wouldn't have it any other way." He talked over his wife, giving Yelena a smile that tried to be reassuring. He set a glass down on the table and yanked the top off the vodka bottle with a pop.

"There is more danger in complacency than in helping," Yuri assured her.

"Would you like some?" He gestured to the drink and Yelena shook her head. Oksana's bristle settled into concentration on her knitting project.

"How do you know Dmitri?" Yelena asked, blowing gently on the soup.

"I never met him in person." He downed his vodka in one gulp, then crossed the room in a few strides to where the legs of a table stuck out underneath a cloth. Yelena sipped her soup. The broth was thin and the meat stringy, but it was delicious. Pulling the cloth back, Yuri revealed a machine made up of knobs and dials, a tarnished metal bar hovering in the air.

She wished she could go back in time to a moment when she didn't know what the machine was. To before the *tap tap tapping*. To those midsummer nights in St. Petersburg. Long days at the university and an evening cigarette hanging off her lips as the southern wind swept in through the French doors, opened to the square below. Nina, asleep beside her on the sofa. The little fingers curling tight around her own. The music warbling from the old record player she'd owned.

That was before they'd seized it, along with her record collection and all her other possessions. Her identification, her passport, her bank account. Seized, never to be returned. Ousted her from her tenure at the university. Locked her out of the Eos database. Wiped from memory. As if she'd never existed at all. More *Ásatrúar* orders, she was sure.

And with Nina gone, soon it really would be as if she never had existed in the *Rodina*—her Motherland. She swallowed another mouthful of thin soup.

"What is it?" Yelena asked, knowing the answer, but not wanting to give herself away. Yuri ran a finger daintily over the machine.

"A way to communicate. From another time." She nodded. It was better, if the two of them were captured, that Eos didn't know how much Yelena really knew. How much she had accounted for, planned for.

"And that's how you and Dmitri..." she trailed off.

"Yes. It's how we coordinate."

Yelena nodded.

"When was the last time you heard from him?" She ran her tongue over her lips, tasting the last of the soup on them.

"Today," he replied, self-assured, but intentionally vague. She felt the nerves returning. Yuri stroked his greyshot beard. Would Dmitri have a beard by now? And Nina would be there? She couldn't believe it.

Her soup bowl emptied, she felt her exhausted eyelids give into the warmth of the fire and droop. Yuri slipped the bowl from her hands just in time.

She awoke to the sound of faint tapping from across the room. Oksana was still seated in her chair, but her needles were still. She watched Yuri at the desk, lips pursed.

With bleary eyes, Yelena looked too, as Yuri recorded the incoming message. When the tapping finished, he leaned back in his chair and dropped his gaze to the paper, running a hand through his beard. After a measured exhale, he spoke.

"Time's up," he grimaced.

"What do you mean?" She sat up straighter, rubbing her eyes.

"It means that the storm didn't cover your tracks. Or else the dogs caught your scent. Either way, the KGC found your trail. They are on the way here, now."

"The KGC?" Yelena gasped, and shot up, Her back ached at the memories of the whip against her flesh, the scorch marks on her legs. How long had she been in the cell before they strung her up outside and let the ice crystalize over the open flesh? She scrambled for her clothes, dry and warmed by the fire. But Oksana was on her feet too, knitting needles clattering to the floor as her hands shook.

"Here?" she asked and Yuri hung his head. "What do we do?" her voice quavering.

"Shh, Ksenia," he cooed at his wife, walking over to her in huge strides and catching her in an embrace. "I will not let them harm you." Soothed, Oksana wheeled on Yelena.

"Who are you?" The woman demanded, her full strength drawn into an imposing posture. "Who are you, that the KGC would come all this way for you? What makes you so special?"

"I'm nobody," Yelena insisted, knowing that it wasn't the truth. Not even close. Eos might be a secret project with a secret purpose, but it was nothing if not important.

However, the truth would not help them if the secret police were on their way.

Yelena shoved her arms into her coat, coiled the scarf around her neck, squashed the hat onto her head, and rammed her feet into the fur-lined boots. All before Oksana had made it across the room to close her hands around Yelena's throat, pinning her against the wall of the *izba*. Yelena's head buzzed as she made contact with the hardwood and behind Oksana's shape a shock of curls, bright like a flash of sunset across an autumn sky, streaked. A laugh like church bells echoed in the cabin.

"Nina," Yelena breathed, reaching for the red-haired girl.

"Get. Out," the woman spat in Yelena's face and dropped her to the ground. She crumpled into her furs, gasping for air.

"Ksenia!" Yuri was beside his wife, an apologetic look in his weary eyes, but he didn't try to restrain the woman. "The damage is already done, wife. Move the machine into the cellar, then you get in after it. Close the door and no matter what you hear, don't open it," he commanded. Then, he turned to Yelena.

"Come," he said and she rose, warily watching Oksana move a corner of the carpet to reveal a hidden cellar. Yuri made for the door.

Yelena zipped her parka and wiggled her hands into her gloves. Yuri placed a weathered hand on the door handle.

"There are snowshoes hanging outside. Follow the tree line until you reach a cave. Don't stop to shelter or build a fire; they'll see the smoke." He thrust a small package smelling of dried meat and a canister of what she hoped was water into her hands. "Ration yourself. It will be hard to navigate in this weather. You may be longer than usual." Yelena nodded.

"Due north of the cave is a stream crossing. Stones set across it. Once you're on the other side, follow the river out of the valley. At the edge of the valley are the mires, with wooden bridges marking the path. If you've gone longer than half an hour without crossing a bridge, you're off the trail."

She scrambled to keep the directions straight. What were mires? Yuri plunged onwards, "The dawn will rise over your right shoulder. Follow her ascent to the border."

"And then?"

"Dmitri will be waiting for you."

"The Research Center?" she asked again and he nodded.

"Last we heard it was in the hands of the Finns, so you should be safe for the night at the Center, ready to move again once you're rested. Don't stop until you get to the Center or we're all dead." He didn't just mean Oksana and himself. He meant Dmitri. He meant her friends still imprisoned in the camps. He meant the entire network of people who had helped to get her out. His grey eyes pleaded with her, and then he opened the door, and winter howled back.

From the cave, through the snowstorm, she could see the lights flashing in the windows while the KGC searched the cabin. She'd been told not to linger, but she couldn't help looking back. It had always been her problem. Always her mind on the future. Never in the present. And it had nearly cost her Nina. It still might. Dawn was going to break in the next few hours, and if she intended to live, she needed to go, now. She took a swing from the canister and coughed. Definitely not water.

As she turned towards the path, a shot rang out, rising above the torrential winds. Her heart slammed against her ribcage, her eyes squeezed shut. In her mind, she could see Yuri's blood crawling across the floor of the cabin, soaking into the carpet and dripping through the hidden floorboards onto his wife's face.

She turned, Yuri's words echoing in her ears about lingering, just in time to see the *izba* ignite. Quickly—too quickly—it was engulfed in flames from all sides. Somewhere, a wolf howled.

The sun had risen and was sinking again by the time she learned what mires were: expansive, windswept, frozen marsh. She was out of food. Out of vodka. The storm had given way to a sunset of brilliant gold, a green-blue tinting the edges that should have taken her breath away.

But Yelena had spent too many years working for Eos to ignore that a sunset in that brilliant color meant their doom was nearer than they knew. That was the reason she had to make it. Even if her daughter never forgave her for choosing work over her own child, she needed to get to Nina and warn her. Because Nina would look at that sunset and see only beauty. Nina didn't know. Yelena had never told her.

How many nights had she wasted, buried in data and observations or on calls with the other Eos scientists? Infant Nina had clung to her breast, content to nurse, buttery skin smelling of roses and wood smoke—warm against her mother—fingering the *Zorya* pendant around Yelena's throat, while she worked into the darkest hours of the night. Then, when Nina was older, curled under the desk with a book pressed to her freckled nose, the pendant around her own neck—a glint of gold catching the unnatural light of the dying world and casting it against the office walls. A precious memory that now soured at how naïve Yelena had been. How much more important her work had been than Nina, when, in truth, she could have been preparing her daughter, educating her on how to survive if things didn't go according to plan.

But back then she'd been so sure of the plan. So sure the radicals would be quelled and the *Ásatrúar* could be controlled.

The sunset passed into night. The howling became more frequent. The wolves had followed her the entire way from the *izba*, catching her scent even after stopping in the day to rest. It was probably the stink of her fear they followed.

As she stumbled across the labyrinth of mires, testing each step for uneven peat, more howls tore into the night. She jumped in her skin, her reindeer-hide boot catching the edge of the icy bridge, slipping. Her boots were thanks to a Sámi friend at the camps, who wasn't only an academic radical, but also had useful survival skills. However, the snowshoes made navigating the bridges cumbersome and slow. And the unusually militant wolves were only waiting for her to slip up.

Above, the sky danced with purples and greens that tiptoed in and out of the atmosphere. It reminded her of trips to Svalbard. It had been beautiful to her back then, but now it was just another sign of Earth's impending finale—that they were so bright and so visible to the naked eye. In the light that the aurora borealis cast across the snowy marsh, she watched for slinking shadows and glowing, yellow eyes.

Righting herself, she steadied her heartbeat and shuffled across the makeshift bridge, frost spiderwebbing the aged, wooden planks in her clunky snowshoes.

This was not what she'd thought she'd be doing when she'd donned her professorial colors for the first time, sashed in velvet. Walked the stage to join the other professors. Nor was it what she thought she'd be doing when she founded Eos. Her exhale turned to smoke in the air, the nighttime temperature so dangerously low she felt herself growing sluggish. The borealis reflected across the ice, and she thought she caught glints of bright orange hair in the reflections.

In fact, there was hair illuminated by the dancing sky above, but Yelena's stomach turned, her thoughts crystalizing clear again as she registered the bodies of Rus and Finn in various stages of frozen decomposition.

Among the relics of war frozen in the marsh were discarded artillery and shells, and what, from far-off, still managed to look like a half-sunk line of long-rusted tanks, run into the collapsed peat.

And a trail of machines and bodies could only mean one thing. That she was nearing the long-contested border. That she was finally nearing the Research Center.

Reaching the other side of the bridge, she took a tentative step down before another howl lifted into the night air. She fixed her gaze on what rose into a hill beyond the mires. She moved quickly, her mind sharpened by the promise of Nina, safe from the howling and the cold, as she hopped from patch to patch of frozen grass. On her final leap, she caught her foot and felt a pop as her ankle caved in, the snowshoe snapping.

"*Der'mo!*" she swore with a gasp, and the rest of her body collapsed atop the unbalanced leg, half in the snow and peat, half clinging to solid ground as she ripped the broken snowshoes from her boots. A heft of panting over her shoulder made her twist her neck around.

Two glittering, yellow eyes sat upon an open smile of teeth, the wolf's tongue hanging out, comically to the side.

The wolf tilted her head as her breaths came out in clouds of silver smoke, almost as though she hadn't decided if she wanted to eat Yelena, yet. She took a step forward, her nails tapping on the wooden board. Yelena went to pull herself up, and the wolf let out a little whine.

"Don't worry, your meal isn't fast enough to run away from you," she joked grimly. But a groan behind the wolf got both of their attentions.

Bloodied face bloated from the cold, a body moved and groaned, a second time. The snow crumbled around him, only recently fallen, it seemed. With a wistful look at her, the wolf lifted her nose to the sky and let out a long, sonorous howl.

Panic set in as Yelena saw innumerable glinting eyes descending from the corners of the marsh, noses to the ground in search of fresh, warm blood. Her blood pounded in her ears, throbbed in her ankle. And she made the choice: she would not die here. Not when she was so close.

Yelena tossed aside the snowshoes, yanked herself up and turned to face the hill, hobbling up as fast as her broken stride would carry her. She tried to ignore the growls behind her, the nipping at her heels and she reached for the winds, grasping at handfuls of snow. A scream penetrated the stillness of the dancing, green-dark marshlands below. She ignored it, letting the adrenaline carry the weight in her ankle, boots heavy with ice and snow as she scrambled toward the summit.

Only when she had reached the top did she turn and catch the glimmer of the wolves, bloodied teeth in the light, ripping muscle from bone as the man let out a final shriek at being eaten alive. It wasn't as loud as she would have expected.

Maybe it wasn't so bad. .... Maybe his limbs were already so frostbitten from hours in the mires, it didn't hurt so much.

The wolf who had been following her looked up, ears twitching. Her nose lifted, and Yelena followed the direction. A split second later, she heard the hum of an engine.

"Yelena!" Dmitri's voice cut over the roaring of an engine, and she whipped around in time for the onslaught of snow-spray as a snowmobile slid to a halt in front of her.

"Dmitri?"

The man pulled down his face mask, his crooked smile and dark eyes alight under the northern lights. She hadn't seen him in nearly ten years, but she would know that gregarious face anywhere. Even with the thick beard.

"Get on," Dmitri instructed and he reached out a hand to help her up. She swung a leg up just as a shot rang out in the air.

"What's going on?" she shouted, with a glance back at the wolves. She wrapped her arms tight around his middle, bracing her hands against one another.

"No time to explain!" Dmitri shouted back, and another gunshot fired. Snow kicked up as she realized the bullets weren't aimed at the wolves. They were aimed at them. Dmitri cranked the engine, and with a wild abandon that almost overturned the snow mobile, they ricocheted off, ping-ponging between snow drifts.

She watched the Research Center come and go, little flickers of light sparking from the towers before the sound of gunshots would reach her ears. It dawned on her that Yuri's information hadn't been good. If she was being shot at, the Rus had taken back the Center.

And whatever had happened here, had happened recently

and it had happened fast. There were bodies strewn in the snow, blood and entrails making pretty little designs the wolves would soon dine on.

Dmitri weaved through the aftermath of the skirmish. Yelena squeezed her eyes shut and clung to him as though it were the time he had taken her and a toddler Nina on holiday, skirting lazy corners of Old Rome's dilapidated streets on the back of his motorbike. The gunshots could be fireworks under the colors of a winking sky. Back when there were such things as holidays and fireworks.

Eventually, she opened her eyes again. They sped until the snow was virgin white powder with the twinkle of a Russian winter. No dead bodies. No signs of struggle. The gunfire ceased, and it was quiet across the tundra, but for the purr of their motor. The snow mobile slowed beneath her and Dmitri turned his head, voice raised slightly over the whine of the engine.

"I'm sorry I couldn't get a message in time," he said, and she squeezed him tightly in response. "It all happened so fast," he added.

"It wouldn't have made a difference," Yelena told him, sadly. "Yuri is dead." Dmitri let out a defeated sigh.

"May he find in death what he searched for in life." It was the only eulogy Yuri would ever get.

"He was good to me."

"He was good to many." Dmitri's jaw flexed. "That's what made him different." There was a pause as Yelena summoned the courage to ask her question.

"Is Nina alright? Did she make it out before the fighting?" A smile twitched in the corners of Dmitri's mustached mouth.

"She's perfectly healthy," he said with a weight in his voice she didn't understand. "She, well, she had a reason to evacuate early, so she was safe long before the Rus got here," he continued. "She's waiting for you at the front line."

"Will she recognize me?" Yelena wondered, and Dmitri answered before she realized she had spoken out loud.

"You should ask yourself if you will recognize her."

"Ten years is a long time," Yelena confessed and bit her lower lip while Dmitri hummed in agreement.

They were silent for a long while, just the thrum of the engine and the northern lights dancing above them until the sun began to cut into the night and whisk away the darkness, one gentle ray at a time. It wasn't the crass, bright colors the sunset had been. This was a soft, pink glow. Something like the pink of a ruby running along the horizon line that cut across the boreal skyline.

As they crested a hill, into the safety of the Finnish line of defense, Yelena saw the flash of red hair, bobbing towards the snow mobile. A man followed in her wake, and Nina glanced back at him, her cheeks crimson in the cold air as she smiled, far wider than Yelena had been expecting.

Yelena clumsily dismounted, tripping in the sun-touched snow as it caved beneath her boots. She rushed to Nina.

They reached each other, both of their hoods fallen back, face coverings blown loose, red hair tangling and red cheeks stinging in the wind. They wrapped their arms around one another, and Yelena felt the wetness of her daughter's cheek against hers, tasted the salt water in the corners of her own mouth. Then, Nina took her mother's face in her hands and pressed their foreheads together, closing her eyes. Yelena's heart thudded. Nina smelled of roses and wood-smoke. She lifted her hands to her daughter's face, feeling the heat of her under her hands.

All those years in the camps. How many times, while in the depths of starvation or as they'd dragged her, delicious from the whipping yards, had she seen Nina skirting around the corner of a building? How many times had she dreamed of her daughter only to wake to the ache of the barracks? But now, Nina was real.

"Mama," Nina breathed, and Yelena felt the air leave her lungs, an unbidden crumple of emotion filling in her at the word.

"Nina." Yelena could hardly dare say it for fear the woman in front of her would dissolve into the frosty air.

By now the man had caught up to her. His cheeks were full and rosy in the morning light, a shock of dark hair pushing out from under the true-blue hat on his head, flaps lined with reindeer fur turned up, leather strings dangling. His eyes sparked and the smile on his face was kind. Nina broke free.

"Mama, this is Biejan." Her hand never leaving Yelena, Nina leaned into him, her voice was strong, true. She was sure of herself to everyone, but those who truly knew her.

And even after the years apart, Yelena could hear the uncertainty underlining it. Even after all these years, defiant, independent Nina wanted her mother's approval for the man who stood beside her. Yelena smiled so wide it threatened to turn into a chuckle at the normalcy of the moment. The innocence.

Before she could reply, Biejan produced a small bundle from the fold of his coat, wrapped tightly in reindeer fur, straps fastened with care, to leave an opening at the top where a pink-faced baby gurgled, deep red hair curling at her temples.

For the second time, Yelena's breath left her chest. Understanding flushed her cheeks and flooded her limbs as they moved forward toward the baby without meaning too, but also without hesitation.

"What?" Yelena breathed.

"Her name is Petra," Nina said and bit her lip, exactly as Yelena had done. And Yelena knew Nina had chosen the Greek name on purpose. How often she'd heard the mythos of Eos from her nest beneath the desk. She couldn't help the reflex. She bit her lip too.

"Her?" she asked after a nervous moment, and Nina nodded. The baby fiddled with something and Yelena chanced a step closer.

"Go on." Nina nodded to her mother. Biejan eased the baby into her arms. She lifted her hand to Petra, who wrapped her impossibly tiny fist around her baba's pointer finger. Yelena bent to kiss her forehead, nostrils filling with roses and wood-smoke.

Then she saw the pendant in her granddaughter's hand. Eos. *Zorya*. Of Dusk, Midnight and Dawn.

FROM SUPPER TO PROMISE
Jessica Erdmann

At fourteen, Yvellios was sure and serious about one thing: he would absolutely hate taverns forever. Packed with not only drunk people but also screaming ones, it always became too loud, too warm, and definitely too hectic. Everyone was taller than him. He was pushed from all sides. People raised their glasses to the ceiling and dropped their beverages in his hair. He could not imagine anyone not feeling dirty in a tavern, unless they were willing to take in the dirt themselves.

"Tavern folk are the most grateful audience, Yve. Always remember: The more wine going down their throats, the less they care about what actually happens on stage!" Luhice had said the first time they were about to perform together. He didn't understand back then, but after months of watching sober men and women, Luhice included, lose their common sense more and more with each glass they chucked down, Yvellios knew what he meant.

While taverns were the latest root of his disdain, their chaos was exceptionally helpful in making him forget about one thing: the fright right before he had to claim his place in the spotlight. The first time, Luhice told him he wouldn't have to sing. He'd just have to breathe, for that's how one plays a recorder after all. What a liar he was. After he became brutally aware of the dozens of eyes that were suddenly focussed on him, Yvellios also had to give his best to fight the numbness in his knees and the aching in his stomach. It was quite gruesome, but also fulfilling. For the first time, Yvellios felt truly alive. For once he was granted the absence of a past or future. There was only him, the stage, and his recorder.

Even now, six months later, the stage still made him nervous. Yet excitement was an equally loyal companion, which seemed to intensify each time he managed to get his shaky hands back under control.

Yvellios fell onto the nearest chair with a deep sigh, grinning from one cheek to the other. Luhice tousled his white hair and laughed at him. With the other hand in the air, the blonde elf gave a signal to a waitress that usually resulted in drinks being brought to their table. A water for Yvellios, a beer for Luhice. It was a ritual they'd established since the day Yvellios gave in and became part of the performance.

It took Luhice several months to teach him how to play the recorder and nearly another year of late night duettes at their kitchen table to make Yvellios enter the actual spotlight. With every show they played, Yvellios ruefully looked back at his former stubbornness. How could he have refused the offer for so long?

A waitress brought beer and water. Luhice grabbed the beer and emptied half of it by the time Yvellios had a chance to sip on his water. It was predictable who would likely sleep in the next day.

"Happy Solstice," The waitress said. "You did a great job.

The two of you." She winked at Yvellios with a warm smile. "It's great to see you out there too" Before she disappeared into the crowd again, she squeezed his shoulder. A gentle and reassuring grip. Yvellios wanted to thank her, but her words made him lose his own. He grinned into his cup instead.

Last year, Luhice and Yvellios followed an invitation to a noble man's solemnity. Luhice was paid to perform, Yvellios was told to engage in conversations with said noble man's sons and daughters.

Yvellios had clearly stated his unease, but Luhice was not to be put out of his mood. "Don't worry, a lot of people here see elves as good fortune! Why do you think my schedule is fully booked every day between Solstice and new year's?"

"Is it not 'cause you're talented?" Yvellios asked. Luhice broke into a laugh, but didn't provide an answer.

With no time to refuse, Yvellios found himself sitting at a table with three unfamiliar children around his age and for the first few minutes, they just stared. Except for one boy next to him who did not seem to find Yvellios' arrival nearly as engaging as the pork chop he processed with his knife. Yvellios' long hair, neatly braided, could not hide anything that night. He tried to loosen some strands at his temple, but his pointy ears stayed exposed.

He felt sick to his core and begged some entity to turn him into dust right on the spot.

"Can you do magic?" asked the girl in front of him. Yvellios frowned, unsure why the question put him so on edge. With the braid sliding back and forth between his fingers, he looked up and, to his surprise, met a friendly gaze.

"Not really," he replied.

"Aren't you an elf though?" the boy next to him asked.

"Half-elf," Yvellios corrected, pulling on his braid more firmly.

They continued to ask millions of questions he did not want to answer. However, they were not rude. Just curious.

Luhice had to perform the whole evening, so there was nowhere else Yvellios could go and linger. Luhice had forbidden him to leave the hall. He should not get lost, Luhice had said. So he remained seated and gave the answers they demanded.

Even though he felt uncomfortable for most of the evening, the chatting, music, and numerous dancing people around him made it impossible to remember what day it was. A quiet Holiday he used to celebrate with no more than two people. That first Solstice without her was the first Solstice that didn't feel like one at all. A part of him was thankful for it. The other felt robbed.

This year, they were asked to perform in a tavern inside the city walls not far from their home. The crowd counted less than a third compared to the year prior but knew how to be just as loud. Compared to all performances he had been brought to, Solstice at the noble family's house was the biggest, yet tamest celebration. Luhice had a strong opinion on that matter: "That's the thing with the rich and popular folk. They are too busy wearing expensive gowns and having conversations with people they don't like, while drinking wine from someone's great-great-grandfather, that they forget how to actually be alive. But that's no surprise. When you consume beverages that are older than a cemetery, you start to act accordingly." By now, Yvellios knew that Luhice had strong opinions on a lot of matters. And the strongest ones were brought up by beverages of the same kind.

Luhice's beer glass shattered against his water cup. "I agree! And you improved!" he cheered, not noticing the mess he'd made on Yvellios shirt. At least it was just water from his own cup. "You get better each time."

"Thank you." Yvellios found his words again and smiled. "I do my best."

They chatted for a while, but after Luhice had emptied a third beer, he vanished in the crowd to join a table of strangers to play cards. Yvellios side-eyed the scene. It only took a short while for two women to appear around Luhice and even less for him to invite them to sit each at one of his sides.

Rolling his eyes, Yvellios turned to the plates that were served to him in the meantime. The freshly baked cheesecake with blueberries and walnuts as a reward for their performance was a worthy trophy. The thick chocolate sauce Luhice had ordered separately was still warm when Yvellios picked the nuts from the cake and dipped them one by one into the silver saucier. For each piece of cake, he fished a walnut out of the sauce with his fork before he shoved both together into his mouth. If Luhice hadn't been otherwise occupied, he wouldn't have resisted making a teasing remark about Yvellios' ritual fragmentation of his dessert.

Half an hour of sitting at the tavern table like a by-stander had passed and so did the previous euphoria. After he had neatly stacked the empty dishes, Yvellios finally got up. With the cake eaten and Luhice not seeming to be done playing cards any time soon, there was no reason left for him to stay.

He pushed his way sideways through the crowd with Luhice's cake plate balancing on the outstretched hand in front of him. "I'm leaving," he announced and placed the cake in front of Luhice, who was involved in a discussion about his cards with one of the unknown ladies.

"Yve! My precious and most talented student!" *Your only one.* He reached over the table for Yvellios' hands, but halted for a second and instead threw his arms for a welcoming gesture into the air as he proclaimed: "Future master on any instrument there is and singer of the greatest tales!" *I haven't written a single ballad.*

"Nothing else was ever expected. You have a reputation, after all," the lady slurred back, not sparing Yvellios a single glance. She swung her arm around Luhice's neck and spoke the next words right into the pointy ear behind the elf's long blonde hair. They were impossible for Yvellios to hear, but made the receiver blush and chuckle.

"Alright," Yvellios mumbled, not expecting any further answer, and turned to leave.

Yvellios figured he liked the city. It was so very different from the village he grew up in. Nothing about the brown walls and grey grounds reminded him of his mother's colourful flower beds. Nothing about the din of each restaurant had anything in common with the memories of her cooking dinner in their small living room. The ceaseless screams of the city nights could never resemble the sounds of spring in their old backyard.

It was only today, on Solstice, that Yvellios considered the city unbearable. He knew the problem was not the city, nor was it the people. In fact, it was a peaceful thought knowing he was never truly alone.

Some groups of chanting and laughing neighbours passed him by. Some recognised him from earlier shows and greeted him with chaotic applause or a slap on the shoulder. Most of them were on their way to another bar. Almost all of them told him to send their best wishes to Luhice.

Snow began to trickle down from the night sky onto his cheeks and nose. From one street to the next, the path cleared up until he was the only one out. A pleasantly icy breeze blew across his cheeks and took the snowflakes with it. He heard the fresh snow softly crunching beneath his feet, and had to admit that this, of all things, reminded him of his snowy forest walks. Two years ago and he could still taste the sweet winterberries he used to steal from his mother's basket. He even smelled the everlasting memories of her breakfast tart.

He saw how the tips of his shoes got buried in the snow with every shuffling step, but there was no grass beneath them. No berry bushes around him anymore. No basket to steal from.

A sudden collision sent him reeling. "Ey! Watch out!" A rough shove sent Yvellios sprawling to the ground.

He looked up. Blinking through the snowflakes, he saw a man in a black cloak and crossed arms looking down on him. Yvellios was not sure what was expected of him so he just stared back.

"What are you looking at? Get back on those fancy boots before I take them as a reward for putting up with you."

Yvellios let out a quiet apology and started to get up again. Out of the corner of his eye, he noticed movement. Then he saw the two other figures in the adjacent alley and another person laying on the ground in front of them. Yvellios immediately knew why the man in front of him was standing there. But Yvellios knew it was for his best not to remain rigid. Another icy breeze let snowflakes dance around his face, and he closed his eyes. He saw nothing.

"Now get those feet moving!" the man hissed.

Back on his feet, Yvellios gave the man a quick nod and hurried past, although the tingling in his stomach tried to persuade him to stay. He knew the pain a too hard surface can cause to a head when both collided a little too quickly. He knew of the curled up body in the middle of a pit of laughter and shame. Yvellios knew all that and wished his anger were stronger than the fear driving the feet that carried him away. He remembered the loneliness. He heard the silent prayers for someone to come. Two would have a more realistic chance than one. But he fled. Two years ago, at this moment, every day.

Yvellios slowed down his pace. This was not the path he wanted to choose, but it was the only sensible one. He never stood a chance back then, and maybe he had just as well lost his mind in that tavern at last. All he saw was the opportunity to be the person he desperately needed all those years ago. Yvellios cursed as he grabbed the recorder from the inside of his jacket and turned back around.

"W-would I be allowed to p-please you with some m-merry music as an ap-propriate apology?" His heart was pounding. His hands shook and dared to spill the truth, but his grin gave its best to undermine the lie his performance was carved from. He wondered whether Luhice would recognize this imitation.

"Piss off!"

Yvellios brought the recorder to his mouth. As the man tried to grab him, he began to dance and jumped to the side.

"What are you doing?" A yell from the alley. "What's going on over there?" They were alarmed. Good.

Yvellios kept playing and jumping in circles around the man who stood guard. He tried to get close enough to the other two, but that was easier said than done. The man's continuous attacks called for him to be as nimble as possible. He only had to finish the last verse and then ... the man's movement slowed until he stopped. His eyes rolled back, and he slammed face forward into the snow. A loud shriek sounded from the recorder as Yvellios backed away. He stood ready in case the spell didn't work properly, but loud snores indicated the man would not get up again soon.

The others stared in shock. For a moment the only one moving was the person on the ground, who began to turn around. The white scales on her face reflected not only the light of the lantern fire but also any absence of fear and inferiority. As long as Yvellios had the men's full attention, she seemed to take her chance and tried to grab one of their legs. But the men already came running. Yvellios could not spare a second thought and made a run for it too. He had only thought as far as that the spell would send all of them sleeping and cursed his naivety.

The two men chased him down the street he'd come from. Yvellios just hoped to reach a busy road before they could catch up.

"Ey!" Yelled a voice from behind, "Will you stop already?" A female voice. Did someone come for help already?

Yvellios turned around, but saw only the men and their bared teeth. He knew the scene all too well from when the cobble stones beneath his feet were forest grounds and the recorder in his fist was only a stick.

"I thought you took care of that!"

"Who knew this beast could take more than a brick wall?"

The men began to argue but were not allowed to finish. A rush of ice-cold air surprised Yvellios and stirred up the trampled snow around him. Their yelling ended with two muffled screams. Yvellios wheeled around in shock. The icy storm almost took the ribbon from his hair. Even the elbow in front of his face offered only limited protection.

A moment later the snow around him settled again. He dared a glance and saw the two lying in the snow with a pained expression on their faces but unmoving. They were breathing, yet their skin had taken on an unhealthy bluish colour.

A snow-white figure in an open purple cloak came towards them. Her head was shaved on the sides. The remaining light grey hair in the middle was tied into a thick ponytail. Yvellios saw the scales stretched from her face across the back of her neck below the collar of her shirt and reappeared at the bottom of her trouser leg to cover her bare feet and clawed toes.

There was no chance he could have guessed her age. Judging by her high-pitched voice, she couldn't be too old.

"Are you alright?" Yvellios asked skeptically.

Her first reply was a laugh. "I surely am!" Then she crouched in front of the men and began to search their pockets with her also clawed fingers. Yvellios counted eight in total. "These fools actually thought they could easily get away with my belongings just like that" He watched her thick tail also covered in big, white scales plough through the snow.

"Aren't you cold?" Yvellios asked, looking at her bare feet in the snow.

"No. I'm half of a white dragon."

"Oh," He replied, pretending to understand. "Thank you for help–"

"Ha!" She held a brown bag in the air and fingered a silver chain out of it. She seemed satisfied with the other content as well and made the entire bag disappear in her own pocket. "Thank you for making this way easier for me." She tossed him a coin.

Yvellios caught it. "Hm. Sure."

"I am starving now. Those guys really were tougher than expected." He had a feeling Luhice would like her. "You better watch out from now on. I hope you won't get involved in any other unpleasantries like this." She stepped over the two thieves with her hands in her pockets and grinned as she walked past Yvellios. He saw the delicate scales also covered most parts of her face, shaved head, and pointy ears. They were longer than Yvellios' ears, and bigger too.
"Have a blessed Solstice," she said and walked off.

Yvellios was left with the two unconscious men. They slowly seemed to get a rosy colour back into their faces.

Yvellios turned to her and called: "Do you like soup?"

Her name was Bilyssa. She was the daughter of a Dragonborn and a baker. "My mother is an incredibly brave fighter," she explained while Yvellios stirred the potato soup. "She is not in the city right now, but she visits quite often. I am living with my father and helping him in the bakery. We sell mostly cookies. Of all kinds. You should come by sometime! But what about you? You live alone?"

"No. With a friend." The soup was done. He reached for the old wooden ladle and got two bowls from the shelf.

"Where are your parents?"

Yvellios froze for a moment. A piece of potato fell from the full ladle back into the pot.

"Food is ready," he announced and quickly filled the bowls before placing both on the dinner table.

"Oh, that looks amazing!" Bilyssa didn't hesitate to take a bite. With a frown, she chewed on the potato pieces.

"Is it alright?" Yvellios tried a spoon himself. "Oh no. This is awful! Why is it so plain?"

"It's not awful ..." She took another two spoons. "See? It's definitely edible!"

Yvellios smashed his spoon on the table. "I don't understand, the soup should be full in flavour and slightly spicy"

"It's just potato soup" It was not just that.

"No! It is my mother's recipe. We always ate this when ... I was young" Theoretically, he still was. Fourteen did not count as old for humans. As a half-elf, he was even a baby. However, he felt like he was aging a year each week, so his own perception told him otherwise. "Her soup was richly seasoned. Spicy a bit. The potatoes were perfectly firm to the bite. And I always ate at least two bowls. It was her recipe." She should have written it down. He should have asked her for it.

"Maybe it's just missing some spices then? Your mother can surely teach you."

"She's dead"

"Oh ..." Bylissa replied. She obviously hadn't expected this answer.

Yvellios stared at the soup. No one said a word. The room was thick with silence. Every time he said it. It was always the same. They all looked at him the same. That expression of shock and pity. The obvious discomfort he caused with the truth.

Bilyssa was the first to say something again. "That soup you told me about doesn't sound nearly as boring as what I have in front of me right now. Just promise you keep practicing. Next Solstice, I can bring some cookies, and you make the proper soup"

"That's in a year."

"Enough time to figure out the seasoning then," she winked and smirked.

The door abruptly opened, startling both of them. "Yve! You are home!" Luhice called into the small room. He slammed the door shut and stumbled over to Yvellios. "You were gone and I asked around and no one saw you leave!" With a relieved sigh he embraced Yvellios' shoulders and forced him into a tight hug.

"I told you I was going home"

"What is it I see over there?" He pointed at Bilyssa. His red eyes gave their best to look straight and sober. "Is that a friend?!" He staggered over to the other side of the table and sat down next to her. "Tell me, my dear, did you know Yve is about to be a famous troubadour?"

Although their profession was no secret, the blood rushed into his cheeks. "Noo! Luhice, please! I am ... not ..."

Bilyssa answered Yvellios' pathetic attempt to protest with raised eyebrows.

Luhice pointed directly at her face. "I hope that's not the only reason you like him for!"

"Luhice!" Yvellios threw his hands in front of his face.

Bilyssa looked slightly amused. Then she giggled, to Yvellios' relief. "This was fun, but I am leaving now" She stood up and went to grab her cloak. "Thank you, Yvellios, for the soup and for helping me." Yvellios smiled. Next to him, Luhice had already claimed Bilyssa's soup as his own. "You should come by and try some cookies by chance." He hoped she meant it.

"I love cookies," Luhice lulled to himself and waved until she closed the door behind herself. "She seems nice!"

"She is." Yvellios took his hands back down. "But you are drunk and embarrassing"

Luhice was munching on the rest of Bylissa's soup and didn't seem to care about Yvellio's embarrassment. "This is delicious!"

Yvellios watched him blow too harshly at the hot soup on his spoon. Half of it splashed over the edge of the bowl on the table. "You don't have to eat that. I messed it up." Yvellios had no intention of telling him everything that had happened that day. Maybe some of it, but nothing that would cause unnecessary worry and definitely not today.

"Are you joking?!" Luhice pointed his filled spoon at Yvellios and spilled half of it. "This is the best thing I could have asked for! You must cook this exact same soup every day from now! For the next week! No! Month!"

The corners of Yvellios' mouth twitched. "That sounds quite expensive. It is not potato season." He took Luhice's empty bowl, who then reached for Yvellios' portion too, and brought it to the water basket they used for cleaning.

"No problem. We just double the gigs." Luhice tipped the bowl and energetically spooned out the last bits. With a satisfied sigh, he pushed the empty bowl away. Yvellios took it and made his way back to the water bucket.

"I'd have a different suggestion on how to save money, since you drink more than I eat," he said while washing both soup bowls.

"Touché!" Luhice laughed. With a tired chuckle he rested his chin on his palm. A bright smile, but eyes closed. "You are so funny" He crossed his arms and finally laid his head on them. While Yvellios watched Luhice's grin fade with each passing second, his own eyes welcomed a familiar warmth.

Luhice was fast asleep. His head resting in an obviously uncomfortable angle on both his forearms. Yvellios hurried to the couch and grabbed a blanket. He wrapped it around the shoulders of the sleeping elf, before he did the same with his own arms. His cheek pressed against a blanketed shirt soaked with cold sweat. His eyes teared up, but for once not due to the sour smell Luhice used to bring home from his night out.

Yvellios pressed his palms onto his wet eyes. As hard as he tried, it could not stop the tears. He let out a whimper with a heavy breath, which did not ease the pain in his chest either. There was nothing else for him to do. There was nothing he needed, but her. He just wanted his mother. He wanted to tell her he's playing the recorder now. He wanted to tell her he made a friend today. Wanted to wear one of her woollen jackets that felt like a blanket to him. But it was all gone. There was nothing left of her. Nothing but one thing.

Yvellios knelt on the floor. He swallowed and slowly opened the lowest drawer of the wardrobe in front of him. Below blankets and abandoned costumes he found his mother's old lyre. Yvellios had never played it himself, only watched her sing his lullabies. He placed the instrument on his lap.

His fingertips glided carefully over the untuned strings. A gentle and familiar voice echoed in his ears with the soft tunes. He could not make them sound a second time.

One time, the sight of the lyre had made Yvellios so angry that he wanted to throw it right out of the window down onto the streets. But Luhice had stopped him. He had grabbed his wrist and snatched the instrument out of his hand. "If you don't want to see it, fine," he had said and shoved the lyre in the very back of the same wardrobe Yvellios found it in moments ago. "But believe me, you'll thank me later." With the lyre pressed tightly to his chest, he was ashamed of the fuss he had made all that time ago, realising Luhice had indeed been right.

Yvellios missed his mother. Right then and there he missed her more than on his birthday or hers. He knew he was hugging a lyre, but it was more than a soulless object. It was the only thing he had and he wanted nothing more than for her to have cooked the soup. For her to have taught him before the spirits had taken her. For her to be there with them, so she could meet Luhice.

The one who stank of beer and all sorts of sweat. Who made him cure his headache every now and then. Who dragged him into bars and taverns. Who laughed at inappropriate times. Who felt no shame and was the root of all his discomfort. But also the one who made him laugh when he didn't want to. Who considered him talented. Who thought he was funny. Who offered his ears and a shoulder whenever Yvellios was in need. Who gave him a purpose. Who gave him a home.

How dearly did he wish for his mother to meet Luhice. For her to know he wasn't alone. That he was safe and, of all things, loved.

Yvellios sat rocking back and forth on the floor with the lyre's tuning bulge pressed to his mouth, and was so, so grateful Luhice intervened and did not let him have his way back then. He knew nothing and no one could ever truly fill the gap his mother left, but Luhice would do his best to close it just a little.

A LITTLE PLACE CALLED THE UNIVERSE
Nathaniel Luscombe

Let's say there are two siblings. We'll name them Lena and Elias.

Early on, they learn to rely on each other. No one else will show up for them. No one else will save them. It's not an easy thing, two kids trying to raise each other, but they survive. Elias shuts down when people treat him harshly. Lena fights back. In this way, they balance each other out.

They age, as kids do, but they don't age as kids should. The world has only shown them its teeth, and they have no choice but to try to bare their teeth back. They are angry and confused and scared. These emotions only grow bigger as they transition from children to teenagers.

You see, time doesn't slow down for anyone. It drags everyone at the same speed and expects each person to find their footing.

There's bound to be a breaking point, and Lena reaches hers on a Saturday afternoon. She's freshly eighteen, and time has made her a bitter, fearful creature. She stands in the middle of her room and feels the way the floor trembles as her mother storms up the stairs. She heard her mother fighting with whoever her boyfriend is now, the two of them high and out of touch with reality. She listened to their bladed words, heard them throw things at each other, watched as the truck tore out of their driveway.

And how her mother comes for her, her anger unsatisfied.

The world blurs as Lena's door flies open. Lena hardly recognizes the woman standing there, chest heaving, face red, a knife in hand. Lena can only see the blade pointing at her chest. When her mother charges, Lena grabs whatever's within reach, her fingers gripping the slippery insides of her small fishbowl. She hurls it at her mother and the bowl smashes into her face with a sickening thud. There's a moment where time seems to pause and Lena locks eyes with her mother's distorted face through the glass. She sees her little fish, the one thing she was able to care for properly, and realizes that she has now failed everything that ever relied on her.

Her mother drops to the ground. Lena drops with her, kneeling on the watery carpet, the bowl turned over the gasping fish. There's mumbling and spreading blood and her mother's eyes turn glassy in the light. Lena can't bring herself to touch her mother. She can only stare and battle the relief and remorse coursing through her.

She's facing the biggest turning point in her life. The choices, though limited, are huge. She needs to escape. She doesn't want to spend her life behind bars. What she really wants is for the ground to open up, swallow her, and spit her out into another life.

This is where we come in.

Let's say time is a concept and the universe is bendable. In fact, let's say that the past, present, and future are three parallel lines that dip in and out of each other. To stop the universe from folding in on itself, we need to set up multiple realities. Lena may only be aware of this existence, but she is one in a million existences, all of them a hair's breadth away from each other without even knowing it.

We don't usually interfere in human affairs. At least not officially. Let's just say that Lena won't be the first to disappear, or the last. All we can do is give her the power to open doors between universes and hope that she uses it to find her way home.

Lena presses a hand to the carpet, mouth open with a soundless scream, and she feels the universe ripple around her. She feels the door, feels the way it opens. She touches time and it stops, then starts, all at the twist of her hand. She could go back in time and undo this. We see the moment she realizes this, her teeth biting into her lip as she considers the consequences of going back.

She knows that someone was going to die in this house today, and going back won't change that. It will only change the body laying on the carpet.

Elias appears in the door. Lena can't even hear him as he speaks. He must be shouting, the way he gestures. She cuts through the universe and leaves it all behind. Everything rests at her fingertips. She leaves her old self behind and sets out to become whoever she wants. Maybe in the future, she'll come back to this moment and become the sister her brother needs her to be.

But for once, she has to be selfish.

If not, she'll take all the universes in her fist and crush the life out of them.

What she doesn't know (at least not yet) is that she

doesn't close the hole behind her. We keep it open. Elias deserves an out too. It wouldn't be fair to leave him to deal with her mess. He's the only person in the universe who knows how to care for Lena.

He follows, developing his own touch for the universes, and this is where we stop interfering. We've set up a story here. Now it's our turn to watch it play out.

Giving them access to every reality could be the end of their story.

Most likely, it's just the beginning.

Lena falls through universes for a while. Time goes forward. Time goes backwards.

Time doesn't exist, remember?

But she finds herself in the past, present, and future. Each time she blinks, she's somewhere else. It takes time to learn how to control it. She figures out how to stay in one place. She figures out how to travel. All she has to do is think of a reality, and the universe guides her there.

She is a needle threading through every universe.

And she is not alone.

There are times she feels incredibly alone. She places herself in the center of a crowd. Any crowd. Nobody ever looks at her. They don't seem to realize she exists.

In a crowd, she watches as bombs drop onto an old city.

In a crowd, she watches as humans first take flight to outer space.

In a crowd, she watches a small spaceship slip into the currents of the universe so it can overtake a star-whale and drain it of its celestial oil.

Crowds always gather around disasters. She enjoys the solidarity. There's always anger and fear simmering between the people. These are emotions she knows well. These are the emotions that drive her to find more disasters. Maybe one day someone will notice her.

She stands on the observatory deck of the *Shreia*. Lately, she's been jumping from spaceship to spaceship, exploring the far reaches of every future. She's grown bored with the past. She wants to know what comes next.

The *Shreia* is a large beast, both a symbol of luxury and a set of sharpened teeth. Just an hour ago, it turned a small moon into a collection of fragments. Lena stood in the middle of a cheering crowd and fought not to scream. People of the future are always sick with the need for power. Nobody wants to be powerless in a universe like this.

To be powerless is to be dead.

She has grown drunk on her power, but at least her power doesn't hurt people around her. She can go anywhere she wants. There's no fear of mortality because in the blink of an eye, she can move to a whole other reality, on another spaceship, facing another sky of stars.

That's why the guards don't bother her. She watches them gather in the reflection of the glass. They're fully suited up and they carry guns and stun sticks. Through their bodies, the stars watch her carefully.

The whole universe holds its breath.

She could leave.

She *should* leave.

She looks over her shoulder. "Can I help you?"

"You're not registered to be on this ship. We need to take you in for questioning."

The voice doesn't come from any of the guards. Lena shifts, finding a balding man at the entrance of the observatory. There's no one else in the room. It's only her, the guards, and him. She meets his eyes and waits. He doesn't dare come in here without knowing what she's capable of.

"Who are you?" She asks.

"The better question is who are you?"

She shrugs. "I'm just passing through. That little display earlier was quite something. Blowing up moons ..." she chuckles. "What's next? Blowing up planets?"

She knows what's next. She cheated and peeked ahead a few years. It doesn't take long for this universe to begin collapsing. Once there's a weapon that can blow apart planets, war turns to extinction.

"That *little display* was only meant for a select group of people. A group that I suspect you don't belong to."

How can she explain that she has never belonged to any group of people, and now she doesn't even belong to a universe? She is a fugitive running from herself.

He speaks into a small device, and the guards start walking forward. Their stun sticks begin to hum. It seems that if she doesn't cooperate, they'll stun her. If she's dangerous, they'll shoot her.

She happily walks the line of fun and danger. It's something she's gotten good at.

All at once, she stands on the other side of the guards. It's a couple minutes ago. She should be watching the stars, but she's here and they're there and the balding man is just walking in.

"Wh—"

Chaos breaks out. The guards turn, guns are drawn, the man dives to the side.

Beyond it all, a familiar face appears. A face Lena has been running from for a while.

She loses her grip on reality. A stun stick rams into her back, and excruciating pain runs through her body. She arches, her muscles locking, and her vision goes black. There's more than one stun stick on her now.

And she can't even form enough thoughts to teleport.

She comes back to life beneath the harsh lighting of a cell. It's laughable, putting her in a cell, but it's preferable to them killing her. Perhaps they would've if they understood who she is and what she is capable of.

When she lifts her head, she locks eyes with a face she missed, yet almost hoped to never see again. It's Elias. He sits against the wall, both scared for her and scared of her.

He's different. Older. His brown hair hangs in his eyes, but she still feels the way he watches her quietly. She feels too much guilt when she looks at him. For so long, she fought for both of them.

Then she killed someone, and left him to clean it all up.

How is he here?

"I've been looking for you for a long time," he says.

Lena was never truly brave, but she's never felt more like a coward than when she cuts through the universe and leaves him behind again.

He follows her.

He loses her.

Not for the first time.

She explores the edge of a universe. There's a drone that follows the curved end, mapping it out for the starship that follows far behind. The drone is capable of carrying several humans. There is no one on it now.

She enjoys the solitude. It gives her time to voice her thoughts out loud. In this small space, where there's nothing but walls and windows, her words are devoured by loneliness. She sleeps with her face to the universe. Except it's not the universe she sees, it's the veil between the universe and whatever rests outside of it.

Is this universe just one universe in a myriad of universes?

Do they spin like galaxies in an even bigger reality?

She's too scared to explore that one.

She stays until her insides try to devour her. She can only survive so long without food and water. She knows she has to leave when she wakes with a fierce rhythm pounding in her mind. An emptiness howls within her.

She's hungry for food and human contact.

Mostly food.

She falls in love.

It's not the first time. She tries not to get attached to people, but she's not completely without a heart. When a man asks to sit with her at a poolside table at a resort, then ends up buying them both food and drinks, it's impossible to not lose herself in his ocean eyes.

Plus his name is Orion. Has there ever been a prettier name?

They get to know each other over the next three days.

Then she spots Elias again. Or at least she thinks she does. When she sees him, she gets so scared she falls in a pool. By the time she's up and no longer gasping for air, he's nowhere to be seen.

Orion wraps her up in a towel and brings her back to his fancy room. They fall asleep on the large bed and when she wakes up in the morning, she doesn't want to leave.

This is love. The gentle tug, the rapid fall, the tired climb out.

She watches the sunlight creep across the ceiling. Long shadows fill the room. They fall across Orion's face, and she can't help but stare. He's so pretty, his face always bright, his very existence almost effortless. They've been dancing and drinking and laughing for several days now, and she has never felt this free in her life.

"You need to leave," she murmurs to herself. She's not ready to face Elias. If he's here, she can't stay.

"Hmm?" Orion rolls onto his back. His eyes crack open. "Did you say something?"

She wants to kiss him, but that would make this hurt even more. "Good morning."

He's too out of it to pick up on the change of words. Lena wishes he would challenge her. If they got into a fight, this would be easier. It's not like she could stay long even if Elias didn't show up. As soon as Orion tries to look into her past, he'll realize she doesn't truly exist. She has no history.

"Do you always wake up this early?" He holds a hand to his head. Before he saved her from the pool, they'd both been a bit tipsy. Clearly he's feeling the effects.

The more she switches universes, the less things like alcohol have an effect on her. It's like her body is learning how to shut down certain feelings. It gives her a sort of freedom, but it also takes away the freedom to lose herself in a meaningless dance with life.

"It's not that early. I hate wasting my time here with sleep." She sits on the edge of the bed. There is a restlessness growing in her like an itch.

He laughs. "Well, what can I treat you to today? We can go anywhere you want."

She's heartless. She's the worst type of monster. She does

things without even realizing how big the consequences are because she's never had to deal with them.

"Lena? Are you okay?" He crawls behind her, his steady hands holding her shaking shoulders.

This isn't the first time she's had to leave someone, but why does it hurt more now? She can't even bear to just leave.

"I think I need to shower. I'll be back." She pushes him away, nausea building in her stomach. As soon as the door locks behind her, she goes back in time. Back to the moment Orion began to approach her table. This time, she turns away from him, and he lingers for a moment, hoping he'll get the chance to introduce himself, but she never looks his way.

Does this fix it? Does Orion never meet her?

Or does the universe split in two: one reality where Orion never meets her and one reality where a part of him always misses her?

The next time she spots Elias, she's walking through a space port. The thick crowds push her every which way. She's looking for a ship to travel on. Something large that she can get lost on.

Then he's there, just a few feet away. He watches her and the crowd flows around him like water around a rock.

She starts rewinding time. If she can just go back and choose a ship earlier, maybe he won't see her. As the people move backwards, he starts walking towards her. Out of everything in the universe, he's the one thing out of her control.

He's walking, he's running, he's yelling.

She's gone.

He finds her again on a little moon colony.

"Please don't leave this time."

"Why not?"

Because we need to talk."

That's what scares her.

She moves into a darker timeline. The whole universe is at war here. Battleships are everywhere, but she chooses to dump herself onto a large cruiser. It's full of people fleeing the war. They're too frantic to notice an extra person joining them mid-flight.

She sits in a room full of sweating, anxious people. A screen on the wall plays footage from the war. Planets are burning, ships are exploding. Every video is full of death. She flinches each time it changes.

What's the point of living if you're stuck in a universe like this?

A hand covers hers. She pulls away, freezing when she meets the familiar sea green eyes. "Elias," she murmurs.

His hand grabs hers tightly, as if he can tether her here. "Are you going to disappear?

Weariness fills her body. "It depends. Are you going to keep chasing me?" Running is so much more tiring when there's actually someone following her.

He laughs, and the sounds of her childhood pull her apart at the seams. She doesn't want to be here, but she'd also rather be here than anywhere else. Where's the sense in that?

"I'm going to keep chasing you. Even when you drag me into some horrible universe where everyone is dying."

She hisses at him to keep quiet. Not too far away, a lady watches them curiously. Lena knows this conversation sounds insane.

"How did you find me the first time?"

"Oh, you mean when I came across you almost dying?"

She blocks the memories. The pain of the stun sticks was a lot. Almost too much to bear. "I only got hit because I saw you."

"And I only let you see me because I hoped you'd fumble enough for me to talk to you. I didn't plan on them hurting you that badly. I've been tracking you for a while, watching from the shadows."

Elias has always been more of an observer. "And why are you following me?"

"Because you're all I know and all I have left."

An alarm begins to ring. It's invasive, the sound splitting through the ship.

Elias freezes. "They're all going to die," he says.

Lena isn't going to die with them. "Find me again," she dares, "and maybe I'll actually talk to you." It's not right for her to taunt him like this, but she doesn't know what else to do.

The ship explodes and everything borders death.

Until she rewinds just a fraction of a second before the explosion and, after making sure Elias is gone, falls through another hole in the universe.

She decides to visit beautiful things.

A garden moon with weeping trees.

A water planet with glass cities beneath the surface.

A space hotel so large it's basically a planet.

In all of it, she's alone.

But not alone in the way she was before. Alone in the way where she feels watched. She is always looking out for Elias, trying to figure out how to talk to him. She has things she has to explain. She hasn't been fair to him at all. But when has being fair ever dictated any of her movements?

And then she gives up. It comes with a realization that she'll always be alone, no matter how many people she meets, because she'll always eventually leave each universe for something else.

There's only one person in existence who can follow her.

She just can't decide if it's fortunate or unfortunate that it's her brother.

She chooses a small planet in a peaceful universe. It's the type of universe where people have chosen to leave each other alone. On a little planet, she finds a small bar tucked away in the corner of an almost non-existent town and stakes her claim in a corner booth.

If he can find her here, she'll feel safe enough to talk to

him. For so long, she has treated every universe as temporary. Maybe she and Elias can make a sort of life for themself in a universe like this one.

Or maybe they'll keep living on the edge, following each other through unknown universes and leaving little marks before moving on again.

When he doesn't show up the first night, she rewinds the day. She does this again and again, then grows bored of the same day and moves time forward. No matter where she is in this universe, he should be able to find her.

She stops moving time when the bar fills up. It's a few days later, and something has changed. She's no longer the only person here. The bartender is busy, and over half of the tables and booths are full. She looks out the window and catches sight of several large spaceships just outside the town. There's a refueling station out there, and the town comes to life when convoys of ships stop by.

Lena finds herself caught up in a jovial crowd. These people don't have the fear of each other beaten into them. There's none of the tension that bleeds through so many other universes she's been in.

She drinks with strangers, her drinks added to someone's tab, and loses herself in this gentle existence.

The night is drawing to a close, a whole day somehow behind her in a haze, when he slips into her booth.

"You chose an interesting place to hide," he says, folding his arms on the table.

"I'm not really hiding anymore. I thought you'd like the atmosphere." She remembers their life back on Earth. Elias always shut down at home, but he had his little escapes. More than once, she found him on the edge of a place like this, soaking in other people's lives.

"I'm surprised you remember anything about me. Do you really care about what I want? Or what I need?"

She ducks her head. She deserves so much worse, but it doesn't make this any easier. "I'm sorry. I didn't mean for this to go so out of control. I didn't mean to leave you behind."

He shakes his head. "I don't believe you. You left me behind *countless* times. No matter how many times I found you, you hardly even let me talk to you."

"I panicked. If you're so angry, why did you keep chasing me?"

"Because I'm not angry, Lena. I'm sad and lonely and scared, but I'm not angry. I just want to understand." He buries his face in his hands, and she realizes he's crying. It's not the first time she's seen him cry, but she doesn't know how to care for him anymore. Somewhere in her universe jumping, she forgot how to be his big sister. Neither of them were built for this.

"Are you still here?" he asks from behind his hands.

She can't stop the tears that begin rolling down her cheeks. "Of course I'm still here." She takes his arm and waits for him to look at her again. "I don't have all the answers for you, but I do know that I won't leave you behind again. I promise this." She searches for the right words, then realizes there are no right words in this situation. She just needs to tell the truth. "I don't know why I kept running. I was looking for a universe that felt like home."

"And did you find it?"

"No. Because everywhere I go, I'm haunted by the fact that I killed someone. I don't know if I meant to kill her."

She slumps forward. She hasn't talked about her mom's death out loud before. She's considered it many times. She could've talked to anyone and disappeared before they had a chance to apprehend her. But now she has to explain it to the one person who has a right to question it.

"Then why did you?"

"She was going to kick me out. I had just turned eighteen, and she knew she didn't have to pretend to care for me anymore. I demanded a couple days to prepare, and she was fine with that until her boyfriend showed up. He must've been part of the reason she wanted me to leave. She would've kicked you out too, you know. But when she came after me, I thought she was going to kill me." Lena breathes. The memories are a lot to deal with. "I didn't think before throwing it. I just needed her to stop and realize what she was doing. I needed to knock some sense into her."

"With a fishbowl?"

She snorts. It's not funny. It's not. She can't tell if she's crying or laughing anymore. It's all a jumble of emotions swirling around inside of her.

Elias takes her hand awkwardly. Even though they cared for each other on Earth, they didn't do things like holding hands. "If it makes you feel any better, I was going to leave anyway. When I turned eighteen. I would've told you, of course, and even invited you to come if you were still around. I wasn't expecting you to stay around, though. I just hoped that when you left, you'd still be close. Not, like, in some other universe trying to run away from me."

"Not you. I was never running from you."

"Right. Well, I just mean that I understand and I forgive you as long as you never run away again. Take me with you next time."

She reaches over the table and pulls him into a hug. Unlike every other time she's gotten close to someone, this isn't going to end. Lena doesn't want to let him go. This is a new beginning for them. She's not going to let the past define her anymore. It's going to be her guide into the future.

"Lena?" He says in her ear.

"Yes?"

"It's your turn now."

"My turn for what?"

She's left clasping air. She looks like an idiot, leaning over her table with her arms wrapped around nothing. A relieved grin spreads across her face. She can sense him somewhere, like a color bleeding through the universe. When she reaches out to cut through the layers of reality, intuition guides her and she allows herself to fall through.

He is a needle threading through every universe.

She is a needle knotting her thread to his.

Let's say we interfere again. Not all of us like happy endings. Some of us hate the way Lena and Elias cheat death again and again. What good is a story if we know the main characters can't die? What if one day we take their powers away? What if we leave them stranded in the middle of nowhere? Maybe on a ship that's about to lose oxygen, or a planet that's about to melt in the face of an exploding sun.

Let's get rid of every one of you who's nodding. If you felt joy at the thought of their pain, you don't deserve this story.

Instead, let's watch from afar as they tackle every universe. They grow old and they grow young as they slip through the streams of our realities. They are needles and they won't stop until they've threaded through every possible existence together.

LITTLE SOULS
Jacob Kelley

Never thought of a time nor a day and nay an event in my life that could alter me so.

The day arrived when a pair of fierce and loving souls, little of foot, but giant of heart, came into my life.

One an inquisitive world seeker, the other a fierce and brave explorer of things both far and near.

Love so strong that even the sharpest steel could never sever the bond I shared with them.

Strong has it made me. I raise my shield to defend and protect them.

For precious are their smiles and joyous are their laughs and warm are their hugs. I would protect my family from all that would seek to sunder me and my kin.

It is these blessed souls from the gods of old that will forever more hold my love, for they are my precious gift.

INNOCENCE
Aisling Revell

"**Well, here we** are." Joey pushed the door open, exposing the spacious living room of his apartment. The room was laid out in a very modern, almost empty way, with trendy, minimalist furnishings, monotonous gray walls, and one flat-screen television with a game console. No family pictures or personal items could be seen among the straight lines and sharp edges. It was organized, not because of any particular tendency, but simply because there weren't enough belongings for it to be disorganized.

He turned to his new roommate, who was still standing in the doorway, as he put his shoes to the side and took off his coat. Her wide, blue eyes took everything in calmly, almost as if she was stuck in a dream. Snowflakes clung to her long, golden tresses and her ears were covered with a bright pink hat with a tassel hanging off the top. Her button nose was still red from the cold weather outside, and a puddle of slush was forming at her feet from the snow off her boots. The red coat she was wearing was too large for her petite body, reaching past her knees like a dress.

She was his seven-year-old niece who would be living with him from now on. His seven-year-old niece he didn't know existed a week ago.

"Uh ... you know ... just make yourself at home I guess," he said, turning away from her. He could hear her fidgeting as she slipped out of her boots and coat, dropping them to the floor at her feet. He sighed, reminding himself that he did in fact tell her to make herself at home. When he turned to gather up her things, he stopped abruptly. Her hat was now gone, revealing a large, purple flower of a bruise, blossoming on the right side of her temple near her hairline.

He averted his gaze, even though he had nothing to feel guilty for. He wasn't the one driving. He wasn't the one who got stupid drunk and decided he was sober enough to get behind the wheel. He wasn't the one who hit a car with a family inside it, sending it sliding off the road and into a tree. He wasn't the one who killed his brother.

He coughed, breaking the silence that was quickly becoming awkward. "Why don't I show you around ...?" He hesitated, realizing he never addressed her by her name. "Eloise." It sounded strange in his own ears. "Eloise? Geez, what were your parents thinking? You're a little girl, not an old lady," he muttered, regretting it the second it came out.

Eloise's cheeks were puffed out and her eyebrows were drawn together tightly. Under normal circumstances, it would have looked funny.

"Oh ... I didn't mean it like that. Eloise is a very ... uh ... nice name."

The young girl shocked him by saying, "I hate it too. That's why I like it better when people call me Ellie."

He sighed in relief, partly because she wasn't offended but mostly because he wouldn't have to use such an old-fashioned name. "Ellie it is then," he said, leading her into the kitchen.

The living room blended seamlessly into the kitchen, gray walls and all. Every stainless-steel appliance shone like it was brand new, and the only sign of living was a greasy take-out container of Chinese that sat in the microwave.

The hallway that branched off from the kitchen led to the bedrooms. Joey originally thought it was pointless to have a two bedroom apartment, but he supposed it was for the best now. His room was rather unremarkable with white walls and the bare necessities. The guest bedroom, which would now be occupied by Ellie, was much the same, other than the addition of some boxes with her belongings that had been delivered the day before. The rest would be coming later. Maybe he would paint it pink. Add some unicorns or fairies. Seven-year-old girls liked that stuff, right?

Noticing it was nearing six o'clock from the microwave clock, he turned toward the cabinets. "Alright, let's find something to make for dinner." He clapped his hands together as Ellie pulled herself onto a tall black stool that sat next to the counter.

The once nearly empty cabinets were now filled with so much food that fitting anything else in would be difficult. He tried looking up fast and easy recipes that children would enjoy earlier that day, and it seemed like it would be relatively simple, but now the brightly packaged food in front of him blurred into a blob of mass-produced mess.

"Papa."

Joey spun so quickly that he nearly smacked his head against the door of the pantry.

"Nooo, no no no! I am not Papa! I am your Uncle Joey! Un—"

Ellie wasn't looking at him. She was staring down at a

picture on top of the counter. It was one of the only things Joey took with him when he left home. After receiving the news about his brother, he pulled it out of its hiding place in the drawer of his nightstand. He figured it could be his contribution for the upcoming memorial service.

The picture was taken at a family gathering while the two brothers were both in high school. One of the last family gatherings his brother went to. Joey was a freshman, while his brother, John, was a senior. Both of the boys were sitting in the grass, beads of sweat visible on their foreheads. Joey was caught in a mid eye-roll, clearly annoyed about just losing the basketball game they played minutes before. John was looking at the camera, one eye squinted shut and a hand up to shield himself from the sun. He had an easy-natured smile plastered on his face, like he always did.

"Papa," Ellie repeated.

Joey was afraid she would start crying, but no sadness could be seen in her eyes. Only an innocent type of curiosity and maybe a little longing.

"Uh, yeah, and that's me," Joey said, pointing to himself in the picture.

"I know," she calmly replied.

Joey flushed with embarrassment. "Oh, uh, right."

Ellie's gaze moved from the picture to a magnet on the fridge. It was a generic looking cowboy on a bucking horse. A coworker got it for him on a trip to some Western state. Either Wyoming or Montana, he could never remember. It was the only somewhat personal thing in the room.

"Mama liked horses," Ellie said.

"Is that right?"

She nodded. "She rode English though, not Western."

Joey remained silent, hoping the topic would change.

"Uncle Joey?" Ellie asked, after a few moments of painful silence.

"Is something wrong?" he asked, as she started to rub her stockinged feet together. Hearing her call him that was just as odd as using her name for the first time. He never thought he'd be someone's uncle.

"I have to go potty," she said quietly, clutching onto her light pink t-shirt that hung loosely on her frame.

"Oh! D–do you need help?"

He silently thanked God when she shook her head no. Ellie remained seated though, fidgeting uncomfortably. Joey was about to ask her awkwardly if she already wet herself, but Ellie spoke up.

"W–where is it?"

"Oh!" he exclaimed, feeling his face turn red. "Right down there." He pointed down the small hallway to the left of the kitchen.

Ellie nodded, hopping off her stool and hurrying to the bathroom. After hearing the bathroom door shut, he took the picture in his hands.

The joint funeral was set for next week, his mother planning everything to perfection. Joey was sure multiple people from their high school would be there, something he wasn't looking forward to. He wondered how many people from Ellie's mother's side would be there. It would be the closest thing he got to their wedding, he morbidly thought.

Had he even processed John's death? He remembered feeling something when the news came out of his father's mouth, but they were soon replaced by an even greater feeling when it was followed by the information that John's wife, who he was unaware of, also died, and that his niece, who he never knew existed, survived.

Not bothering to hide his anger, the corner of the picture became crumpled in his hand.

When the lawyers revealed that Ellie had been left to Joey in the will, he was beyond furious. It wasn't enough that he played second fiddle to John his entire childhood, always just second best, or that he caused the family to unravel completely after he left, since his parents' pride and joy was gone. Now he wanted to saddle Joey with a kid he had no relationship with.

How did he get himself into this mess? What did he owe John? What did John do for him? After high school, John just disappeared, leaving an astronomical mess for the family he left behind.

To say John disappeared was probably unfair. John tried to reach out. First with his old number that Joey still had memorized. Then with what Joey was assuming was a new number after John was removed from their family's plan. Then by email. Then by letter. All the while, their father was looming in the background, making it clear what he wanted Joey to do. So, Joey ignored it all. Rejected the calls, deleted the voicemail without listening to it, set his email to spam, and threw the letter straight in the trash, never opening it.

John could have tried harder is what Joey told himself. If John really wanted to have a relationship with him, he would have made it happen. Their father's wrath shouldn't have stopped him.

In a way it stopped Joey from trying harder too, but something else was at play. Something that still kept him up at night. He wanted John to be out of his life.

He loved his brother. He did. John was Joey's biggest defender, and Joey wasn't sure if he would have made it through his awkward adolescence without his big brother there to support him. It was just that John was perfect. Good looking, athletic, stellar grades. A typical example of girls wanting to be with him and guys wanting to be him. In contrast, Joey was average at best. Living in his shadow during childhood was miserable, and after he disappeared, Joey finally had the opportunity to be seen as his own person instead of John's little brother.

After John's disappearance, Joey expected that all of his father's strict expectations would land on his shoulders now, and he was eager to prove himself. Joey was never given the opportunity though. His father stopped caring, and it made Joey feel like he wasn't capable of shouldering the burden. He resented John even more because of it. That resentment cost him his brother.

How would things have been if he tried a little harder? If he answered the phone. Looked at the email. Read the letter. Would John still be there?

To this day Joey never found out why exactly John left. Why the straight-A, exemplary son with a football scholarship just vanished. All he remembered was one day waking up on the morning the family was supposed to go to John's school to pick him up for summer vacation his sophomore year. Instead of finding the SUV packed, all he found was his dad, sitting on the recliner with a disgruntled look on his face. His dad quietly said they wouldn't be picking up John. Joey first thought that his dad was just upset that John made some summer break plans he never shared with his parents. He didn't know he'd never speak to his brother again. Joey wasn't sure if he'd ever learn the whole story, unless his dad spilled his guts during one of his drunk, late night phone calls. It probably had to do with John dropping out of college, completely disregarding the wishes of their father who demanded excellence.

Then there was the mother. Alice. Joey suspected she had something to do with John's untimely ruin. He was learning more and more about her everyday. She was from the town John went to school in and Joey assumed they started dating before the fallout. She was beautiful, with the same blonde hair and blue eyes as Ellie. She was artistic, exhibiting her watercolors in multiple small galleries. And apparently she rode English. Whatever that meant. She, like John, had no relationship with her family. Joey didn't know all of the details, but abuse was involved somehow. The families must have been dysfunctional if he was considered the most capable of raising a child.

"She must have been something special, John," Joey said to himself.

"Who's special?"

Joey jumped and was shocked to find Ellie standing directly behind him.

"No one. Don't worry about it, kiddo."

Ellie reclaimed her seat on the stool and Joey resumed his search for something to make for dinner.

He tried his best to ignore Ellie's gaze, but her eyes were glued to him as he moved about. The worst part of it was that those eyes reminded him so much of John's. Not so much in looks. John's chocolate brown irises were nothing like Ellie's crystal blue ones. It was that stare. That innocent, yet wise and all-knowing stare which seemed to absorb everything.

It was the same way John would stare at him. The way he would get Joey to reveal who he was crushing on or how he secretly took one of their dad's beers. A seven year old should not have eyes like that.

Could she tell what he was thinking? That he thought of her as a hindrance to his life and was still questioning whether he should have taken her in.

Joey wasn't sure what his face looked like when he read the letter that was left with John's will. The one that said he wanted Joey to become Ellie's guardian. Surely he looked even more surprised than his parents. Probably confused as well. Maybe even angry.

He wasn't sure why he accepted the role. It wasn't for his brother, he was sure of that. He was still upset with John, even after all these years. When his parents offered to take her though, he couldn't let that happen.

So, here he was. Trying to figure out dinner for the girl he would now be raising.

The labels on all of the boxes and cans may have well been in a foreign language because he couldn't figure out what he was looking at. He could hear Ellie's foot tapping incessantly against the side of the counter, irritating him all the more. He couldn't even decide on a simple thing like dinner. How was he going to raise a child?

A bright blue box on the top shelf drew his attention upward and he reached up to grab it so he could get a better look.

Unfortunately, the pantry was so packed that when he was pulling the box down, it knocked against another, making it tumble to the floor. He tried to catch it, but his elbow banged against a lower shelf, sending many of the contents it held to the floor as well. To make matters worse, a can rolled out of the pantry, landing on his head.

"Damn it!" he yelled out, completely forgetting about Ellie's presence.

"Pfft."

Ellie was biting her lip and grabbing onto her forearms, trying to stop herself from laughing. Soon though, it became too much to keep in, and it all came spilling out. Her laughter was high pitched and pleasant, sounding like bells.

It was the first time he saw her smile.

Joey found himself laughing as well, and something about that shared moment made it all click for him. Maybe it was because it finally made him see her as the child she was, and not some random burden to deal with. Maybe it was because it reminded him so much of John's own boisterous laughter, while also being completely her own. Maybe it was because he couldn't help but think that if she could laugh after everything that happened to her, then he could take her in and figure the rest out later.

He was going to love her in the way an uncle is supposed to love his niece and he was going to make up for all of the lost time when he didn't know her. He could never replace her perfect father, but he would be the best Uncle Joey he could be, even when it was hard.

He may never know why John chose him, but he could trust that he had a reason.

"How 'bout some McDonald's?"

Ellie managed to contain her laughter enough to nod. He helped her down from the stool and after cleaning up, they headed back out into the cold weather outside.

Things would be alright.

ALTERNATE REALITIES
Jenni Sauer

Do you think you're my brother in every universe?
That in an infinite number of realities
We share genes and memories
And I love you until it bleeds?
Or can there maybe be one
—I'm just asking for one—
Where I'm free?

THE SPIRIT AND THE SISTER
Cassandra Hamm

The shipwreck is young, not yet covered in coral or algae—too healthy to sink but for a hole in the hull.

I kick harder, letting the ache chase away the ocean's chill. My lungs stay still and silent, just as I trained them to be, surviving on the oxygen I gulped down at the surface. I focus on the burn of my legs instead of the pain lodged in my chest.

The wreck looms before me. Cannonfire punched holes in the mahogany siding and shivering sails. The mainmast spar is almost severed from the deck, hanging over the side like a giant, ominous rifle.

I run my hand across the wooden siding. Though the crimson paint is starting to flake, the garish lettering glares out at me: *Swift Passage*. The fastest ship in the empire, supposedly. But not fast enough to outrun pirates.

Wyn...

My lungs seize, threatening to breathe and take in water. I focus on the creaks and moans of the sea, the dust stirring below me with each kick, the push and pull of the faraway currents. My body calms.

Bits of broken wood jab into my suit as I wriggle through one of the larger holes. My brain slowly adjusts to the tilted floor. Abandoned bunks rest against the wall closest to me. Casks press against the ceiling, swaying back and forth with the movement of the water.

Bronwyn's spirit is here. It has to be. Spirits don't change until three whole days after their passing, when the ocean calls them to a new form.

But where are the spirits? Have they already changed into sirens? Was I too late?

I turn my head to find a limp, bloated mass, not yet buoyant, lying at the bottom of the cargo hold.

I flinch, my arms cutting through the water as I hurtle away from the body. There must be a trapdoor leading to the next level. There has to be. I can't be stuck in the hold with this—

The square outline is nearly blocked by a floating cask. I shove the barrel aside and push on the trapdoor, muscles straining. The door shrieks open.

I enter the lower deck and nearly let out a scream. Three more corpses litter the ground, hair swaying around their faces, flesh swollen and bone-white. I claw my way down the tilted passageway, far away from the bodies, but their hideous forms linger in my mind. *One might be Bronwyn.*

I would have come to the wreck sooner, but the thought of entering the water where my sister had drowned made my lungs seize, my limbs freeze, my heart drop into my stomach. If not for the three days almost being up, I would have stayed in the fresh, cool air.

But tonight, the dead will change to siren or mer, and I have to make sure it'll be the latter. So I shove the terror to the back of my mind and let my body take over. Kick, stroke, don't breathe.

I'll find her. I have to.

The water before me changes from pale gray to silver. I flip my body so my feet are in front, kicking frantically to prevent collision.

The spirit is a broad-shouldered young woman, no more than twenty, with ghostly, shoulder-length curls. She uses the hand signals of our people. *I don't want to be a siren,* the motions say. *I don't want to drown anyone.*

I wish I could help her, but I only have breath enough for Bronwyn. If I can even find my sister.

I'm sorry, I sign back with shaking hands. *Do you know a Bronwyn? Can you show me where she is? I have to find her before—*

Help me! Her hand movements are a blur. *Please!*

The ocean swirls around the spirit, a fierce whirlpool that blurs her incorporeal form. I swim away, knowing it is too late to stop the change. Her body solidifies into silver scales, her legs into a powerful tail. *Siren.*

My arms churn, stroke after stroke, as I dart across the lower deck, back toward the bodies. Hissing echoes through the water in sibilant waves as the siren completes her change. And she is just the first.

I swim through the still-open trapdoor leading to the cargo hold and yank it shut behind me with a *screeeeeeech.* I fight to keep my lungs from seizing with terror. The door won't hold the newborn siren for long, and I know more sirens will soon be forming. My freediver training will only last a few more minutes, and then I'll have to breathe. But I can't leave without finding—

A chill brushes my skin, different from the ocean's usual ebb and flow. Skin prickling, I turn. The body and I are no longer alone in the cargo hold. Another spirit, pale and ethereal, gazes at me, but this one has my sister's face.

Wide-set eyes. Rounded, upturned nose. Thick, bow-shaped lips. Heart-shaped face.

Svana? the spirit signs. *What are you doing here?*

Grief clogs my throat. My sister is truly no more.

I knew, yet seeing her like this ... It makes me want to curl into a ball, to let the ocean take me too. I don't even care if I'd become a siren. At least as a siren, I would only feel rage, not this clawing, all-consuming pain. The hole in my chest where my sister used to be.

Svana? Bronwyn surges forward like the tide, coming so close I can see ghostly freckles on her cheeks.

How did it happen? I ask.

I know only the bare details. Pirates looted and sunk the *Swift Passage*. There was speculation that they'd taken some slaves, the women for more ... salacious reasons.

Part of me is glad she escaped that fate. That would be worse than death.

The captain said I wasn't womanly enough. Bronwyn's see-through form trembles. *Not enough to tempt him or any warm-blooded man.*

Where is he now? Can I stab him?

So they decided I wasn't worth living and stabbed me through the heart. Bronwyn's last sign indicates her blood-stained chest. *Now here I am.*

How can she say that with such casualty? I want to rage, to raze the ship that pillaged hers, to destroy every man who deemed her not pretty enough to live. She was more than her face. She was strength and kindness and power. She was a diver and a sister and a human. She would have changed the world.

Thud. The trapdoor splinters. The siren must be hurling herself against the door. It won't hold for long, not against siren strength.

I sign frantically. *Your time is almost coming. I won't let you become ...* I pause, pointing toward the door. *That.*

You can't stop my fate, Bronwyn replies.

But there has to be a way. I know I've seen more than just fearsome sirens in these waters. There are mer, too, kind and strong and good, assisting the shipwrecked and fighting off sirens and caring for the sea. They didn't succumb to the sea's siren call. They fought the fate thrust upon them.

Fight back, I sign, my fingers a blur. *Fight back, Wyn. This doesn't have to be your fate. You can become a mer.*

I am already so close to becoming a siren. Bronwyn's ethereal form ripples. *My three spirit days are almost gone.*

You don't have to become a siren! I know it's possible—

She slices a hand across her throat, indicating that I should stop. I freeze. *You should leave before it is too late,* she signs. *Once I shift, I can hold off my sister so you can escape.*

I stiffen. *That creature isn't your sister. I'm your sister!*

I'm sorry, Svana. Bronwyn shudders more violently this time. Her form starts to harden into scales, then changes back to vapor. *This is my fate.*

Bits of wood spew from the trapdoor as the siren batters my sanctuary entrance. I know I don't have much time, and not just because of my aching heart. Soon, my lungs will begin to work whether I want them to or not. I need to be above the water when they do.

I swallow hard as I look at the ghostly form of the sister I once dove alongside. Even as a mer, she wouldn't be the Bronwyn I knew, not really. But at least she wouldn't be consumed by rage.

I have to stop her!

But I can't. She has to make the choice herself.

I love you, Wyn. So much. My hands shake with each signal.

Bronwyn presses her lips together, as though trying not to cry, even though she can't in this form.

You're strong, Wyn, I sign. *Strong and beautiful and brave, no matter what those men said. Please ... remember who you are—*

The trapdoor bursts open. The siren dives inside, her powerful tail churning the water. Black spots bleed into the edge of my vision, forming a dark halo around the siren. Her teeth are bared, her eyes reptilian slits, her claw-like hands outstretched.

This is what my sister will become.

Bronwyn surges toward the siren, her body rapidly solidifying, and this time, it stays. Her legs fuse into a powerful tail, but her humanoid body stays scale-free. Her tail turns dark and cartilaginous, like a shark. She barrels into the siren, knocking the creature away from me.

A mer. Bronwyn is ... a mer!

With one last glance at Bronwyn's glorious new form, I slip through the cannonball hole I'd originally entered. My body is frigid, almost numb, as I swim toward the pale surface.

My lungs finally break free of their freediving training

and inhale. Water blazes through my nostrils, down my throat.

I saved you, Wyn.

A pair of powerful arms catch me around the waist. A thick tail whirs next to me, *swish, swish, swish.* I am so tired. So cold. So weak.

I crash through the glassy surface into the night air, but my lungs refuse to take it in. They have been trained not to breathe, and they will listen to the training.

Thick arms brace around my sternum and pump, pump, pump. Water spills from my mouth as my ribs crack. Pain lances through my body, but it's nothing compared to the burning in my chest and the sting of fresh air. I gasp and choke, trying to adjust to the pain of being alive.

The mer drags me toward the shore and lays my body on the coarse sand. I blink up at her with heavy eyelids.

She is Bronwyn, and yet she is not. Her nose is still upturned, and her eyes are still too wide-set, but there is a strangeness to those slitted eyes. She smiles with pointed teeth. *Sister,* she signs.

Sister, I sign back.

The tears I've kept buried ever since I heard the news come flooding out. My broken body shakes with sobs, each movement a fresh agony. Through tear-fogged eyes, I see this beautiful, strange creature signing to me.

You will see me again, Svana. Then Bronwyn disappears under the glittering sea.

HEAR MY MEMORY
Myka Silber

When I go to fetch Auntie, she's dozing quietly in a folding chair under the Memory Tree with a blanket on her lap. As usual, I put a hand on her shoulder to wake her. She has become so ancient now that sometimes I worry she won't stir when I go to rouse her, so it's always a relief when her hazy eyes blink open.

"Time for dinner," I say, signing the words as I speak. Auntie can lip read, but it always feels more considerate to sign at her anyway. It also helps break the stillness of our life. There's not a lot left that can move these days.

Her expression is wistful as she gazes up at the old, gnarled branches of the Memory Tree, bedecked in a multitude of metal, crystal, glass, and ceramic creations. A gentle wind blows, swaying the wind chimes and suncatchers, creating dazzling displays where the light of the twin suns refracts in the crystal and glass. It's late in the day, and both of the suns burn red near the horizon. I ignore the gentle clangs and tinkles of the chimes.

"It sounded so beautiful," Auntie signs, seemingly caught up in a dream. "I remember the chimes outside my door growing up."

Sometimes she gets lost in memories of when she was a child some eight decades prior. Before everything happened. Before the comms relays went dark and the great spacefaring vessels stopped coming to our world. Before the wars. Before she lost her hearing in an explosion that had left half her face looking like melting wax.

Before we were alone.

"Tell me about them," I say and sign to Auntie.

She sighs, smiling faintly. "They were metal, with a pattern of vines and roses, and the clapper was a singing bird. They sang clear notes in the wind, and that sound would cut through anything else. Those chimes *wanted* you to hear them." After a brief pause, her hands hovering in the air like uncertain birds, she asks, "Describe these ones to me?"

I pause and consider the variety of chimes swaying above us. Each one has been placed in the tree by someone from our town who lost family or friends in the wars. Or lost them to the grueling misery of existence that came after. My eyes stray to the chimes I made for my mother—made of scrap metal from a downed satellite. The bright purple I used to paint flowers on them has faded with time.

Each chime and suncatcher is sentimental to a bond. No two are alike. Some have been hanging for years, their threads fraying with time, those who once hung them in sorrow and remembrance long gone themselves. When those old memories fall amidst the knotted roots and the brown grass, I always replace their thread and hang them up again. I don't know why I bother. Maybe I can't bear the thought that someone's love will no longer be remembered.

"It's chaotic," I say first. "There are so many different chimes that all have their own voice. It's like ..."

Long-buried emotion stirs in my chest, clogging my throat. I'm glad I don't need to speak for Auntie. My hands still work, and that's easier. I sign, "They sound like they're looking for someone. .Someone they love, who is gone. Like they're crying."

Auntie's gaze sharpens, and I know she's fully with me now. She places both hands over her heart and holds my gaze. I know what she's saying—that my pain is her pain—that we both miss my mother, Auntie's niece. That her absence is a hole in our hearts.

Unbidden tears spring to my eyes, and Auntie stretches her arms out to me. I crouch down next to her and let her wrap her arms around me, simply holding me. She hums faintly, a tune I've never known the words for, a lullaby she hummed to me when I was a child. For a moment, I can see my mother's smile, hear her bright laughter in the tune; but that can't be, it must just be the chimes, and the memory fades.

We stay wrapped up in each other for a few moments, until my knees protest at the continued crouch. As I shake out my legs, I wipe my face on my sleeve. Auntie's cheeks, one smooth and melted, the other wrinkled with age, shine with tear tracks. I offer her the handkerchief from my pocket. Her gnarled hands wrap around mine for a moment as she accepts the cloth and then carefully dabs her eyes and cheeks. When she hands it back to me I'm half-tempted to frame it, label it "Auntie's Tears", so that when she's gone some tangible piece of her will remain. It's a foolish, childish thought. I'm too old for it—old enough that I should have my own family, children growing into adulthood.

That was another thing the wars took from us. Radiation

turned our insides against us and killed us, made us sterile. A child hasn't been born in years. Our entire world, all of us left anyways, will disappear. It won't even be that long from now. All that will be left of us for future spacefarers to find will be ruined cities and the Memory Trees. I duck my head so Auntie can't see my face as I struggle to compose myself in the face of unavoidable erasure.

I only look up when she signs again. "I don't want chimes."

Her expression is somber. Puzzled, I ask, "What do you mean?"

"When you bury me," she signs, "and put something in the Memory Tree for me. I don't want it to be chimes."

"Why not?"

She frowns, and her hands momentarily still on the blanket on her lap. Then she signs again with renewed vigor. "I want my memory to be joyful. I will be at rest, in peace, with everyone I have loved who has gone before me. The very earth of this world will cradle me. I want ... I want you to put up a suncatcher."

My throat feels thick with tears once again. She's never spoken about this before. Like this. I wonder if she knows her time is close. I squash the thought before it can take root. "What kind of suncatcher?"

"Something with wings and colour. Something like a beautiful dream."

"Okay Auntie," I promise. "I will build you the perfect suncatcher." It will mean days spent scrounging through the abandoned houses and storefronts of the town, but I would do anything for her.

She smiles warmly at me, her mind clearly eased by my

words.

I don't want to think about this anymore. I sign to Auntie, "Come, dinner's getting cold."

Slowly, painfully, she rises to her feet as I fold her lap blanket and drape it over my arm. As she begins limping to our small home, one of the few houses still occupied in this town, she asks, "What is it today?"

This, at least, is a familiar game. "Guess."

"A plate of roast pricklepig and steamed greens in a curry sauce."

"No, guess again." That kind of meal hasn't been possible in decades.

She scrunches up her face as if deep in thought, then exaggerates the gasp of revelation. "My mother's recipe for Hundred Cake."

I laugh and answer, "You can't eat cake for dinner."

"Says who? I am old as dirt and can eat what I want!" she signs back with good humour.

The conversation has taken us to our door, and I let her go in ahead of me. For a moment, I pause and glance over my shoulder back to the Memory Tree. I've never learned what kind of tree it is—but it feels old and weathered, like it's been here since this town was settled.

I will put up a suncatcher for Auntie one day, but there will be no one to hang anything for me. A shiver runs through me as I watch the few sickly leaves sway in the wind. I step into our home and close the door firmly on the sight of the ancient tree.

It is dinner time, and Auntie needs to eat, even if it is only a ration tin of beans I scrounged in an abandoned store on one of my trips into town cooked with what few stunted vegetables I can convince our garden to yield. A poor excuse for a dinner, but Auntie will no doubt make it into a feast with her words as she always does.

The thought pulls my shoulders back and raises my chin. I follow Auntie to the small table in the kitchen, where we have eaten together for years, just the two of us. For now, we are together. Tomorrow is still far away.

COME BACK AT BEDTIME
Tristan Durant

Come **back at** bedtime
And tuck the sheet up under my chin
Tell me a story of brave men and noble deeds
In hushed tones of whispered reverence
Sing me a lullaby to usher in sweet dreams
Press a kiss to my forehead
Even the bravest soldiers need their mother's kisses
Murmur goodnight
The creak of the door as you slip out
Your footsteps on the stairs the last thing I hear
As I drift off, at peace
Oh how I long to be your little boy for just one more night, mother please, is there a version of the story where you don't leave?

NIGHTMARES
Abigail Hawthorne

To Mama. You always said that if you could take my pain, you would. This one's to your love.

CARRIE – 18 Years Ago

Long, death-like fingers snaked around me, clouding my vision. I brushed them away. "Not now, Agnes. Please."

The wisps recoiled, providing me with a clear view of the most beautiful thing on earth: my newborn daughter. I heard a sob from somewhere behind me and smiled. Even the shadows found her lovely.

Bridget smiled and cooed, content in whatever little baby-dream-world she was in. I dashed at a tear before it could fall down my face and onto her perfect little cheek. No, her dreams would be safe. Distant. Foreign.

She wouldn't carry on my legacy.

Noah, my husband, slipped an arm around me. Agatha slithered away, giving us space. "She's so beautiful," he whispered in my ear.

I nodded, tears blurring my vision. "We'll keep her safe,

right?"

He kissed my temple. "Of course."

Of course. I'd keep her safe.

BRIDGET – Now

Whoever said you didn't need a college degree to succeed was right. I think. I wouldn't know, because I was dumb enough to think I should be a lawyer. And they generally didn't let lawyers practice with nothing but a high school diploma.

So here I was, shuffling into sophomore year with a chip on one shoulder and a backpack full of textbooks I probably wouldn't read on the other. Don't get me wrong, I really do enjoy law. It's just the myriad of not-law classes that make me wish I could pitch a fit like I was still two years old.

"I'm an adult," I mutter as the stairwell door slams behind me. "I'm an adult." I drop into the second row of chairs in my eight A.M. sociology class.

"Still wish you were two?"

I force a smile—or the closest I can manage at this forbidden hour of the morning—at the girl who slinks into the seat beside me. She's lanky, with long purple waves of hair that frame her angular face. She looks familiar—did we have a class together last semester?—but I can't remember her name.

"Somedays, yes," I say. I take a long *glug* of my canned iced coffee. "But then I wouldn't be able to drink caffeine."

"But you wouldn't need it." She smiles, revealing impossibly white teeth, and holds her Styrofoam travel mug up in a toast. "I'm Stella Rey. Never did manage to get a nickname, you have to say the whole thing."

Stella Rey. The name is so familiar it hurts. Where—

"And you're Bridget, right?"

"Yeah—yes. I'm sorry, have we met before?" I can't take my eyes off her as more students funnel into the classroom.

"Seventh grade." Her eyes are so haunting. I can see now that they aren't brown or blue or green or any normal color. They shimmer an iridescent black. "You were in your slightly-goth phase."

There's nothing *slightly* about Stella Rey. From the black tie-dye crop top to the skull and crossbones necklace to the winged eyeliner, she's just the grown-up version of middle-school gothic.

My hands twitch, wanting to text mom or Yasmin and see if either of them remember Stella Rey. I remember her clearly now, sure, but not ... not in real life. She was a dream, a figment of my imagination, a way my 13-year-old mind had found to piece together little bits of information as I slept.

Stella Rey had never been real.

CARRIE – 16 Years Ago

"She's sleeping like an angel," Noah said, sinking onto the couch beside me. He slipped an arm around my shoulders. "You'd never know she was fighting like a demon ten minutes ago."

I elbowed my husband's side. "Shush. She's a darling."

"Uh-huh." He grabbed the TV remote from the coffee table. "Movie time?"

"You know it."

He scrolled through several films, pausing on a few just for me to grunt my disapproval. Finally he landed on a horror flick with the word "nightmare" in the title. "How about this? Adam said it was really good—"

"Let's not." I burrowed deeper into his side, wishing the stupid shadows away. They saw the word "nightmare" and sprang to life. Agnes, the ringleader of my living dreams, ran a shadow finger along my face.

"What's wrong with nightmares, sweetheart?" she taunted.

I swatted her away, trying to disguise my movement so Noah didn't notice anything wrong. She'd haunted me since childhood. She was the monster under my bed, the footsteps in the night, the terror in the closet. And she was as real as me.

My father had been imprisoned by his own versions. I knew because I'd heard him screaming. He's the one who'd finally told me I wasn't crazy for seeing the nightmares while I was awake. He did, too. So did his father. And his grandmother.

It was our family legacy.

As Noah scrolled through a dozen more movies, I listened to the utter silence from the baby monitor. Maybe my daughter would be the end of this family lineage.

BRIDGET – Now

"Mom, do you remember a Stella Rey? From when I was in middle school." With my phone tucked against my ear, I pick my way around the puddles in the school's cracked sidewalk. I have an hour before my next class, which means time to go back to my dorm room and study. Or nap. Probably nap.

"No, why?" she asks. Her voice crackles through my phone's broken speaker.

"I just met her in sociology class. She seems super familiar, and she says she remembers me from seventh grade." I pause, rationalizing the weird nagging in my gut. "You're certain you don't remember her? Purple hair, dresses goth."

Mom laughs. "I think I would remember that. Your only friend in seventh grade was that nerdy boy who had a secret crush on you. Devin, was it?"

"Yeah, yeah." I wince. I didn't meet Yasmin until eighth grade. Seventh grade had been torturous—new city, new school, no friends except for the gamer geek that, as it turned out, only wanted me around if I would date him. "Then why does she remember me?"

"I don't know—"

Mom's next words are chopped off by my shriek.

"Honey, what's wrong? Are you okay?"

I clench my phone in a death grip and stare at the monstrosity that's blocking the sidewalk. It's a dark, hairy blob of green, with eyes that pierce my soul and two horns that twist far above its head. It towers above me, fills the width of the sidewalk.

"Bridgy, answer me." Mom's voice crackles in my ear. "Are you okay?"

"Mom, I—I—"

I can't take my eyes off the horror. But, in my periphery, I see other students walking past like nothing's wrong. One bumps into me, muttering an expletive as he passes.

Then he walks straight through the beast.

The monster slowly looks down at the space where the student walked through. Then he refocuses on me.

What on earth is happening?

"Mom, I promise I'm not on drugs," I say.

She laughs, but it's terse. "Honey, I know. Just tell me you're okay."

"I—I'm fine. I think." I step forward, towards the monster. Another student on a skateboard flies past me and runs straight through him. Again, the beast looks down, then back at me.

I take two more steps forward. I could reach out and touch him now. But I don't, convinced that no one else is seeing this.

"Mom, I'm going to switch to video call," I say. "Tell me if you see anything, um, weird."

"Okay."

I switch the call and hold my camera up. Even on my phone, I can see the monster. He cocks his head, like he's confused. "Do you see anything strange?" I ask.

"Does the dude in nothing but a Speedo count?" Mom asks.

"Nope, that's normal. He's just out for his morning run."

"Glad I didn't go to college. No, everything looks fine. Sweetie, what's wrong?"

I switch back to voice mode. "I think I'm hallucinating?"

"Okay." The word is slow, drawn out. "What makes you think that?"

"I'm seeing a monster on the sidewalk."

She gasps. "All right. That ... that'll do it. Honey, tell me what you see."

After a fortifying breath, I walk forwards again. I'm so close I'm all but touching the monster now. One more step and I should be able to walk through it, just like everyone else. I try it.

But I run right into its furry, solid body. It chuckles. The hallucination *chuckles*.

"You really think that's going to work, Bridget?" it asks. Its voice is deep enough to send a shiver of fear down my spine.

"Mom, I don't know what's going on. Maybe I'm having a stroke? I can feel the monster and it's talking to me."

"Can you sit down somewhere? I need you to stay with me." Panic edges into her always-calm voice.

She thinks I'm on drugs. Shoot, *I* think I'm on drugs. I look away from the monster long enough to spot a bench a few paces behind me. "Yeah." Once I'm seated—still watching the beast as more and more students walk through it—I say, "What do I do? Did someone drug—"

"I have a strange question for you."

"No stranger than this."

She laughs, even though it sounds strained. Why is she

laughing? I'm having some sort of medical crisis.

"Honey, does the monster look familiar?" she asks. "From nightmares when you were a little girl or something?"

I squint at the giant beast. "Maybe?"

"And this Stella Rey. Do you think you ever dreamed about her?"

"Yeah, that's what was odd. That's the only place I remembered her. Dreams."

"All right. I'm going to tell you something I've been hiding for years." She inhales, then sighs loudly. "My family has a … a weird characteristic. A family trait that gets passed down. I thought you'd missed it, and I was so glad. But I suppose it only showed up late."

"Is it a susceptibility to strokes? Because I'm pretty sure I'm stroking out."

"It's not a stroke. It's about our nightmares." She pauses, and I can feel my blood pressure shooting up. Her voice is trembling, like she's about to cry. "They … they come to life. They're real."

"That doesn't make sense. Dreams can't be real."

"They are for us. But only for us. That's why I can't see your monster. Only you can. But, I promise you, it's as real as you or me."

"That's—that's—"

"Completely insane, but also the truth." Now I'm certain she's crying. "I've been living with my nightmares since I was three years old. Maybe younger, I just don't remember. Your grandpa is the same way."

I focus on controlling my breathing as I hold eye contact with the monster. "How do I get rid of them?"

"You don't. You learn to live with your nightmares."

CARRIE – Now

"Agnes, get in here." I snap.

The shadowy figure slips into the kitchen, wrapping around me. "Yes?"

She doesn't talk often, and I'm grateful for it. Her hissing voice sends shivers up my spine. But I need her now.

"I had a dream once that I could take on someone else's nightmares. I need to know how."

She laughs, the silvery sound flooding the otherwise-empty house. "That would be foolish, Caroline."

"If I dreamed it, it could be real." I slam the lid on the beef stew and whirl around, facing her. She doesn't have eyes or any facial features for that matter, but I can make out what passes as a head. The shadows narrow to form a neck, then expand into almost an oval shape. I stare there, a tactic I learned in high school—it was the same time I named her Agnes. The more human I make her, the less frightening she is.

"Not everything you dream is real." Her voice shifts into an almost sing-song tone, mocking me.

"But there's the possibility. I want to know how to assume someone else's nightmares."

"Their nightmares would be more frightening than your own." To prove her point, she shifts into a taller, less human shape and towers over me.

I sidestep her and move to the fridge. "I don't care."

"Well, then."

"Is it possible?"

"Yes. But it's never been done."

"Don't care. Tell me how to do it."

She slams her wispy hand on the fridge's handle. "Why?"

I try to open the door, but it won't budge. "Please move."

Her shadows ripple in the stir from the A/C, but she doesn't remove her hand.

I sigh. "Bridget has started seeing her nightmares. I don't want her to live like that."

She cackles, the smell of her musty breath overwhelming. "She'll learn. Just like you did, and your father did, and his father, and his mother, and her father—"

"I get it." She finally moves her hand, and I pull a handful of carrots out of the fridge. "But I want to break the cycle."

"This isn't a drug addiction, Caroline." She still hovers near me, her wispy form brushing my arm as I turn around. "There's nothing to break. Just let her live out the legacy."

"It's not a legacy I'm thrilled to be passing on." I snatch my favorite cutting board from where it was drying beside the sink. "Are you going to tell me how to take her dreams or not?"

When Agnes sighs, her whole body shivers. "Fine, my dear." She stretches each word out. "It's really quite simple. But it can only be done once. Bridget can never take the nightmares back."

"I wouldn't want it any other way." I finish washing the carrots and grab my chef's knife. "Tell me what to do."

BRIDGET – Now

I skip the rest of my classes for the day. I bunker down inside my dorm room, grateful that my roommate has a packed schedule on Tuesdays, and eat Lunchables while I read syllabi. But I can't focus. The monster stayed on the sidewalk, I haven't seen Stella Rey since class this morning, and my mom hasn't called back after our insane discussion. Maybe it's all a joke. Maybe my roommate slipped drugs into my water bottle while I was getting ready this morning. I don't really know her all that well.

I shake my head to clear it. No, this is real. The monster and Stella Rey were real(ish) and the talk with Mom was definitely real.

Maybe it was a freak incident. Mom did say that everyone else in the family had their first experiences with their nightmares before they were my age. Maybe I'm special, and it'll just be a one and done deal.

The door creaks open, and I shove all of my trash onto one corner of my bed. Then I flip the lamp beside me on. No use having my roommate know I'm living like a slob.

I wait a moment, expecting her, but she doesn't step through the tiny hallway and into our room. "Layla?" I call. "Is that you?"

Heavy footsteps—much louder than tiny Layla could ever make—pound down the little hall.

I gasp and yank my covers up to my chin at the figure before me. He's tall, broad, and wearing black sweats that do nothing to hide his strength. He grips a long, curved knife in one hand. But his face ... his face is weirdly non-existent. Where it should be is a swirling mass of features. Eyes, skin, mouth, nose, everything. It shifts into one face, then melts away into another. None of them are fully human.

"Who—what—what—are you?" I stutter as I cower under my pile of blankets. I know the answer, though. If Stella Rey was my way of coping through the friendless middle school years, and the beast on the sidewalk was the monster under my bed in preschool ... then this hideous man is the terror that chased me down in every nightmare as a child, teenager, even into college.

"What do you want?" I ask.

He doesn't speak. I know he won't. He never has. His face shifts into one that's familiar. It reminds me of the creepy neighbor I was terrified of in second grade. Then it turns into the high school boyfriend who tried to assault me when I was sixteen. Then it melds into something horrid and completely unrecognizable. Still he comes closer. Each step is in slow-motion.

"Please, just leave." My voice pitches up. I feel my skin grow clammy.

The nightmare edges closer, reaches out, and touches me. Nausea overwhelms me as he brushes my face with a gloved hand.

This is not a hallucination. I can feel every thread in his worn gloves. I can taste his putrid breath as he steps right up beside my bed.

Then he's gone. Not like you would expect a dream to dissipate, but like a person would leave the room. He turns around, walks out, closes the door behind him.

I curl into a ball and start sobbing. Is this how I'm supposed to live?

CARRIE – 3 Weeks Later

Bridget comes home for a long weekend, and I barely recognize her. Dark circles crowd her once-vibrant eyes, she jumps at every noise, and nothing makes her laugh. Noah notices it, but he doesn't understand. I explained the whole thing to him years ago, when Bridget was four, after he found me sobbing in the bathroom at three o'clock in the morning. He believed me, but his blessedly normal mind can't comprehend what it's like to live under our curse.

I haven't told anyone about my plan. Not Noah, not my dad, and certainly not Bridget. She would fight me if she knew. But I hate the pain in her eyes, and I would do anything to take it away.

I've run over Agnes's instructions a million times. When Bridget falls asleep on the couch halfway through *The Man Who Shot Liberty Valance*, I know it's time.

I wait until Noah steps out for more popcorn. This will be quick.

Smoothing my daughter's hair off her forehead, I lean into the cushion behind me. Eyes closed, inviting all my nightmares in. Agnes leads the pack, her shadows filling the room. I can sense them even without seeing her. I hear the murmurs and footsteps of everyone else, from the friendlier creatures to the dragon to the gang of murderers that all look like they belong on *Star Trek*. Then I take Bridget's hands in mine, hoping I don't wake her.

Deep breath. Imagine all of her nightmares. All of her fears. Invite them.

When I open my eyes, my living room is packed with terrifying sights. New characters and beasts stand between familiar ones. A tall girl with purple hair flashes a haunting smile. The beast she described on the sidewalk fills the doorway. One faceless man swings a giant, curved knife at my dragon.

I feel the terror trying to flood my senses, and I let it. I've lived with nightmares since I was a toddler—the fear never goes away, and I can handle it. But this is different. The horror holds me to my seat. The dreams keep morphing, turning into something worse than I'd first seen. Worse than I'd ever seen or imagined.

Bridget shifts, laying her head on my shoulder. I look down at her and see a smile creeping onto her sleeping face. It's the first smile I've seen since she came home yesterday.

Her nightmares begin to disperse, finding new homes in my mind and my house. Shivers race up my spine as they brush past me. One meets my eyes, and my blood runs cold. But I'll be fine.

I drop my daughter's hand. I embrace the fear.

I break my family's legacy.

RED RAINS
Kelly Hellmuth

I have not left the cellar in Leroy Green's feed store for some time. Jimmy told me to stay put. I have to trust him, even though it turns out I never really knew him.

I was only eight years old the day Papa brought him home. It rained for the first time in months, and the sudden cloudburst coated everything outside in a layer of red dirt. There was a boy standing on the front porch that didn't belong there, and I made sure Mama was aware of his presence, all soaking wet and stained Oklahoma copper. I had never seen a kid quite so caked in dirt before in my life; I told him all about it as Mama shooed me into the kitchen and handed me a knife to peel potatoes for supper while she drew him a bath. Papa sat down on a kitchen stool next to me and peeled, not saying a word as gritty brown potato skins fell to the ground at his feet. I examined his tired, weatherworn face, desperate for some answers.

"Why is there a dirty boy in our washroom, Papa?"

"I found him out in the far cornfield, Florence. He's all

skin and bone. I couldn't just leave him."

I thought about it before picking up my knife. "Where do you suppose he came from?"

He sighed. "I can't say for sure, but no one was with him, and he's not much of a talker."

I scoffed and went to work on my potato. "Who in their right mind would leave behind a child?"

Papa smiled just a little, pausing for a second as he looked me deep in the eyes. "Sometimes people don't take care of their own, Florence. The best we can do in the moment is to step in and try our best to help, just as the good Lord tells us to."

I rolled my eyes and resumed peeling. "Could the good Lord have sent us someone a little cleaner?"

It was weeks before the boy's skin and hair returned to something resembling a natural color. His hair was still the color of pennies. Mama insisted he had to be out in the dirt longer than we expected. All the scrubbing in the world couldn't seem to get the stains from the Oklahoma clay out of his skin. He said little at first; mostly he just repeated short words back to us like "yes" and "no". Papa started calling him Jimmy after Oklahoma's pride and joy, and Jimmy didn't seem to mind. "If Jim Thorpe can come from nothing to take over at the Olympics, so can this kid," he said. Though Jimmy never told us where he came from.

Mama insisted one of those traveling circuses where no one spoke English had left him behind. "It isn't the first child that those folks have abandoned, and I can guarantee you it won't be the last," she said to Papa one night early on when she thought Jimmy and I were long asleep. "We can't take in every stray they abandon on their way to Amarillo!"

"We may not be able to take in every stray, Mabel, but this one isn't going anywhere. We're the only family he has. There's no changing that now. We take care of our own." Somehow, Jimmy understood that, and he was loyal to Papa from that moment on.

A special kind of bond happens when people go through hard things together, and the Great Depression didn't help. Jimmy was family, picking up with ease what it took to take care of a farm. It was difficult work. Mama often took it upon herself to toughen Jimmy up. "This world is hard, and you're going to have to just get used to it." Papa would sit quietly by, bringing us along to pluck slaughtered chickens or detassel the corn. We toughened up, and we depended on each other. Jimmy grew more and more like Papa every day. Willing to learn. More loyal than anything. When the big drought hit in the summer of 1930, we were all thankful to have Jimmy around. Farming would become near impossible.

Papa and Mama insisted Jimmy and I find another way to help, so we both got jobs at Leroy Greene's feed store in Lawton. It wasn't long before rumors started flying around about whether Jimmy would ever propose to me. Mrs. Sadie Greene would hound me all the time about it. "You'd do well to lock that Jimmy down sooner rather than later, Florence. He's a good-looking young man. Emma May Johnson was watching him behind the seed counter just yesterday." I would simply smile and remind her that girls didn't marry their brothers. Jimmy would watch me and grin just a little. There was never a need to talk about it later.

The next spring, the hopes of just a little rain overshadowed all fears of an active storm season. Jimmy had returned to the same dusty red color he was when we first found him. But to be fair, everyone and everything had turned the color of rust. Piles of crimson dirt filled the corners of every building and every street. The winds were relentless, the once beautiful blue cloudless skies now hazy with an unholy auburn hue. The tension in the atmosphere echoed within the hearts and minds of the people of Lawton. Jimmy was the worst of us all.

He never stopped looking at the sky like he knew a storm was coming. But most Oklahomans are born with that sixth sense, and all I could anticipate was more dirt. Jimmy had always been a man of few words, but he grew strangely quiet that spring. One morning in particular, I awoke to find him emerging from the underground cellar on the farm. He said nothing of it but left a note for Papa and Mama sitting on the kitchen table before we left for Leroy Green's. A lone cloud hung in the sky. "How did you know that was coming?" I asked as we walked to work. He didn't answer.

Main Street in Lawton was abuzz with excitement all day. Emma May Johnson spent the morning talking about the cloud with her little crew in the corner of the feed store, glancing over at Jimmy every once in a while to see if he was paying attention. Both Leroy and Mrs. Sadie went on and on about the possibility of rain. As the atmosphere heated, the cloud grew and grew. The winds didn't relent, but somehow the cloud was stationary in the sky.

Mrs. Sadie threw open the glass doors of the feed store, gabbing to anyone who would listen about the miracle cloud building overhead. As the energy around this meteorological phenomenon spread, Jimmy grew more and more uncomfortable. I pulled him toward the door, trying to get in on some of the bustle outside.

"We are finally getting some rain, Jimmy! C'mon!"

He didn't budge. "Don't go out that door, Florence."

The sky darkened as the cloud obscured the sun, and thunder clapped overhead, rumbling the foundation of the feed store. Cheers erupted as all of Lawton lifted their arms and welcomed the coming rain. Emma May Johnson lifted a shout of "Hallelujah" which was echoed up and down the street by everyone around. Leroy and Mrs. Sadie led a chorus of Amazing Grace. Only Jimmy and I stood indoors, and I ached to join them. But Jimmy was insistent.

Giant crimson drops fell from the sky, the rain capturing the dust that filled the air and sending it crashing to the ground. Emma May Johnson declared, as the drops ruined her perfect curls, she could see blue skies again! Mrs. Sadie prayed loud prayers of thanks, with a refrain of loud Amens affirming her words as rain soaked through her clothing, any bits of modesty gone in celebration of this joyous event. Leroy Green proclaimed for all to hear that it would be a good growing season and that everyone should come into the feed store and buy seeds. I beamed from ear to ear and rushed to hold the door open.

Jimmy yanked my arm back and locked the door behind us. Outside, the intensity of the rain increased, and the harder it fell, the more red it became. Shouts of joy grew quiet for a moment, then abruptly shifted into terrifying screams.

I stood and watched in horror as everyone outside became coated with a thick scarlet substance. It was no longer rain.

Leroy Green charged the doors to his shop, pounding so hard on them I thought he might break them down. The viscous liquid trailed down the glass with each hit, leaving crimson streaks in the clay-covered panes. I could feel my stomach jumping into my throat, but Jimmy simply stared at him, placing himself between me and the door. Leroy first pleaded for us to let him in, but his cries quickly turned to curses, his anger increasing exponentially every second. I snatched the key from Jimmy's hand.

"No! He isn't our own!" he cried out.

"We have to help him, Jimmy!"

"It's too late, Florence!"

I looked deep into Leroy Greene's eyes, which had grown desperate and wild. I couldn't turn the key. Blood-red moss grew rapidly over his entire body in what felt like an instant. It entered his mouth and his ears and his eyes, his body rapidly disintegrating into a festering pile of scarlet moss that pulsed on the doorstep of Leroy Greene's feed store. Main Street was silent other than the sound of a heavy rain. Emma May Johnson. Mrs. Sadie. They had all disappeared. I couldn't speak.

Jimmy wrenched me away from the door just as the moss ate away the glass and joined what remained of Leroy Greene. The parasite throbbed and took shape, building upon itself as it developed into the form of a man. Leroy Greene. Out on Main Street, I could see blurry images resembling people that I once knew rising out of the rains.

Jimmy leaned over and whispered in my ear. "You have to get underground, Florence. Now!" He whisked me toward the back room and down into the cellar, as portions of the roof dissolved above our heads. I was in shock. He shoved me down the steps and started to close me in.

"Wait!" I yelled, and Jimmy paused. "How do you know about this?"

He thought for a moment, and his body shuddered, transforming blood red.

I could not breathe. "You're one of them." I said.

He nodded, shivering again, turning back into the Jimmy I knew.

"What happened to my parents? Are they okay? Why are you doing this?"

Something resembling love washed over his face. "I am taking care of my own. Stay here until I return. Don't make a sound. I'm going to check on your parents." He closed the door. I heard him scoot a nearby desk over the hatch.

That was at least five days ago. I've lost track. I hear the desk scraping across the doors overhead. The lights are blinding as the hatch opens, but I can make out the silhouettes of three figures staring down into the cellar.

THE GREATEST STORY NEVER TOLD

Tristan Durant

The greatest story never told

Is the one where we were happy

Where she didn't leave

And he wasn't distant

The one where we were a family

Not three people sharing blood

And dysfunction

The one where I didn't worry

About the implications of loving like them

Where I grew up happy and healed

In a home, not just a house

With warmth and traditions

Where I got to have a childhood

And maybe even a sibling

The one where my memories are old friends

Not monsters that hunt me at all hours

HOW FAR I'LL GO FOR YOU
Lexie Kauffman

Work to prove your worth, they declared, shoving a mop into your hand.

You will never leave this house, they said, installing locks to keep you *in* rather than others *out*.

You are nothing, they proclaimed, laughing as you begged for freedom.

But you're something, and that is the fire that burns through your veins as you swing one leg out of your bedroom window. The brick digs into your exposed ankles. You stare down at the pieces of your life stuffed into two measly bags in the dewy grass below. You glance back at the only room you've ever known and wonder if it's always been that small.

The gray walls are faded and the cheap excuse for a bed takes up most of the floor space. When you were little, those four walls could be anything—a castle, an airplane, a boat. Now, all you see is the prison that has tortured you since you dared speak your mind. Since you wondered why you couldn't go to public school like the neighbor girl you see through the window. Since you wondered if differences make people stronger than weaker. Since you met him.

He's everything your parents are not. He's kind and gentle. He would never raise a hand towards you. But like everything else, your parents took him away, filled his head with lies. You know he's not waiting for you. He might have been your entire life, but you were simply a blip in his memory.

But you're not doing this for him. If it was for him, you would've left years ago. You're not even doing this for yourself. You take a deep breath and look down at the sleeping figure strapped to your chest. The bruises left by your mother shine, purple and blue, in the moonlight. You lean down and kiss the top of her head, her matted blonde hair the perfect mirror of her father. You are now living for her.

With one final glance into the room, you swing your other leg over the windowsill. You lower yourself onto the grass, your hands grasping the windowsill while your legs swing and stretch to meet the ground. Once you do, you pick up the bags and pull them over your shoulders. Then, you run into the night.

LETTERS TO LESLIE
Darby S. Fisher

Dear diary,
Friday.

I need somewhere to share how I'm feeling. I'm so un-happy with life right now. My job is boring and pointless, and it's getting harder to leave my bed. This morning, my sister asked me how much gas is left in the car.

"Not enough."

I walked away from her after that. She had filled the tank at the beginning of the week (we share my car). I only drive to work and back, which doesn't use much gas.

This gloom is making me weird.

Dear diary,
Wednesday.

My sister got mad at me. She had the keys to the car in her purse, which she keeps in her room, which she locks while she sleeps (she works nights). I ended up an hour late to work.

She made me sick with her glare when she finally opened the door. I wish I had called out, but the manager, Rob, has a short temper.

When I walked into the office, I clocked in and sat down. No one said anything about me being late, not even Rob. Usually, they tease people about flat tires or aliens, but I didn't get a word.

I saw girls online calling themselves "lucky girl" and manifesting good things to happen to them. I wish life worked that way.

I wish I was lucky.

Dear diary,
Saturday.

My sister, Leslie, started taking walks before work. She invited me to join her, but I don't want to go.

I wish I could rewire my brain to be proactive. Leslie seems to have that mastered. She's so confident. I peeked over her shoulder the other day and watched her apply for new jobs like it was no big deal. I could never.

I read a post online about space studies. They are researching deep sleep so we can reach a new planet. The guy who discovered it wants to call it "Zed-Alpha." I don't know how they come up with names for this stuff.

Dear diary,
Wednesday.

I did some research on the sleep study, and they are accepting applicants. There's one a couple hours away. The pay looks good, and it's three years long.

What's a few years? When I think about three years ago versus now, not much has changed. I live with Leslie. I'm at the same office job. I don't have friends.

Imagine how nice it would be to fast-forward time? I might wake up well rested and with money, if I'm lucky. I need a break. Money's too tight for one right now, and I don't see that changing soon.

I could take six months or more off of work and figure out a new job. Leslie could have the car and the apartment to herself.

Maybe I'll wake up a different person.

Dear diary,
Thursday.

Two days in a row? It's an anomaly.

Yesterday, my computer at work deleted all my emails, and Rob screamed at me. Apparently, I've been doing everything wrong for the past four years that I've worked here. No one ever noticed until yesterday. I guess I was "lucky."

I spent a few hours filling out the application for the deep sleep program.

Once I talk myself into it, I'm going to submit it.

Reasons why I should: I won't get picked anyway, the money, a break, no more office.

Reasons I shouldn't: change is scary, I might get picked, three years is a long time.

Or is it?

Dear diary,
Monday.

At nine, I got an email from the space company asking me to fill out a survey. They're interested in seeing if I could be a "great fit" for the study.

It's a much larger scale than I realized. They need a range of people because they have colonization planned for Zed-Alpha. If I knew how likely I was to be picked, I don't think I would have submitted it.

I have to tell Leslie. I feel like a kid again, waiting to show Mom my report card. Maybe I could set up a shared bank account so she could still get my half of the rent. I know she can't afford our place on her own.

I'll tell her this weekend.

Dear diary,
Happy Friday!

Surprisingly, I'm in a good mood. The survey the study sent me is five hundred questions long. It only opens on my laptop so I've been staying up late to work on it.

After these questions, they are going to decline me for the study. I'm trying to stay honest, but it's fun to click answers I know they'll hate. How do I feel about tubes? Hate them. How do I do in confined spaces? Terrible.

Tomorrow when Leslie wakes up, I'm going to tell her. I'm not sure how she'll react, but if I don't do something different with my life, I'm going to go crazy.

Crazy isn't the word. I'm not sure what the word I want is. Nothing is going to get better for me. I'm a fly in a jar with no lid on it, but somehow, I can't get free.

Leslie has found her way out. I don't think that can be taught.

Dear diary,
Wednesday.

Leslie did not take the news well, but it could be worse! I think she was in shock. When I brought up that it was a three-year study, she rolled her eyes.

She offered to help me go through my stuff. She might not live here in three years, but she said she would save a closet for me wherever she goes.

Also, I sent in the completed survey! They sent me a confirmation email. I should hear back from them in a few weeks. I'm sure they aren't going to ask me to participate, but Leslie keeps saying, "you never know."

Dear diary,
Tuesday, again.

Every time I get a notification on my phone, my heart skips a beat.

Work has been extra terrible lately. When I'm in the parking lot, I want to cry. Going inside is getting harder and harder with the idea that soon I might not have to go.

Leslie has been clingy lately. It's nice but awkward. We grew up in the same house with the same parents, but we're polar opposites. She's optimistic, competitive, and athletic. I'm none of those things. I don't mind spending hours alone, and I'd rather work with people than against them.

I've tried being optimistic like her, but it never worked.

Maybe she took all of my luck at birth.

Dear diary,
Monday.

I had a good weekend with Leslie. We talked until midnight about things we used to do as kids, like sharing candy apples and braiding our hair.

My parents were saints to put up with all of our differences. I hated having the overhead light on; she said she couldn't see without it. She wanted all our jackets to be brightly colored (we shared them), and I wanted neutral tones. We get along better as adults.

I think my parents were shocked when we said we were moving out together. Coming to Jacksonville was one of the only things we could agree on.

The email from the study should be here next week.

Dear diary,
Happy Monday!

I got an email from the sleep study at six this morning. They accepted me. They want me to pack my belongings and travel to the center as soon as I can. Also, they gave me a number to call if I need anything, even a ride there.

The man who signed the email, Levi, sounded excited about my survey results. If they want more people on

Zed-Alpha in the future, they need to accommodate people who are scared of tubes and tight spaces.

I can take on a new identity in those character traits. They might be true. Will the medical equipment freak me out when I see it? Will they put me in a tight pod to sleep in like they do in movies?

I have no idea.

I need to write a letter of resignation for Rob. Neither of us will be heartbroken.

Dear diary,
Friday.

Rob didn't care. I gave him a two weeks' notice, but he said I have some time off to use and not to come in again.

I asked Leslie when we could drive to the center. She made me work for an answer. I told her that they offered to come get me, but she was adamant about going with me.

We made a shared bank account, and I filled out the payment information so that the account gets half of my money. She says she doesn't need it, but it makes me feel better.

I'm relieved that the center wants to store my things for me. I emailed Levi that I should arrive Wednesday afternoon.

He said they'll be expecting me.

Dear diary,
Tuesday.

Leslie has been moody since last Monday. She gave me a hard time about having to take off of work to go with me. I offered to pay her for it, but she's not accepting anything, and I can't say anything to get her out of her mood.

We are going to leave tomorrow morning at ten. It's the earliest she's willing to wake up.

I expect it to be an awkward, quiet drive.

Dear diary,
Friday!

I feel at home here.

They took my blood on Wednesday once I arrived and then again on Thursday. Levi greeted me at the door. He explained that all over the nation, they set up these centers to study deep sleep. My center's name is Palm, like the tree.

I like it. There are ten other people here. They expect to have a group total of fifty by the end of the month.

In the meantime, he wants me to keep up with you. When I confessed that I already had a diary that I updated once a week or more, he was ecstatic. He wants me to update you more often, but I don't see that happening.

They're encouraging us to spend our free time in an activity room. They have games, streaming services, and coloring in there. The group's interactions will help their research.

They aren't sure when these colonies are going to happen, and they won't say much else.

Would I want to go to Zed-Alpha? I don't know. I've tried learning more about it, but all I've learned is that it's similar to Earth.

I'm relishing this whole experience.

Dear diary,
Tuesday.

The more people who arrive here, the more structured our schedule becomes. They mainly serve us 'health food' and supplements to prepare us for deep sleep. I overheard some guys talking about how no one here has food allergies. I'm not sure how correct that is, but they are determined to ask everyone here.

The last two people are arriving Thursday night.

Everyday has been something to look forward to, but the researchers are making us exercise and requiring us to learn more new things to see what we will retain in three years when they wake us up. It's a lot of work.

Some of this stuff is complicated like engineering. Other stuff is simple gardening and composting.

Leslie would thrive here. It's hard not to, but wherever we went, she found fortune. One year when we were young, she grew sunflowers all over the backyard. Dad made her cut them down, but she sold them and turned a profit.

She paid for us to go out for dinner and let me pick the restaurant.

Maybe we can go back when I wake up.

Dear diary,
Thursday.

In fourteen days, we're going into these pods (yes, like the movies) for deep sleep.

Since there is a risk that we won't wake up, they encouraged us to write letters to our families and friends. I'm going to write to Mom and Dad this week. Next week, I'm going to write to Leslie.

I'm not sure what to tell her.

Dear diary,
Friday.

The first batch of letters are off. I started my letter to Leslie, but I tossed it. Staring at the paper, I realized I'm angry and jealous of her. She's had a very lucky life.

I don't want to send that to her. She's my sister; we're buddies. I'll have to keep it short. I can't imagine not writing to her since I wrote to our parents. She deserves better.

She's always made an effort to be nice to me, even when I pushed her away (sometimes physically). I wish I wasn't angry at her. It would be easier if she wasn't mad at me for leaving.

I couldn't live like that. Here, I have friends. People pay attention to me. Not too much, but people look at me and smile when I sit down with them. They encourage me during our morning runs.

Maybe I should tell her that … I'm happier here.

Dear diary,
Tuesday.

I barely finished Leslie's letter in time to send it. At least she can't be angrier at me for ignoring her.

This Thursday, we are going into our pods. They are going to let us into the room where they are kept tomorrow. I would say that this is the point of no return, but we all signed the paperwork.

Levi got us some markers to decorate the insides. We can't put anything on the outside, but he encouraged us to write our own name, the group's name (Palm), and draw some things that we like.

Three years is going to go by in literally a blink of an eye for me.

Dear diary,
Wednesday.

I'm only writing this because I was told to, and everyone is writing something.

    Sight: forty-nine other people, white paper on brown tables.
Smell: tight, old carpet, unscented soap.
    Feel: nervous, dread. I don't know what I'm going to do once this is over. It's like summer camp but with blood work and college classes.
    Taste: chocolate. One of my friends gave me his piece.
    Sound: quiet, pen on paper.

    I won't write tomorrow. We'll get into the pods and go to sleep. I wrote my name, Palm, and drew little stick figures of my family.

    I put sunflowers around us.

Dear diary,
Unsure.

I'm shivering. It's cold here. I expected to wake up at the center, but I don't know where we are. The staff is missing, too. There's a skeleton crew, wearing face masks. Are they worried about giving us something? Maybe the deep sleep suppressed our immune systems.

I want to see the sun, but they say it's too much for our eyes right now.

Everything is dim. The rest of the Palm are like me: shaking, cold, and confused. No one will give us access to the outside world.

I wish I was home.

Dear Leslie,
I miss you.

I'm full of regret. My dreams are us in the kitchen or on a walk.

There's a bad feeling in the air. The Palm have become tighter. We sit closer together.

The skeleton staff asks us to do things, and we decide as a group if we will do it. Yeah, there are fifty of us in total, but we feel like one unit.

They asked us to run around an auditorium. We declined. They asked us for blood samples. We declined. They threatened us. We stood together. They gave in quickly.

I think the threat was always hollow. They will get what we will give them, nothing more.

I hope you're well.

Dear Leslie,
I'm sorry.

I'm sorry for leaving. I'm sorry for being jealous and angry. I'm sorry for being miserable around you.

If I knew what would happen to the world, I would've stayed.

The skeletons finally told us what happened today to get us to cooperate with them better. We shut down. The door of our bunk room is barricaded until we feel up to opening it.

The deep sleep has changed our bodies. We don't sleep as much as normal, or eat, and we're always cold.

I would have written you a better letter if I knew I probably won't see you again. Life is extremely lonely without you.

Dear Leslie,

I'm becoming closer with a man named Gabriel. He's one of the "main brains" of the Palm. He helps me feel warmer. Not warm, because I'm never warm. None of us are.

Gabe points things out to me, like there's an equal number of men and women in Palm. He also told me what I already knew.

It's likely once the war broke out and the event happened, they had to expedite the research. The skeletons haven't told us yet, but we don't think we are on Earth.

My loneliness is deepening. I'm not sure how I'm supposed to go on with life knowing we aren't on the same planet anymore. We may not even share the same heartbeat.

You are the only person who knows what I know: our parents, the way our room smelled, the sounds of the birds outside our house.

I can't breathe.

Dear Leslie,

The skeletons threatened to take our food away. They would be at a loss if we perished, but some of the women have started to feel hungry again.

We won't let them be hungry. Gabe and the other brains are making negotiations with the skeletons.

They don't have a choice other than to work with us since we are, what the brains suspect, fifty out of a limited number of people from other studies. That is, if the other groups made it to Zed-Alpha.

A million things could have gone wrong between Earth and wherever we are. I cry every night. Gabe has his own things to cry over, but he comforts me in silence. A lot of us cry when it's time to sleep.

We don't enjoy sleeping or eating. The only things we like are art and storytelling. There's something about suffering with people that makes you feel close.

Dear Leslie,

Gabe told me that he used to work at one of the places you applied to before he was accepted to the study. You would have liked him. He's an intelligent, protective man.

I feel like our luck switched the day I arrived at Palm. My terrible luck morphed into your excellent luck. I'm still alive, I have Gabe and others who value me, and I'm doing as well as I could be for the circumstances.

I still wish you were here.

Dear Leslie,
I think another week has passed.

The skeletons have told us of a place for us to colonize. They made a deal with the brains to show our group to a window tomorrow so we can see Zed-Alpha.

Part of me doesn't know why we distrust the skeletons so much, but lying about what happened on Earth (or delaying the information) and the suddenness of it all put us on edge. Though, more of us are used to the "new normal."

Some of the skeletons have been putting extra effort into bonding with us. They took down their masks so we could see their faces. I know they are just people, scared and displaced like us, but they aren't like us.

Gabe wonders how long we slept. They are trying to get a clear answer from the skeletons tomorrow.

I think the skeletons are afraid that we'll get angry. They're scared to let us grieve. There's fifty of us in total, but I don't know how many they have.

Maybe you should be here instead of me.

Dear Leslie,
We saw the sun today.

It's not our sun, but it was light from a star. Greenery grows here. It's uncanny how much it looks like it could be Earth, but we are all painfully aware that it's not our home. Our families aren't here. Our friends aren't here. We are here.

Also, the skeletons told us the correct Earth year. It's so far in the future that it feels wrong. I refuse to write it.

So, even if we could go back to Earth, I would never see you again.

I hope you know that I never meant any mean thing I ever said to you. I hope you know that I wouldn't have left if I knew it meant never seeing you again.

As miserable as I was, I felt better being known by you.

Dear Leslie,
We are going to the settlement.

I wish there were better words. Settlement, colony ... Are we pilgrims?

Gabe and I were joking about what they used to wear. He's my best friend. I feel lucky.

Sometimes after I feel happy, I feel guilty. Should I be laughing about pointy hats when so much evil has happened in this universe? But if you don't laugh, you never stop crying. Life goes on, the world (Zed-Alpha) keeps turning. The skeletons think that we can be friends or allies.

I feel bad that they can never be Palm.

Dear Leslie,
It's been a while.

We've learned that the women who first felt real hunger again are pregnant. We didn't know that it would come so easily after deep sleep, space travel, and all of the changes that have occurred. The skeletons have noticed and provided extra supplies.

We have more answers from the skeletons. There are five hundred people total on Zed-Alpha. Most of the deep sleep studies ended when the war broke out, but a select few continued. When the first nuke hit the country, we were loaded into ships and sent off to Zed-Alpha. Earth is a "radioactive wasteland" according to them.

We have no choice but to believe them. They have taken off their protective gear and helped us break land to build our homes. Thankfully, we do remember what we learned from our classes.

Because we aren't sure what wildlife is like here, we are building our homes facing away from each other with a wide backyard for our gardens. Everyone helps in any way they can. Some of us are still suspicious of the skeletons, but the relationship is improving.

We are building fifteen houses in an oval. Most people are more comfortable having four or five in a house than just two or one.

We're starting to explore hunting and making traps for wildlife.

Hopefully, we'll have meat again soon.

Dear Leslie,
Our house is built.

Gabe and I are living together.

My appetite is back. The feeling of hunger rumbling in my stomach scares me. I'm not used to it, and I don't know if it means I'm pregnant. I don't want to broach the idea with anyone. Thankfully, I have you.

I'm worried about the timing. There's so much to do, and until the garden produces crops, food is limited, even with the addition of meat. Small game is the most reliable, but the animals are close to a large hare in size. It doesn't go far among fifty.

There's no doubt in my mind that Gabe would give me the last bite of his meals if I asked for it, but he's not a small man and he works harder than I can.

I've been sleeping more, too. I can't hide it. Part of me believes that he knows, even if he only knows deep down.

The skeletons are staying at the base where we first woke up. We aren't far from there so they visit often and ask if anyone would volunteer for getting blood drawn.

We keep the pregnant inside when they come. The idea of them wanting to take our children to run tests fills us with anger.

What good does running tests do now?

Dear Leslie,
All the houses are completed.

Our first crops are growing. The soil here is fertile and rich. Our herb garden looks wonderful.

Since our people spend so much time outside now, we're less cold. We like to sit around the garden and chat in the afternoons.

No one in Palm is bold enough to try the native greenery of Zed-Alpha. Two of the skeleton men are determined to try everything in this area. They give us papers every other week with the details.

Gabe has noticed the changes in my body. He offers me the last of his food when we eat together and encourages me to rest. I've decided that if the baby is a girl, her name is Leslie. Gabe can pick her middle name. I just want to hear your name again.

I haven't said any name from our family aloud since I tried to talk to you in the car. That was an awkward ride. I wish we had spent that day together.

Dear Leslie,
I'm halfway through the pregnancy.

We believe that the first woman who got pregnant should give birth in the next month. Thankfully, or suspiciously in Gabe's words, two of the Palm women are midwives and one of the men is a registered nurse. We're in good hands.

The brains keep trying to get information from the skeletons on whether this whole ordeal was planned from the start to give our country a jump on space colonization. We don't have concrete proof that the Earth is a wasteland. They offered to show us videos and articles about the events, but computers can generate realistic images and videos.

We need more time to process, decide, and heal before we trust them.

Dear Leslie,
The skeletons asked to live with us.

I guess they are out of food or close to it. They made a
list of what they can offer to us in exchange for joining the
group: medical supplies, solar panels, and the base.

The brains are considering it. Since it would be cruel to let
the skeletons starve to death, they are willing to work something out. They don't want to demand that certain medical
equipment be destroyed, but we've all agreed that we don't
want the new generation to become lab rats.

I don't think the skeletons will have a choice but to yield
to our demands if they want any food from our garden.

Dear Leslie,
I talked about you today.

Gabe and I had a long conversation. I don't know why
I felt like he had something terrible to say to me when he
asked if we could talk, but I was on edge for a couple hours.

We sat in our room and discussed everything. He asked
me what I thought about him, and I was honest. I love him.
He told me that he considers us more than partners or lovers. I guess we got engaged. I'm not sure if anyone here is
ordained or if that matters anymore.

Anyway, then we talked about baby names. He suggested
a few, and I told him I wanted to name her, if she is a girl,

Leslie. Immediately, he asked "who is Leslie?"

I cried a little, but I enjoyed telling him about the luckiest girl I've ever known. I hope that you were lucky until your last day.

Dear Leslie,
The skeletons have their own homes now.

We got some of our stuff back that we put into storage at the center on Earth. It's all small stuff, mostly jewelry. You'll never believe what they gave me.

It's your butterfly necklace, the one with the aquamarine! I don't know if you put it in my stuff on purpose or if it accidentally got mixed with my things, but it was like a breath of fresh air. I can imagine you tearing apart your room looking for it.

You were organized with everything except your room and purse. I bet you had the car looking like a second bedroom within a month of me leaving. I hope you spent all of the money in the account on coffee, but knowing you, you saved it for me.

Anyway, the skeletons have homes that function like end caps for our neighborhood. They are starting to blend in with us.

We are less cold and look healthier.

Dear Leslie,
She gave birth today.

The first baby of our group is a boy! She named him Isaiah. In a few weeks, she'll let everyone meet him properly. The father and midwives are taking good care of her.

From what I heard, the baby is normal and healthy. I hope he's as perfect as the sunrise.

Dear Leslie,
We got a big one.

Gabe went out with some of the Palm on a hunting trip. They left at the first sign of light and came back as darkness started to fall. They carried an animal that weighs roughly two hundred pounds.

Everyone, even the skeletons, gets to eat well tonight. I'm over the moon about it.

Dear Leslie,
Sorry I'm writing less often.

Since we are settled, everyone has fallen into a sense of normalcy. We aren't interested in anything that could bring conflict.

I think we all want peace and calm for a while. Baby Isaiah is doing really well. He is so loved. I feel like Palm is one big family.

A lot of Palm believe that I'm having a girl based on how the baby is carrying. More women are getting closer to birth in the upcoming months. I'm learning a lot from them.

Dear Leslie,
I gave birth a week ago.

The baby's name is Leslie Lynn. Her middle name is Gabe's mom's name.

He's been a wonderful father. It's amazing how a stranger becomes a friend and then the father of your child. Baby Leslie is more beautiful and perfect than I could have imagined. I feel like you sent her to me.

I never would have had so much happiness without your luck. Thank you for being my sister. I hope in the next life, and every life, we are sisters again.

Your sister forever, Ruby.

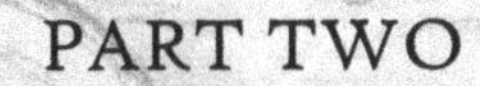

Meet Cutes and More

HOT BOSS
Michelle Bulsiewicz

The text message that will change my life forever arrives as I'm walking back to my towering steel and glass office building after my lunch break on a Friday afternoon. My chunky heeled, strappy sandals clomp on the sidewalk as the intense heat of the Phoenix sun beats down on me overhead. It's only May, but the high today is already in the triple digits.

The text in question comes from my best friend, Kim. I stop at the crosswalk of a busy intersection to read it before the light changes.

Kim: *Have you told hot boss yet?*

How could such an innocuous text change my life? You'll see.

She's referring to handing in my notice. After working as the executive assistant for vice president Oliver Torres at a corporate law firm for the past five years, putting myself through coding boot camp and web design classes for two years of that time, and building up my clientele for the past twelve months—I can finally kiss my nine-to-five goodbye. I get to go off to be my own boss as a freelance web developer at last.

Is it terrifying? Am I going to have to pay for my own health insurance? Will filing taxes be an absolute nightmare?

You betcha.

But I'm going to get to work from my house in comfy pants. Or no pants at all if I so desire. I can sleep in and set my own hours. My cat will never have to be alone again. It's going to be more than worth it.

Once I work up the courage to tell my boss.

Not because he's a horrible tyrant. Quite the opposite.

Kim and I nicknamed him "hot boss" on the day of my first interview for the position. Since then, I've discovered that beneath his tall, muscular frame, square jaw, and sensuous mouth—he's a genuinely sweet, humble guy who I've been so glad I got to know.

He's young for his position, early thirties, and soft-spoken. He's a genuine listener who always defends me if someone else in the office comes after me for something I didn't do. He readily admits his mistakes and is open to criticism and outside ideas. He's honestly amazing. If I didn't detest my commute and dress pants, there's no way I'd be leaving this job.

Before I can type out my reply to Kim, I also get a text from said hot boss.

Oliver Torres: *I'm heading into a meeting with a client now. Shouldn't be long. Could you get the PowerPoint for my three o'clock to me by the time I'm back? Thanks Nicole!*

I tap out a quick *will do* in response, and then the light changes. I put my phone away to cross the street. Don't want to be one of those pedestrians getting hit by a car because I can't take my eyes off my phone. Still, I'm formulating my response to Kim in my head as I walk. Once I'm on the other side of the road, I pull out my phone to type it all out:

Me: I haven't told him yet. How do I say, "Hot boss, you're one of the best people I've ever had the chance to know and I'm a little bit in love with you. I'm going to miss you so much and these last five years have been everything, but your passion and enthusiasm for your job has inspired me to start my own business, and I'm outta here. But also call me," without sounding like an obsessed person?

Then, because I'm texting and walking, I accidentally run into someone coming in the opposite direction—they clock me on the shoulder so I'm startled from my focus and press send on the message earlier than I meant to.

"Sorry!" I turn to the older man I ran into with a sheepish smile. He glowers at me before continuing on his hurried way.

Now, standing still on the sidewalk, I look back at my phone, and realize with dawning horror that I've just made a huge mistake.

I never left the thread with Oliver. I typed out the message meant for Kim inside it. I *sent* the text meant for Kim to my boss.

The text where I say I'm in love with him.

I stare at my phone as ice cold panic pools in my belly. He wasn't supposed to find out like this. About me leaving, about my feelings for him. He was *never* supposed to find out about my feelings for him. Yes, he's single. Married to his job, really. But he's successful and hot and rich and about a thousand light years out of my league. Not to mention he was always my boss, so I had to keep everything I felt for him tucked away all these years. So, yes, I'm going to miss him when I leave this job, but also it's going to be such a relief not to have to restrain myself around him all day, every day anymore. I can move on. I can find someone else I actually have a chance with.

In the meantime, I still have to work at this job for two more weeks, and I will not be able to survive facing Oliver for every single one of those ten working days if he sees this text.

The flow of foot traffic moves around me as I stay frozen to the spot on the sidewalk, eyes glued to my phone screen as if I can will it to unsend that text. To change the new reality I've gotten myself into.

It's still marked as unread. He hasn't seen it yet. But he will. He *will*.

Except. He said he's going into a meeting with a client. He never brings his phone into client meetings, preferring to work on his tablet, not wanting to get distracted by another screen. It should still be on his desk. I'm still ten minutes away from the tenth floor of the office building where I work, if all goes well. But that should be plenty of time. He's had me help him with so much for the past few years that I know all his passwords. I can get to his office, unlock his phone, delete the text—he'll be none the wiser. It can be like it never happened.

There's still time to fix this.

But I need to start moving.

Next thing I know, I'm sprinting down the sidewalk harder than I've run in years, possibly ever. I'm more into yoga than running, and I may or may not have done more walking than running when forced to do a mile around the track in high school. Thus, in a matter of seconds, my breath is like daggers in my lungs, and I can almost taste the blood pounding from my ill-used cardiovascular system.

Still, I keep going, driven by adrenaline and pure fear, until one of the straps in my sandals gives out, my foot fumbles, and—like in slow motion, my arms flailing about me for purchase—I slam into the concrete below me.

A kind, middle-aged lady in a pant suit stops to ask if I'm okay. I assure her I am, but accept her hand as she helps me to my feet. I wipe at the gravel on my clothes, notice a stinging scrape on my shoulder where it made contact with the sidewalk, and lean down to pick up the remnants of my now broken sandal.

"Do you need help?" the pant suit lady asks.

I give her a tight smile. "No, my office is right there." I gesture to the building. "I'll be alright. Thank you."

Once she's gone, I glare at my traitorous, useless sandal, and start limping the rest of my way to my office. I still have plenty of time. Surely Oliver is still in his meeting anyway. It's only been a few minutes. There was never any need to run. I was just being dramatic.

I reassure myself of these things over and over as I finally make it to the main doors of my office building. I'm hot, sweaty, tired, a little bloody and dirty, and half bare-foot, but I'm here. I let out a huge exhale as I walk through the automatic big glass doors—only to run headlong into someone carrying a fountain drink, which smashes into my chest and spills all down my front.

I gape at the mess dripping down my clothes in utter disbelief. I'm cursed. There's no other explanation. How can all of this keep happening to me?

"Oh, no, I'm so sorry!" It's a young guy in a polo shirt who's trying to mop at the stain on my shirt with his hand until I glare at him and he pulls away. "Let me—let me go get you some paper towels." He turns around like he's going to rush back to the restroom or something, but I stop him.

"No, it's fine. I'll take care of it. It's no problem." I have to repeat myself about three more times before he finally lets me go.

Now literally dripping and sticky in addition to everything else, I hurry over to the elevator.

Only to find the biggest crowd waiting by the doors. I don't know if everyone got back from lunch at once or if there are a ton of people visiting someone's office for some reason—regardless, I take one look at the amount of people trying to cram into the next available elevator and I know I'd have to wait at least ten minutes to get on one of those, not mention having to stop at I don't know how many floors along the way.

I can climb ten flights of stairs faster than that.

I have no choice. If this day insists on throwing all the shit my way, then I'm just going to have to barrel my way through it. Mess and all.

Setting my jaw, I head for the door to the stairs, thrust it open, and start making my way up as fast as I can.

Which quickly slows to a heavy, slogging step by the fourth floor. By the time I've made it up to floor ten, my thighs are burning, I'm even sweatier than before, and I know I'm going to barely be able to move tomorrow. This is more cardio than I've gotten in ages. Possibly ever.

Gasping for breath, I throw all my weight into opening the door to the tenth floor. I spot my office down the hallway and start dragging myself toward it. Almost there. So close.

"Nicole! What happened to you?" Bob Price, a senior attorney and the office busybody blocks my way as he strides up to me from where he was obviously just chatting with another coworker. He grins with glee at the sight of me, and I can already hear his loud, braying voice telling everyone in the office about my disastrous appearance within the hour.

Not knowing where to start and still out of breath, I hold up my broken sandal in one hand. "Fell." It's the most I can get out as I press my hand into a stitch in my side.

Bob looks me up and down. "I can see that. You need a band-aid or something? A towel?"

I wave him away. "I got it." I start to shoulder my way past him.

He tries to stop me. "Hey, wait, you can't just leave it at that. Give us the story!"

"Later." I throw a hand over my shoulder without looking back.

Oliver's office. I need to get to Oliver's office. I can see it, just yards away. The door's shut and the blinds are drawn on the windows, but he has to still be in his meeting. He has to be. It's like I'm moving through drying cement, every movement slower and more difficult the closer I get.

At last, my hand is on the doorknob. I turn the handle, the door swings inward and—

Oliver is standing at his desk, his phone in his hand.

Every muscle in my body goes limp. My broken sandal slips from my fingers, falling to the floor with a thump. Oliver looks up, an unreadable expression on his face.

He's gorgeous, as always. He fills out his light blue button up shirt from his shoulders to his chest to the sloping V of his abdomen. There's a slight dark shadow to his defined chin—his beard is thick enough that he can shave in the morning and look like he didn't only hours later. His dark, wavy hair falls across his forehead in that cute, purposefully messy way. His chocolate eyes home in on me standing there, looking like a complete wreck.

With everything inside me bared out in the open for him on the phone in his hand.

"Are you all right?" he asks, taking in my disheveled appearance at the same moment I blurt out, "Is your meeting over already?"

Then we both respond at the same time.

"Yes, I just fell," I say, right as he says, "It never happened."

I blink for a moment, taking in his answer. "It didn't happen? Why not?"

He shrugs. "The client had some emergency and cancelled last minute."

Just my luck today.

"Are you sure you're okay?" He wrinkles his forehead, eyes scanning over the scrape on my shoulder. "You need me to get you something?"

I shake my head. "No, I ..." Then the reason I'm here, looking like this, all comes flooding back to me and I realize he didn't say anything about the text yet. For a split second, I let myself hope. Maybe he hasn't seen the incriminating message yet. Maybe I can rip the phone from his hand. Maybe ...

But before I can act on these thoughts, he glances down at the screen in his palm then back at me.

"You're leaving?" The hurt and sadness in his voice pierce my heart to the center. I'm hypnotized by the sound, by the depths of his pupils on me. I can no longer tell if I'm out of breath from climbing ten flights of stairs or from the presence of this man. I can feel my heartbeat in my teeth.

I take way too long to respond, just staring at him, dumb. Then the floodgates burst. "I didn't want you to find out like this. I meant to send that to my friend, to Kim. You know Kim, she came to the last Christmas party with me because I didn't want to bring a date and you guys talked for a while and—"

"'Hot boss?'" he cuts me off, thank goodness, cocking an eyebrow at me.

I squirm, unable to meet his gaze. I hear the sound of people talking out in the hallway and have the sudden where-withal to shut the door to his office behind me. And we're alone.

"Look, that's just a little inside joke between me and Kim. It doesn't mean anything."

He's not done. "You'll miss me?" Now there's something almost timid in his expression. I notice he skipped over the in-love-with-him part. Maybe that's too much for even him to face. Maybe he's just being nice to me, sparing my feelings just a bit.

"I—" But before I can come up with some half-baked lie to cover my own ass, Oliver's talking again.

"I'll miss you, too." There's something so heartbreak-ingly earnest in his voice, his eyes. My throat thickens with tears. Actual tears, building heat behind my eyes.

Damn it, I think I really do love him.

"Oh." It's the only syllable I manage to make.

In two strides, Oliver covers the space between us, takes me by one arm, and brings his mouth to mine.

It's better than I ever imagined—and, boy, did I imag-ine it, hundreds and thousands of times over the past five years. No matter how hard I tried not to, Oliver infiltrated my dreams, waking and sleeping. I couldn't get him out of my head. Now, here he is in real life, that familiar smell, the familiar touch of his hand, and the new sensation of his taste on my tongue as the kiss deepens ever-so-slightly before he pulls away.

He takes a step back, running a hand through his hair. "I'm sorry. I shouldn't have done that."

"No ... it's ... it's all right." More than all right. Amazing. Incredible.

"You still work here. I'm still ... your boss." He shakes his head.

"Not for long." A small smile tugs at the corner of my mouth and his eyes meet mine, something hopeful and even a bit mischievous there.

"You know, I ... I'd love to take you out to dinner sometime. Once, you know, once you don't work for me anymore." He lets out a shaky, quiet little laugh.

"Yes. Please." I giggle a little at my own eagerness. "I'd love that."

I can't believe this is happening. It occurs to me for a split second that maybe all those disasters that led to him reading one little text that was never meant for him weren't a curse. Maybe it was fate, playing its hand.

"Great, uh ..." He looks down at his phone, then back up at me, a huge grin spreading across his cheeks. "I'll text you."

PULCHRITUDE
Brett Salter

Child of nature
The skyline trapped in your eyes
Wrapped in a blanket as I'm wrapped round your finger

My finger trembles
It searches your cheek
And gathers endless tresses behind your ear

Whispers into an ear
Marvelous wonderful sounds
Escape from the smallest space between gemstone lips

Your lips are vanguards
They rouse and stir the rest to wake
A sudden dance of limbs releases a sylphlike hand

Breathtaking touching of hands
Lead me up the dreamy ascension
To immerse my body in the comfort of your nature

WRITTEN IN THE STARS

A Rasaverse Short Story

Effie Joe Stock

"Do you see the way the sun reflects off it and casts rainbows?" Pavati tilted the kelp she was holding. The lazy afternoon sun struck it, then separated into hundreds of dancing rainbows on the rocky beach.

Shania tilted her head, careful to keep her horns from bumping Pavati. She narrowed her eyes, raking her memory for the name Pavati had called the plant an hour before. The kelp's dazzling sheen, so similar to Pavati's scaled skin, distracted Shania. "So, this is *mulauw yáfuw-doziz* kelp then?"

Pavati's excited smile made all the hours of listening and learning worth it. "Yes! I'm amazed you remembered. I threw a lot of names at you at once."

Shania's eyes lingered on Pavati and the way the sun caught her blue dreadlocks. Finally, she dragged her attention back to the kelp. "Of course I remember. If it means something to you, it means something to me."

A pink blush raged across Pavati's ocean green cheeks as she looked away, letting the kelp drift back into the shallow tides. "I know, but I figured something so mediocre might be a bit boring for someone so—" her gaze shifted to the pan flute dangling at Shania's side.

"Barbaric?" The word scrapped itself off Shania's tongue as she subconsciously pushed the flute out of sight.

Enjoyment turned to horror on Pavati's face as quick as a fish's tail flick. "I'm sorry, I didn't mean that. I just ... I was trying to say ..."

A heavy sigh escaped Shania's lips as she scratched around the base of her horns. They were still growing in and would itch until they'd curved down around her long ears. With sharp nails, she detangled a stick bug from her thick curly hair and set it free on the rocks beside her. "No, you're right. We *are* barbaric. It's not a secret." Hearing Pavati say "barbaric" made her stomach roll, but she would never show how much it bothered her. She'd rather shoulder the word's burden than shame Pavati for saying it. Careful not to scratch her delicate skin, Shania touched Pavati's cheek. The ocean water felt cold on her skin and a shiver ran down Shania's spine.

Seeing as the frown had yet to leave the mergirl's lips, Shania did her best to reassure her. "Really, it's fine." She grinned, making her eyes sparkle with all the sincerity she meant.

Unsure, Pavati smiled back, but didn't present the other piece of kelp she'd brought. Instead, she let it drift away, taking some of Shania's hope with it. The air blew a little colder around them now, the embarrassment of the interaction taking some of their warmth with it.

It wasn't Pavati's fault Shania was so different. It wasn't either of their faults.

Their Kinds were both called the Sházuk—brethren of the forest. And according to legend, both were descendants of the stars. But that was where their similarities ended.

Pavati was of the ocean: scales across her skin, dreads of hair that moved like kelp in clear water, a tail instead of legs, gills in her ribs and little fins along her arms. Shania was of the forest: thick curly hair spiraling from her head and around her curving horns, bare chested with smooth skin, thick fur on goat legs, hooves well built for dashing among rocks and thorns, and a little tail that wagged when she got excited. One confined to water, one to land, both held together by an invisible bond neither knew how to define.

But in moments like these, Shania felt the distance between them like the ocean from the stars.

"Are you excited for the eclipse?" The words jumped from Shania's lips before she could stop them. The hurt on Pavati's face mirrored how she'd felt moments before. Eclipses marked important celebrations to the Sházuk people; they were a time to spend with family and friends. To spend with your tribe. Only, Pavati had no one to spend it with. "Stars of old, I shouldn't have—"

Pavati smiled through tears which mingled with the ocean spray. "No, it's okay. It's been so long you'd think I'd move on." She laughed as she brushed the salt water from her face, but the sound, usually so musical to Shania's ears, sounded dull and painful instead.

Shania wrung her hands in her lap, wishing she could reach out and hold Pavati. Instead, she curled her hooves further under her, the sharp ground beneath digging into her skin despite her thick fur. She wondered if Pavati thought the water she swam in was cold, or if she preferred it to the rocks Shania was constricted to. "Losing family never gets easier. It's alright if you're still sad about it."

"I don't think sad is even the right word." Pavati stared into the distance, perhaps to where her pod used to live. Not that Shania would know. She couldn't swim.

Desperately she wished she could help Pavati find the right word. Perhaps putting her pain to words would ease it somewhat. But though she didn't think a word like that even existed, she did understand the agony of feeling utterly alone.

A long horn call rose in the trees, curving over the land like a warning. The sound would be familiar and welcoming to the rest of Shania's Faun tribe. To her, however, it was the bitter sound of captivity. Instead of responding to the call, she closed her eyes and took in a deep breath of salty ocean air.

"Don't you have to go?" Pavati's words, though almost dismissive, were heavy with regret.

As their eyes met, their pain mirrored each other's.

"I do. But maybe ..." Shania's hand moved closer to the edge of the shore, closer to where Pavati's hand held her close to the rocks.

"You can't stay any longer. You know that." Shania *did* know that. She also knew she wanted to jump into the water and swim away with Pavati far into the depths of the ocean and never look back. But she couldn't. The world itself stood between her and Pavati and neither had the strength to move it.

Shania tasted salt on her lips, unsure if it'd come from her tears or the spray of the ocean. She let her fingertips trail the ebb and flow of the water as the tide slowly rose. Soon the rocks she sat upon would vanish underwater once again, driving her back into the forest, into the growing nightmare she struggled to call home. Unlike every other Faun she'd ever met, Shania hated the forest. She hated the damp dark decay of it and the never-ending rows of trees reaching to swallow her whole. To other Fauns, the forest felt like a warm, safe haven. To her it felt like a cage.

Cold fingers touched her cheek, and she looked up, her forest green eyes meeting Pavati's shining blue gaze. Shania's heart skipped a beat as her gaze roved over the scales sparkling on the girl's skin and the way her sea blue dreads haloed her shoulders in the water.

"Please don't cry. You'll make me cry too." A small smile lifted Pavati's lips, then quickly vanished as small oceans pooled in her own eyes anyway.

"You're already crying, Pavati. The ocean can't hide that from me." Shania mimicked Pavati's gesture and touched the sea girl's cheek.

For a moment, just a moment, they mirrored each other, their souls so similar they could've been a single girl looking at her own reflection. But they weren't.

"I don't think I can face them. Not tonight. Not tomorrow." Shania bit her lip as her gaze wandered to the forest. Already she could hear the heavy drums and intoxicating flutes filling the trees. "Not ever."

Pavati drew herself onto a rock, her fish-like tail splashing Shania's curly hair and budding horns. Usually she'd apologize, but a little bit of ocean spray seemed a small inconvenience when their dreams were being unraveled by the second. She planted both of her palms on Shania's cheeks, her webbed fingers gently tickling her skin, and stared deep into her eyes. "At least they are there for you to face." She could no longer hold back the tears. They streamed down her cheeks, catching the suns and turning the rays into rainbows. "Some family is better than no family."

Shania bit her lip as she leaned into Pavati's cold touch. The chill of the ocean felt so much warmer than the fires of her tribe. "You're my family." She choked on her emotion. "You're the only family I need. The only one I want." The urge to wrap her arms around Pavati and pull her onto shore, to steal her away deep into the forest crashed over her like a tidal wave. "I want to spend every minute of every day here on the seashore." Shania's voice cracked. "I'd trade *everything* for that. I'd give up ever seeing my tribe again if it meant watching the suns play tricks on the water or hunting sea-shells with you, my *yáfuw luk*, for eternity."

A different kind of pain filled Pavati's eyes as she brushed away Shania's tears with her webbed fingers. "You wish for something you don't understand. The pain your tribe inflicts upon you stems from a place of love. They may misunder-stand you, but they're trying their best. It's a horror to live in where you don't have anyone to follow you to the places you must go."

Shania clenched her jaw and dug her nails into her bud-ding horns. The itching had grown nearly unbearable, and she wanted to rip them from her head before they grew any bigger. "I would follow you there."

Pavati squeezed her eyes shut. "I know. But you can't"

Worthlessness settled into Shania's chest. After today's eclipse, Pavati would have to migrate to warmer waters for the coming winter. With a pod of merpeople, the trip would be routine, but alone ... Pavati's chances of surviving were ex-tremely slim. And even if she managed to return next spring, Shania would already be stuck in the loveless marriage her tribe had arranged for her.

Time had run out for them.

"And besides." Shania sniffed. "My tribe doesn't love me. They don't listen to me. And they hate how much I love the sea and how much I love ..." she swallowed around the lump in her throat. "How much I love ..." A sob left her lips as she sucked on her cheeks, unable to form the last word.

Pavati smiled for a moment, then let her lips fall into grief. "I know." She touched her forehead to Shania's and they held each other, as close as the ocean and sharp rocks would let them. Their hearts ached with the distance, with the inches that felt like miles between them.

"Do you remember what I taught you about the stars? About how to navigate the ocean by them?" Pavati's soft voice calmed the chaos in Shania's mind as she nodded. "Then you'll always know which constellations to look at. You'll know we're looking at the same stars no matter how far apart we are."

Despite the pain in her chest, Shania couldn't help but smile. She believed the legends that said their Kind, the Sházuk people, were descendants of the stars. With all her heart, she believed no matter how different their forms looked on the outside, all Sházuk people would return to the stars when they died, taking up their home in the heavens once again. Someday, she and Pavati would be together, no longer separated by physical forms, and though she hardly had the patience to wait, it gave her the hope she needed to survive each day.

"Do you think the stars listen to us?" Shania looked up. A few stars peeked out through the dusk-colored sky.

Pavati bit her lip the way she did when thinking hard.

"I think so. I know the Centaurs listen to them, so why wouldn't they listen to us?"

Shania smiled, liking the idea. Perhaps even a fabled star deity of Hanluurasa would answer if she spoke to them. "Do you remember the song I taught you about the forest?" Shania brushed a lock of Pavati's waterlogged hair behind her sharp ear. The song was one of the few she still sang—the only song her mother had left for her before disappearing into the forest one day and never returning. To this day, the tribe shamed her mother for her actions, but Shania knew better. Her mother had been discontent with the hard traditions of their people and had left in search of a better life. She'd never returned, but Shania hoped she'd found what she was looking for.

Pavati cocked her head and smiled, lips folding over sharp white teeth. Shania wondered how they would feel across her lips, then banished the thought when she remembered she'd never find out. Humming softly under her breath, Pavati started singing the song, letting her light, airy voice carry over the waters. Shania would follow that voice to the deepest ocean, to her death if it were.

"That one?" Pavati winked and gently flicked Shania's forehead as the Faun shook herself from the gentle trance she'd sunk into.

With a deep sigh she nodded. "That's the one. If you sing it every sundown, we'll always be singing together."

A small, strained smile spread across Pavati's lips. They both knew the suns would set at different times for them once an ocean lay between them. But neither voiced the grim thought.

The Faun tribe's horn sounded again. Dread dropped

Shania's heart, shattering the tender moment.

Cold panic washed over her, sending shakes down her spine. "I can't." Hysteria rattled her voice as she clung to Pavati's smooth, scaly skin. "I can't go back there." Her tribe had been pressuring her to finish the mating process, to become the next chief's mate. But every moment she spent with him made her lose her will for life. He squashed her dreams of sailing on a ship, mocked her for her distaste of the forest, and shamed her for her mother's abandonment years ago. His voice was deep and brash, the opposite of Pavati's light gentle trill. His hands were needy, strong, harsh, relentless—everything Pavati's wasn't. He represented everything Shania hated and feared: power, control, a cage, a dead life in a dark forest where she was expected to perform for everything each and every night, expected to conform, to be someone she wasn't, to love someone she didn't love. "Please, Pavati," Shania cried. "Please don't make me go."

Pavati choked back a sob as she pried herself from Shania's grasp. "You have to. There's no other way. There's nothing we can do. People like us ... they aren't meant to be together."

Shania's heart broke. "Don't say that. Please don't say that. Don't let me go. Let me stay."

With a final push, Pavati separated herself from the Faun and drifted back into the water, rivers of salt running down her cheeks to join the ocean. "You can't stay somewhere you've never been. Our worlds are too different. You have to let go. It's over. There's nothing we can do. Only the stars and gods could help us now."

Shania's hooves clacked against the rocks as she jumped up. She slipped on the wet rocks, trying to follow Pavati as far into the water as she dared. If she fell in, the ocean would claim her and all her small hopes and dreams; the thought didn't seem as bleak compared to the forest doing the same. A choked sob leapt from Shania's lips as Pavati swam further from her reach.

She wanted to tear the world apart to change their fates. But no matter how much her heart hurt, and lips screamed, Pavati was right. Shania had never been in Pavati's world and Pavati had never been in Shania's. The only place their love existed in time and space were these few feet of rocky shore where the ocean met the land. Outside of that, it didn't, *couldn't*, exist, and they would be fools to think otherwise.

They'd known this from the start, from the moment they stumbled upon each other, two wandering hearts trying to find a home. But their hearts had ignored all logic.

"Goodbye, Shania." Pavati hid her emotions under the sheen of water, letting the ocean wash over her face as she dipped into the ocean. Her tail flicked the surface of the water once more before she disappeared entirely.

Shania screamed to the waters, then collapsed to the rocks and added her tears to the ocean. "Please," she sobbed, turning her face to the winking stars above. "Please don't let this be the end of us. Please don't forsake our love."

She waited. And waited. And waited. Waited for the gods to save her, for the stars to rewrite their fate. Waited for Pavati to return, to crack a joke and promise she'd never leave again, to promise their little love would be safe at the edge of their worlds.

Seconds passed into minutes and minutes into an hour after the suns had set.

Neither the gods nor the stars answer.

And Pavati never returned.

Dark numbness filled Shania's heart as she dragged herself upright and forced herself to descend into the depths of the forest. Shadows reached out, entangling her in their grasp. Decaying sticks and leaves crunched under her steps. All sounds muffled in the thick underbrush and the world fell into silence.

Until she moved closer to her tribe. Its chaos crashed down upon her, crushing the silence and darkness with her.

Swarms of Fauns grabbed her with warm, sweaty, clingy hands, pulling her into their furious, vibrant dance. A drum passed into her hands but when she refused to play, another Faun took it and brought it to life. Two hands grabbed hers and yanked. She felt something pop in her shoulder as the world spun around her.

Lights blinded her. Throbbing music pounded in her head. Trilling flutes rang in her ears. Loud hollers and singing burned in her blood as the heavy beats of hooves drove her dread deeper and deeper into her heart.

The dance dragged on, and on, and on until the moons hung high above them and the forest stank of sweat and drink.

She wanted to lay down, to give herself over to the forest and let the tribe trample her into the dirt until moss grew over her bones and mushrooms devoured her skin. All she could taste and feel were the cold salty tears rushing down her cheeks. When the sensation reminded her of the ocean, the tears only flowed thicker.

Then hands reached for her body, touched her chest, groped her, helping themselves to her body. She screamed and flailed, fighting against the strong arms holding her tight.

Senses snapping into the present, she found herself staring deep into a pair of familiar golden eyes.

"Julius, get off me!" She screamed, desperately trying to pry his hands from her body. Frantically she searched the crowd for help, but the other Fauns were either too busy drinking or dancing. Some even looked proud.

No one moved to help. No one dared defy the chief's son.

"Get off you? By the end of next season, you'll be mine." Julius pressed her body to his, trapping her in his sweaty embrace. The stench of alcohol tumbled off his breath and her stomach rolled.

Bile rose into her throat as her hands slipped on his chest, her fingers tangling in his coarse fur. "Right *now*," she begged. "Get off me *now*."

He only held her tighter and leaned closer. When he pressed his lips to her ear, his horns knocked the side of her head painfully. "Best get used to it."

She couldn't take it any longer. Night after night he'd come for her, trapping her, caging her, violating her. But she'd suffered enough today, losing the girl and freedom she loved. It was all too overwhelming, too much to handle, too much to hold in. One moment she was shrinking under his touch, the next she was free, the contents of her stomach splattered on his chest, sticking to his hair, covering his horns, coating his hooves.

The tribe fell silent. All eyes turned to her. A deep rolling rage rippled through the Fauns as the chief's son roared in anger.

Hot tears raced down Shania's cheeks as she took one, then two steps back. After whipping her mouth with the back of her hand, she spat next to his hooves. "You make me sick. I hate you."

The back of his hand struck her hard across the face, sending her careening into the mossy dirt. The stench of rotting leaves made her gag again.

"You're worthless to me," he hissed, hysteria lining his voice as he dragged a leaf across the vomit on his chest. "I need an heir. The *tribe* needs an heir and all *you* can think about is that wretched mergirl in the ocean."

Shania staggered to her feet, wiping dirt and blood from her chin as she waited for the words to dig deep into her soul.

"It's ... It's ..." His flashing eyes met hers as he gritted out the words with venom—words spoken behind her back since she met Pavati seasons ago, but never to her face until now. "It's an *abomination*."

Anger replaced the fear and dread in her veins. She thought of the gentle way Pavati touched her—never straying too far, never going anywhere Shania hadn't already guided her. Or the way Pavati looked at her—with nothing but patience, love, acceptance, and adoration.

Then her body remembered the way Julius groped her with relentless lust and disregard, and the way he looked at her now with disrespect and disgust.

Yet they believed the way she loved Pavati was the abomination?

"What did you call her?" Eyes burning, Shania dug her hooves into the ground and straightened her form, standing as tall as could despite him being a foot taller. She forced herself to stare deep into his eyes, ignoring every cell in her body revolted from him.

"She's a filthy, disgraced, abomination." Pure hate filled his eyes. "Hanluurasa will never accept you or her for the crimes you've committed."

"Don't you ever call her that again."

"Or what?"

She didn't bother answering.

Reaching out, she shoved her fingers in his eyes, eliciting a scream. In his confusion, she wrapped her fingers around one of his own budding horns and yanked with all her strength.

The force threw him to the ground. He flailed, trying to throw her off him. But she wouldn't be deterred. This was revenge for herself. For her mother. For Pavati.

Planting a hoof against his head, she jerked on his horn, once, then twice, then a third time until she felt the shell crack.

His screams chilled her blood and echoed through the forest. One of his hooves kicked her stomach, sending her to the dirt a few feet away but she bounced back up, for once grateful for the agility in her goat-like legs. With the viciousness of a predator, she lept back onto him, latched her grip onto his breaking horn and pulled until it gave way.

Again, she tumbled back into the dirt. Scrambling to her hooves, she stood, eyes locked on the broken, bleeding horn in her hands.

The tribe froze. All eyes locked on her. The only sound in the forest was Julius' pitiful groans and cries.

Then the chief broke into the circle around them and screamed. "Get her!"

Her eyes locked on Julius' bloodshot gaze. Before the first hands could trap her, she raised his horn above her head. "This is for Pavati. And if the stars reject me for it, then so be it." and brought it crashing into his temple. Blood trickled down the side of his head as he lay dazed.

She dropped the horn and ran.

The tribe raced after her, crashing through the forest, jumping over fallen logs, and towering boulders with unbridled agility. Any other Faun would've been caught by now.

But she knew the way to the ocean better than any of them.

Trees gave way to grass, then rocks, then open air and a straight drop to the ocean. She skidded to a halt, her hooves knocking little rocks into the crashing waters below. The high tide thrashed against the cliffs below.

"Shania, come back, please. I'm sure something can be worked out." The chief's voice rose over the others as he stepped out of the forest and stalked closer. But though his words promised reconciliation and forgiveness, his tone assured her of the opposite. Lust for vengeance shone in his eyes. He'd never risk the embarrassment of letting her back into the tribe. At the very least, they'd shave her horns and outcast her. The very worst and she would die for her crimes.

Her gaze drifted to the waters below, and for a moment, her mind wandered. She wondered where Pavati slept at night. Was she sleeping now? Or had she already started on her long journey to warmer waters? Would she even know how her sweet land lover would meet her end? Would she even care or would death bring some form of relief for the living?

But whatever regrets Shania may have formed, whatever words she'd left unsaid between her and Pavati, whatever life she could've salvaged in the tribe faded away. She looked up to the stars and found the Centaur constellation Pavati told her about. Legend said a powerful Sházuk deity once resided in that constellation. Tears streamed down her face. Hanluurasa's stars and deities hadn't answered her cries earlier, but maybe in the naked night they would see her now and understand her grief. Maybe they'd even still accept her into Hanluurasa when she died. Or maybe they wouldn't, and her dreams would end at the bottom of the sea to become nothing more than food for the fish.

It was too late to go back.

The time for apologies and reconciliation had passed.

The time for hope and dreams to take flight had come.

She sent one last plea to the gods above and made her leap.

The fall felt surprisingly long. The water had seemed closer than it truly was. The moons and stars glistened beautifully on the never-ending waters and Shania's heart fluttered knowing she would die in this beautiful place rather than suffer in the forest's cage.

Then she hit the water. The waves beat against her mercilessly until her lungs flooded with their salty embrace and everything fell dark.

In the darkness, Shania knew no pain, nor sorrow, nor grief. She stared into the void and watched as little winks of light sprung to life around her. Some seemed close, while others looked miles and miles away. They all breathed in sync, each breath a sound more beautiful than any Faun's music. Their movements complimented the others as they morphed and changed into beings unlike any she had seen before.

She tried to move toward them but found her limbs slow and unresponsive. Pressure wrapped around her along with the sensation of water, though she breathed fine and saw none around her.

A ball of light drew closer and closer until a face formed from the mass and stared deep into hers. A dozen eyes blinked back at her as she stared in awe. Colors familiar and colors she'd never seen before nor imagine dance across the surface of its skin. It looked something like her, half humanoid, half animalistic, but then she'd blink, and its form would change again. It seemed to move in and out of existence as if not all here, but not all *there* either.

For a stretch of time longer than she could measure, the eyes searched her. Its gaze pried gently into her thoughts, memories, heart, hopes and dreams. Nothing remained hidden from this creature. She waited for it to judge her sins and reject her from Hanluurasa. But the judgment never came.

Instead, a smile grew on its strange, changing face.

In a language she'd never heard before but understood deep in her soul, the creature spoke her sentence. "A soul displaced, and a love cut short. This will not do. Your fate is written in the stars, little Sházuk, and it's not yet finished. Go back and love freely."

Then the darkness claimed her once again.

"Shania." A muted voice called to her. She tried to ignore it, tried to find the pocket of darkness she'd found solace in. "Shania!" The voice came again, this time sharper, clearer.

The sensation of water pressing in on her filled her senses. Her eyes snapped open, and she took in a sharp gasp, water rushing into her body. Panic set in and she fought against the arms struggling to hold her. She tried kicking but found her legs wouldn't work. Screams and bubbles escaped her lips until hands shook her shoulders and that voice rang out once more.

"Shania, it's me, Pavati! You're okay. You're alright!"

Everything in Shania froze. Her eyes focused onto the creature in front of her and she sobbed. Beautiful gentle eyes stared back, wide with joy and adoration.

All panic and confusion left Shania. Nothing else mattered but the girl before her.

Without thinking, Shania threw herself upon Pavati, pressing their bodies as close as she could as she laughed and cried in relief. Her hands found the familiar long thick dreads and entangled themselves there. Her lips found her cheeks, her forehead, her neck. "I thought I'd never see you again. I thought I'd have to spend the rest of my life with that horrid monster or dead under the water. I wanted to follow you. I had to try, even if I knew I wouldn't succeed."

Pavati's crystal-clear laugh rang out, bringing tears of pure exaltation to Shania's eyes. "I don't think that'll ever be a problem again."

Shania drew back, looking at Pavati quizzically. "What do you mean?"

Pavati shook her head and pointed to Shania's body.

Then Shania realized for the first time her own transformation. No longer was she a Faun. Where her goat legs had once been now grew a tail the color of purple berries. Where her hair had once grown, now marched sleek sparkling scales. Little fins protruded from her side. The skin between her fingers webbed had grown longer into webs. The skin above her ribs parted into ridges of gills, effortlessly breathing in and out water. Her hands flew to her head. Gone were the itchy horrendous horns she'd resented. Instead, she felt a head full of silky hair flowing around her, tangling in the water.

Shania gasped and sobbed. "I can't believe it." She couldn't stop touching her new form—one that matched the way she'd always seen herself on the inside. "They heard me. They did it."

Pavati took her hands in hers and twirled her around, helping her test out her new tail. "Who did what?"

"The stars." Shania laughed in disbelief. "They gave me a second chance." Her entire being focused on Pavati. "They gave *us* a second chance."

Pavati's face grew serious. "You'll be giving up everything you know above water. That life is dead to you now and you'll never get it back. Are you sure that's what you want?" Doubt shone in her eyes. She didn't believe she deserved Shania to give up everything for her. Determination settled in Shania's heart; she'd spend the rest of her life convincing Pavati she was.

Shania cupped Pavati's face and took in the beauty of the girl who'd loved her for who she was on the inside, not the outside. "I've never been more sure of anything in my life. Wherever you will go, I will follow, and I'll always have everything I need right here by your side." Then she did what she'd longed to do for so many seasons and pressed her lips to Pavati's.

For a moment, Pavati didn't move, her eyes wide open in shock. Then a laugh parted her lips, and she pulled Shania closer.

When they drew away, Pavati wrapped her fingers tightly around Shania's. "Well, *da me ayuwuk?* Are you ready for our first adventure?"

Shania kissed the back of her hand and grinned, eyes sparkling. "I've always been ready. Lead the way, *yáfuw luk.*"

As they set off for warmer waters and a new future, the stars winked and smiled down upon them, a new future full of opportunities written in their constellations.

MY SOUL MATE
Marion Cedar

Before you
I thought my soul was complete
No missing piece
But when I met you
I felt whole
and now without you
My soul feels torn
You are the one I think of when I fall asleep
and the first thought
when I awaken
When we lock eyes
I can feel our souls touch
and when we dance together
our souls are dancing too

A CURSE OF SPINES
K. R. Yauger

Chapter One

I soaked in the first rays from the sun spilling over the desert. Sand shifted around me in a playful breeze. Stifling a sigh, I shook sand from my spines, though I knew it was pointless. Sand was the indomitable one here, just like the sun in her glory above. I rose and stretched my muscles. I danced like my mother had taught me to, my hands above me, my feet tapping rhythms in the hard packed sand.

Bats and moths pollinated my purple tube-like flowers at night and ate my fruit. During the day, snakes and hawks used my growing buds for shade. No human had seen me for many years. I stopped dancing and let the breeze have its way with my shoulder length hair. Tattoos of dashes and dots ran from my shoulders, down my arms, and spiraled around my stomach. Ink streaked across my face, accentuating my deep brows and angled jawline. A bone needle pierced my nose and two pierced my ears. I was proud to wear my heritage on my skin even if I wasn't part of my tribe any longer. I didn't even know if they existed anymore.

I retreated into myself, letting my thoughts run like the

river miles and miles away. I missed my mother, my tribe, and the cave where I'd lived. I missed Tala. The curse had taken them all from me. I furrowed my brows and wrinkled my nose. An odd scent bloomed in the air. Sweat was normal to smell off a running coyote or its prey. But this smelt worse. I stiffened.

The sand shifted to my shaded side as a woman sat down. She hummed to herself and ran her fingers through her long thick hair. Heat rushed into my cheeks, and I averted my eyes. She had no idea I was here. She took off her shawl, her outermost layers of clothing and laid it in the sun to dry. I waited for her to leave, but she stayed for a while, sipping water from a gourd flask. Finally, she stood and poured a small bit of water around my roots.

"Thank you for your shade. May the sun make you grow big and strong." She whispered.

Then she grabbed her clothing and wandered back the way she came. The sand was warm from where she'd been sitting. I watched her till she was out of sight. A small part of me wondered if I'd ever see her again.

Chapter Two

Waking nightmares chased sleep from me, and I had no dreamcatcher. I blinked at the stars roaming the heavens and wondered if they cared about me. Owls roosted in my top pads and waited for desert mice to scurry by. I turned over, listening to the coyote's lonely wails echoing the ache in my own soul. Tears leaked out of my eyes. That small contact with the woman had awakened something in me, and I didn't like it. I was strong like my mother had prayed for me to be. She always told me that strength came from the heart, and I had plenty of it.

Bats fluttered around me, hoping to drink some of my nectar. I reluctantly opened a couple of blossoms and let them feed. Small moments like this were like the gentle brush of my ancestors hoping to ease my pain. I tried to remember the woman's humming and shook my head.

I stared at the moon and hoped she could see me. She'd done nothing for me before, but maybe she would now. I settled back into fitful sleep with my memories jarring me.

The moon hung huge and low in the sky as if she was interested in the night's festivities. Drums pounded in the village, and fires blazed. I nervously ran my hands through my hair. Tonight was Tacho's night; not mine. My name hissed through lips, and I turned to see my mother staring at me. She furrowed her brow and shook her head. She'd braided her long hair to rest on each side of her face. A colorful shawl wrapped around her shoulders.

"What are you doing?"

"I'm getting ready."

"You look fine. You don't want to be late."

I nodded, following her out of our small cave. Excitement thrummed in the air, and it ran in my veins. It was time. Tonight, it would be known. A solemn hush filled the crowds as Tacho joined the throng of drummers and dancers. He adjusted the coyote pelt that rested on his head and shoulders.

He held a wooden staff in his hand and thumped it against the ground in the same rhythm. His deep dark eyes searched the crowd and narrowed when they found mine. I startled. My mother's eyes darted to me, and she gripped my shoulder.

"What did you do?" She hissed in my ear.

"Nothing mother."

"Tonight was supposed to be a night of celebration and feasting, but instead it is a night of betrayal." Tacho cried, his voice ringing in the silence he'd created.

"I chose Tala to be my wife; but she refused me, and I know it must be because she loves another . The spirits decreed she would be mine."

"Don't you dare invoke the spirits about my daughter!" The chief roared, rushing to the shaman.

"I am the spiritual leader of this village." Tacho replied, resting his staff against the chief's chest.

"Just because you inherited this role, doesn't mean you can do whatever you want." The chief growled, flaring his nostrils.

Tacho clenched his strong jaw, and he rolled his shoulders. Red paint shone under his narrowed eyes. Tala clutched his arm, tears streaming down her face. I stared at her beautiful round face and flat nose. Her eyes were pools of obsidian, her teeth bleached bones. I rested my hand on her shoulder to comfort her, but she shook her head. Fear lit in her eyes like a deep fire, and I realized her reluctance. She tried to mouth a word to me, but her lips shook so hard I couldn't make it out.

"I shall curse the one who has betrayed me and the spirits!" Tacho cried.

"No!" Tala pleaded, kneeling at his feet. "Please don't do it."

The shaman raised his staff and glared at me. My heart thudded in my chest as thousands of terrible things sprang to my mind.

"You are cursed to be alone and thwart anyone who would love you. You will never find solace for the rest of your days."

"Please Tacho have mercy!" Tala begged.

"The curse will be broken if you can find true love." Tacho answered, leveling his gaze to me.

Tala mouthed the word "no" and sank to the ground. Loud sobs emanated from her body as she buried her face in the dirt. Itching and dryness chafed at my hands, but I couldn't tear my face away. Tears streaked down my own cheeks. No matter how much I'd hoped, Tala didn't love me. Not like I loved her.

Chapter Three

My feet thudded on the sand as I ran. I didn't want to be around anyone right now. My dry throat ached and threatened to close. My body felt like it'd been lit on fire and my bones were piercing my skin. I retched, hoping my blurry eyes would clear. I glanced at my arm and gasped. My skin was mottling green, and weird bumps protruded from it. I ran until my feet dragged into the sand and wouldn't move anymore. I looked up, realizing I was near the ridge. My arms stiffened and shook with the effort of movement. Screams tore from me as spines erupted from my skin. I would've collapsed from the pain if I could move.

Fibrous membranes raced through my body and filled my lungs. Grey threatened to overtake my vision. I tried to scream for help, but I knew no one would come. My spirit slid onto the sand, and I turned to see what Tacho had done to me.

Tacho had turned me into a cactus. Tears slid down my cheeks.

I walked back toward the village, but my spirit was yanked back by an unseen hand. I wailed into the night knowing the spirits wouldn't beckon me. They listened to the shaman. I closed my eyes, letting myself try to dream, but only my darkened eyelids greeted me.

I was truly alone and would never be loved again.

She came again, this time at night. She rolled out some maza and jerky and ate it by the light of a small fire. She made sure not to get too close to me. She hummed softly. I noticed her tattoos this time were like mine except for the color. Mine were black like a warrior's, while hers were dark purple. I did not know what this meant. I was too afraid to ask.

"May I take one of your fruits?" The woman asked.

I stood still, unsure if she was talking to me or asking ritualistically.

She held her hand up as if waiting for an answer. Sweat beaded my forehead, and my limbs began to tremble. If she found out about me, what would she do? Think I was a skinwalker or an evil spirit and try to kill me? Kill me anyways? I looked deeply into her beautiful dark brown eyes and searched. I found only sincerity and kindness, which scared me more than greed or evil. She was just a hungry woman. I let one of my fruits drop into her outstretched hand. Part of me wondered if her hands were smooth or calloused. She murmured thanks and bit deeply into the fruit. Juice dribbled down her small chin and sloping neck. I turned my burning face away so she could eat in peace.

She turned her face to the moon, whose loveliness rivaled

her own. Frustration mounted within me. She was just a woman enjoying some peace and quiet beside a cactus. She had no other reason to be here.

The woman grabbed something from a small bag at her waist. She began to weave threads together with some beads and feathers. After a while, I realized she was making a dreamcatcher. She must suffer from nightmares too. I watched her delicate deft fingers weave, and her frow pucker in frustration as they tangled on the threads. I lost track of the night as I sat nearby watching her and making sure nothing came near to attack her.

Satisfied, she stood, brushing sand from her clothes. Then she hung the dreamcatcher from my spines.

*"**I know you** can hear me."*

I kept my back to Tala. I couldn't face her. I was afraid of what Tacho would do to her. She knelt beside the cactus and wiped the tears from her eyes.

"I'm sorry Tacho did this to you. I tried to stop him. He was so angry when I refused him and assumed that I loved you because we're close friends. I do love you, but not in the way Tacho wanted me to love him. I don't love any person that way. I love everyone in the village the same. I'm so sorry."

Words clogged my constricted throat. I opened my mouth, but knew only anger and grief would pour out. I stayed silent. Tala wept beside me.

"I thought our friendship meant something to you, but it must not if you won't speak."

Tears spilled down my cheeks, and I couldn't stop them. Every word she whispered punched me in the stomach. She didn't love Tacho or me like we wanted her to. I wanted her to be free, and I hoped her father protected her.

"Father is keeping me safe, but I'm afraid the spirits may have something planned for him."

Her lips quivered as she spoke, and I wanted to still them. I wanted to squeeze her shoulder as I'd done a thousand times since we were children. I clenched my trembling hands into fists.

"Spirits guide you."

Tala rose and left. I watched her go back to the village, wondering if I'd ever see her again.

Storm clouds rolled across the sky like a dark blanket. Rain always flooded the desert, and I worried if my roots could take another drenching. Thunderbird raked his claws across the skies, and his mighty wings rang out in thunder. Rain poured down, and I danced in it, knowing no one could see me. It reminded me of the dancing festivals my village held during a good hunt or after the rains.

I titled my head back and breathed deeply. My existence was wearisome, and sometimes I didn't drink water at all, hoping I'd cease to exist; but small things like this made it worth it. Sometimes. I hoped the woman who visited me was safe from the storms. The water could flood the caves my village had lived in. It was quick and deadly.

It stormed for days. Hail thudded to the ground and made hollow marks in the sand. No animals searched for shelter under my pads or tried to burrow near my roots. Wind whipped through and tore off my flowers. I huddled in myself, hoping the storms wouldn't rip me from the ground. I didn't want to go that way.

A forceful gust ripped the dreamcatcher from my spines and tore it away. I watched the threads fly off into the desert and hoped the woman's spirit wasn't flying with it.

Chapter Four

"I was hoping you'd made it through the storms."

The woman's voice was rich like the syrup made from my fruit. Her warm eyes searched over my pads and spines. She gasped when she saw that a couple pads had almost been torn off completely. I quickly ran my hands through my hair. I was bruised but still alive for whatever it was worth.

"I'm sorry, but I need to tear these off."

I braced myself as pain lanced through my body. She peered over the edges and sighed almost in relief.

"There's no rot so that's a good sign. I'm going to use these pads if that's okay."

I was glad that a piece of me was going back with her. She smiled softly, and I stared at her full parted lips. I looked away feeling foolish. Even though she'd been visiting for months, I didn't know this woman enough to have feelings for her. I'd loved Tala because I'd known her my whole life and had a deep connection with her.

"Do you want to know my name?" she whispered.

Everything in me froze. I wanted to know everything about her. I bit my tongue to keep from responding. She stared and squinted as if she could see me. She stood and gently traced one of my spines with her finger.

"Aponi."

Tears slid down my face at the gentle name. It reminded me of the sun arching through the cave I'd lived in, the smooth stones in the bottom of the stream, the droplets left over from the rain. I whispered her name in my mind over and over, grateful for this bit of human connection.

"Can I tell you a story?"

My pads swayed in the breeze as a nodding response. I wondered if she saw.

"A long time ago there was a shaman who was new in the ways of the spirits. He tried to lead his village as best he could, but he was anxious and angry. He loved a girl, but she didn't love him that way. He cursed someone to be a cactus, and to break it, they had to experience true love. After some time had passed, he regretted his decision and implored the spirits, but nothing could be done. He told the story and passed it down to the next shaman hoping they could fix his mistake. After many years, it was passed to me."

Terror gripped my gut as realization dawned on me. I was too focused on her beauty to notice the way her eyes keenly sought me. Her eyes like Tala's.

"I know who you are," she whispered.

Chapter Five

Tala came to *visit me once more. Dried tears had snaked down* her face, and her eyes only showed despair. It had been months since she'd visited me last. She stood in front of me and wrapped her arms around her middle.

"My father was killed in an accident, and there's been no one to protect me from Tacho," she rasped.

Grief and anger filled me, and I clenched my fists. If he'd even touched her, I would find a way to kill him. The wind whipped around us, kicking up small dust clouds.

"I'm bearing his child. I refused him, but he wouldn't stop. I screamed for help, but no one came."

Tears streaked down my face, and I tried to reach for her shoulder, but my hands shook. My fingers almost brushed her bare shoulder but were jerked away by an unseen force. I cursed under my breath. Spirits take Tacho. Spirits torture him for the rest of his days.

Tala stared at my cactus and brushed tears from her eyes. I wished I could bear her grief for her, but there was nothing I could do now. She smoothed down her deerskin skirt and walked away. She never came back.

Aponi stared up at me as if waiting for a response. I felt my insides clench, though I knew it was just my spirit. Why did she tell me this? Maybe she wanted me to be afraid. Maybe she wanted to put me out of my misery. I opened my mouth, but words failed me. Her long, braided hair danced in the breeze. Even now, I wanted to run my hands through her coarse tresses.

"Can I ask you a question?"

I bobbed my pads in response.

"Can I ask your name?"

Fear danced in my belly. I had no reason to distrust her. She'd never harmed me even though she was a shaman. I trembled slightly. I'd never wondered if she'd break the curse or if she even wanted to. I knew a lot about her, but she knew nothing of me.

Tala had loved me as a friend. I felt Aponi loved me too, but it hadn't been enough to break it. I'd loved Tala, but mine was a selfish love. I'd wanted her to want me the same way, and didn't let her love me the way she did. Tears slipped down my cheeks. I'd been unable to break the curse because love wasn't selfish. I'd hidden from Aponi because I was afraid to trust her. Tacho had meant romantic love when he cursed me, but maybe the love of a friend was enough.

I slid from the cactus and let her see me. She gasped, but the brilliant smile on her face made it worth it. She stared at my tattoos, and tears welled in her eyes.

"My name is Kai."

She reached out her trembling hand, and I took it. My spirit wavered under her touch, and I saw how translucent I was. She brushed her thumb over my hand and kissed it. Heat rushed under my skin as my heart threatened to burst from my chest. My knees wobbled as she traced her hand across my cheek.

"You're even more beautiful than I imagined," she breathed.

"Why are you doing this?" I whispered.

"Because I want to," she replied, her voice thick.

She stared at my lips, and I licked them.

"Why do you want to?"

"Because I care about you. I wandered from my village because my spirit was restless, and I found peace under your shade. I didn't realize who you were till I had a dream about a crow leading me to you. I've spirit-walked many times, but after I met you, I always came here. I couldn't see you at first, but the longer I've been with you, the stronger I can sense you. Your form was like a flickering flame. Now I can see you since you bared yourself to me."

"I'm sorry I hid myself for so long, Aponi. I was scared. I loved what we had and didn't think I could cure the curse."

Aponi smiled sadly.

"You had a reason to be afraid. I'm a shaman, and my forefather cursed you."

"But you won't harm me?"

"I want to help you."

"How?"

"Do you feel loved, Kai?" she whispered, her voice hot on my neck.

"Yes," I breathed.

I pulled her into my arms and held her. She wrapped her arms around me, and sobs racked my body. She ran her hands through my hair and her fingers down my back. Warmth filled me as my form solidified again. She held my face in her hands and stared deeply into my eyes. Love and passion flickered in them.

I whispered her name as she threaded my fingers between hers. She tugged me away, and my feet trembled. We walked away from the ridge, and laughter bubbled up my throat. Aponi grabbed me in her arms and twirled me around before gently sitting me down. Though the sand was hard, and the heat fierce, I relished being in my body again. I stared at my skin. Tiny pockmark scars ran under my tattoos. Aponi ran her fingers over them and kissed my hand.

"Thank you." I whispered.

"I'd do anything for you Kai. I'd cross the desert, fight the spirits, and swim the rivers if it meant I'd get to be with you forever."

"You broke a curse for me. You love me. That's enough."

"Did I say I loved you?" She asked, her bronzed cheeks flushing,

I stammered a response.

Aponi grabbed my face and kissed me. It was like lightning sizzling my body, gentle rain on my skin, and warm drink in my stomach. I kissed her back, wrapping my arms around her. We held each other for a long time just enjoying being together.

"Let's go home." She breathed, smiling up at me.

"Home?"

"I have a cave across the river. It's close to the village."

"It's been years since I've been to a village. My family is all gone by now," I whispered.

"Their legacy is in their children's veins, and Tala's is in mine," she replied, squeezing my hand.

"What happened to her?"

"She passed from heartbreak shortly after her child was born."

I knelt on the sand with my face in my hands. Sobs shook my body. I wept for Tala and her pain that I couldn't protect her from. I wept for the life that Tacho stole from me. I wept for never getting to see my mother again. I wept for freedom from the curse. I wept for getting to love Aponi and to share a life with her.

Aponi wrapped her arms around me from behind and rested her arms under my wrapped chest. She whispered comforts in my ear and kissed the back of my neck.

"Good can come out of evil," Aponi whispered. "Tacho paid for his horrible actions. From what I've been told, the spirits haunted him till his dying breath."

I closed my eyes and took a deep breath. I slowly released it. I couldn't forgive Tacho for what he'd done. But I could move forward. A crow with a painted wing sat on the cactus and cocked its head at me. I nodded respectfully, and Aponi smiled.

She reached out her hand, and it alighted on her shoulder. It nuzzled its beak across her cheek.

"She's my spirit guide. Her name is Azarca."

"Nice to meet you, Azarca."

The crow flew off into the distance. The cactus crumbled to dust at our feet. The dust settled into the sands and blew away in the breeze. I stood shakily, still getting used to a solid form again. Aponi wrapped her arms around me and steadied me. We stood in the sand till I could take steps on my own. Aponi whispered encouragements in my ear as we walked.

"My village used to hold a celebration when a baby took their first steps," I said chuckling.

"Mine does. Maybe we can have one for you when we get there."

"I don't know if I'm ready to be around so many people."

"We can do it ourselves," Aponi replied, squeezing my hand.

I grabbed Aponi's hand and danced with her. Our steps were different, but the meaning was the same. Aponi led me down the slope, and I could see tiny fires in the distance. We waded across the cold river, and I relished the feeling of the water against my legs. We stopped outside of a cave with a brightly colored rug and a small hearth. A bundle of blankets lay in the corner. I breathed in the smell of dried cactus blossoms and smiled.

"Welcome home, Kai."

I stared deeply into her beautiful brown eyes and traced her jaw with my finger. I kissed her gently and pressed her body against mine.

"I'm home when I'm with you, Aponi."

She laughed, and it was the most beautiful sound I'd ever heard.

"IF I WAS A WORM"
Bethany H. Watson

"If I was a worm would you still love me?"
you ask, and to that I say no.
For I love you for more than the mind you possess
and more than the body you own.
I hold love for your soul and a worm has not one,
nor heartbeat like yours nor your stammering tongue.
I love you because you are like me and yet
different, unique, with depths enough
for me to unearth my whole life.
For among the animals was no helper for man
for man was not meant to love worm,
but human hand to human hand reaches
as waves upon waves rush to sand beaches.
Certain I am, I would not love you
if you were a worm and I still a man.
But if I too was worm, then maybe, perhaps,
most definitely, I'd love you in the dirt and the mud.

THE RED THREAD
Aisling Revell

Sonya always knew they were doomed to fail. She knew he would never really be her's, no matter how badly she wanted it to be so. She knew the moment they met that she would just be left in heartbreak.

She knew it when they made their relationship official, so she did her best not to think of what was to come, forcing herself to be content with the present moment.

She knew it when he started to think about the future, hinting about getting married and having a family. By this time, she gave up on distancing herself because she had fallen so much in love with him.

She really knew it when she realized she was dying, and he stayed by her side even when it was hard. Even when *she* made it hard.

Despite always knowing it would fail, it didn't hurt any less when she met the love of her life's soulmate.

Soulmates are real. Some don't like to believe it (Sonya surely doesn't), or even refuse to, but it's true nonetheless.

The nonbelievers can't be blamed. Afterall, it's such a far-fetched notion. Over eight billion people in the world, and there is only one that you are meant for? It's illogical. Despite the disbelief, sometimes even those people find their soulmates.

Romantics are thrilled by the idea. They have been since before pens were first put to paper to compose sonnets. Someone being out there to complete you, like a puzzle piece. It's a thrilling, and even comforting thought. You don't have to go through this life alone. They are always delighted when they find theirs.

But, just as soulmates are real, it's a fact that not everyone has one.

Where does that leave those who don't have a soulmate?

She was born with a gift. Or curse, depending on how you looked at it.

As long as she could remember, Sonya was able to see who someone's soulmate was by a thread that connected them. She didn't know what this was at first, until she realized it was more often than not shared between couples or those with deep, romantic bonds. Sometimes the thread bound two people in close proximity, and other times the thread spread out from a single person, stretching to an unseen location in the distance.

The thread was red, tied around the left ring finger. Wispy and almost ethereal, it would break apart like mist if an object moved through it, before forming together again. They reminded Sonya of the annoying spots in your eyes.

They won't go away no matter how much you rub your eyes, but then they dash away the second you try to focus on them.

Her parents had it. Stretching out the door when one of them left for work, and messily intertwining when they held hands. Her grandfather had one, but it was cut short, and she noticed that whenever they visited the cemetery, it stretched out for her grandmother's grave. Everyone was surprised when her childhood best friend called off her wedding to be with the boy she once despised in middle school. Everyone except Sonya because she had seen the thread that connected them since adolescence.

She used to tell her parents about this strange phenomenon when she was a little girl, but they assumed it was just the product of a child's overactive daydreams, and applauded her imagination, so she kept her strange ability to herself. It became her special little secret, and she liked to come up with stories for how these couples met, and wonder what adventures their futures held.

She truly enjoyed it, but what once was an amusing trait, turned into an anxious foreboding for one simple reason.

Sonya didn't have a thread.

She wasn't the only one. She occasionally came across others who didn't have it, others who were destined to live this life without someone connected to their soul. When she was younger, she thought, hoped, the red string would one day appear. Maybe after she got in a relationship it would materialize. Her high school and college flings quickly dispelled that hope, and she became burnt out on the idea of romance. It was hard to date when you could clearly see your significant other was meant for someone else. At twenty-five, she gave up on the notion, thinking love was just not meant for her. She did her best to distance herself from men.

Then came Ellis.

"Hi!"

Sonya looked up from her untied shoe to a young man. Brown hair that appeared like it was normally shorter but was in need of a cut. Hazel eyes and an earnest smile that hid nothing. In his right hand he held a red leash connected to a large golden retriever. On his left hand there was no wedding ring, but it didn't matter with the just-as-red-as-the-leash thread that flowed from it. It led out of the park and down the street. She resisted the urge to sigh as she finished tying her shoe, standing back up.

"Hello," she said, not even bothering to take the one earbud out of her right ear. Heavy metal blasted through, loud enough for others to hear. She originally started listening to it only as a distraction from the world, but it grew on her.

"Sorry, I just had to come over to introduce myself." He gave a boyish, apologetic smile, holding out his hand. "I'm Ellis."

She took his hand, but didn't return the smile. "Sonya."

He didn't seem deterred. "It's nice to meet you Sonya. This is Ruby." He looked down at his dog, who was wagging her tail excitedly.

Sonya's heart warmed just a little bit. "Hi, Ruby." She'd always liked animals since they didn't have red threads that tormented her.

"Do you come here often?" Ellis asked, keeping up with

Sonya as she continued her walk.

"Hm," was her unenthusiastic reply.

"I'll have to start coming more." Sonya could see him looking at her from the corner of her eye, but she refused to return his gaze.

"I know this is pretty forward, but can I have your number? I'd love to talk to you more."

She sighed. "Sorry, but I'm not really looking to date right now."

"Say no more. Too soon, I get it." He held his hands up, showing no offense was taken. "I need to get going, but I'll see you tomorrow hopefully!"

She shouldn't have gone back the next day. She should have found a new place to walk so he would get the hint. She knew all of this, and yet there she was, in the exact same spot as the previous day at the exact same time, walking a little slower than usual.

It couldn't be because he was unphased by her cold demeanor or because his smile was so open and warm or because she couldn't stop thinking about the touch of his hand. She told herself it was because she wanted to see his dog again.

Their relationship started like any other. Awkward getting-to-know you conversations over food you were too nervous to taste. The unsure pause at the end of the night, wondering if a goodbye kiss was appropriate. The butterflies when that first kiss finally happened.

Before long, there was no uncertainty. Ellis effortlessly blended into her life, holding her hand with no hesitation and getting along with her family as if they knew each other for years. It felt easy. Something she thought would never happen. From time to time, she would glance down at their hands, hoping that just maybe things had changed. That there would be that red thread connecting their fingers and souls. She tried to lie to herself about her disappointment when it never turned out that way.

She tried to ignore it then. To act as if it didn't exist. She would just enjoy her time with him, and who knew? Maybe his soulmate lived in Timbuktu and he would never even meet her. There was nothing to feel guilty about. She wasn't depriving him of anything better. Besides, she had a hard time believing that anyone could love him the way she did.

Still, no matter how hard she tried, *it* was there. Every time she saw it slightly slacken from the corner of her eye, she tensed up, wondering if *she* would be right around the corner, lying in wait to steal her greatest joy.

After nearly two years of dating, she was finally starting to feel comfortable when she had her accident.

"Sonya!"

Ellis came rushing into the room, his face more pale than she had ever seen it.

"I'm fine," she tried to reassure him from her spot in the

bed. She wasn't going to tell him about the whole incident, but her mom called him.

"What happened?" he asked, brushing her hair back and placing a hand on her forehead, as if he was checking for a fever.

Sonya took his hand in hers and gave it a comforting squeeze. "I just got a little dizzy. I'm sure it was nothing." She was at work when everything suddenly went black. Next thing she knew, she was waking up in an ambulance. Dizzy spells became common for her in recent days, but that wasn't surprising considering sleep had been almost impossible for the past week. Accidentally finding an engagement ring your boyfriend stowed away in one of his shoe boxes will do that to you.

"Miss Simmons?" A nurse walked into the room, holding a clipboard. "We're just going to run a few more tests and you'll be free to go."

Sonya swore she could feel her heart stop. Just when she was starting to feel safe. *Her.*

"Sonya?" Ellis squeezed her hand when Sonya only continued to stare at the nurse.

Sonya snapped out of her trance. "Sorry. Yes of course, thank you ..."

"Tracy." The nurse smiled. She was short and cute, with dirty blonde hair in a messy bun and blue eyes. Standing in direct contrast to Sonya's tall frame and darker features.

"Tracy."

Tracy. Her boyfriend's soulmate.

Sonya wasn't sure what she was expecting. For Ellis to look at Tracy, be mesmerized and immediately break up with her on the spot. Of course that wouldn't happen. He couldn't see the line connecting them.

Still, it didn't change the fact that Tracy was Ellis' soulmate. She glanced between them nervously, trying to sense some kind of irresistible connection, but Ellis only showed Tracy the same courtesy he showed everyone, and Tracy spoke to him like she would talk to any patient's loved one she assumed. Ellis certainly didn't smile at her the way he smiled at Sonya. There was nothing to worry about. They would leave the hospital and, hopefully, never have to see her again. Nothing had to change.

Maybe a small part of her felt guilty for this, but Ellis was happy, wasn't he? Why change that? Soulmates be damned, she was a good girlfriend, and she would continue to be one. And when Ellis offered her that ring, she would accept, and they would spend the rest of their lives together. She had been unsure, but seeing *her* face to face made Sonya almost eager for him to propose.

Nothing would stand in the way of their happiness. Not even his soulmate.

"Let me help." Tracy quickly moved to her side, attempting to move the pillow in a way that would make Sonya more comfortable.

"I've got it," was Sonya's short reply, as she sat up on her own and wrenched her arm behind herself uncomfortably to adjust her pillow. Her stubbornness left her breathless and with a sore shoulder, but she refused to let it show. From the corner of her eye she could see Ellis and Tracy share an awkward look. As Sonya's dislike for Tracy became more and more obvious, these shared looks became more frequent, and they pierced Sonya a little harder every time. Maybe Ellis would break up with her for her rudeness.

"Of course. Let me know if there's anything else you need." Tracy smiled before leaving the room, and what killed Sonya most of all was that it was a genuine smile. Not one that was used to cover for offense or hurt feelings. It was a smile that said she understood why Sonya was acting the way she was.

Even though Tracy left the room, the thread that connected her to Ellis was still there, dancing over her own bed-stricken body in an almost flirtatious way. She brought her hand down roughly on the sheets to rip it in half, but it only misted around her, before forming again. The stupid thing was teasing her, she knew it.

"Are you ok?" Ellis asked, probably thinking she was just simply letting out her aggravation.

"Other than the obvious," Sonya started, attempting to make light of the situation. "I'm fine."

Ellis gave her hand a reassuring squeeze before kissing it. "You'll be home soon. I know it."

It didn't get to be that simple. What she thought was a simple inconvenience ended up being much more serious. Numerous tests and multiple doctor visits, and no one could tell her exactly why her body was deteriorating. Why she had no strength and her organs were starting to fail her. Idiopathic was the word the doctors used to describe it. Eventually, she became a permanent resident in the hospital. And who was there for her through it all? Of course it was Ellis. Never letting her go to an appointment alone and always being there to hold her hand.

Another person who was there was Tracy. Sonya knew she shouldn't take her anger out on the poor, unaware girl, but she couldn't help but be short with the pretty nurse every time she checked on her. Ellis and Tracy seemed to chalk it up to just simple frustration over her situation and had no idea a more personal motive was at hand.

Did she really have to die just so Ellis could be with this girl? Why did soulmates even matter? Would Tracy know how to make grilled cheese exactly the way Ellis liked it, with the bread slightly burned? Would she be able to listen patiently to him as he prattled on about whatever his newest video game obsession was, all with an amused smile on her face? Would she know that when Ellis said he wanted to be left alone, it really meant that he needed you more than ever? Would Ruby even like her? Tracy was probably a cat loving, video game hating person who undercooked grilled cheese. Ellis would be miserable with her.

Of course, all of the lies Sonya told herself about Tracy turned out to be false. Tracy was allergic to cats, with two dogs of her own that she excitedly showed Ellis pictures of when he asked. Not only could she tolerate long talks about video games, she played them herself, and she and Ellis bonded over their excitement of a new release coming out next month. There was still hope that she couldn't properly burn grilled cheese, but it didn't comfort Sonya much.

Most of all, Tracy was the kind of person who knew exactly what someone needed. Years of being a nurse probably helped with this. Unlike Sonya, who had to learn how to be there for someone after isolating herself for so long, Tracy had an effortless compassion about her. She could tell when someone needed their space and when they needed a shoulder to cry on, even if they claimed the opposite.

It's what made it so hard for Sonya to keep hating her. The young woman was truly a remarkable nurse, always making sure Sonya had everything she needed. Before long, she found herself being kind to Tracy. Tracy was moral support, if not a friend.

Sonya was dying. She didn't need some thread to tell her. She could feel it, and despite how unfair she thought it was, her anger wouldn't solve anything. Her acceptance, however, could help Ellis.

"Marry me," Ellis sleepily said, gazing at her through tired eyes from his spot on the recliner next to the bed.

Sonya smiled, wanting to reach out to smooth his bedhead, but not feeling strong enough to do so. "No."

It was a daily ritual for Ellis to propose now. He wouldn't admit it, but it was because she was dying. Because he wanted to share that with her before she left this world forever. A part of her wanted to say yes, because she so badly wanted to be his wife, but she couldn't do that to him. Losing her was going to be hard enough for him. It would be even harder if they got married. He would feel a sense of commitment, and wouldn't be able to move on.

If she asked him to never be with anyone else after she was gone, he would do it, with no regret or resentment. A selfish part of her wanted this. Wanted him to belong only to her, even when she was dead, but she knew how big his heart was, and his capacity to love others. She didn't want him to be as lonely as she had been for the majority of her life.

Something she once dreaded was now something she needed to help happen. She had to make sure he was going to be ok after she was gone. Even if it meant choosing to let him go.

Sonya stared at Ellis as he slept, his head leaning against the back of his chair and one hand loosely wrapped around hers. He'd lost weight during the past weeks, and there were dark circles under his eyes. She wanted to sleep too, but she took this time to memorize his features, hoping she could take the image with her when she was gone.

"He really loves you."

Sonya looked up to Tracy, who was standing in the doorway of the room. Her shift was supposed to be over an hour ago, but there she was, smiling and checking in on Sonya.

Sonya examined Tracy for a moment before returning her gaze to Ellis.

"Yeah, he does." The thread spread over her again, reaching from Tracy to Ellis. Instead of feeling like she was being torn away from Ellis by it, she was comforted from its presence.

She took a breath, giving Ellis' hand a light enough

squeeze to not wake him up, but a tight enough one to reassure herself. "Tracy, can I ask you to do something?"

"Of course." Tracy entered the room, standing next to Sonya's bed.

"This has all been really hard on Ellis, and it's only going to get harder ... when I'm gone-"

"Sonya—" Tracy tried to interrupt, but Sonya wouldn't let her.

"When I'm gone," she firmly said, and Tracy didn't argue this time. "He's going to need all of the support he can get. It might take him a while to open up, but can you be there for him when he's ready? As a confidante, or a friend, or ..." She paused, taking another breath. "Whatever he ... and you need."

Tracy didn't argue. She didn't ask why Sonya was trusting her to look after her boyfriend instead of a friend or family member. The young woman couldn't possibly know all of what Sonya meant by it, but Sonya knew, somewhere in the future, when Tracy was struggling over her guilt, she would remember this conversation, and it would bring her peace and the confidence to pursue what she was meant to.

She wasn't sure how long it would take Ellis. Knowing him, it wouldn't be an easy process for his heart to heal. It could possibly take years, but when it did happen, Sonya wanted Ellis to be sure that she would be happy for him, even if they couldn't be together.

Tracy glanced at Ellis, then looked back at Sonya, nodding. "Of course."

With her free hand, Sonya took Tracy's. The thread curled around Sonya's fingers as she held both of their hands, connecting them.

"Thank you."

She would love him with everything she had while she was still here, and when she was gone, she would let him go, confident in the fact that even if she wasn't his soulmate, their love was real.

/WARNINGS OF A FALLEN EMPIRE/
June Elliott

What happens when the object of your desire
becomes your downfall?
When every drop of blood in you is screaming
warning you away from him?

When you know he would be your destruction?
You would go down in flames if you just touched him
Burned to the ground
ashes of who you once were

Oh, but what a glorious bonfire you would be
you'd burn bright and fast
He'd raze the entirety of your character
leaving a trail of desolation and regret

The Roman Empire went out in a blaze of glory
Fierce they fought and lost
An entire civilization / never to rise again

This is how it is with conquerors

They are an inferno
They build roads entirely changing the landscape
of every inch of your skin
until you're all smoke and no flame

The Roman Empire is dead
and so too will be your soul
if you let the object of your desire conquer you
His is a fire you can't come back from

ESCAPING SHADOWS
Michaela Bush

I swirl the amber liquid in my glass a moment, studying its rolling, velvety texture. I down it, a burn trailing down my throat.

Might as well be the last thing I feel.

I wipe my mouth with the crumpled-up napkin left on the table from a meal prior, then brush a finger against the worn mahogany surface. Something from a thrift store. Battle scars, knife slices, liquid rings, and stories I'll never know. We were never home to use it for long, and now? There's no chance of planting new memories on this table.

I chuckle softly, waiting for the elephant in the room to speak up. When she doesn't, I do.

"You're here to kill me," I finally announce to the shadow lurking behind me. "Do it right the first time."

"No, I'm not."

Ava. Once my partner at the force. Once an operative for one of those alphabet soup agencies—there, she became known as the Crimson Angel. Once my wife. Until the amnesia agent Stromausfall took her from me. And I've been escaping both the clandestine shadow government and Ava since then.

It's no life to live.

And I'm tired.

"It's your order. Do this and you'll be named the right hand to—who? Your little puppeteer." I don't remember his name anymore, if I ever had the right one to begin with. I spin out of my chair, pulling the revolver I have taped to the underside of my table. And I hold it out to her, grip first. "So do it."

I can't say it and look her in the eye at the same time or I'll choke up. So I finish my last words and then meet her cool, blue gaze.

They used to be warm.

But I've given up that memory. It cuts like knives.

"No." Ava's gaze flickers over my gun, and I wait for her to snatch it despite herself. It's when I finally take a good look at her. She doesn't have a gun, unless it's tucked in her boot. Nothing on her hip, thigh, or beneath her arm. But she has a packet of papers, and she's holding them out to me. "Take this and live."

My brows furrow. "Take what? I'm not accepting gifts from your little—"

"Take it, Reese."

She could've just slapped me. It would've hurt less than her saying my name. I imagine the other, softer ways she's said it before. Tell myself I'm lying when I wonder if she tried to fight the amnesia and remembered those gentler times.

But this revolver would end my pain and keep her alive.

And that's the best I can hope for. Does she want to deprive me of that too? Does she even know how much it burns to hear her say my name?

She rolls her eyes at my frozen state, but I'm not touching it, whatever those papers are. She rips the rubber band from them and unfolds the wad, moving past me to smooth the stack out onto the kitchen table.

Three swipes across the folds to smooth them, like she used to smooth out bills and mission orders. Our marriage certificate, even. *It's not fair.*

"It's a new identity," she explains. "It took everything I had to get this. Use it." She flicks a gaze over the house quickly, then shakes her head. "Find somewhere far away and go there."

"No." I suck in a breath, but I'm still drowning. "No. You're going to end this now."

"I'm *trying*," she snaps. "If you'd just take the—"

"I don't want this! I don't want any of it!" An awful thought creeps in. "They'll know you didn't eliminate me. They'll retrace your steps and know. They'll kill you."

Fear flickers through her eyes, and she nods stiffly. "I know. They murdered my person for the new ID cards this morning. Which is why you need to go. Now."

If they caught up with the license manufacturer, they already know what my new name is. I don't even look at it; it's useless to me anyhow. "The day I die, my obituary will read Reese Blaire. Not anything else."

"Then that's what you'll do! And then I—" Ava cuts off short.

She's staring at the fridge now, across the room. A picture from our honeymoon is stuck with a magnet. We found a stranger on the beach to snap a picture as the ocean foamed behind us and Ava's blue sundress and blonde hair billowed.

I couldn't take it down in the past year since I lost her.

And out the window, an SUV rumbles down the long driveway, dust trailing behind it. Still half a mile out.

"Why did you do this?" I ask her. "The new ID. This."

She jerks out of her trance. Blinks, confused. "Something inside screamed an alarm when I got the orders. But I couldn't fight them or they'd know something was wrong. I decided to do this instead, because I–I just can't shake you. And then ..." She picks at a loose thread on her black cargo pants. "I–I had a memory," she finally admits.

My brows fly up. A *memory*. "What of?" I ask. The SUV is still coming. Urgency tingles along my nerves.

"That." She lifts a finger toward the photo. "Well, no." Her face scrunches in confusion. Fights the fog stealing her from me. "The wedding. The white dress."

I want to marvel. My knees want to buckle in relief, because if she has even one memory intact, it's worth fighting for. But the SUV is coming.

I push the revolver into her hands and run down the hallway for my gun cabinet, unlocking it quickly and pulling my 9mm and a couple boxes of ammo for the both of us. I spin around again and find she's trailing me. Not the skilled assassin and agent I knew, nor the spitfire woman I married. Someone who's lost and trying to figure her way back home. Someone trying to escape the shadows she's lived in for so long.

I shove one box into her hands.

"Can I trust you with this?" I ask. She nods sharply.

"But Reese ... why? It'd be easier if you just took the ID and left me figure out the mess I'm in—"

I talk fast. "I'll show you why if you give me a chance." I've prayed and begged every day that she would remember me. I'll try to make her fall in love with me all over again every day if that's what it takes. With the unknown effects of the amnesia drug, I might just have to.

Would it be easier to run? Simpler? Less pain in the long run? Possibly.

But my Ava, just a glimpse of who she once was, stands before me. I promised to be there in the good and bad. She learned to love once, amidst a broken home and a job that proved the worst of the human race ... but she can do it again if she just trusts me.

We can do it again.

And whatever's waiting outside can't possibly compare to the pain of losing her again, or worse, disappearing and letting her die.

I lock eyes with her. "But it might involve taking down a shadow government. Just like old times, Crimson Angel."

A faint smile flickers across her face as the back door is kicked in.

FEED
Charleigh Frederick

Energy isn't given. It's harvested. Carefully curated by a master hand and the gentlest of touches. And Harrison was of a species with the touch.

Step one is to find your meal. Step two is to get them close to death, where it's easier to feast.

They walked up together, as Harrison promised. His meal tonight was nervous, jittery, but that didn't affect the taste.

He needed to feed soon. Harrison didn't like how weak he felt along the way, relying on the boy more than once to help support him. But they both made it.

Harrison guided them around stones, into the second row of death. Unlike a theater, there's no higher price to be near the front. The gate the bodies want lay above the heads of the dead, an equal height away for all, and just out of reach for those alive.

The two stopped at Harrison's lead. The boy hadn't noticed it at first, but once he saw it, it was all he could see, his eyes glued to the stone, refusing to back down.

"It's really here." The boy sank to his knees in the dark of the graveyard, his hand reaching out as he traced a finger over the etched letters spelling his own demise in the last hour of the day.

Step three is where things got interesting.

Harrison knew the boy was ready, but that made none of this easier. He had targeted the boy long enough to know his weaknesses. Harrison promised something he would never know if true. "They'll be there to greet you as soon as you arrive. They can't wait to see you again. We're getting you out of this school, and back to the people who are your home."

The boy shifted his weight, leaning heavily on his left knee, a debate playing in his eyes. It's one thing to agree, and another to see it laying out in front of you, welcoming you home. No one likes to see their own headstone.

Harrison may have grown in graveyards, may have felt most at ease amongst the looming mounds of dirt, but he knew for those like the boy, this was not a place to feel at home, but one to feel dread. Sadness. Despair.

The boy looked up from his grave, his eyebrows drawn together, his lips a thin line. "Harrison, maybe ... I don't know. I mean ... what if I'm not ready, and something goes wrong?"

"You are ready. Nothing will go wrong." Harrison locked his hands behind his back, looking up at the full moon overhead. It lit up the graveyard, making it feel much earlier than it was. Harrison knew the pressing time constraints. If they waited much longer, the death date would be inaccurate, which would bother him to no avail until he got a chance to fix it. Despite the amount of graves around them, he knew fixing a date wasn't quick, and would raise more questions than he cared to answer.

That, and he needed to eat soon, or else he risked collapsing.

Feeding took time, unless you wanted an impure meal. People that will go unmissed often don't have the best of souls. It takes planning, care, and cleverness to pick someone pure whose absence won't ruffle the school's feathers. But he risked dying himself if he waited too long between feedings. And this time, Harrison was stretching how long he could go. He never needed to lean on a human before today. He didn't want the feeling to linger.

"It's so ... permanent," the boy weighed.

"No more so than life." Harrison looked to the larger grave next to him, and to the beautiful woman sitting perched atop the stone, blending into the night as if she emerged from the shadows, newly birthed by her mother, the moon. Her legs dangled down over the name, obstructing it from view.

Harrison was one of few people who knew the girl, Raven, was older than he was. You would never guess it by her ageless, never changing appearance. Being young helped her feed when she couldn't live off his table scraps. This was his meal, but with it, they would both leave satisfied. She wore all black. Her lips were coated in a layer of purple that smudged in the left corner.

"Everything happens in stages." Although Harrison spoke to the boy, his eyes remained trained on Raven. "It's inevitable for your kind to end up here, surrounded by the leeches of the world."

"Leech is such a cruel term," she let out a laugh, though they both knew that was what she was called. "Don't look at me like that, Harry. Mine don't want him either. Except in death."

"I don't want one of your kind here for this," Harrison

said. It wasn't that it was Raven. In truth, he loved the girl. He didn't want her to see him so weak. He waited too long to feed.

She rolled her eyes. "You do this every time. A girl is going to start to think you don't like being with her. Though, I know that's not true." She gave a devilish grin, her purple lips twerking up on one side. "Are we killing him or not? Either you can shoo me away, or you can make sure that end date stays accurate. You don't have time for both."

Harrison nodded his head and turned back to the boy. "Stand up."

"Will it hurt?" the boy asked as he stood, his legs shaking. "On the field, it looks painful what you do."

"You've seen the fields?"

The boy nodded. "That's how I lost my family."

Most don't see the fields and survive. Harrison heard enough stories to know how to calm the boy down, despite himself not ever going there. "On the field we are in battle. We are going for speed, not grace. It's most important to move quickly and trap the soul. Here we will go slowly and gracefully. This will not hurt. It should feel almost freeing." Harrison began to unwrap a strip of fabric from around his left hand, putting it in his pocket before he moved onto the right.

"I'm glad I won't die in the fields," the boy said.

Harrison finished unwrapping his right hand and tucked away that fabric too. "You are lucky," he agreed as he placed a hand in front of the boy's chest, just below his breasts. He could feel quick breathing, a sensation Harrison himself hadn't felt in a long while. "Do you have any last words before ...?"

The boy shook his head, and pinched his eyes shut, like a child waiting for a splinter to be dug out of their finger, except Harrison was taking more than a sliver of wood.

Harrison closed his eyes, placed his hand on the boy, and focused. A gray mist appeared around his hand that grew until the cloud cocooned the boy completely. Harrison lifted his hand from the boy, slowly and carefully drawing it back. The cloud moved with him. As it left the boy, the boy's body slumped to the cool earth, unmoving, unnaturally still, tossed down like a rag doll. The cloud seemed to react but settled after a moment and Harrison smiled. He brought his hand encased in the fog toward himself, until he was touching his own chest, in the same place he touched the boy's. The fog moved in around him as in the distance the old church bell gave its first of twelve chimes to issue in the new hour, the new day.

They made it.

The fog was gone, dissipated into Harrison's body. He felt better. His energy returned to him. The night embraced him like its own child, calling to him, and letting him in. He felt stronger now that he had fed. Like himself once more.

"Is it done?" Raven asked from where she perched. "Am I safe to ... be a leech?"

"I shouldn't have called it that."

"You get snippy when you're hungry. I'm glad you've fed."

Harrison turned to look at the woman. She nearly fell off the headstone in surprise as his blue eyes glowed in the dark. He smiled, and blew outward a gray cloud, like a puff of cigarette smoke. "You have never seen my breed work in the dark, I take it." They normally worked during the day.

"It's startling," she said. "I've only been near your kind for one year."

"War brings us all together. Are you coming tomorrow?"

"It's not fair they get to go home when we don't. But yes, I will be there. It will be interesting to see who the fresh blood is."

"Try not to change anyone on the train. Your kind is so ... messy."

She gave a laugh. "Headmaster's head would pop off in fury if I did."

Every year, by what Harrison could gather, the trains came bringing new students into the school, offering them up as fresh meat. Killing them, feeding off them, was illegal. They were there to learn, and to transform into one of the species housed at the school. To become like Raven, like Harrison. And once they were, the only way they were allowed to leave the school was to go to the field and fight. Graduation was a death march into battle.

"What could the headmaster do? It's not like you can be killed twice." Harrison pulled out of his pocket a new long black piece of fabric that he carefully unrolled, rerolling it around the hand he had used to touch the boy and then himself. He liked to change fabric after he ate.

"The house leaders can kill me though."

"Pity." Harrison finished the wrapping and pulled another sheet of fabric, identical to the first, starting to wrap the other hand.

"Are you done then? With the boy I mean."

"Hm?" Harrison looked down at the body, unmoved from where it fell out of the smoke. It fit in better here now that it was no longer breathing. You can't be at home in a graveyard with breath still in your lungs. Perhaps that was why he was always at home here. Perhaps that was why he liked the girl. It was a reminder that there were more like him, without breath on this planet, then those with it.

Harrison looked back to her, the eagerness in her red eyes. "Feel free to do as you please. His shell is all yours."

"Excellent. I knew hanging out with you tonight was a good idea." She hopped down off the grave, making her way first to Harrison. She stopped before him. Her hand traced up his chest, electrifying his nerves. "You told the boy it doesn't hurt."

"I did."

"You lied."

"I did. You find it attractive when I lie."

"Harry, you are a naughty boy." Her hand reached up, cupping his cheek as she looked into his eyes, the glow fading out as the buzz of a fresh feed wore off. "Have you ever tried to feed like a leech?"

"That's not how I eat."

"Pity. I think you'd look cute with blood on your lips. A little color to offset how pale you are."

He didn't answer, so she went over to the boy, her sudden absence chilling Harrison. She crouched beside Harrison's meal, careful not to get her knees dirty as she examined the remains.

"Perhaps I should meet you back at the dorms," Harrison offered, though he wanted to stay with her.

"Weak stomach?" She looked up in surprise. "You're the one who killed him, not me."

Harrison shook his head. "I don't enjoy getting dead

men's blood on me."

"Not really a man yet, was he?"

"Still." Harrison turned without another word, but he didn't leave. Didn't want to. Couldn't.

He could hear her fangs tear into the flesh behind him. And then the sucking sound, like a straw without enough in the glass.

She was a quick eater, part of why Harrison let her tag along in the first place on his feedings, though the rest of the school didn't know that they did this. If they moved in the shadows, no one had to know.

The boy was a new student, left orphaned from the war. No friends to speak of, and he lived in a single room. Perfect bate. No one will notice he's gone, until he starts to miss class. The staff will think he eloped to the cause and joined the front line. That's where they assumed all of Harrison's victims went. And then months later, maybe years, someone would notice the gravesite. Case closed. They'd think to themselves how they wished they had known when the funeral was so they could have gone. That wish was all the closure anyone would need.

The sounds stopped. A moment later her hand traced up Harrison's back.

"Do you want a taste?" she whispered in his ear.

Harrison spun around. Her lips were no longer purple—that smudged off onto the boy's body. They were red now.

She let out a yelp, but not one of protest as he grabbed her by the hips, holding her. Their lips met. The metallic taste of blood left his mouth bitter as he sat her on the top of the boy's headstone. The boy's torn apart body lay at their feet. But that's not where Harrison's focus was.

His focus was on her.

On devouring her.

On kissing her like he needed her to live.

He never understood how a leech can have body heat, especially when he did not, but it offered a source of comfort against his mouth he hadn't known he needed until the first time they kissed.

Her hands tightened in his hair. Then all at once they were gone, and she was shoving at him. "Harrison," she said, but not in the way he would have wanted. "They're coming."

He turned. The bob of a walking flashlight bounced up the path.

No one was supposed to come looking for the boy yet. He carefully planned it, carefully selected his meal. His curation skills were on point. What was missed in his hunger?

"I can't get expelled," she hissed, jumping off the grave.

The boy's body lay at their feet, her lipstick all over the torn apart and gutted corpse. They didn't have time to hide it. So instead, "We need to hide."

She blended into the shadows, but like him, her species didn't have any special skills in hiding. They were predators, not dinner. Evolution didn't account for headmasters and house leaders.

The only place for them, if expelled, would be the front line.

Harrison moved behind a headstone, getting himself out of view of the path just as he started to make out the two voices of the flashlight owners.

"I swear I saw someone up here," a crisp female voice said. Valerie Maycomb. House leader. Not Harrison's house, but that hardly changed her power over him.

A deep, yet still distinctly female, voice answered. "I'm not doubting you, Val. I'm just saying we don't have that many students here yet, and it's rather unconventional for them to be sneaking up here to drink already. Once the train comes, it would be more believable." The headmaster.

The beam of the flashlight illuminated around the stone behind which Harrison hid. In the dismal light, he could make out where Raven was hiding, two stones down. The stone between them was that of the boy. And that's where the light ended. Even from where Harrison was, he could see the blood staining the ground. He took his sleeve and wiped his mouth.

Neither Valerie nor the headmaster screamed. The light stayed there for a moment.

"Well," Valerie spoke first. "Someone wants to be sent to the front lines."

"This was the Rubel boy," the headmaster said. "He hadn't started classes yet."

"A leech killed him," Valerie incorrectly assessed. "Leeches don't leave before the blood is dry. They should still be around here somewhere."

"He was so young. His aunt sent him here to keep him safe."

"If we start looking, perhaps call a few more house leaders, we should be able to catch the leech and get rid of the problem. Are you listening?"

A pause. A shuffle.

Then silence.

Nowhere to run. Nowhere new to hide. Just to wait.

The light didn't change. Harrison didn't see her until it was too late. Until Valerie grabbed his arm and dragged him up on his feet. "Harrison?" she demanded as her fingers dug into his arm. Fighting right now would make everything worse. "You're not a leech."

"I am not," he confirmed.

"Did you kill the Rubel boy?" headmaster asked as Valerie dragged him back over in front of the boy's grave. 'Mark Rubel. Hwensler 2E, 1382 - Klensler 1B, 1398' The date was accurate. Harrison was proud of that. Dig into his finances, you wouldn't find that Harrison paid for the stone. By all records, the boy bought his own grave.

No matter what Harrison said, they would keep looking for the leech. "Don't be ridiculous. You know my kind thrives over gravedirt. I came here to relax, and was doing so rather successfully before you hauled me to my feet."

"Did you see anyone else?" Valerie asked.

"No."

"Did you talk to Mark at all?" the headmaster asked.

Harrison shook his head. "He was dead when I got here. I think his spirit called to me as it left the world, and that's why I was drawn here tonight. You know how it is with my kind. The souls are like a drug. Catch whiff, and here we come. Perhaps my arrival scared the leech away."

Valerie put a finger to her mouth.

"What?" Harrison asked. He knew what. But Raven needed to hear him, to leave before she was caught. It would be harder for her to talk her way out of this.

Valerie went to the grave on the other side of the boy. That was where Raven had been hiding. But she must have moved, as Valerie kept looking.

Even the headmaster waited and followed Valerie's lead, though Harrison knew the woman was a puppet for the generals. Give them a school, a refuge, but don't really run it. Those were the orders Harrison discovered last week when he went snooping for student files in the headmaster's office. The house leaders stepped up, filling in the gap of leadership and turning the school into a place where those who went against house leaders were expelled to the front line.

There it was only a matter of time before death finally took them too.

Valerie sulked amongst the graves.

"The leech probably went home by now. They don't tend to stick around long after feeding," Harrison offered.

"No. They stay until the blood is dry, drinking every drop they can get," Valerie protested.

Headmaster nodded, though she seemed in such a daze it was hard to tell intention until she spoke. "Harrison is right. We should head back to the school."

Valerie pounced like a cat behind one of the gravestones, coming up once more, with Raven in her grasp. "I found a leech," she said proudly.

"Let me go!" Raven squirmed, but unless she attacked a house leader, she couldn't do much as Valerie led her back to Harrison and the headmaster.

Valerie took in a long sniff. "I can still smell the boy's blood on her."

"What do you suggest? Front line?" the headmaster asked.

"No!" Raven objected. "I didn't kill anyone."

"Then who did, leech?" Valerie said. Harrison knew that she knew Raven's name.

Raven's eyes met his.

One of them wasn't going to make it out of this. Someone needed to go down for the death of the boy. The headmaster discovered the body. Somehow, Harrison's sloppiness led them right to a feeding. But there was no reason both he and Raven had to be sent to die. No reason at all. One of them had to be braver.

"Harrison killed him. I cleaned up the scraps," Raven said.

Apparently you really can't trust a leech.

"We already asked Harrison," the headmaster had a gentle tone, as if explaining something hard to understand to a child. "He didn't do this."

"Why is his word worth more than mine?" she objected.

"I'm not a leech," Harrison said.

Headmaster nodded. "It is tricky to find the truth. Valerie, what do you think?"

Valerie looked to the headmaster. "Permission to issue a punishment?"

"Permission granted."

Valerie wasn't really asking for permission. It was for appearances. She was in charge here.

"Harrison will punish the leech. A life for a life," Valerie said.

Harrison's mind began to swim. "You don't mean ..." he trailed off. Raven looked pale.

"It's really quite simple. You have to feed, Harrison. And here we have a willing candidate. You said you don't know each other, so it's no big deal. Just take her."

"She's a leech," Harrison argued.

But Valerie looked unphased by his objection. "Your species consumes leeches all the time on the battlefield. It's not as strong as a human's life, but it does work. Like an appetizer. You will issue the punishment and end her life."

Harrison met Raven's eyes. They'd been together for so long. Doing this for so long. Perhaps she had been the one to be sloppy. She sold him out the first chance she had gotten.

No matter how they got here, they were here all the same. If he objected, they would both either be killed or sent to the front line. If he did this, at least one of them could live.

Raven had a crazed look in her eye that only comes when faced with an unwanted death. "We can take them," she hissed to Harrison. "Come on."

"I like appetizers," Harrison said to Valerie. His life was dependent on one more feeding for tonight. He unwrapped his hands, starting with the left. They didn't both need to be unwrapped, but he preferred it. Feeding was one of the few times it seemed okay to let his hands breathe. Even in the bathroom of his private dorm he worried about fully unwrapping them in case someone snuck up behind him.

Raven's eyes grew wide. "You bastard."

He had just finished his left hand, the dark fabric going into his pocket when Raven lunged at him, teeth out. She tackled him, knocking him down to the ground. He put his arm up, blocking her, holding her up over him, too high for her teeth to reach his weak flesh.

His left hand pressed against her. A gray shimmer appeared around her body.

She let out a scream as she stopped fighting him, going for retreat instead.

Taking from a leech was far slower than taking from a

boy.

Raven sprang up off him, the gray cloud sucking back into her body as she gave a whimper, moving away. Valerie stood behind her, stopping her from running. Stopping any sort of real escape.

"She nearly bit me," Harrison growled as he got to his feet, his eyes on Valerie. "Perhaps you ought to do the honors."

Valerie shook her head. "You almost got her. That round is a draw."

"If I get bit and don't die, I become one of them," Harrison pointed out. "Kill her yourself, or hold onto her so she doesn't come at me. Leeches don't have much to take, it's like ripping tape off a hairy chest and not wanting the hair to come with it."

He hoped Valerie would say to forget it then, but no such luck. She tightened her grip on Raven, grabbing the girl and holding her arms behind her back. "If she bites me, she'll face a fate worse than death."

Harrison didn't doubt that.

Raven looked exhausted. Apparently almost losing what little is left of your soul does a number on anyone. Her head sagged, but she looked up as Harrison drew near.

He started to unwrap his right hand. His powers felt stronger in his dominant hand, though he knew that wasn't how it worked. It was like writing in a way. He knew his left hand could write, could be taught to do what the right knows, both equally strong, but that didn't mean he wanted to grab a pencil and scribble out a manuscript with his left. He would still use his right.

"Harrison," Raven whispered as he shoved the fabric into

his pocket, both hands now free. "It's me."

"I know," he said.

He lunged his hand forward, grabbing for the flesh of the neck, holding steady.

Valerie's grip on Raven released as a gray cloud emerged from her body, swirling defiantly around his hand.

"You'll regret—" Valerie was only able to choke out the two words before Harrison tore her free from her body, moving his hand away from her, the gray cloud coming with him.

"Oh my," the headmaster muttered from behind them.

Raven sank to the ground, a laugh billowing in her throat as she rolled over onto her back, staring up as Valerie's body collapsed in a heap on the ground. Valerie's gray wrestled against Harrison's grasp.

Guiding Valerie was harder than it had been with the boy, but she was tethered to his hand until he chose to release, either into him, or out into the world as a ghost.

Her gray cloud absorbed into his chest, his eyes glowing, his body buzzing. He hadn't fed so much in one night since before he came to the school.

He closed his eyes, feeling her in him. He felt strong. Good. With gentle release, he blew out a plume of gray smoke.

Harrison turned to the headmaster, the weight of what he did, his split second decision to save Raven, sinking in. "The student body won't like that she's gone. But I'm not going to the front line. Neither is Raven."

"Okay," the headmaster agreed. She would agree to anything while Harrison had his hands unwrapped.

"You will make me a house leader," he ordered.

Raven's scoffed. "Are you serious right now?"

It was a risky plan, but it was his only chance at survival.

He would be free from any consciousness of his actions here today if he was a house leader.

His body was still buzzing from so much energy. Perhaps it was his glowing blue eyes, or the way he bounced, but he knew the headmaster's answer before she even said, "I can do that."

This was the only chance they had at making it.

"By the power vested in me as headmaster of this school, I now pronounce you, Harrison, as a house leader, taking over Valerie's post," the headmaster said. As she spoke the air around them glowed brighter. By the last word, the graveyard had a noon light about it. The headmaster clapped their hands. On the first clap, the light vanished, zapped into her hands. On the second clap it was released into the air like a flare on a battlefield, a hissing sound accompanying it as he flew upward, and exploded in a firework above their heads. A rain of green danced down and fizzled out.

It was visible from the school.

Meaning the student body, at least those here, would know that he was now in power. He would be a house leader when the train came.

"You can leave now," Harrison told the headmaster.

She looked to the boy's body, at young Mark Rubel, hesitating, before her gaze once more met Harrison's. "I hope you know what you've asked for."

Harrison pulled the fabric out of his pocket and began to wrap his left hand. "Power," Harrison answered.

"With power comes enemies." She turned, heading back the way she came, out the graveyard gate, and back down the path to the school, flashlight in hand.

"She's right you know," Raven said and got to her feet. She strolled over, stringing her arms up and around his neck. "You were clever, Harry. I'll give you that. I thought you were really going to kill me. I should have known you'd never hurt me."

He felt he should tell her that wasn't true. That he meant to kill her. That he hadn't been clever like she was giving him credit for. He'd been foolish. Rash. A little bit lovesick. But cleverness hadn't guided his actions tonight.

Telling her wouldn't change anything for the better. All it would do would be to prevent their future. He leaned down, using his lips to kiss her, instead of to confess.

Now, he was a house leader. This would make getting food easier. Almost as easy as the pipeline of leaders to the front line.

Raven pulled away, and Harrison felt his whole body try to protest, his grip around her tightening as she looked into his eyes with her red ones. "Do you mind if I ... you know. Before we ...? It goes bad if you leave it for too long."

"Right. Of course." Reluctantly, he let go of her.

She moved past him to where Valerie lay.

Harrison didn't have a grave for Valerie. No stone to mark where she was, for people to find and wonder what fate brought her to her close.

The boy served his purpose.

Valerie served him a hard fate.

The future was unclear, but for tonight, here in the school graveyard, he was safe. That was the real step one. Step two, Raven was safe. Step three, they were both fed. And that was all that truly mattered.

"FOR YOU, I"
Bethany H. Watson

if I was a sculptor,
I would scrape my fingers raw on stone of you,
carve every inch of you,
desecrate these delicate fingers.

if I was a singer,
I would scream my voice raw on song of you,
loose every line on you,
vibrate these resounding cords.

if I was a soldier,
I would bleed my soul raw on siege of you,
waste myself on want of you,
emaciate this war-torn flesh.

for you I would shed my leaves in winter's little death.
for you I would be drained on some forgotten altar.
for you I would dig through dirt

so we may lie together
in earth's nurturing embrace
one another,
fertilizing forever.

for you, I would do,
for you, I would be done;
for you, I would build mountains,
for you, I would let mountains fall on me.

for you, I would be everything,
stretch myself thin around the world.
for you, I would do anything,
fold laundry and bury bodies.
for you, I would lack nothing,
but I'd lose it all to be lost in you.

for you, I would.
for you,
all, always
for you.
all, always
you, I,
all, always
you.

you, all you,
all I need
one word from you.

/ LIPSTICK MARKS /
Effie Joe Stock

always told i'd need a "special" person
told i'd have to search real hard for the "one"
told "options are slim / but don't give in / don't settle in"
but please just don't die alone, hun

always believed women were catty / hateful / bitches
felt the heat of their burning whispers / touches
promises made / broken
broken bones / hearts and wishes

hated them like they hated me / before i even tried to see
to be friends with a creature in undeserved pressure
twisted / forgotten / cast out
lurking in the deepest parts of the sea

until i opened my eyes
adjusted to the darkness,
reached into the void,

and left my hate in the bleakness

i kissed your cheek / your skin so soft / a lingering moment
shutter flashed / blinded our eyes / our hearts
burning away the hatred / igniting in me wonder
"the only kiss I'll ever get from you"/ i whispered / heart
pounding thunder

"I'll kiss you right now" you laughed

eyes lingered on yours and the mark i left

"You'll get lipstick on you" i whispered / touched your cheek

"I'm wearing some right now. What's a little more?"

warning bells rang / clashed / quieted

lips so soft / more than lips / souls pressed together

drew apart blushing / laughing / joking

ignoring souls bared / promises twisted

you'll return to the man who gazes at you

obsessively / wantingly / lovingly

and I'll return to the darkness of the sea

watching / waiting / patiently

so i vow to remember what you taught me:

a woman's heart burns in many ways

hateful / painful / acheful

powerfully / timelessly / gently

but most of all i'll remember

love was never uncommon / limited
options were never slim / prohibited
if only to dare again to chance / look outside / brave the sea
and trade lipstick marks with me

GIVE IT TO ME
Lorelei R. Jensen

It was not unexpected for Do-hyun to find Adeline in the library with a book by the window. She sat at a table on the fourth floor by herself. Rain crashed against the window, and the wind howled, but that was the perfect weather for reading in the library. At least, that's what Adeline had said last year during midterm season before tying their grades again.

It was not unexpected to see her chocolate-brown hair braided over her shoulder, or that her notebook was opened and filled with notes and doodles. She seemed like a book fairy in the library. Something about her amongst books was magical and beautiful. Maybe fairy was the wrong word for her since fairies are small and cute.

Adeline was not small or cute. She was tall. Almost as tall as Do-hyun. Though, he was an average height for men. Adeline was not small, and she was not cute. He hated how he thought of her because no one had the right to be that ethereal. Especially not someone who he battled against so often.

Do-hyun found it disgusting to admit that he found such comfort in her habits, or that he couldn't imagine a more beautiful woman. Adeline should be nothing more than his classmate. Maybe even his academic rival, but only that. He shouldn't know her habits or come to the library at the same time as her just to see her. It was unbecoming of him.

However, there was one thing he didn't expect today though. It startled him because it didn't suit Adeline at all, not the cheery and good natured person she is. The hollow emptiness in her eyes was unexpected, and it made something in Do-hyun's heart falter. The usual icy blue of her eyes, that usually flustered him because of how warmly they stared at him, seemed colder than usual as she stared off in the distance.

He languidly sat next to her, drawing her attention. He shrugged off his uniform jacket and placed it over the back of the chair. Running a hand through his black hair, Do-hyun made himself comfortable next to her.

"Do-hyun," she greeted, but it wasn't as warm as normal. Not that he wanted her to greet her warmly. It just confused him. What made her change?

"Studying for the *Hamlet* test?" He took note of the book she was reading. The pages were yellowed and the spine was cracked. Her little thoughts lined the sides, and pen highlighted different lines that impacted her. Again, this was not unexpected of Adeline. Her love for literature was cute. No, not cute, admirable. No, not admirable, annoying. He really needed to get hold of his thoughts about her.

Adeline nodded. "Yeah. I'm not worried about it, but it doesn't hurt to review."

No, that wasn't right. Her voice wasn't filled with her usual emotion. Her eyes didn't glance at him with the usual smug little look. Something was off, and it shouldn't bother Do-hyun, but it did. It bothered him because it wasn't the usual her.

He couldn't even stop himself from asking. The thoughts left his mouth before he had the chance to think. "Adeline, what's wrong?"

Her eyes widened, and she stared at him in confusion. "What do you mean?"

"You just seem a little off." A blush crept across his cheeks.

"How so?"

Do-hyun cleared his throat. Does he just admit it or pretend nothing happened? It really bothered him, but he didn't know what he should say. Her eyes seemed so distant. A piece of hair fell out of her braid and into her eyes.

Without even thinking again, Do-hyun brushed her hair out of her face, tucking it behind her ear. He needed to get himself under control. "You're not as cheerful as usual. You seem not quite there."

Shock flashed across her expression, and he thought he saw a little hurt. He could tell that the hurt wasn't towards him though. Do-hyun hated whoever hurt her. His blood boiled at the idea that someone caused her pain.

"Addy, what's going on?" He leaned forward. Worry laced his voice as he took in her appearance. Her eye bags were incredibly dark as if she hadn't slept in days, and her face seemed thinner. No, her whole body was thinner. "Have you lost weight?"

"I'm fine." Her voice cracked.

The air in the library grew tense as they stared at each other. He wanted to make her talk, to spill her emotions to him, but he knew that wouldn't help, so Do-hyun sat back in his chair and sighed. There was so much he wanted to say, so much he wanted to hear from her, but he kept his mouth shut about this subject.

"Test me for the exam," he finally said, breaking the tense silence.

Adeline nodded. She opened her well-loved copy of *Hamlet* and flipped through the pages to some of her highlights. He leaned closer, touching shoulders with her, and read through her annotations. Some of them were studious and about potential foreshadowing and symbolism, but others were cute little thoughts and comments. Her handwriting was beautiful among the printed words.

"You seem to have a lot of thoughts on Ophelia's death," he pointed out, leaning in to read some. Shifting slightly to face her, he realized how close their faces were. Their noses almost touched. With a shaky and surprised breath, he moved away.

"I understand her sentiment, I guess."

Do-hyun's eyes widened. "What do you mean by that?"

She shrugged. "I just relate. She realizes her voice means nothing to the people around her. That she means nothing to the people who are supposed to care about her. Ophelia wanted the best for her loved ones, but Hamlet goes and betrays her love, and then her father is murdered. In her love, she found her only choice was to die. Maybe she finally got the attention she wanted when she drowned."

"In what ways does that relate to you?" His voice was low and filled with worry. He prayed that she didn't mean what he thought, but with how lifeless her eyes were and the obvious lack of sleep, dread filled his eyes.

Adeline's voice echoed in the empty library. "I've just come to terms with my situation. My voice, my needs, my wants mean nothing to the people that are supposed to love me. Why else would they treat me like this? Does life really matter when you're not even a person in their eyes?"

His heart broke. No longer was he afraid of how he came off. No longer did he care that it made him weak to be so influenced by her. All he cared about at this moment was Adeline. "You don't mean ..."

"What does it matter to you?" Her voice cracked. Tears formed in her icy blue eyes. "What does it matter to anyone? It doesn't. Nothing matters. Not me, not my feelings."

"You know that's not true."

"Name one person who cares." Tears streamed down her cheeks. "My family only sent me to this school so I could make connections for them, and my friends only hang out with me because I help them with their homework. And don't try to argue against that because I've heard what they say behind my back. I have been and will always be alone."

His heart dropped. She really thought she was alone. They made her feel like she had nobody. Did she have anyone? Did she really not have someone to rely on?

Using the back of her hand, she wiped her eyes. "I'm so tired of this. I'm so tired of pretending to be okay all the time. I'm tired of having to be there for everyone, and no one being there for me. I'm so done with all of this. I just want to be cared for. Is that too much to ask?"

Do-hyun honestly had no words to say. How was he supposed to comfort her when she was so distraught?

"I can't take the emptiness any more." He almost didn't catch her saying it. She whispered it so quietly as if more to herself than him. Maybe all of this was for herself, and not to him. "I don't want to do this any longer."

"Please. Please don't say that." Do-hyun grabbed her

hands. "I'm begging you. Don't say that. Don't even think that."

Adeline watched him in confusion.

"I understand you're hurting, but please, I need you. If you're so done with your life, give it to me. Please, just don't leave me. I'll make sure you never feel alone again so give it to me." His voice shook with emotion as he kissed her fingers. A sob escaped Adeline's lips. "If you can't find a reason to keep going, let me because I don't want to be in a world where you are not."

With shaky hands, he pulled her into a hug. Though she hesitated for a moment, Adeline crumpled against him. Her sobs filled the quiet library as she clung to Do-hyun. He wrapped one of his arms around her waist, while the other one held the back of her neck. He placed a soft kiss on her forehead.

"I'm so sorry I didn't see how you were hurting," he whispered into her hair. "I'm so glad you held on for so long. You don't have to be strong anymore."

She nodded slightly as she buried her face into his shoulder. His grip tightened around her.

"Everything will be okay now, my angel." He doubted she believed him completely, but he would do anything to keep his sweet Adeline here with him. He was going to do anything in his power to make sure she didn't feel alone because he couldn't imagine a world where she didn't grace the library or beat him on a test. He didn't want a world where her beautiful laugh was missing, where that gorgeous smile didn't exist. "I've got you now. I'm sorry it took so long."

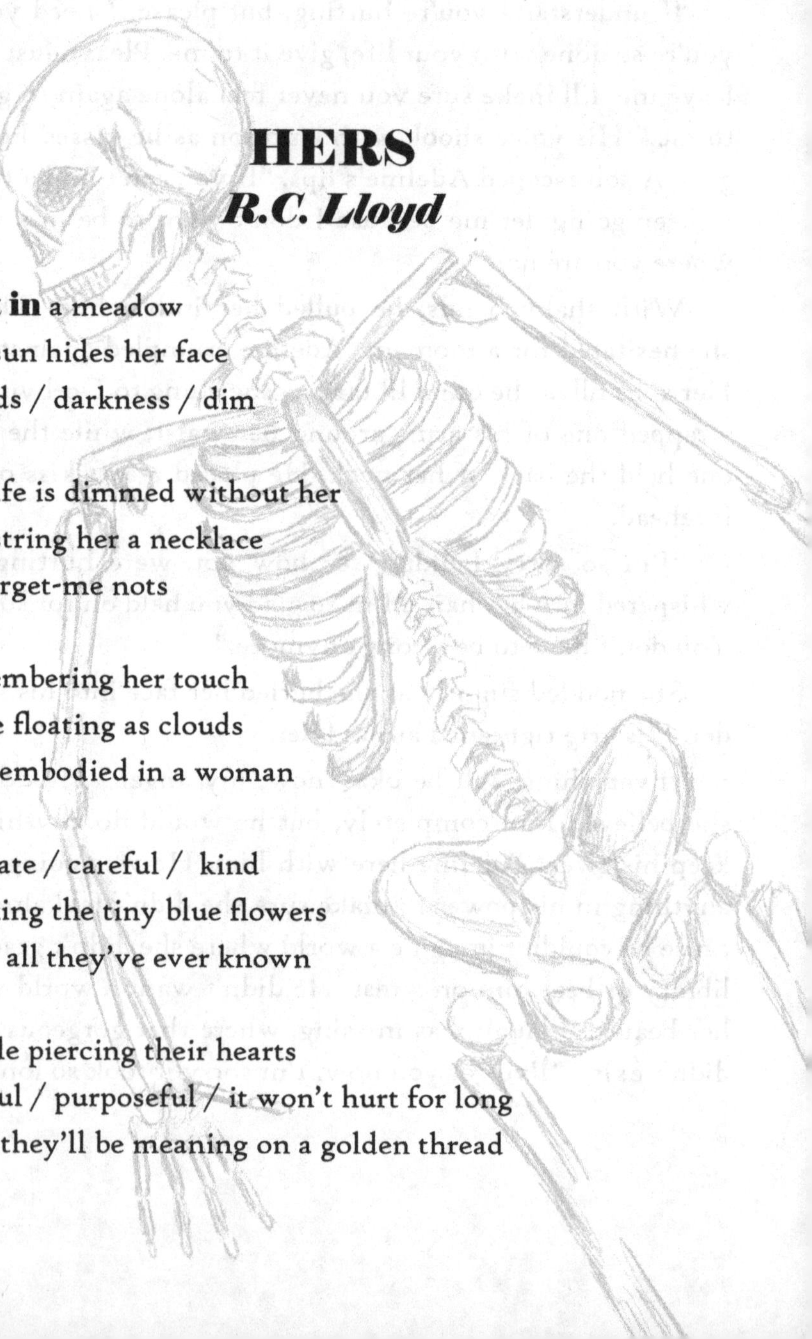

HERS
R.C. Lloyd

I sit in a meadow
The sun hides her face
Clouds / darkness / dim

My life is dimmed without her
So I string her a necklace
Of forget-me nots

Remembering her touch
Voice floating as clouds
Love embodied in a woman

Delicate / careful / kind
Plucking the tiny blue flowers
From all they've ever known

Needle piercing their hearts
Painful / purposeful / it won't hurt for long
Soon they'll be meaning on a golden thread

My hands are still nimble
My aging slowed / my feet grounded
Anchoring my heart to this plane

When it belongs to the next
Where my wife holds my daughter
Where I long to hold them

Soon I'll be in her arms
But for now
I live for her

Draping breath over the blossoms
Draping the necklace on her grave
Draping my tears at her feet

I'm not in a meadow
I'm in a cemetery
Staring at my empty plot next to hers

NEBULOUS
Kit Aldridge

The drawer hitches on its janky track, and Arken has to slam it shut with a *bang* that sounds more like a gunshot. He looks up at me, eyes burning like the neon lights outside our fourth floor flat. He's frozen in the kitchen, and I hate myself for the hurt in his voice when he asks, "What did you say?"

Annoyance flutters in my chest. I'm always repeating myself with him. I wish I could fool myself into thinking that he did hear me, that this is a chance to backtrack, to speak some kinder, more amiable thing. But anger takes hold of my tongue and wields it like a knife, and I repeat myself with lethal enunciation: "Are you cheating on me?"

Something breaks between us. I can see it in his face: he's heartbroken, insulted, quietly distraught that I would ever even think such a thing.

"Is that a serious question?" he breathes.

"You're gone long into the evenings, and I hear *nothing* from you."

He splays his palms helplessly. "I'm working."

I slide my phone out of my pocket and wave it in front of his face. "Does this not work anymore?"

"I've told you," he implores, stepping around the counter

so that there's nothing between us. "Sometimes my hands are full and I can't get to my phone. If I could text you, I would, but I'm tied up with these experiments."

"You could text when you're on the tram."

"My phone died, otherwise I would have."

I fold my arms over my chest. He's not helping himself. "It just seems really convenient that whenever you're out late, so is Marathine."

He blinks, confused. "She's ... my lab partner. And why are you keeping tabs on her anyway?"

"You work a lot of late nights with her, right? She talks about your 'dinners' together, then you sneak into bed without so much as a 'hello'. What do you expect me to think?"

Arken halts on a response, lips thinning like he's trying not to shout. He inhales deeply. An airtram whizzes past the building, shaking my paintings on the walls and scattering fluorescent lights through the windows. It's ridiculous, but all I can think is how grateful I am that these trams go too quickly for their passengers to make anything of the city but blurring colors and lights. When the apartment falls dark again, Arken finds his voice.

It's hard. Trembling ever so slightly, like he's on the verge of crying. "I expect you to trust me. I've never given you any reason to doubt my loyalty, yet you're so suspicious. How long have you felt this way?"

Months.

I say nothing, and the crestfallen look on his face is too much to bear.

"Raya," he tries after a moment. I shake my head, biting back venom, sucking my tears dry. He says my name again, and I grant him the briefest of glances—full of blazing anger.

"I promise," he whispers, like I might suddenly pounce with outstretched claws, "nothing has changed how I feel about you. About us. I know I work late. You're so patient with me, and you don't know how grateful I am for that."

I snap. "You've taken every bit of my patience. From the moment we started dating, I've done nothing but wait for you, your text, your call—anything to show me that you're alive, or that you care to reach out. Do you know how humiliating it is, to be the one stuck here, *waiting* for you to come home while I'm not even a fragment of a thought in your mind?"

"I love you, Raya." His eyes are glassy.

I can see every word stabbing deeper, twisting more violently, but I can't stop myself now. "You're asking me to believe in what I can't see. How ironic is that, that you'd declare some grand faith in us, when all this time, mine has been *dying*. Maybe it meant something to you once, but I don't think it does anymore."

Arken knits his brows together. "What are you saying?"

"If you love your work that much, maybe you should be with someone who loves it as much as you do."

"No, will you please just hear me out? I want to talk about this—"

"I can't—I won't stay here." Interrupting him feels horrible, but I let my rage burn a deeper chasm between us. "Why don't you call Marathine? I bet she'd love to see you. God knows I can't even look at you right now."

I leave him with those hateful words, not even bothering to grab my coat. It's cold outside, wet with rain that makes the city lights glisten and glare.

I'm too angry to think. Too hurt to see where I'm going

as my feet trace a beaten path down the stairwell and into the parking garage. The slam of my door sets off another car's alarm, and I speed out of my parking space. Traffic is slow and congested as people return home after a long day at work, but once I make it onto the streets, I lean my foot further against the accelerator.

Rain batters my windshield in waves. The city is distorted beyond the glass, and these old wipers are of no help. Adverts stretch at least ten stories high on all sides, reflecting off the tempered glass roads of the second and third tiers of traffic. The highway becomes a garish kaleidoscope of LEDs, a cesspool for nighttime joyriders who blast their music through subwoofers and loudspeakers.

I need silence. Darkness.

I floor it and weave through the ground level of traffic. Halara City never sleeps, and it's precisely that frenetic energy that pushes me to tear through the streets. I skid around corners. Slip beneath yellow lights. I could drive past the bounds of the city if I wanted to. Chase down the places where the lights go dim and the stars come out.

But nearly an hour of rage driving bores me, and soon my thoughts creep back. My hands relax around the wheel. It's when I start circling the same familiar block around my workplace that my fight with Arken resurfaces.

I replay our words. Bite my tongue to suppress the anger—but in its place comes guilt. Quiet at first, then consuming. Torturous.

I can't even look at you right now.

My stomach drops in horror with myself, and I'm overtaken by a sudden urge to turn this car around and plead for forgiveness. I'll beg on my knees if I have to. Arken has my whole heart; he's given me so much of himself in return.

How could I have been so cruel?

This car is old and lacks the handling for the second or third tiers, but I take the ramp up anyway. The Intuitive Driver's Assistant chimes in, "Warning: Unsafe terrain. Please direct the—"

I punch IDA into silence.

After squeezing through a narrow window between a cargo truck and some skimpy low rider, I ride the middle lane and plaster my eyes forward. I block out a chorus of alarmed honks and adjust myself in the driver's seat. I won't be here long. My exit is just two miles down.

I speed past the right lane, wondering whose bright idea it was to construct roads from glass. At nighttime, Halara City is a bejeweled light show that drowns out the lane dividers, bounces off the upper roads, and blinds the driver. Cars like mine aren't meant for roads like these. It's damn near impossible to see anything when a set of headlights glares in my rearview mirror, and I am wholly unprepared when a light-biker swerves into my lane.

My foot slams the brake. Something crashes into me from behind—hard and fast enough to send my car flying.

For a moment, it's like I'm floating inside a planetarium. Being confronted by my own impermanence, the infinity of the stars and worlds just beyond reach. Colors and lights and rain glaze the windshield, and I feel my body shatter like glass when the car spirals off the highway.

I wake with no pain. No visible injury. No memories to tie me back to whatever brought me here.

I'm in an empty, circular chamber. Every surface is pristine, almost like a hospital, but unlike a hospital, there is an alarming lack of ... anything. Any*one*. The bed supporting my weight is plain, and nothing but a thin white sheet covers me. I'm wearing the same clothes I was before ...

Before *what*?

No sooner than the confusion echoes in my mind does a figure make itself known in my periphery. I blink rapidly and sit up—only for a blinding pain to split through the back of my skull. I wince and drop my head into my hands, but I hear my solicitor rush forward.

"Slow movements, Miss Yeung." The speaker is neither male nor female. Their hand rests on my shoulder, and I am too absorbed in my own ebbing agony to shrug them off. Their voice is concerned yet impartial, like a stranger who witnessed another stranger take a fall down a flight of stairs. I feel them tuck a lock of hair behind my ear, and it reminds me so violently of Arken that I recoil into the wall.

"Raya!"

Agony shudders through me, but I hold my hand out, warding them away. I lift my throbbing head and stare into a striking, gorgeous face. My first thought is *Arken*. But when I blink in disbelief, their face shifts again into a stranger's, then again into someone vaguely resembling my mother. Their eyes are colorless and depthless, as if the ocean were sitting atop a pane of glass, and the moon was spilling all her borrowed light down into it.

"Who are you?" I manage.

"My name was lost to my memory long ago." They must sense my discomfort, because they offer a flash of a smile and amend, "You may call me Nexus, if it eases you."

"Nexus." My vocalization of their name seems to bring them no joy or displeasure, and I continue warily, "Where am I?"

"Somewhere between life and death. Not an easy feat for someone like you. You're the first of your kind to cross through this place."

My thoughts tangle. "The first of my—"

"Humans are quite fragile," Nexus interrupts. "Most do not linger here. Death calls too loudly."

They straighten at the waist and hold a hand out to me. Gingerly, I take it, and they lead me from the bed with unlikely strength. Their bare feet, nearly concealed beneath a wispy, formless gown, fall silently as they walk. My own footsteps sound and feel like an elephant's in comparison. Nexus pulls me toward a blank spot on the opposite wall, and with a wave of their hand, an image swirls into view.

It's me.

I'm lying on my back, surrounded by glittering shards of glass. Rain soaks my face, mixing with the blood from a scratch on my cheek. My hair fans around my head in sodden black ropes, and a pool of something dark seeps from a wound I cannot see.

My heart starts pounding erratically. I feel like vomiting, but I can't look away. Paramedics lay me on a stretcher, then load me into an ambulance. My injuries must be severe; the tires retract into the vehicle, and a pair of wings unfurl from the sides of the cab. Highway traffic on the second and third levels is halted to give clearance for the ambulance, and the last thing I see is the red emergency lights twirling into the dreary storm.

I clutch my head in one hand, my heart in the other. Nexus levels a somewhat sympathetic look on me. "You're taking this well."

"I ... Am I—I mean, did I—"

"You're not dead," Nexus says. "You're close, but you've been granted a choice."

"A choice?"

Nexus nods, eyes sparkling. They look like my first year philosophy professor from my undergrad days now. Dr. Fray was a quirky, if eccentric man, and I can't help but wonder if Nexus has plucked this face from the files of my memory to better impart some bullshit wisdom.

"All of you have unfinished business to address, but rage stole you away from your work."

"All of ... me?"

My parroting doesn't seem to bother Nexus. They nod, and with another wave of their hand, dozens of windows blink open to reveal some fresh, new horror. I turn in slow circles, my jaw slack and agape.

Countless versions of me lie on operating tables. A host of doctors and nurses scramble around my body; someone affixes an oxygen mask to my face. Bruises riddle my arms, one of which is broken. There's so much blood—

"Raya!" a voice calls through one window.

A voice that makes my heart stop altogether.

I surge forward as *Yeye* strains against the arms of hospital staff. Fear contorts my grandfather's face, and tears well in his eyes as he calls my name, curses the staff, ignores my parents' attempts to console him.

"Yeye," I breathe. He's been dead for two years now. The

loss of his wife was too much to take, and he killed himself not a month after she passed. His death shook my father so badly that it's all my mother can do to help him rise from bed every morning.

But there he is—*Yeye*, screaming. Afraid. *Alive.*

I turn, blood roaring, toward Nexus. My voice sounds wholly unlike mine. "What the hell is going on?"

One corner of Nexus's mouth flicks upward, as if they're suppressing a grin. Without speaking, they gesture toward a different window. Another image of my half-broken body grows cloudy, and when it clears again, I recognize a scene from my past: I'm a senior in college, and I'm presenting my portfolio in an art festival.

I remember this day clearly; it was only weeks after *Yeye* had died, and I was distraught. I flubbed every question the judges asked. Curious eyes noticed my art, but when they spotted me, a hunched figure mere moments from breaking down, they bounced toward a more composed artist.

But here, I watch another version of that day play out like a movie. I speak with a confidence I've never known. My interpretations impress the judges. My voice carries like a solo instrument over an orchestral accompaniment, and a crowd gathers to listen to me speak of what inspired these "masterpieces," as one of the judges names it. Over dinner that night, I celebrate my success and bask in the praise of my family—whole again. My father beams with pride while *Yeye* drags the entire waitstaff to our table so he can show off my portfolio. At my side, my mother can't stop smiling.

Through yet another window, I see myself partying in a nightclub with Strylla and Vayu. I don't remember this, but a flood of new memories tells me that we're celebrating my last night in Halara City. I'm opening a private gallery to feature my art and the works of other underprivileged, undiscovered artists. I've signed a lease to open my own studio and tutor my own students, too. My friends, close as sisters in this life, are overjoyed for me, and I've never been happier. Everything I've ever wanted for my career has just ... fallen into my lap.

"Do you understand now, Miss Yeung?" Nexus sidles up beside me. Music from the nightclub fades into the unsettling silence of this liminal space, and it takes every effort for me to tear my eyes away and face Nexus again.

They look like my father now—from the years before *Yeye* died. I swallow hard and avoid looking in their eyes. "These are different timelines, different lives. But they're all mine?"

"Or some version of you." Nexus shrugs one shoulder. "Every choice you made, consciously or not, branched into another reality. People *you* know might be strangers to another Raya. And to another Raya entirely, you might be the very picture of all she never wanted."

I'm trying hard to understand this, but my mind is twisting itself just to make sense of it all. The windows replay moments from my life—familiar and not—but they all wind up in the same place: on a hospital bed, fluids pumping into my veins, blood staining the sheets.

In all of these, my family is gathered in the waiting room. Sometimes *Yeye* is there with my parents; sometimes he's not. Strylla and Vayu appear in some windows—either together or alone. But I notice a glaring absence: "Where's Arken?"

Nexus lifts a brow. "You expected to find him here?"

"Yes, because—" I stop myself short. My own memories are coming back, piercing through the haze like a ray of light through morning fog.

Arken and I fought. He insisted he wasn't cheating or lying; I insisted he was. He told me he loved me; I stormed out in anger. I took my car and left him alone in that apartment, alone with his thoughts and anger and hurt.

I left him.

Fear stems from my chest, then oozes through the rest of me until my limbs are heavy and leaden. Why would he be there, when I was so horrible to him?

"What about the others?" I ask, fighting to keep my voice steady. "I'm sure he'd come to me if he knew I was hurt." I amble toward another window, waiting for Nexus to show me Arken, but my hospital room remains empty. No one joins my stone-faced family in the waiting room. "Will they not allow visitors? Arken would be there."

My hands clench and loosen anxiously, but my stomach drops altogether when Nexus says, "I cannot show what does not exist."

They stand beside me, their presence comforting and eerie all at once. Touching a fingertip to the window, they conjure another rippling scene. It takes me a moment to recognize the setting, but it surges back like high tide.

The bar where Arken and I met, where I drunkenly cried to him over the then-recent death of *Yeye*, is as crowded as I remember it being. But when I search the throngs for me, I only find Arken. He walks in like he has nowhere to be and finds a seat at the end of the bar, right under the dying neon sign that reads HAPPY HOUR 9-11 PM.

He orders a drink, ignores the women—and men—who

try to chat him up, and leaves after tossing fifteen dollars onto the counter. The digital clock above the front door reads 22:57, but I recall Arken and I leaving that bar at midnight.

It's cold and rainy outside. This I remember well, because Arken had wrapped me in his jacket and held me close to try and soothe my crying. But again, I'm not *there*, not with this version of him.

An uneasy feeling prickles in my chest as he walks down the slickened street with his hood thrown over his bowed head. He's a dark shadow in a storm-black night. On the out-skirts of downtown, the traffic lights pulse like dying stars. Visibility is low in the rain, but I don't miss the flare of head-lights that split the darkness—or the squealing tires of the car that tries to miss Arken.

I spin away from the window, one hand slapped over my mouth. Even here, where I've fallen to my knees, I can see this scene playing out in other windows—too many of them.

The car strikes him hard. Sends him windmilling into the darkness while the driver straightens the vehicle, pauses deliberatively, then speeds away.

A nauseating silence follows.

I'm whispering "No, no, no," when Nexus kneels before me. Their hands cup my shoulders, a gesture that is meant to comfort but that only frightens me further. I flinch, and their fingers curl tighter into me.

"The one called Arken," Nexus murmurs, "is dead in every life that offers you an unbroken family, or a thriving career, or friends who will pledge themselves to you for a lifetime. You recall I said you have a choice to make?"

My throat grows tight. "Don't make me do this."

"You must."

"Can I not save them all?"

By "them," I mean, of course, my family. *Yeye.* My father's happiness. My mother's peace of mind. My friendship with Strylla and Vayu. Arken.

Nexus answers, "The universe was never so generous. Every timeline has led to this place of convergence, this paused breath between life and death, and now you must choose which life to return to."

"What happens to the others?"

Their silence is my answer: every other Raya will die, leaving behind a life of promise and potential far greater than I could ever anticipate—what with my half-assed barista job and mediocre art that I'm too shy to share with anything but the walls of Arken's apartment. Only in one life can I spare my loved ones the devastation and heartbreak of losing me. And there is no timeline in which everything is so neatly and beautifully whole.

It should have been obvious from the moment I awoke here. I feel so utterly foolish, but I get it now. I'm being forced to sacrifice countless lives—somehow all my own—in order to return home.

Whatever that looks like. Whatever I choose.

"Raya Yeung," Nexus says, a warning tone creeping into their voice now, "the longer you stay here, the further from life you drift."

I can already feel the removal they're alluding to: the weightlessness of death filling and emptying me all at once. It's a pull on my chest—a thread tying me to the fabrics of the universe, calling me back to the very dusts that collided to create me.

It hurts so much. I want nothing but silence. Stillness.

I could choose *nothing*.

I examine Nexus's face and whisper, "Would that be so horrible? To drift away?"

Nexus lifts their chin and inhales deeply. I don't think they were expecting this question, but instead of answering, their face shifts. Rapidly.

In dizzying succession, Nexus mirrors the faces of everyone I've ever known and lost: my father, when he was happy. My mother, before she grew weary. Strylla. Vayu. *Yeye.* Arken. Their voices pour through every window, too: a discordant symphony of desperate pleas for me to live, to fight, to come back.

Before I can muffle the noise, Nexus seizes my face in those broad, firm hands. Their thumbs peel my eyelids back, and I see whorls of color—brush strokes that smear across my vision and blur into the next scene, where my fingertips dance through blushing sunlight, reaching for a hand that I recognize as Arken's. My laughter echoes into an overhead view of us dancing in the living room of his apartment while the lights of Halara City shimmer through the sheer curtains. The airtram that always wakes me in the night whizzes past, shuddering the building in that precious, familiar way, but I don't think anything of it when I spin into Arken's embrace. He smiles and pecks the space between my brows, and when he spins me away again, the vision shifts.

Arken is alone now. The apartment is dark, and rain slaps against the windows. He's slouched on the couch, eyes fixed on the coffee table without really seeing anything, and outside, an ambulance soars through the storm.

I cry out his name, praying that he can somehow hear me. He does not.

He grimaces at the flaring red lights and mutters something, stomping over to the windows to yank the curtains shut.

I shove hard against Nexus as darkness falls. The vision shatters like glass, and I cradle my head in my hands. Tears are streaming down my face now. Like a lost child, I whimper, "Why are you showing me this? I know I screwed up, okay? I know I don't deserve him—or anything I took for granted."

Nexus towers over me, their face an indurate mask of marble. "Do you not wish to reclaim your life?"

"What—"

"You've taken every bit of my patience." My spine tingles. Those are my words they're stealing, *my* voice they're using, but before I can process what's happening, they say, "If you won't muster the courage to go home, then I shall do it for you."

I scramble back as Nexus surges down toward me, seizing my wrists and pinning me in place. "You've no idea what it's like, *feeling* yourself fade out of existence. Watching the world you called home slowly forget you. No one I loved remains. I've forgotten their names, their faces, the sounds of their voices."

I can't get free. Their eyes are burning with the light of a thousand suns, and their voice turns my skin to gooseflesh.

"You yearn for silence, for nothingness—but you've no idea how *unbearable* that is. Millennia have passed since I arrived here. I thought I'd never speak to another soul again. Thought I'd be confined to eternal solitude—and then you came along. Just as lost, just as desperate for escape as I was. But there was no one to guide me. No one to warn me of what would happen if I lingered too long."

"Let go," I gasp. My hands are losing feeling, they're gripping me so hard. I search frantically for my window home, but the room is spinning. A sudden wind blows and whips hair about my face.

I'm locked in Nexus's grip, and horror sinks into me when their face morphs into my own. It's my voice that falls from their lips: "I watched you fight. I watched you leave. Then I watched you fall. I've watched you amble through all these years as if you had infinite chances. I know what you have to lose, and I won't make the same mistakes you did."

They discard me like a used tissue and walk with chilling assuredness toward a lone beacon of light that shines through one of the windows. I can't tell if it's mine, or where it will lead. All I know is that if they walk through it, I'll be trapped here.

Forever.

I launch myself at Nexus, chaining my arms around their waist. Pain lances through me when they jab their elbow against my collar bone, but I don't let go. I can't. They will take everything I love, everything I took for granted. They will leave me here to rot away until all the worlds fall down.

Nexus, still straining against me, waves their hand, and the window before them yawns into a taller archway. This is not my world; *Yeye* paces furiously in the waiting room while my parents speak in hushed tones to my friends. My throat tightens at the worry on their faces.

How can I abandon them?

I think of Arken. The dulcet baritone of his voice. The feel of his hand sliding into mine. The way his body curls against me when I reach for him in the night. I think of all the times I gazed at him and thought, *I would love you for the rest of my life if you'd have me.*

I've lost so much already. What little scraps of family and friends I have can be salvaged—but I cannot, I *will not* lose Arken, too.

Nexus has their hand halfway through the archway. The image ripples like water at their touch, and I can feel my own consciousness expanding. Widening. The fine, precious minutiae of my own life slips beyond my reach, like I'm grasping smoke, and I feel Nexus take a full, refreshing breath. Their eyes—*my* eyes—are alight with childlike wonder. Aching hunger. They're wearing my face. Shaping their body into my own.

I muster every ounce of strength and plunge two fingers against their knee, where an old injury I acquired from a bicycle accident years ago permanently damaged the joint. Nexus cries out and stumbles, but I use the momentum to spin us around and hurl them into the center of the room.

I have seconds before they recover.

The archway gapes open. I turn away from it and scan the windows—all indistinguishable now.

My hand closes around my chest. I think of home. Of Arken, the one last blessing I haven't lost yet. I can still fix this. I can repair what I broke. I just need to find him again.

One window among hundreds. One life splintered into thousands. One chance to make this right.

Home. Take me to Arken.

Nexus has regained their footing. Their face morphs with grotesque ambivalence between my face and something entirely inhuman. They're charging toward me now, reaching for the archway, and I don't have time to think or stop them.

I can only hope I'm faster.

I squeeze my eyes shut and throw myself through the window over my left shoulder. The sensation of being plunged into arctic waters halts the air in my lungs, and everything falls silent as I tumble through open space.

Hot, salted tears spill down my temples and into my ears. A mask covers the lower half of my face, and my chest convulses with a sharp gasp.

The room constructs itself in sensory spotlights: a heart monitor *beep, beep, beeps* to my left; the drone of an HVAC echoes from an empty chamber that fades into the back of my mind like a bad dream; a tiny pinprick of pain pulses in the back of my skull—

A hand reaches through the dark and meets my cheek. Soft. Warm. Familiar. A quiet voice draws fresh tears to my eyes.

"Raya?"

FREE FALL
Rhyker Dye

I hate the feeling of freshly washed silks. The fabric loses its grip when it's washed, and it stretches for the first hour of practice. There's an unspoken rule among circus artists: we don't talk about how often we wash our fabric. The ones at the studio get washed once a week for hygiene purposes, but our personal silks are a different story altogether. If I'm asked how often I wash mine, I lie and say biweekly. It's like when you ask a girl how often she washes her bra. Guys that grew up with sisters, like I did, know the answer is never; but that's gross, so she'll fib and give you some arbitrary number that's not disgusting.

I curse at myself for leaving my own fabric at home, abandoned on my bedroom floor as I tore through my duffel looking for kevlar armbands for a fire spinning gig. Now, I'm at the mercy of the studio silks that smell like sunshine instead of sweat. I'm sliding out of handlocks I normally can perform in my sleep. I pull my knee to the fabric and dip my head back, trusting the silk to catch at my hips as I free fall towards the ground. The moment of weightlessness on the way down is my favorite part. A cocktail of uncertainty, regret, and thrill about what will happen next even though I chose to let go.

No matter how much experience I gain, I'll always feel my stomach drop. Is it fear, or is it butterflies? Does it matter?

Circus is all about trust. Trust in yourself. Trust in other performers. Trust in the assumption that your silk won't stretch out so much that your head smacks into the corkboard floor with a resounding thud. But freshly washed silks aren't trustworthy so it's really my fault for not having better judgment.

Technically, the silk did its job. My hips are locked securely in place, just closer to the ground than planned. I pull my head up from the floor and massage my jaw, pendulum swinging upside down for a moment. This is what I get for not using a crash mat. It's always *Safety First!* when it comes to other performers, but I slack when it comes to myself. As I hear the studio door chime open, I tuck my chin and place my elbows firmly on the ground, disentangling my legs from the silk above me and slumping out of the fabric onto the floor like a rag doll.

"You should've rigged your daisy chain higher. You know yesterday was Wash Day, Ollie."

"I didn't want to flip into the silk each time. My arms are still sore from fire spinning at the fall festival this weekend," I admit, glaring at the orange fabric swinging idly above my head.

Celeste steps into view, glancing down at me with disappointed amusement. Even cast in the warm morning light from the wall of windows, she still looks as worn out as I feel. Her fiery hair is pulled up in a sloppy bun, and she chose her outfit from the comfy side of the closet instead of one of her overpriced matching sets. Neither of us will be taking any promo videos for the studio's social media today. Can't let the bachelorette parties know that Circus isn't all glamorous outfits and instrumental music. Sometimes it's ratty sweatpants and rap blasting through the speakers.

I grab the loop at the bottom of my silk and pull myself back to standing. Celeste is already walking towards the ladder hanging on the back wall. While she releases it from its straps, I roll out the kink forming in my neck from the failed drop. Instead of taking the ladder to one of the silks still suspended across the studio from a restorative yoga class, she brings the ladder directly to my right. I quirk up an eyebrow at her in question. Studios are kind of like urinals; it's polite to leave a gap between you and the next person if there is space.

"Do you want to practice the Halloween flow?" she asks while opening the ladder.

I want to say no because I'm still worn out, both from today's practice and the festival, but we haven't had a lot of time to smooth out the bumps in our routine since October is a busy month in our line of work. That's definitely the reason I agree to rehearse (not the fact that I couldn't deny those green eyes if I tried).

Once Celeste and I have both adjusted our daisy chains, raising the silks to head height, she coyly slides crash mats under both our fabrics with a pointed glare. I roll my eyes and pull up the music on my phone. We take our positions in front of the studio mirror, eyes finding each other in the reflection in a mental check in before we begin. She has a soft smile that makes my cheeks heat up. I start the music before she can notice.

Partner performances are always harder and more frustrating. Solo flows are forgiving. If I fumble out of a grip or forget the next shape, I simply freestyle into the next major pose. Even if other performers notice that I made the mistake, the audience is none the wiser. They are just impressed that I'm a man who can do the splits, and that I plummet towards the ground with no hands.

Partners take away the grace period. They require patience and understanding (two skills that I am sorely lacking). They make me feel too seen and itchy from exposure. There is nowhere to hide. Each person's shortcomings are on full display to each other, and if it goes poorly, the audience will notice too. A partner's performance is in my hands just as much as mine is in theirs.

It's risky. It's terrifying. Sometimes, it's worth it.

Celeste is one of those people who makes me think it's worth it. We have a synergy that I find difficult to feel with other performers. She's a beauty in the air, which is great because it takes some of the attention away from the more technical moves I have to perform during the routine. If I miss a beat or a move just doesn't pan out like we wanted, she rebounds for me instead of freezing. I never feel like I'm going to trip her up. I don't think I could if I wanted to. She's too quick on her feet. She takes what I can give and spins it into something magic. I joke that her middle name is Midas since everything she touches turns to gold.

The music crescendos as we both climb higher on our own silks, tangling the fabric around our legs to prepare for a drop. Out of the corner of my eye, I see Celeste arch her back and flourish her arms in time to the music. She's gotten into position before me as always and is buying me time to get set.

On the beat drop, we release our leg holds and brace our cores for the impact of the silk snapping to catch us. I only hear the whip of one fabric which means that we dropped in sync this time instead of her being a hair ahead of me like normal.

"Nice!" Celeste calls out as she gracefully grounds herself and dances across the floor towards me while I move onto the next shape.

My arms are screaming at me as I pull myself through a complicated series of wraps to prep for Celeste's weight. I should have warmed up my rotator cuffs a little more for this routine. Celeste is small, but she's all muscle. When she grabs my wrists and flips through the space between our arms, my shoulder tingles. She must notice my wince because she lets herself flip completely through instead of remaining suspended like we planned, landing softly back onto the ground in an elegant side split. Magic. Gold. She makes all my fuck ups look planned.

When the music fades, our arms are locked across the chasm between our silks, using each other as counterbalances for the standing scorpion pose that marks the end of the routine. The sound of our heavy breathing fills in the newborn silence. Our foreheads rest against each other, neither of us pulling away even though we've both lowered our lifted back legs. Her hair smells like coconut. I can picture the blue bottle in her shower even though I've never stayed over long enough to use it.

After a moment that feels awkwardly long, I lean back and grab onto my silk for support with one hand, making sure that Celeste does the same before I let go of her. Her eyebrows are scrunched together like she's trying to figure out a particularly frustrating transition. It's her thinking face. Her gears are turning, and I'm sure she's about to grill me for my sloppy performance.

"I heard back from Carnival," she finally whispers.

I'm in free fall, plummeting towards the ground. No crash mat in sight.

"Oh, really? So soon?"

I hope it sounds nonchalant. I slide down into the loop of my silk. I kick out my feet to sit in it like a beach hammock, praying it looks relaxed. Celeste mimics me, placing her back on the opposite side of her silk so that we can face each other. She brushes a few strands of hair that fell loose during the routine behind her ears.

"Yeah," she says. When her eyes meet mine, there's a storm brewing behind them. "They want me to start in December for Christmas."

I shift uncomfortably, deciding to hide my jitters by pretending to roll out my shoulders. You never think about the last Christmas you'll spend with someone. Last Christmas Eve, I kissed her under the mistletoe after working as sugar plum fairies at a Nutcracker themed party downtown. She had glitter on her cheeks that made her eyes shine like stars. We went back to her place that night, but I left before she could wish me a merry Christmas in the morning. I felt like I only deserved moments like that if I planned to stick around, and I wasn't ready then to take the leap with her. She's been patient, but I've always been a solo artist. Scared of blue shampoo bottles and morning afters I suppose. If I had known that I'd be losing her to a luxury cruise line the next year, I would have been braver.

I choke down the plea on my tongue. It would be cruel to ask her to not leave when I've had every opportunity to give her a reason to stay. Instead, I plaster on a smile. I know from the way her mouth turns down that she can see that it's my stage smile though. I don't have it in me for it to be genuine.

"That's great! I'm so proud of you. You're gonna be amazing." Two truths and a lie.

She fidgets with the fraying drawstring of her sweatpants. The gears are still turning, and I am left wondering what else she has up her sleeve.

"There's more ..." she starts and then the words fall off.

I wait for a moment for her to keep going. When she doesn't, I attempt to draw it out of her, "More?"

"Yeah, the troop is looking for more male aerialists, and I told the manager I would talk to you." She stops fidgeting and steels herself. She locks eyes with me, and she's bold as wildfire, "I want you to come with me, Ollie. Is that something you might want?"

Risky.

Terrifying.

Worth it.

"Yes." My mouth runs faster than my brain, and my stomach drops.

Is it fear, or is it butterflies?

It doesn't matter.

This feeling of weightlessness is my favorite part.

TRUE RELIGION
Rhyker Dye

I feared God before I feared the dark,
Knew that my Savior bled for me before I sang the alphabet,
Memorized scripture before I could quote my address.

But when I fell, God did not catch me.
When I screamed, my Savior did not hear me.
When I cried, scripture did not comfort me.

I lied bare before jade eyes,
Wept onto tan collarbones,
Balled fists into auburn hair.

I knew then that love is the only true religion.

Devotion is a God.
My darling is a Savior.
His voice is scripture.

I stand in rapture,

Fall to my knees in prayer,
Speak in tongues against his.

I calcified amongst the pews in the chapel waiting for the
Holy Ghost.
I drowned in the front calling out to Christ.
I ascended between raspy breaths whispering his name.

My crucifix is a ring around my finger.

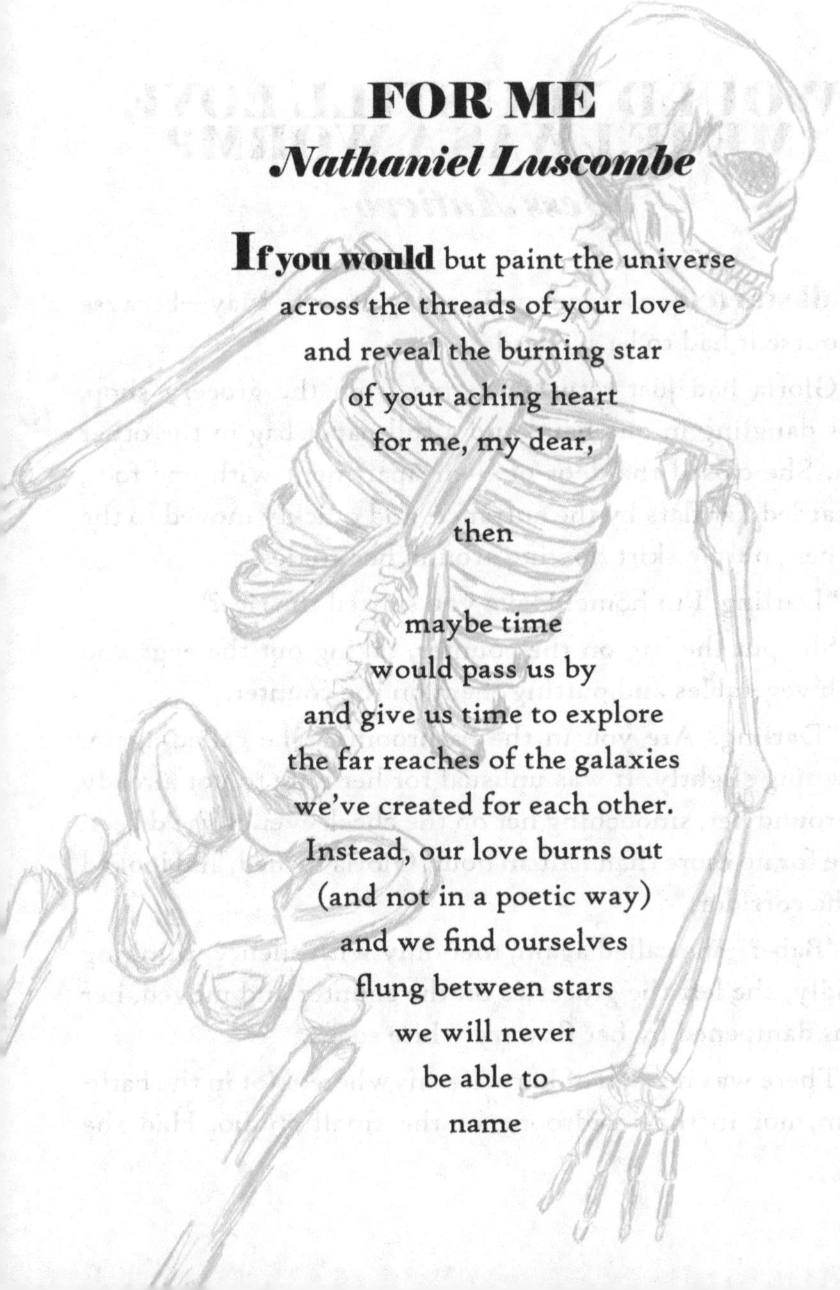

FOR ME
Nathaniel Luscombe

If you would but paint the universe
across the threads of your love
and reveal the burning star
of your aching heart
for me, my dear,

then

maybe time
would pass us by
and give us time to explore
the far reaches of the galaxies
we've created for each other.
Instead, our love burns out
(and not in a poetic way)
and we find ourselves
flung between stars
we will never
be able to

name

WOULD YOU STILL LOVE ME IF I WAS A WORM?

Jess Autiero

It all started on a random Tuesday of early May—because of course it had to be a Tuesday.

Gloria had just returned home from the grocery shop, keys dangling in one hand and a full paper bag in the other arm. She closed the door of their apartment with one foot, discarded her flats by the entrance, and quickly moved to the kitchen, purple skirt flowing around her ankles.

"Darling, I'm home! Have you started the rice?"

She put the bag on the counter, taking out the eggs and fresh vegetables and putting them on the counter.

"Darling? Are you in the bathroom?" She called again, frowning slightly. It was unusual for her wife to not already be around her, smooching her on the cheek even if she'd been gone for no more than half an hour. Gloria turned, and looked at the corridor.

"Babe?" she called again, met only with silence. Blinking rapidly, she left the groceries on the counter and moved, her steps dampened by her flowery white socks.

There was no sign of her wife anywhere. Not in the bath-room, nor in their bedroom, or the small studio. Had she left? Where to? The pot was already on the stove, filled with water and ready to boil. Her keys were still hanging by the entrance. She moved to the living room right by the kitchen. Her mobile was still on the coffee table. Then where ...

Her gaze fell on the discarded clothes on the floor. How strange. Her wife never, ever left any mess behind, being too much of a neat-freak to do so. She loved this about her, of course, and it perfectly balanced her own need for an organised-chaotic mess life. As she picked the t-shirt from the floor, the sight underneath made her shout in surprise and disgust.

An earthworm, thick as her thumb and long as her forearm, was wriggling among the clothes. Its shiny body caught the reflection of the light, making it appear even more slimy.

Gloria shuddered at the sight.

"Yuck! How did you get inside?" She moved around it, eyes fixed on the little creature. What could she do? She couldn't just throw it outside—she lived on the fourth floor, and the poor thing would certainly meet a very nasty ending. But she didn't even have a big enough pot to just let it rest. She mumbled, and then decided to take the bucket she used to wash the floor. She filled it with some planting earth her wife used for their plants, and, using the longer spatulas she had, tried as gently as possible to lift the worm and put it in the bucket. She would release the poor creature afterwards. Right now, she needed to find out where her wife was.

Rummaging in her head, Gloria tried to think about the whereabouts of her wife, but nothing came to mind. Focused as she was, she almost missed her wife's mobile vibrating quite aggressively. A name she knew well appeared, and without thinking she answered.

"Liz! Thank God you answered!"

"Hi Fiona! Sorry, Gloria here. Do you know where Lizzy is?"

There was silence for a few seconds, followed by a curse on the other end of the line.

"Is there a worm in your house?"

Gloria blinked, her gaze going directly to the bucket.

"Yes, how—"

"Don't throw it out!" Fiona's voice was so high Gloria had to move it far away from her ear. "It's Liz!"

"What is Liz? Where is my wife?"

"It's Liz! The worm is Elizabeth!"

Gloria blinked rapidly—a new habit induced by her current situation.

"... is that some kind of joke?" she huffed, rolling her eyes. "I swear, if this is an elaborate joke by you two you can tell her—"

"Shush woman! Haven't you heard? It's, like, all over the internet!"

"I—no, what?"

"Just ... check your feed, okay? I'm coming over." With that, the call ended.

Gloria stared quite long at the screen, a picture of her and her wife hugging lovingly. Fiona's call had stirred some uneasiness in her. She'd never been prone to rudeness or agitation, but she'd been both on the call. What on Earth was going on?

She fetched her mobile, logged into her social media account, and began scrolling to understand what was happening.

Her eyes widened as more and more posts and reels appeared. They all said the same thing.

People were turning into worms. Earthworms, to be specific.

That must have been a joke, she thought. A big, international joke that had taken over the internet, and people had just collectively decided to tag along. But when Fiona arrived, short-breathed and with her usually well-kept hair in a mess, and told her that one of her own friends had also turned into a worm and had almost been thrown out on the street, she had to accept the reality of the situation. That her wife had, for some strange and inexplicable reason, turned into a wriggling worm.

After saying goodbye to Fiona, Gloria sat next to the bucket and stared deeply at the worm, now half covered by earth. What was she to do? Of course she would not throw Lizzy out, that wasn't even a question, but she hardly knew what to think. Lizzy had always been the practical one, not her. The furrow on her forehead deepened. She sighed, and took out her mobile to take a picture of her wormly wife, and post it online for their friends to know. After that, she opened a new tab and started researching how to keep her wife alive, at least until a cure was found. It was the sensible thing to do.

As the days passed by, she changed Lizzy's home from a bucket to an old fish tank that her elderly neighbour gave her. She filled it with earth, and covered the top with grass and moss, making it as habitable as possible. She learned to use the kitchen scraps to feed her wormly-wife. In this way, she could almost imagine they still shared a meal, though the idea was bittersweet in her heart.

June arrived, and with it less time spent working and more to be spent at home with her wormly-wife. It was on one of these days, as Gloria returned home from her last day of weekly work, that she heard it. A tiny, almost inaudible screech, coming from the living room.

Gloria peeked at the window. Had the upstair's cat fallen on their balcony again? But the screech did not come from there. As it sounded once again, Gloria slowly turned to face the tank.

"... babe? Is that you?"

Another screech, this time a little higher.

"You gotta be kidding me." If she was prone to cursing, she would have done so in that very instant. She took out her mobile and pressed play.

"Babe, could you do that again please?" she asked, hoping that her wormly-wife would understand her, and that it wasn't just her imagination.

When her wormly-wife screeched again, she was sure she wasn't hallucinating. She sent the video to Fiona, as she had kept their friend up-to-date with anything new that happened.

Fiona answered back with a series of random letters smashed together to form complete and utterly nonsense.

[Gloria:]

Fiona, please, use English. I don't like it when you do that.

[Fiona:]

OMG!!!

When did this happen???

Is she talking???

OMG?!?!?!?

Did you upload it? I think the world needs to see this.

Gloria furrowed her brow, but, since she had no one else to turn to, she agreed with her friend and uploaded the video on her profile, with the caption: *Can your wormly-partner also do that?*

She was amazed by how many people reached out to her, by comments or messages, to describe the similarity of their situation, or to ask how she got her partner to talk back. Of course, not all of them were positive, as she had happened upon several rude messages containing conspiratorial theories and calling for this huge hoax to cease once and for all—even though, apparently, the Prime Minister's wife had disappeared from public events since this nonsense had started—but she had learnt to ignore the half-wits and focus on helping and supporting others in the same situation as hers.

From that day on, Gloria started having conversations with her wife. Rather, it was mostly her talking, and her wormly-wife screeching softly back, but it gave her a sense of normalcy that she had terribly missed.

By the end of June, the situation hadn't changed at all. Wormified-partners were still wormified, and the Government had done little to nothing in the sense of discovering why this had happened or why it appeared to be so random.

Gloria hummed a song as she took one cupcake over to the tank, a fond smile on her face.

"Happy birthday, dear. I baked you some cupcakes. Tried to make them with vegetables, as I didn't want you to be sick on sugar for your birthday. I hope you like it." She took half of it, crumbled, and dispersed on the earth. Her wormly-wife was soon on it, feasting as if it was a delicacy—the cupcakes were actually pretty decent, and Gloria could say she was impressed by how much her culinary skills had improved over that short time. She sighed as she thought back to Lizzy preparing dinner for her. She missed her wife's dainties dearly. Daydreaming as she was, she almost missed the screechings.

"What is it dear? You want some more?" she crumbled the other half part, but her wormly-wife was still screeching.

"What? You need to be more specific, you know I can't really understand you."

The screeches intensified. Gloria sighed, half a laugh escaping her lips.

"Of course I love you, dear. But if it's a kiss you're asking for, I won't do that. You are a worm now, and, frankly, kissing you in your current state would be disgusting."

As she said that, her wormly-wife did something she had seen her do just once before: she writhed on herself and kept screeching in an agonising way.

Gloria huffed, and rolled her eyes.

"Unbelievable. You can't keep being this dramatic, you know?" As her wormly-wife kept on being dramatic, she sighed deeply and put a hand inside the tank.

"All right, all right. Come here, you crybaby. I can't believe being a worm hasn't changed your antics at all."

The sliminess didn't make her nauseous as it had at the beginning of this bizarre adventure, but it still made her highly uncomfortable. She took a deep breath, maybe two, well three, before closing her eyes and kissing her wormly-wife on what she truly hoped was her head.

A blinding flash erupted in the room. Gloria found herself on the floor, massaging her arse after falling on it.

"What the actual fuck just happened?"

Gloria stopped mid-massage, eyes widened as she traced the source of that voice that she knew too well.

"... Lizzy?"

Her Elizabeth was there, stark naked in front of her, covered only in dirt.

"Babe!"

For once, Gloria didn't mind her clothes being covered in soil, nor did she mind the earthly aftertaste in her wife's mouth. Tears formed in her eyes as she kept holding her wife, frightened that it was only her imagination playing a very sick joke on her. But when Fiona was called, and she dashed over to hug and sob all over her wife, she was sure that her wife had finally returned.

Of course, the online community divided as she posted an update on her no-longer-wormly wife. Most of them resorted to negative comments, accusing her of having played along for the sake of fame, running on the wave of real sufferers, calling her a hoax and a liar, branding her a fake. Those who believed her reached out in private, asking her for directions or support. Most were able to turn their partners back from their wormly state, and those thanked her profusely, but alas not everyone succeeded.

In the end, even some dark-suited agents contacted her, as apparently she had been the first one to successfully turn their partner back. She had given them a detailed account over all that had happened, from the discovery of her wormly-wife to the kiss that had turned her back. They had also thanked her, and asked her to keep the conversation private, to which she agreed.

Months later, the situation had slightly improved. The Government released a statement in which they asked the afflicted people to try and be more affectionate towards their wormly-beloved ones. Which, of course, had unleashed some of the most horrid people online to comment upon the idiocy of their Government, and call for sabotage and new elections. People who listened, though, found out that being more affectionate could indeed help. More and more people transformed back and were reunited with their loved ones, and therapy groups for both partners and former-worms were created to ease the reintegration into society.

Gloria and Lizzy, hugging on their sofa, spoke in hushed tones as to why it had happened to them. They loved each other so much, expressing their love through gestures and sweet talks. Was it not enough? What else was there to prove, if not what they were already doing?

In the end, they both agreed that this would remain a truly remarkable, although bizarre experience.

ETERNALLY, HE PROFESSED
Ava Lauren Grayson

László **spent his** entire life saving hers. The first time Princess Elyzabeth almost died, she was ten years of age. She was chasing a butterfly in the fields beyond the palace walls and was nearly trampled by a stampeding herd of wild horses, but she wasn't. Because László was there. He pushed her out of the way. A stable boy, he was then. But after the second time he saved her life—when the fifteen-year-old László rescued Elyzabeth from drowning when her attempt to escape her imprisoned life as a royal failed—László was promoted to Princess Elyzabeth's personal royal guard. The king thought that the boy had saved his only daughter's life so many times on his own account, he should be the protective shield that would keep Elyzabeth safe eternally.

And although László, the day he first laid eyes on the princess, holding her in the grassy field after he yanked her away from that oncoming stallion, made a vow that he would not only love Elyzabeth for the rest of his life but that he would rather die protecting her than die any other way, he had no idea what his promise would truly mean.

"I'm getting married."

Elyzabeth's pronouncement made László want to faint, explode, and crumble all at the same time.

"Oh, are you now?" he teased, trying to mask the quaking in his voice. Somewhere deep inside of him, László knew this conversation would arise at some point in the young guard's life, for the princess was not his to claim, only protect. But he didn't dare give it much thought. Until now.

"Does it surprise you?" Elyzabeth plucked a rose from a coiled bush, overgrown and reaching into the marble gazebo under which the princess and her guard now hid beneath, protected from the night's downpour. The soft spoils of rain caressed the shadowed gardens beyond the arched marble overhang and drowned out the ghosts of obligations always shouting at Elyzabeth from the palace walls. Out here, it was just Elyzabeth and László, and though they both secretly wished that they could pretend that they were not princess and guard for one night, one moment in time, that could never be. Because to pretend would be to cause irrevocable destruction that they could never repair.

As the princess plucked the ruby rose, the tender flesh of her finger snagged on a thorn and she winced before laughing, looking at the smear of blood. "That someone as ungraceful and doomful as I could attract someone as highly-esteemed as Prince Oramus?"

László snorted and drew closer to Elyzabeth as he tore a strip of white linen from his own tunic and firmly grabbed hold of Elyzabeth's hand to cradle it in his as he wrapped the gauze around her wounded finger. "You're a dangerous type of beauty, you know that, Elyza?" His deep olive eyes caressed her copper ones, and he took the rose from her. "Who will protect you when you're married?"

The young woman scoffed yet didn't draw her hand away, even after László finished tending to her wound.

"First of all, I don't need protection. And secondly, *you* will be." Her raven brow that matched her curly hair, loose around her shoulders, furrowed in confusion. She hadn't expected László to step down, to relinquish his power as her royal guard once she wed. But of course, he would. He couldn't stand beside the princess for the rest of her life while she stood beside the man that she was now tethered to for the rest of *her* life.

"The ball tomorrow ... it's for your betrothal." There was no question in László's voice. And when Elyzabeth did not respond, he knew he had his answer.

Elyzabeth would marry another. In that moment, he wanted to ask his princess why she wouldn't run away with him, disappear into the forest, and never look back. But there were two reasons: one, she had a kingdom to rule one day, and being the only heir to the throne, she could never abandon such a responsibility. She tried once. And László stopped her. He'd regretted his actions every day since. But then again, he wouldn't have gotten to spend the last six years being beside the only person he would ever love. Then, there was the second reason. László did not have a *gift*.

As commanded by the king a hundred years ago, every royal that governs the kingdom must have a gift, a magical power bestowed upon the person through ancestry. Only certain, worthy bloodlines in Hungary had these powers, gifts of healing, gifts of water-bending, gifts of prophesying, or gifts of light-yielding. Elyzabeth could paint anything into existence. László ... László was not born with a gift. He could never marry a woman of royal blood. He was not worthy.

"Well," László swallowed down the urge to fight for a woman that, between his societal stature and lack of magic, was far out of his reach. Instead, he drew her soft hand to his dark lips. "I congratulate you. I do. May you and Oramus be happy until death do you part."

Until death do you part.

László's words would echo in Elyzabeth's mind all night. Even as the sun crowned the pale cloudy sky in golden shine, she could still feel his words heavy on her shoulders, bitter on her tongue, painful in her ears. Because the truth was, she was already bound to someone until death. But it wasn't Oramus.

Yet, as corroding as László's words were, Elyzabeth knew she couldn't run away this time. László showed her that— that her trying to run from her inevitable fate as monarch would just turn her into a coward.

So she put on the crimson corseted gown laid out for her and took her father's arm for him to escort her into the candlelit ballroom in the belly of their cobblestone palace. A flute, fiddle, and cello beat loudly in the room as couples clapped and stomped their feet, spinning around in merriment. László followed closely behind like the loyal hound he was. Elyzabeth would not dare to look back. For she knew that if she took one look at his toned figure clothed in his long navy jacket and pants tucked into his high boots, his shaggy chestnut locks, and his squared jawline, she would give in to the coward she wanted to be.

"My daughter, might I present to you, Prince Oramus, your betrothed." King Zoltán dropped Elyzabeth's arm to allow Oramus to forcefully kiss both of the princess's cheeks. The tall, mysterious prince had tousled dark hair, a short cape draped over one shoulder, covering half of his obsidian vest and trousers, and a lustful grin tugging his lips.

"Végre," the prince breathed. "I've been so eager to meet you."

Clearly, László's face read.

"May I have this dance?"

As Elyzabeth was escorted to the floor by Oramus, László's intuition spiked. At first, he wasn't sure if he was simply being plagued by jealousy, but a moment passed, and he realized it was something more. You see, László didn't just save Elyzabeth's life all those times because of mere coincidence. No. He felt *compelled* to be somewhere at a certain moment. An instinct beyond his comprehension would warn him that the princess would be in danger. And that same instinct was screaming at him now.

Before László realized what he was about to do, he found himself taking a partner to the dance floor. A cello rumbled, and a violin growled to match it as the partners stepped forward and back and spun around. László never took his eyes off of Elyzabeth, who noticed yet didn't peer his way. Something burned deep inside of László when Oramus took note of László's far too possessive gaze at his betrothed and tugged her closer to his body. Elyzabeth snorted with irritation and pushed back, forming a wider gap between the two of them. The moment that the dance called for partners to switch, László did not waste a beat and snatched Elyzabeth into his arms as Oramus was forced to take another partner.

"What are you doing?" Elyzabeth snarled. "I'm not in the nursery, László. I do not need a nursemaid."

The folk music sped up, and Elyzabeth and László quickened their stomping and spinning. They instinctively careened into one another as Elyzabeth twirled, and László caught her. "I'm not jealous, if that's what you're thinking."

Elyzabeth quirked a brow up at him as she peered into László's eyes over her shoulder. "Okay, fine. Perhaps a little. But this isn't simply that. Oramus ... He's here to kill you. You need to leave now."

"I'm not leaving. You can't tell me—" Elyzabeth opened her mouth to correct László on his misinformation, but then László spun Elyzabeth around to face him and snugged his arm around her waist, drawing her in. The princess didn't pull away, letting Lázló go on.

"He was hired by your cousin. To seduce you and kill you so that your cousin would be heir, next in line for the throne."

Contemplating, Elyzabeth folded her lips together as László intertwined his warm fingers with hers and led her forward in dance. Oramus glared daggers at the two.

"How do you know that?" Elyzabeth challenged.

László's jawline went taught. "I just do."

Before Elyzabeth could say anything more, the dance called for the changing of partners once again, and Oramus charged to take hold of the princess. But László walled himself between them.

"Excuse me, sir, but I believe it's my turn to dance with my betrothed." The two men locked glares and stood their grounds. Now the crowd and dance partners had, too, noticed the altercation and stopped to watch, though the jolly music trailed on.

"Really?" László's words snapped. "Because I think it's actually time for you to leave. Before I expose why you are truly here."

The dark prince scoffed and quirked his head in a confident challenge. "Ah I see. A jealous lover."

All eyes flicked to Elyzabeth as gasps circled the ballroom. "Do not fret, dear princess," Oramus continued. "No one blames *you* for such an affair. I'll protect you from now on." The prince held out his gloved hand and waited for his betrothed to take it. But she didn't. Instead, Elyzabeth raised her chin and crossed her arms over her chest.

"Is it true?" the princess impugned Oramus. "You were hired by Andor?"

Breathing through his nostrils, Oramus rubbed his face, taking a moment. Then his eyes shot up. "Yes."

In one swift movement, the assassin drew a blade from his belt and pinned László beneath his arm while resting the blade against the tender flesh of the guard's neck. Traitors, hidden in the form of guests, drew their swords and pointed them at Elyzabeth, her own band of guards formed a huddle around her. The musicians halted in shock, and the guests drew back in fear.

"Give yourself over now, Elyzabeth, or he dies." Oramus enjoyed the pleasure of counting László's pulse beneath his fingers. His wicked grin told him so. Elyzabeth, now hidden behind the backs of her guards, rose on her toes to look over their shoulders, peering with fear yet rage at the man threatening to cut her heart to pieces. "You have three seconds."

"Elyzabeth, don't!" László choked out just before the blade began to saw away at his skin, drawing trickles of crimson. Elyzabeth's body shuddered at the sight. Without a second thought, she was shoving her way past her guards.

"Let me through. Now! I order you." The princess charged through her protectors and stood with vulnerability before László and Oramus.

"*Elyzabeth,*" the young guard breathed out as a diamond of saltwater fell from his cornea. The princess smirked.

"I didn't run this time." Her eyes flicked next to Oramus, changing from tender to deadly. "Now let him go."

Oramus jerked his chin toward his men and they drew forward, collecting Elyzabeth by her arms.

Elyzabeth, what have you done?

Instinctively, László took his moment to fight. Not for him, for he knew he would not be released as promised. For her. To protect her. To the end.

László's hand flew to Oramus's, wrapping around the dagger still resting at his throat. The two struggled over it, muscles quaking, teeth grinding. The blade drew deeper into László's neck for a moment, pain seeping into his skin, before László's power won out and the guard twisted Oramus's wrist around, forcing him to drop the dagger. On his knees, László twirled around, caught the falling blade, and drove it into Oramus's abdomen. The assassin grunted in pain as László drove the dagger deeper, blood staining his jacket sleeve, before he ripped it out and let the prince keel over in death. As everyone watched in horror, the princess's guards were quick to use the distraction to seize Oramus's men and sweep the princess away. As soon as she was safe from harm, Elyzabeth barreled toward László, who let the dagger fall from his hand as he wrapped his arms tightly around Elyzabeth's waist, pulling her into an embrace, letting his head nuzzle into the crook of her neck, and burying his face in her now-loose hair. The two never did say anything to one another. They never got the chance. Because as László pulled back to let his eyes gaze into Elyzabeth's before falling to her lips, Death played a wicked trick on the lovers. Oramus was still alive—alive enough to use the dagger to pierce László's chest in a deadly stab of revenge.

"László!" Elyzabeth cried as the guard's breath shuttered and he sank to his knees, the blade protruding from between his shoulder blades. Oramus was seized by the new set of guards barreling into the ballroom, but it was too late. Elyzabeth cradled László's limp body in her arms as the guard began to die. The princess bent her head over his, tears streaming from both their eyes but for different reasons. László kept his promise.

Till death did them part.

The moment László took his final breath, Elyzabeth collapsed into herself and plummeted into darkness.

Elyzabeth painted László that very night. They took his body away to make preparations for his funeral. Just before the sun came up, when the night was still potent, Elyzabeth hid alone in her chambers. Stained with his blood, she tore her dress from her body, stripping down to her chemise.

Though her hands were still caked in blood and quavering with earthquakes, Elyzabeth hurried to her easel and oil palette. With a fresh sheet of canvas before her, she frantically mixed pigments and dug the worn bristles of her brush into the thick clumps. With tears blurring her vision in a kaleidoscope of mourning, the princess painted László's portrait until dawn broke. When she finished, it was messy and quick, but it was still an impressive likeness. With a clutter, she threw the palette and brushes to the ground and hovered her paint and crimson-stained hands over the painting, willing it with her magic to come to life. Willing László to come back to her. But unlike her usual paintings, which glowed with magical rebirth, this one didn't breathe with life. For the very person she painted was not alive to come to her.

Or so she thought.

A cry of sheer agony escaped Elyzabeth's throat as she collapsed onto her scarlet-dressed wooden bed, burying her face into the sheets. She did not cry, but wailed, for a broken heart was far more painful than a grieving one.

"Elyzabeth?" Upon hearing her name, the princess shoved herself upright with a startled gasp as László stood before Elyzabeth. For a long while, the princess was convinced she was dreaming, for László looked like himself but stronger, more golden, with white feathered wings protruding from his back where his wound was no longer. His neck and bare chest were clean, not blood-stained, and he floated above the ground.

"László is dead." Elyzabeth spoke with coldness to the golden phantom as she cradled her arms around her legs, still perched on her bed. "Do not taunt me."

The young man fluttered forward with such grace he

could have been a cloud; then he gently drew his hand up to brush his knuckles along Elyzabeth's cheekbone.

"László is me. I promised I would always protect you. Even in death, I will never leave you." Words like deep amber honey rolled off his tongue. Elyzabeth could barely contain herself. Feeling the warmth of his love upon her face, she flung herself toward László, who caught her confidently in his arms as the princess eagerly pressed her lips to his. With passion, promise, and earnestness, the two kissed for the first and last time. For, you see, László *was* born into a magical bloodline. But his powers never revealed themselves in his life; only in his death did he find his purpose. Being Elyzabeth's divine protector. In life, he possessed the clairvoyant, supernatural powers to know how to protect hers. And in death, he would devote all of eternity to doing the same. This was the last time Elyzabeth would ever see László on Earth. The last time he would be permitted to show himself to her. But even though Elyzabeth never saw him again while she ruled over her kingdom, he was always beside her, always protecting her. Chasing butterflies together. Eternally.

VÉGE

Blood of the Covenant

IT TAKES TWO
Judy Liu

"Hey, how's it going?" Yarlo responded, uncharacteristically professionally on the other end of the call.

Sarai paused. "Are you at work already? It's so early!"

"Yes, there's a big deal going down so I came in. One moment. Let me grab a separate room."

She heard a door close on the other end before Yarlo came back with a tone change.

"Helloooo," he greeted her in a sing-song. Sarai laughed.

"You didn't have to pick up if you're at work!"

"No, no, this is a good break that I needed. Those guys are so dry. Plus it's been forever!"

"Right? Catch me up!"

Sarai and Yarlo had been friends for eleven years. From him organizing her birthday dinners to her helping his parents when they got locked out of their house, Sarai and Yarlo had been there for each other throughout their teenage years into adulthood. If someone needed a plus one to an event last minute, they were each other's people. Over the years, they'd maintained their close friendship despite being in different cities. One minute they'd be laughing silly and the next they'd be ranting about how the world worked.

While listening to Yarlo regale her on his new job and the next new city, Sarai looked out her window at the rolling hills of tree roots and absentmindedly pet her skimmer Tat, a two-foot-long yellow salamander with black stripes and a mane of external gills on either side of his head.

"How's Auntie and Uncle?" Yarlo asked, referring to Sarai's parents.

"They're good. They ask about you from time to time."

"Aw, well of course." Sarai could hear his grin across the line.

"They've been hounding me to be more serious in finding a partner so that I can receive the government pension," she laughed, "but I tell them I got them, my friends, my own shop, and Tat here." She looked down affectionately at her skimmer.

"I know what you mean! Amma and Pa get on my case, but they're truly enjoying the empty nester life too. Sometimes I'm the one asking them to not stay up too late socializing!" They laughed together. "By the way, Sarai," Yarlo added. "On the topic of the government pension, I've been meaning to tell you."

Oh?

"I'm getting engaged."

That sentence reverberated in her ears so deeply that Sarai thought maybe she heard wrong.

"Wait, are you being serious? Or are you joking?" *Who is this all of a sudden! Has it been that long since we've caught up that I don't know about a relationship? A relationship to the point of engagement?*

"I'm being serious, Sarai. It's actually partially why I moved to Parstat. To pursue her. I wasn't sure if it'd work out, and time's running out before we hit the cut-off year, so I didn't tell anyone other than friends in Parstat." His sentence ended in a small laugh. "But yeah, I really like her. I really do. And luckily for me, she likes me too! Once we tie the knot, the government marriage pension is a plus!"

"Oh, wow!" Sarai felt something break inside her. "Congratulations!" Her tone was high and exuberant, but it took all her effort to put the voice behind it. She cleared her throat. "Well, who is she? What is she like? And how could you not tell anyone!" she asked playfully.

He laughed sheepishly, and Sarai pictured the way his eyes always wrinkled with a sideways glance when he laughed like that. "I haven't told anyone about it. You're the first. But she's met my mom, and they get along. She's great. She's driven and ..." but Sarai had tuned him out.

Later that evening, as the sky turned into an orange hue, and Sarai returned from her apothecary, she immediately slumped back into her couch and laid an arm across her eyes. Tat crawled into the shallow stone pond in the living room for his evening soak.

Why am I feeling this way? You knew this would happen. It always does. Your guy friends get engaged, and you lose a dear friend. Inevitably, with a mutual understanding, the friendship fizzled and both sides distanced themselves. Sarai wasn't bitter—she understood that relationship dynamics were complicated and difficult, and she respected whatever happened. But accepting it didn't mean it didn't make her incredibly sad. Sarai had always delighted in getting to know her friends' partners, but she felt a pang each time she noticed a shift. One day, without either of them knowing, he would call with that singsong greeting for the very last time.

She felt a lump tickle the back of her throat and took a shuddering breath. *Yarlo's not the first. Two other friends had gotten engaged in the last three months.* Though she hadn't reacted in this way to her other friends' news, it felt as if Yarlo's announcement was a final blow after a series of punches in a boxing ring. She heard a small splash and tiredly lifted her arm from her head to see Tat crawling toward the couch and onto her. He made a few spins on her stomach before settling his large head on her chest and stared at her with imploring bulbous black eyes.

She placed her hand onto Tat's spiny back. "Thanks, Tat. I don't mean to stress you. I'm okay." Her voice broke on the last word.

She then wrapped both arms around Tat's thick neck and cried softly into his feathery gills for the treasured friendships past and gone.

The government cherished children and held them in the highest regard. As such, the government enacted the Marriage Pension program where they offered couples who got married before the age of thirty a life-long pension, distributed biweekly like a paycheck. If the couple produced a child, then the pension increased. The pension was enough for living expenses and medical care; anything additional, such as food, travel, and enrichment still required people to have their own earnings, but the pension made a huge difference in quality of life. The government had the formulas and legal caveats for regulating this program meticulously spelled out to prevent people from cheating the system.

Because of this, understandably, people were consumed with finding love and having children before turning thirty years old.

To Sarai, it was a cruelly unfair system that favored youth and those who could bear children. Those who couldn't have children had to get fertility doctors or surrogates and at that point, they had to calculate if it was even worth it on a cost-basis. Those who didn't get married or have children ended up working three times more than their married contemporaries to make enough to live at the same level of comfort. Those who did get married and had children would later realize if it weren't for the pension, they might not have wanted children.

Sarai turned twenty-nine this year, meaning she had only one more year to find a partner if she wanted the pension. It was probably too late for her to consider even trying for the child pension supplement, and her parents were starting to worry.

She would protest but she knew they wanted what's best for her. To them, that meant having the pension for stability and making sure she didn't become the aged lady who lived alone with ten skimmers.

"Not a bad way to live life, though," Sarai thought to herself every time her parents mentioned their greatest fear, imagining a house full of plants and ponds for cute, ginormous salamanders.

Unlike the majority of people in their twenties, Sarai hadn't focused on finding a partner. She assumed whoever was meant to be for her would naturally be for her and placed her trust in the universe. But before she knew it, nine years had passed, and she hadn't imagined the likelihood that she'd be single at the pension cut-off year either.

She'd been in relationships before, and she loved each of them, but she also realized she was most at ease on her own. She had a habit of putting others before herself, to the point where she disregarded her own needs and boundaries. So when she wasn't in a relationship, she was free. She focused on herself and *her* wants. She flourished.

As Sarai aged, she'd also found herself increasingly reluctant to date because she found the early stages of a relationship nerve-wracking. People talked about the giddiness and excitement of early love, but it stressed Sarai. She wanted the romance but found advances scary and off-putting. She knew that it was normal for people to want that kind of intimacy, but being ace combined with her personality, she needed more emotional intimacy before she was ever comfortable with it. Her discomfort often manifested physically into gagging fits. Her timing with physical intimacy sometimes had people thinking she wasn't interested. Or ... they simply lost interest because she took "too long." And Sarai was fine not communicating her asexuality or history—it was too exhausting to explain it all every single time. She knew not everyone had bad intentions, but her previous experiences on some horrid dates made her flinch physically whenever she thought of her courtier making a move on her.

It was easier for Sarai to shower affection on her friends and family. She made a concerted effort to schedule meals with friends, make it to their events, or to keep in contact and support them emotionally. She loved them deeply.

But a change in her friendships over the last few years made this year different. She lost friends as they got married near the cut-off year. Close friends slowly drifted away, and although they called often, it wasn't the same. The other friends were always there for fun, but never there for the depth. Sarai didn't view friendships as a quid pro quo, but she found herself unfulfilled. She willingly extended herself to foster and nurture these relationships, but when she needed them, they didn't pick up her calls or said they were too busy. Over the last few years, Sarai stopped reaching out to check-in and stopped planning group trips. She noticed, without her drive, those friendships slowly dissipated. They never noticed.

As such, Sarai started to expect less and less, and the friendships that had warmed her heart slowly hardened it instead.

She didn't mind being alone, but she'd found loneliness creeping in like a fog in the night. When asked for an emergency contact on official documents, Sarai didn't know who to put down. If her vehicle ran out of air or she got sick, there was no one in town to help her. She handled all of this alone. It was during these moments that doubt would take root in Sarai's mind.

Perhaps having anyone would be better than having nobody at all.

At her parents' incessant requests, Sarai had gone on dates regularly that were set up by the town matchmaker. The men were all nice, but she was always scared. Scared she was being too friendly. Scared they were going to make a move before she was ready. Scared about how to confront them and advocate for herself. Scared of their reaction. Scared of how she'd make them feel. Scared they'd internalize it. Scared she would seem aloof to them, when in actuality she saw partner potential. Scared she wasn't respecting her own boundaries. Scared they wouldn't reciprocate the vulnerability she put forward. Scared they wouldn't understand her. Scared of being misunderstood.

It was so much easier staying home with Tat.

Sarai was handling an online order at her apothecary, grinding softshell turtle shells with her mortar and pestle, when she heard the front doors slide open. *Already?* Sarai had been hoping for a quiet morning of seething. Tat had defecated all over her kitchen (yes, even the counters and cabinets) this morning and her supplier of silver-ear fungus had called saying they were hit by a plant disease that wiped their supply. They wouldn't be able to ship to her for another three months. Sarai wasn't in the best of moods, and she wanted to be alone.

"Good tidings," she stated on autopilot. "How may I help you today?" She continued her arduous task of grinding the shells.

"Um," came an unsure response, "it's my first time here."

Okay ... so what? Sarai looked up and saw a man of average height and stocky build with the expression of a lost traveler. She heaved a sigh. *I don't have time for this. So much to inventory. I have to notify clients of the lack of silver-ear fungus.*

Maybe if I finish early, I can go home and deep clean the kitchen before dinner. The front door slid open again for a group of young teenagers.

"Sure. Take a look around and call when you need me." Sarai moved onto portioning the powdered shell with some dried yams into crisp paper parcels and called a half-hearted greeting to the new group.

The man's eyes glazed over as he wandered aimlessly within her tight shop. Sarai spared him a glance to see him graze a jar of dried orange peels with his thick coat in passing.

"Watch out!" she yelped, prepared to hear the crash of shattered glass hitting the floor. To her surprise, the man had turned quickly enough and shot a hand out to catch the jar.

"Thanks for the warning." He grinned apologetically. The last thing Sarai needed was an accident at the shop too today, so she beckoned the man toward her. He carefully maneuvered between the narrow rows of ingredients to the register kiosk at the back of the shop which was an expansive wall of small wooden cabinets.

"What do you need help with? I can't help if I don't know what you're looking for." At that, the man seemed to look past her, unfocused.

"Excuse me, miss? Could we order first?" one of the teens in the shop called out. Sarai looked at the man with a quirked brow.

"Of course," he said immediately, putting a hand out to allow the others to go ahead of him.

Sarai took their order for five bowls of bird's nest soup. It was her bestseller. Herbal remedies took time to prepare, but her customers knew that Sarai's apothecary was a place to slow down and savor the present so they didn't mind waiting. It helped that Sarai had preparation methods to speed up the process. Nothing took more than an hour. That's what set her shop apart from others; in addition to packing prescriptions for people to take home, she could also prepare it for them to consume at her shop. No other apothecary did that.

Sarai wanted to get customers out so she could go back to her own thoughts and simmer on this morning's unfortunate events. She motioned to the man to follow her to the backroom.

He looked at her, then glanced behind him before turning back to her and pointed at himself with both brows raised.

"Yes, you," she answered impatiently. "Come with me and tell me what you're looking for while I prepare their order. It's five people so instead of having you wait this whole time, you can talk to me while I work."

The man dutifully lifted the detachable part of the front counter to follow her to the backroom.

"Oh wow," he breathed, looking around. There were soups brewing, half-opened drawers of herbs, baskets of fresh harvests, hearths heating, and hanging strings of drying persimmons and jujubes. At that, she gave a small smile.

She checked on the birds nests that had become translucent and noodle-like from being soaked overnight, and then grabbed the jujubes and rock sugar to simmer with it.

"What does that do?" the man asked.

"It's high in antioxidants and chock full of nutrients. It's a natural medicine for coughs, and our books indicate that it may enhance bone strength. Oh, also cell regeneration."

"Okay, that sounds TOO good to be true."

She laughed at that and when she looked up, she saw him smiling back at her, and a warmth tugged at her heart.

"It's not a panacea, nor a one-time wonder drug if that's what you're thinking. But it really is quite beneficial if taken every day."

He nodded, brows furrowed as if he were straining to mentally note this.

Remembering he was a customer, Sarai asked again. "Tell me. Has anything been ailing you? Maybe I can prescribe something to help."

He took on a distant expression. "I'm not sure what I'm looking for." He gave a small smile that didn't reach his eyes. "Well, I don't know why I just said that. I do. Well, I don't anymore." When he looked back at Sarai, he was met by a concerned but patient gaze.

"I was waiting for someone," he continued. "But, she said no more. So, I don't know what I'm looking for anymore. This was six months ago, but I'll still close my eyes and hope when I open them, she'll be there."

"Oh, sorry," and Sarai truly felt sorry she asked. She wasn't good at these things and emotions. Additionally, as the anti-Marriage Pension person, she probably wasn't the best to talk to in his state.

He smiled wanly at her. She hadn't noticed his ghostly complexion and gaunt face with his stockier build and brighter expressions until now.

"Today's my first day out in a while. When I saw your shop, something pulled me in."

Sarai was thankful for the shift away from his break-up. "It's okay to not know what you're looking for. Give yourself some space and time." *Please, don't treat me like a therapist.*

Please. Otherwise, I need to start charging him for the time ... But he continued spilling thoughts.

"I thought she was everything. Without her, I'm feeling lost. I know she's gone, but I can't grapple with the fact that what I imagined for us would never be. I feel like I should have done something else while we were together. That I'd been wrong this whole time. Time's running out."

Sarai's grandmother's gravelly voice rang in her head. "You should be putting more time into dating. You should have put in more effort in your youth. Time is running out. You should be starting a family." Sarai forcefully pushed it away.

"I've recently had similar thoughts. I've been wondering if I've been doing it wrong for the past nine years." When Sarai met his gaze, she saw him looking intensely at her, urging her to share more. She kept her mouth clamped; she already shared more than she intended to.

"What do you mean?" he exclaimed with fervor upon her silence. "You own this gorgeous apothecary," he waved around in admiration. "Do you not?"

I do. Sarai looked around as if absorbing it for the first time again and felt a sense of pride swell in her chest. Seeing the hundreds of stacked, square wooden drawers spanning the walls, the scales set around the room, the ceramic jars of rare goods, the wooden beams supporting the ceiling, the wafts of smoke billowing from stone cooktops, and the smells of earth and warmth—many wouldn't call it gorgeous compared to modern apothecaries of minimalist sleek designs, but she definitely thought it was. With her mind weighed down by worries of her age, her gradual loss of friendship quality, and the likely loss of the Marriage Pension that would potentially affect her for the rest of her life, she'd forgotten that all those years of focusing on herself led to this shop. Her dream shop.

"What's your name?" she asked him quietly.

"Attica." He ran a hand through his wavy black hair. "And you?"

"Thank you, Attica, for reminding me," Sarai whispered gently. "I'm Sarai. But back to you, I think I have an idea of what you need. To help with how you're feeling." Sarai had no treatment for heartbreak, but she could help strengthen his body from the inside and build him back up.

He looked at her with a slightly quizzical expression. "I think you've already helped with that," and he broke into the first genuine smile she'd seen, briefly shedding the dull pain that had a vise-like grip on his heart.

She quickly looked away and pretended she didn't hear him.

"Watch this pot while I go find the right herbs for you." She hastily shuffled to another section of the room to grab some loquat and mulberry leaves and came back to find Attica humming while meticulously stirring the pot of bird's nest soup.

"I'll prescribe you this mixture," Sarai held up a wad of leaves, "and we'll go from there."

Before she could go into more detail, one of her many timers chimed softly.

"Could you please tell the other customers that it's almost done steeping, and we'll be out shortly?" Sarai asked of Attica while she busied herself with grabbing bowls.

"Absolutely," Attica stepped out of the backroom.

Sarai scooped out the contents into double-walled metal bowls. She served up five and paused before grabbing a sixth bowl to serve.

"Done!" Attica announced as he came back.

"Great, thanks. And this one's for you." She handed Attica the sixth bowl. He took it in both hands, wide-eyed.

"Wait, what!"

"On the house," she said with the wave of a hand. "For the help."

"I barely helped!" he laughed. "But I'll take it. I think I'm getting the better deal here." They both grinned at each other while she placed the other five onto a wooden tray and took it out to serve the customers.

When she came back inside, Attica hadn't tried the soup yet.

"What's wrong? Does it smell funny? Is there a bug in it?" *Though we often use bugs in our remedies so even then, a fresh bug isn't that big of a deal ...*

"Not at all!" he responded quickly. "It looks amazing. It's just scalding hot!"

Sarai rolled her eyes at that. "Don't be a wuss. That's when it's most delicious. It's amazing as you feel it burn down your throat."

He shot her a dubious look. "You have a weird definition of 'delicious' if it includes burning my insides." But he blew on his bowl a few more times and took a small sip.

Attica's eyes immediately brightened, and he stared at the bowl wondrously.

"Good, right?" Sarai nodded knowingly.

"Good? It's so refreshing and lightly sweetened, and the texture of this clear noodle in it is so bouncy. I feel better already!"

"Don't be so dramatic," Sarai laughed.

When she opened her eyes from laughing, she saw that he was staring straight at her.

"No, I really do feel better now. And not just because of this soup. I'm glad I walked in today."

Sarai couldn't help but beam back.

"Well, I guess now I should tell you what bird's nest soup is made from. Those aren't noodles. You're eating hardened bird saliva."

He spit and some of the noodles flew out his nose. Sarai roared with renewed laughter.

Attica started coming in more regularly. At first he came to report on his health and get new packets of herbs, but eventually he started staying longer to simply chat or watch her work. Sarai found herself looking forward to his easy company while she busied herself among the shelves of herbs. Before she knew it, several months had passed of him coming regularly.

"Sarai!" Attica rushed in through the doors one day. "I found this yesterday. It kind of looked like something you've shown me before." He held his phone up to her with a picture of a translucent fungus. It looked like shards of ice with wavy edges that had frozen in a clump.

Sarai grabbed his phone in disbelief. "That's the silver-ear! I've been short on these for months because the supply chain is being impacted! Where did you find these?" she demanded.

"Ah, geopolitical issues trickling down to affect everything." Attica raised a brow and rolled his eyes before looking back at her. "I found it while I was hiking. What do you say to us going foraging?" He grinned ear-to-ear.

Her heart lifted. "I would want nothing more than to do that!"

She closed her shop for the afternoon, and they set out. Seeing the clumps of ice-like fungus was a dream to her, and she hopped around like a gremlin while Attica laughed.

They brought their basket of goods back to her place when she saw a broken window. A rogue root had invaded her house via the window, and Tat was spooked, wreaking havoc inside.

Sarai lived on the edge of an animated root forest. It had ideal soil for growing herbs but the downside was the occasional moving roots that shoved or broke things.

Seeing the broken glass and her furniture upturned with pond water everywhere, Sarai's mind started buzzing with everything she had to do, and her shoulders started to tense when Attica picked up a machete that every household had to address root issues.

"Let me help." Without another word, he started hacking at the rogue root inside her house, allowing her to tend to Tat before cleaning the rest of the living room. Attica chattered about everything and nothing while they cleaned, soothing the tense air that surrounded Sarai with his familiar voice.

Reina, one of Sarai's best friends who lived an 8-hour flight away, called.

"Are you okay? I saw the alert just now after work!" Sarai had to hold the phone farther away from Reina's loud frantic voice.

"I'm fine, Reina. It was just a root. Thank you for checking, though. Means a lot." Since Sarai and Reina both lived alone, they had set up home alerts for each other's homes so that they could watch out for each other.

"Do you have anyone who can help you?" Reina asked. "I'm sorry, I wish I could be there! The glass everywhere and having to deal with the window will be annoying."

"Don't be sorry about that, Reina! And actually, yeah. A friend happened to be with me, and he's helping. Don't worry, I'm not alone." Sarai smiled at Attica as he shot her a thumbs-up while sweeping.

By the time Sarai wiped the floors, refilled Tat's pond, and reset everything to its rightful place, Attica had also finished sweeping up the broken glass and covering the window with a tarp he found. *Wow. It all goes by so much faster with someone helping.*

The moon was halfway across the sky by the time they were done. Sarai felt bad about keeping Attica and also wanted to thank him, so she offered him her spare bedroom for the night. Hours of foraging in the mountains followed by hours of hacking at a thick root and cleaning—it was best he got some rest.

After he graciously accepted, she insisted he sit on the couch and rest while she whipped something up from the silver-ear fungus.

Tat curled into the nook of Attica's legs as he sat cross-legged, and they chatted while Sarai prepared the tremella soup made of silver-ear fungus, goji berries, and dates.

They'd exhausted conversation by the time the soup was done. As they quietly sipped their tremella soup, a warmth that had been growing in Sarai's chest blossomed. Over the last several months, their friendship had become something she cherished, and this quiet companionship put her at ease.

Sarai woke before Attica the next day and set to prepare congee for breakfast. It was still dark when Attica got up. They settled on opposite ends of the couch while they waited for the congee to heat up. There was something about the darkness and quiet that caused people to speak softly and open up. So they shared their passions and fears and thoughts with one another until the sun started peeking over the horizon. Attica turned his head toward one of the windows admiring the colors outside.

"Gosh, isn't that gorgeous?"

Sarai looked at his profile, now being hit by slants of soft sun rays and saw how it lit his eyes into a mahogany brown and highlighted his cheekbones.

"Yeah, it's beautiful," she agreed while looking at him. And together, they savored the stillness before the world came awake.

Years Later

Sarai's phone rang. She checked and saw it was Attica. She'd moved to Parstat for three months to check out the local herbs and to conduct research on Parstat apothecaries while also visiting friends. The other day, she'd grabbed dinner with Izry, a dear friend who she'd actually met first through Izry's husband, Yarlo.

"How's the shop looking?" Sarai greeted Attica on call.

"Let's just say I don't know how you run this shop yourself while being your awesome self. Like, I have no time for myself!"

She laughed. "I'm sorry. I'll make it up to you! Thank you again so, so much for watching it last minute. You're the best." Sarai lauded him with praises which she knew would soften him.

"All right," he huffed good-naturedly. "I know I'm the best friend anyone could possibly ask for but, yeah, make me some super special herbal soup or something or I'll never do this again!"

She laughed. "Love you, too, Attica."

"Yeah, yeah, love you and your overachieving-turd-wad-self, too," he laughed as well.

She trusted in the universe.

DEEP IN THE WOODS
Charleigh Frederick

Deep in the woods, darkness shadows their heads.

March on little ones, march. Do as you're told.

Deep in the woods, darkness shadows their souls. The joyous memories once held dear trapped in the sacks on their backs.

March on little ones, march. Do as you're told.

Deep in the woods, two girls traverse, one older than the other. How strange if they were to be born the exact same minute of the exact same day.

March on little ones, march. Don't let the forest win.

Deep in the woods, they do as they're told. Not seeing what lies under the bark of the trees. Under the moss of the rocks. Under the birds of the nests and snakes of the ground.

March on little ones, march.

Deep in the woods, the rain breaks through the branches above. "Come on," calls the littler one. "Come on."

Run on little ones, run. Don't get caught, little ones, don't.

Do as you're told.

Deep in the woods, our girls find shelter. The storm picks up, the wind wild around them.

"Don't cry," says the older one. "Don't cry." Do as you're told.

Deep in the woods, the storm rages around them. The chill bites at their skin, and they cling to each other.

They can't march on. There's nowhere to go. You're trapped in the woods, little ones, trapped.

Deep in the woods, the littler one mutters, "I love you."

Deep in the woods, the older responds. "I love you too. You're my best friend."

Deep in the woods the littler shrugs off her pack. Opens the top.

Deep in the woods, the girls pull out their memories to stay warm, bundling in their glow, golden threads around them.

Stay warm little ones, stay warm.

The wolf isn't ready for dinner just yet.

THE CHASM
Honora Quinn

I don't quite know where to start. How do you cut to the chase when the story has never ended, but the beginning is too far faded to coherently recall? How will I explain to those passing through my life like ghosts, those that are but temporary replacements for you? How will I explain the feeling? The sound of your laugh, but not your normal laugh, the one from that one random day. It was snowing, and we dyed your hair. I got the pigment on my shirt, causing the words on the surface to change meaning in an arbitrary but stupid way.

Yet you had thrown your head down as you howled at my misfortune. This was before you'd cut your hair short—the look people know you for. It covered your face like a curtain. Now, those long-jagged lines of ink bond us, your clothes are stained like mine.

The chasm was but a crack in the sidewalk, something we would joke about superstitiously in the summer heat, yet barely give a passing thought. You and me, we're forever.

How do I accurately portray the change of the octave, that it normally was deeper but for some reason you freed it? How do I transfer the memories? How can I live in someone's head and get them to properly understand what it feels like to live on the same earth as you? I get sidetracked while talking to the ghosts, a short anecdote blossoming into tangent. Wrapping myself up in the context that no one else on the planet understands or rather cares about. They don't understand that one day we were in your bathroom, and now you are impossibly far away.

They don't know who you are. They don't know the ache, they don't know me, not in a way that matters. They don't care.

Now it has been impossibly long. Why hold onto the past when you can live for the future? Replace her, replace the memories, and enjoy your life. It has been impossibly long when you finally respond to my texts. Suddenly, we are children again. Younger this time, wandering, speaking in our own tongue. Mixing metaphors and references to the point they barely make sense to either of us. But we laugh together, you laugh again in a different way. How do I explain myself when I call you the wrong name? You were in the room next to me, now you're states away. I backtrack, say that I called her your name so many times over that she thinks that she knows you.

You don't understand. You say that you do but I know better.

Now how can I explain what *you've* missed? The chapters that never made it into your copy of my life, giving you a skewed view of who I am. The chasm tore away at the remaining land, but I won't let it take us, not entirely. We're in the same state now at least, moving ever closer as your promise to text regularly. A rock breaks away by my feet as the ghosts say to not get too attached again, *you've been burned,* and this time is no different.

A week later, when out with work friends, I realize that I don't remember your middle name. Something so sweet and simple I called you a million times as a joke as you said mine back. You've taken that story from me and thrown it into the pit. That was only the first you took from me, one by one my tangents shorten, turning tomes into essays, paragraphs then sentences. I let you have them.

I spent so many years tearing at my being, pulling at every loose thread I could find. All to fit you and your shiny world that I have lost my form. Broken and twisted, while your sharp corners gave you the world.

How do I tell people I knew you, back when the chasm was just that crack, that you were one of us? They give me those looks, thinking me a loon trying to dirty your coattails as you march ever forward.

How can you send me presents then pretend I never existed? How can you cut your way through the crowd, back down to earth, just to remind me of the tales I lost?

All I can do is smile; this isn't real anymore. It hasn't been for a long time.

I'm a bridesmaid in your wedding. It's one of the photos I use at parties to prove our connection, to show myself that it hasn't all been a dream, long and cloudy. My dress was a slightly different shade of violet, I thought that you were finally claiming me back. But it could have been a mistake to pose me as an outsider.

When you posted it online you cropped me out of all the photos. Erased me from the narrative to call me a liar, since the only alternative lives on my phone. How do I further explain that that phone got run over by your mother's car and now the photos are really gone?

I let you take that story too. Since I don't get invited to those parties anymore.

Now I no longer tell people about you. Spinning my tales for the awaiting spirits no longer has any meaning. Where do you end, and where do I begin? Even with history, there never really is a beginning. Just factor after factor propelling you ever backwards until there is nowhere to go but forward.

I'll give myself to the chasm, if that is what you want, you need. I know you'd do it for me, you would have, once upon a time.

We were girls once, we were friends.

But how is anyone to ever understand?

/TO MY ARMY/
R.C. Lloyd

God knew I was lonely / So He recruited an army

To the spontaneous ones / He assigned my spirit

Dancing into the night / Losing myself in the thrill of it all

To the patient ones / He assigned my heart

Broken / Weary / Learning contentment / The definition of insanity

To the soft ones / He assigned my femininity

Flower crowns / Friendship bracelets / Have courage / Be kind

To the strong ones / He assigned my actions

Foolish in love / Fearful in life / Reckless in the moment

To the brave ones / He assigned my nightmares

Wild / Clawing / Dragging insecurities into the daylight

To the quick ones / He assigned my words

Angry / Bitter / Jaded with heartbreak

To the wise ones / He assigned my soul

How to spend a life / How to leave a legacy / How to be a friend

So to my army / Thank you for your service / We ride at dawn

THE BEST MAN BLOWUP
Katie Fitzgerald

"We definitely made the right call about the reunion," Dave told Isaac as he pressed on the spade with his foot and made space for another marigold next to the tombstone. "Small talk and cocktails with people we don't even really remember would have been awkward." Dave felt that planting fresh flowers at Imogen's grave was a much more fitting tribute to their high school years than a twenty-five-year reunion in some restaurant's event room.

"Told you," Isaac said, as he shook out the roots of the flower and planted it in the hole Dave had just created.

Dave leaned on the spade and observed the symmetry of their planting so far. Not bad. But it was a little jarring to see how historical his late wife's grave looked. "I don't understand how she's been gone for eighteen years," he mused. "I don't feel that old."

"Well, you look it. The short haircut isn't fooling anyone. We all know you're going gray." Isaac smirked playfully.

"Thanks, buddy," Dave said. "My hair's doing better than your face. A flock of crows called. They want their feet back."

Isaac tossed a hunk of dirt onto Dave's shoes, and Dave

kicked it back at him.

"I get what you mean," Isaac said, standing up after a minute. "It hits me on our birthday. She stopped aging at twenty-four, but I just keep going." He shook his head. "Time is strange."

Dave nodded. Grief was strange, too. He and Isaac had gone through this together every step of the way, but just as Isaac didn't know what it was like to become a widower before age twenty-five and raise a daughter on his own, Dave had no idea about the pain of losing a twin. The closest he could ever come to understanding was to think about what it would be like to lose Isaac, and he didn't like to entertain that thought.

"What do you think?" Dave gestured with the spade. "Geraniums here and here?"

"If it were up to me, we'd have left them in the pots they came in," Isaac said. "It's your call, Danny Tanner."

"You're going to need to stop calling me that after the wedding, you know." Last month, Dave finally proposed to Fern, his other best friend. He was looking forward to being a husband again. No longer would he have to do all the cooking, cleaning, gardening, laundry, and parenting of his daughter, Grace, on his own. Better still, Isaac would no longer have any reason to tease him about being Mr. Mom.

"Why? It won't bother Fern. She loves you and your oven mitts and your Swiffer broom."

"Because maybe it bothers me. Honestly, are you in denial that this wedding is happening? Because you never seem to acknowledge it."

"Oh, lighten up." Isaac said, rolling his eyes. "It's just a wedding. What do you want me to do? Throw you a party?"

Dave scowled. Instead of arguing, he started to dig in the places he had indicated. When the holes were deep enough, he knelt down to place a geranium in one, and Isaac did the same in the other. Then, as they knelt side by side in the grass, he spoke.

"I want you to be my best man."

Isaac's head swiveled toward Dave. His eyes widened, and for a minute he didn't say anything. Dave stood up and waited in awkward silence. Why was this more nerve-wracking than proposing marriage? Because, he realized, he had known Fern wouldn't say no.

"Can you even have the same best man twice?" Isaac asked, also getting to his feet.

"That's the response you want to go with?" Dave shot Isaac an irritated look. "I don't think there are rules, man. You're going to need a better excuse."

Isaac sighed. "I didn't say I wouldn't do it. But ... isn't it weird? Whose best man is their dead wife's brother?"

"Mine, I was hoping. What's weird about having the same best friend for thirty years?"

"I know you don't have much family, but Fern does, right? You're marrying into her family."

"I guess ..."

"And out of my family. You can't change that by dragging me into your wedding."

"Wow." Dave stepped a little away from the gravestone, trying to adjust to everything he was hearing. He shook his head. "Seriously?"

Isaac glanced at Imogen's grave for a long moment, and Dave started to think maybe he'd forgotten he was here. Then, suddenly, Isaac said, "We are not talking about this in the cemetery. It's creepy."

"Okay, then where ...?"

Isaac clamped a hand on Dave's shoulder. "Come on. We're going bowling."

As he started collecting the gardening supplies, Dave groaned inwardly, knowing Isaac was going to wipe the floor of every single lane with him, but he didn't betray his annoyance. Honestly, it'd probably be easier to sort this out if they didn't have to look at each other while they talked. "Whatever you say. I'll see you over there. Just take a minute to think on the drive."

"Yeah, yeah," Isaac said. "Let's just get out of here."

At the bowling alley, Dave tried really hard not to imagine the toe fungus he was probably picking up from his rented shoes. Isaac spent forever choosing the exact perfect ball, determined to break his all-time scoring record. Dave grabbed the first non-pink ball he found and carried it to their lane.

"You go first," Isaac told Dave as he added their names to the scoring screen.

They each bowled several turns without talking at all, and Dave was unsure who was meant to continue the conversation. Finally, just as Dave was about to refuse to bowl again until Isaac told him what on earth his deal was, the man spoke.

"So like I was saying," began Isaac, watching as the pins he'd just bowled over were swept away, leaving just one behind. "You're starting a new family."

"I'm adding one person to my family," Dave said, but Isaac held up a hand.

"You and Fern together will be a family. And Grace. The Bennett family."

Dave nodded. "Right ..."

"And I'm not a Bennett," said Isaac. "We're not really brothers. You do know that, right? You haven't forgotten we're not actually related anymore?"

Dave laughed in surprise, but his laughter was thick with irony. "Geez, Isaac, tell me how you really feel. Who cares if we're related? You're still Grace's uncle. If I say you're family, then you're family. Nothing is going to change that."

"You will have in-laws. Maybe more kids. Who knows? But people don't stay friends with their ex-in-laws."

"Maybe people don't. But I want to." Dave had no idea how to fix this. How long had Isaac felt that their relationship was temporary and conditional? Dave had always felt it was the one thing he could count on, that Isaac would always support him in all things, as he had for practically three decades.

"Look. You married my sister, and then she died. Imogen is what we had in common. If you had gotten remarried sooner, we would have drifted apart. It only feels funny to you because it took so long. It's always been inevitable."

In that moment, Dave went from feeling sorry for Isaac for misinterpreting their friendship as something convenient, rather than a priority, to wanting to punch him square in the face.

"Where is this coming from?" He shook his head in disbelief, and he wondered how often the police got called to bowling alleys to break up fights. He was becoming increasingly angry by the second. "I met you first," he said. "We've been brothers since before I even knew you had a sister." The ridiculousness of the words leaving his mouth was not lost on him. But they were true. If anything, his marriage to Imogen came about because of their friendship, not the other way around.

"Watch out," Isaac said, picking up his ball, ready to bowl again to avoid this conversation.

Dave would normally yield to Isaac, who was taller, and bigger, but not this time. "No," he said. "You're not going to insult me and then just keep playing like nothing happened."

"Insult you? How? By stating facts?" He tried to go around Dave, but Dave stepped into his path.

"By responding to an invitation to be my best man with all this crap about how our friendship doesn't mean anything to you!"

"That's not what I said."

"Well, it's what I heard."

"I'm warning you. Move, or I'll move you."

"Go ahead," Dave said, and he stared Isaac down right up until Isaac grabbed him by the shoulders and shoved him out of the way.

Dave's bowling shoes had almost zero traction, and he slid backwards. His arms spun as he tried to maintain his balance, but it was a waste of energy. He landed hard on his tailbone against the polished wooden floor. Isaac pretended he didn't even notice, and bowled his spare.

Dave, who had been keeping his hurt feelings mostly under control, found it easier to react to a physical assault.

"What the hell is your problem?" he shouted, getting to his feet and avoiding thinking about how hard it was going to be to sit down for the next few days after that impact.

"You are my problem," Isaac said evenly.

"What, are you jealous?" Dave asked, wracking his brain

for any possible clue that would help this make sense. "Is that it? You've always said Fern was beautiful. Did you want her for yourself?"

"Don't be stupid," Isaac spat. "I don't care that you're marrying Fern."

"Clearly, you don't care about anything but you." Dave shook his head. "Bowl by yourself, Jackass." And then he did something that, even ten minutes ago, he couldn't have imagined ever doing. He walked out on Isaac, limped to the car, and went home.

That night, Fern came over, and Dave poured out the whole story.

"This doesn't make any sense to me," his fiancée said as she gave him a back rub on the couch to help with his tension headache. "You two have been so close the entire time I've known you. Even when he had that truck driving job, you still heard from him all the time."
Dave sighed, feeling utterly defeated. "He'd rather cut me out of his life than tell me what's wrong."

"Probably because it would mean telling himself first." Fern gave Dave a knowing look. "I seem to remember you having the same problem admitting your feelings for me. Neither of you is great at this stuff."

Dave groaned. He didn't like being reminded of how stupidly long it had taken him to realize he was in love with Fern. But it was possible she had a point. "So, what? You think he *is* jealous?"

"I think he liked you guys both being single. He likes showing up at your house at four in the morning to demand that you go fishing with him. He likes that when he's lonely, he can count on you to go throw axes, or shoot pool, or play mini golf, or whatever. And now he's assuming you won't want him to do those things anymore."

Dave closed his eyes and leaned into Fern's touch. "But I never said that," Dave said. "I said the opposite. I told him nothing would change."

"But that isn't true," Fern pointed out. "Maybe he'd feel better if you acknowledged that things will be different, but he'll still be a part of them."

"I don't see why he needs to hear that. Isn't that what asking him to be my best man means? It's what it meant last time."

"Last time," Fern said, "you married into his family. This time, you're essentially marrying out of it."

Dave turned to look up at Fern, flabbergasted. "How did you know that's what he said?"

"I didn't. But that's what all this brother stuff is about, isn't it? Even I refer to him as your wife's brother. When we're married, it won't make sense anymore."

"But he's also my brother!" Dave said. "Is this what fighting with your sister feels like? Honestly, being an only child didn't prepare me for this stuff."

"Just give him some time," Fern said, kissing Dave's cheek. "He'll realize he's wrong. My sister always does."

Dave really wanted Fern to be right, but he had his doubts. Those doubts dissipated around midnight. Fern went home at ten, and Dave went to bed shortly thereafter, falling asleep reading a John Grisham novel with the bedside lamp still burning. When he was startled from slumber by the doorbell, he jumped and dumped his hardcover book onto the floor, then jumped again in response to that sound.

By the time he got into a robe and went down the stairs,

noting with every step how much his tailbone ached, Isaac was already letting himself in.

"Come to finish me off?" Dave said as Isaac stepped over the threshold. "I'm still able to walk."

Isaac closed the door, then fixed his eyes on Dave. "I came to say I'll be your best man."

Dave snorted a sardonic laugh. "You think the offer still stands after the way you treated me?"

"I do, actually," Isaac said.

"That's how pathetic I am, huh?"

"Not pathetic," Isaac said, looking down, his voice very soft. "Loyal."

"You reached the limit of my loyalty when you put your hands on me." Dave was still in shock over that. That was not normally how they communicated at all. The occasional playful punch, sure, but not what had happened today. That was almost more hurtful than the refusal to be in his wedding.

"I said I'm sorry."

"You didn't, actually."

"Well, I am. Of course I am."

"Of course?" Dave crossed his arms, feeling defensive even as he saw the sincerity in Isaac's eyes.

"I didn't mean for you to actually fall over," Isaac said, smirking. "I forget how weak you are."

"Not helping, man," Dave said. "Do I need to ask you to leave?" He put his hand on the doorknob, ready to throw him out.

Isaac held up his hands in surrender. "I'm joking. Trying to lighten the mood. You know me."

"I thought this might be one thing you'd actually take seriously. Stupid me." He crossed to the couch and sat down. So much for Fern's back rub. All that tension was coming right back.

"Dave, come on."

"No, you come on!" Dave raised his voice. "I don't know if you've noticed, but my circle is pretty small. My daughter, who is away at college, my future wife, and my best friend. And today you tried to tell me one of those doesn't exist."

"I didn't mean it, all right?" Isaac sounded irritated, but Dave suspected it was directed mainly at himself.

"Why do you want to be my best man?" Dave demanded.

Isaac wandered over from the doorway and took a seat on the opposite end of the couch from Dave. "Because you asked me," he said.

"Not good enough," Dave said, frowning.

"Fine," Isaac said. "It's because, of the two of us, I know what it's like to have a sibling, and it's exactly like this. I don't want to lose that a second time. It's not like my life is so full of long-term relationships, either."

Dave felt a few tendrils of anxiety loosen in his body. "Fern thinks you need to hear me say that we'll still be friends even if everything changes. Is that the problem?"

"Well, it'd probably be easier to swallow than the rosy b.s. you were giving me about nothing changing. It's like you think I'm stupid."

"Sometimes you are," Dave argued. "Do you honestly think, after nearly thirty years, I'm just going to ditch you? If I was going to do that, I'd have done it by now. Many times." Dave glanced at Isaac and saw that he was laughing knowingly. "But it's not stupid to put faith in our friendship.

Best friends, brothers-in-law, honorary brothers—whatever the title is, it's all the same thing."

"Hey," said Isaac, "none of this honorary stuff." He stuck out his hand. "Okay? Real brothers."

"Then none of this handshake stuff." Dave opened his arms for a hug. Isaac made a big show of pretending he didn't want to hug him, but then he gave in.

"We should have just gone to the reunion," Isaac joked. "This was way more awkward than telling strangers I work for a pest control company."

"Seriously," said Dave, clapping Isaac on the back, then pulling away from the hug. "Though if you'd shoved me at the reunion, someone would have taken a picture. That would have sucked."

"Are you actually hurt? I didn't push that hard."

"Just bruised," said Dave, and he realized this applied to his physical and emotional injuries. He'd get over both. "How about you?"

"Well, I guess it's a pretty big deal to be a guy's best man twice," Isaac said. "I should probably trust the guy who has stuck by me for thirty years when I'm such a jerk."

"Probably," Dave agreed. "Imogen isn't the reason we're friends, you idiot. Losing her brought us closer, but our friendship isn't about her."

"I know that," Isaac said. "I just ... needed to hear it, I guess. I do actually care about something other than myself. I just don't like talking about it."

"No kidding," Dave commented. "But if you can't talk about your feelings, that might explain the lack of long-term relationships. You could probably settle down, too, if you tried."

"Well, maybe I'll meet somebody at your wedding. Fern probably has hot friends, right?"

"Probably. But you need to learn to say what you feel. Not everyone has had thirty years of practice figuring you out."

"I'll work on it, all right?" Isaac said. "And when I get married, you can be my best man."

"I'll think about it," Dave said, but he started laughing right away, proving he didn't mean it.

"Are we good now?" Isaac asked.

"As long as you promise to keep your hands to yourself, we're good," Dave said. "Do you want to hang out and play cards for a bit?"

"In the middle of the night? That's not like you. Don't you need ten-point-five hours of beauty sleep every night?"

Dave waved a hand. "It's the weekend. It's fine. And maybe I'd like some proof that we can do something together without coming to blows." More than that, Dave wanted to prove to Isaac that he would still make time for him, even at odd hours of the night, if that's what was necessary.

"Well, then we'd better not play Uno," Isaac said. "You know how you get when I make you draw four."

Dave laughed. That was true. He took draw-four cards personally every time. "Definitely not Spades," he said. "We've had enough of that for one day. Old Maid?"

"Is that another dig about me being single?"

"Maybe," Dave said.

"Well, help me out at the wedding, then."

"I can do my best to play wingman, as long as playing groom comes first." Dave turned to look at Isaac, realizing he'd just summed up this entire day's conversation in one pithy phrase. Being a husband didn't mean he couldn't still be a friend. "Okay? I can do both."

"Yeah," Isaac said, opening two decks of cards from the drawer in the coffee table. "Okay." Then he dealt out all the cards and started a game of rummy, which they played, following their own rules perfected over many years, until the sun came up.

IN THE BRANCHES OF YGGDRASIL
Seren J.H. Wolfe

like serendipity, we met at the Crossroads,
in between the tempest of the present
and the ashes of a false future.
the Fates, my sister, entwined us readily,
our bond forged
in the welcoming, rich grounds of Aïdes.
we are daughters of Magick and Night,
the bridge that shepherds hearts
weavers of stories from silk and burlap.

our mettle has been challenged
by villains aplenty —
of monsters born from draconian lineage
of death sentences disguised as glory
of man wearing the masks of changelings.
of Pandora's Box, we have triumphed!

and still more will we conquer

afore our journeys must wind down;
crimson lips our armour, iron words our weapons
laid down for the next generation
of witches.

shieldmaiden to queen,
goddess to goddess,
this I promise thee:
in the branches of my ash tree,
you will always find solace.
in the storms of absence and
the absolute,
you will always have safe harbour
on my docks.
in the triumphs you proclamate,
you will always find fierce pride
in my words.
and when you can only taste tears,
you will always find my sunshine
you only need to call.

I'm Happy for You
Abrigail Julian
I say I'm happy for you
And I mean it,
Even though there's tears in my eyes.
My silence is for you,
Since you seem to prefer it,
But it hurts me more each time.

So many little things
I would ask or say,
But I don't want to lose my friend.
Not that it matters anyway,
The things that I think,
The pain of loving you is worth it.

You make me better,
So even if you go,
I'm not a mosaic of scars left behind.
The little things before
That scarred me and hurt,
You touched each one unbeknownst.

My healing friend,
I sorrow in silence,
Because the pain is void of sting.
You still love me
In your own easy way.
You just don't need me the same.

I miss you, it's true;
No lie, no secret.
If I could, I'd never let you go.
I love you too much,
For you, mainly, I do.
But to love you for me? Pure vanity.

Your silence hurts,
But you don't mean it.
At least you're honest, I'll give you that much.
I'm here for you,
To love and support,
And I still will be when you want me again.

LUMINOUS RAGE
Cassandra Hamm

Rhea was going to murder this batch of dough. Rest in peace, loaf.

She blew out a long breath, her hands resting in the sticky mixture. Now, inhale—shouldn't the scent of spice and cinnamon soothe her? The soft crackling of the fire in the oven, the knitted throws on a nearby chair—all cozy and warm and *Not. Helping.* She'd almost rather be outside in the near-blizzard conditions. At least the biting wind understood her rage.

Rhea dropped her mental walls enough for telepathic transmissions to enter through their respective bonds. A message was already forming in her head, something about how baked goods were going to be the death of her, when she realized who she was about to send it to.

Addien. The whole reason she was rage-baking in the first place.

Rhea folded the dough into itself, over and over. She could almost hear Addien laughing at her for even attempting a loaf by herself, asking if she was trying to make a weapon with how burnt and crunchy it was going to be. A flash of longing, quickly replaced by fury.

Fury was good. Fury was fuel.

A transmission slipped over Rhea's mental walls, accompanied by a stab of pain. **I'm sorry,** Addien said through their broken bond. **I miss you.**

Rhea yanked her walls back up, hands fisting in the dough.

It'd been months since she'd heard her best friend's voice in her head. Once, sending thoughts back and forth had been as easy as breathing. Now, the crack in their telepathic bond turned every transmission into a pinprick of pain, though maybe that was the wrong word. More like being jabbed with a sharp stick.

At least the stick-jabbing went both ways, afflicting both sender and receiver, so Addien was experiencing her own flash of pain right now. If only some of that pain could be inflicted on Sylas too.

Rhea swallowed hard, remembering the wrongness of Sylas' presence inside her mind, like a touch she hadn't asked for.

No. She would *not* think about that. She would think about dough and rage and Addien but never, never Sylas.

Wintry wind howled outside the hut as Rhea shoved the thoughts to the back of her mind. She threw herself back into kneading the shaggy mixture, pushing, pressing, folding. Maybe she could add "punching" to the list. The act might ruin the bread, but at least she could expel some of the rage burning in her chest like her own miniature oven.

A thought tendril prodded at Rhea's mental defenses. She stiffened, nails digging into the dough.

"Rhea Mae!" Granny Jestine's voice rang out through the hut. "Don't you dare close your mind to me!"

Rhea immediately lowered her walls. **Sorry, Granny. I thought you were someone else.**

Miss Addien? Granny Jestine drawled through their telepathic connection.

Yes. Rhea pushed a lock of hair, pale enough to blend with the snow, out of her face and returned to kneading. The dough had definitely thickened, but was it thick enough? She'd never done much baking. It just seemed like such a good way to release her feelings. Beat up some dough. Eat some bread. Win win.

Granny Jestine shuffled into the kitchen, a blanket layered over her fur-lined coat and her white hair stuffed into a knit cap. She looked a bit like a fluffy snow-bison trundling about.

Rhea looked at her dough, then at her granny, suddenly feeling judged, even though Granny Jestine hadn't said a word about the baking.

Granny Jestine's red eyes narrowed. **And have you answered Addien?** she asked through their link, despite their proximity. There was just something more intimate about speaking inside one's head, a sign of trust and care.

She and Addien used to talk inside their heads every moment of the day.

Have you? Granny Jestine prodded.

No. Rhea's arms ached. Was this normal? She could ask her granny, but that would be admitting defeat.

She's all alone, you know, Granny Jestine transmitted.

She's not alone. She has Sylas. Even just thinking his name made Rhea's heart race.

Granny Jestine harrumphed. Rhea could sense the disapproval even from that one, drawn-out sound.

What did Granny Jestine want her to do? Allow Addien back into her life and, therefore, Sylas? Absolutely not.

I was like your friend, once, Granny Jestine sent. **It's a lonely place to be.**

Right. Before Granny Jestine met Rhea's grandfather, Granny had bonded with a cruel, controlling boy. Rhea couldn't imagine her granny falling for someone like that, but she hadn't imagined Addien doing so either. Maybe no one ever thought they would.

Another transmission from Addien. **I wish you were here, Rhea. You could help me sort out my thoughts.**

Like Addien would even listen to her. She hadn't listened before, not when Rhea tried to tell her how Sylas had broken into her head. Past Addien's voice rang in Rhea's mind—*"He would never do that. The only head he wants to be inside is mine. Get over yourself, Rhea."*

The coals sparked and throbbed inside Rhea.

Granny Jestine hovered over Rhea's shoulder. "What are you doing to that poor dough?" Her speaking voice was so much frailer than her mental one.

"Kneading it." Wasn't that what one was supposed to do with dough?

"You've kneaded it enough," Granny Jestine said. "Can't you see how smooth it is?"

Well ... now that Granny Jestine mentioned it ... Rhea formed the dough into a ball. Very ... doughy. Rhea poked the substance experimentally. Her finger left an impression only for a moment as it popped back into shape. Odd.

"You'll make it too tough, working it too hard." Granny Jestine clucked her tongue. "Good thing I saw. Without me, you'd be baking a rock."

Maybe I could purposely bake a rock-hard loaf and throw it at Sylas' head. But that would require seeing Sylas again. With a faint shudder, Rhea set the dough onto a cooking stone and began lifting it.

I think … maybe you were right about Sylas, Addien transmitted.

Rhea dropped the stone. It clattered to the table, knocking the dough askew.

Was Sylas hurting Addien? Or had she simply opened her eyes to what he truly was? Was she ready to leave him?

You're mad at her, remember? Rhea's thoughts whispered.

But she couldn't help herself. Concerned Best Friend Mode had reemerged. If Sylas hurt Addien … The coals flared hotter.

What's she saying, Rhea? Granny Jestine asked.

Rhea shook herself out of her trance and eyed the cooking stone, wondering if she'd manage it better this time.

Rhea Mae. Granny Jestine propped her hands on her hips. A strand of white hair stuck out from her cap, almost like an icicle.

She's just trying to get me to trust her again. Rhea flattened her hands on the table. **None of it is real.**

But what if it was? Addien had to be so scared, realizing that her lover was a monster, not knowing how to break free—

She's the reason Sylas found you in the first place! She told him about the cave.

That in itself was another betrayal. The bioluminescent cavern was *theirs*—Rhea and Addien's secret spot. As kids, they'd been exploring the system of tunnels outside the village and stumbled into a glowing offshoot. For years, they'd kept the secret, but then Sylas came along and Addien just *had* to tell him.

Now Sylas had ruined the cave.

I know she hurt you. Granny Jestine picked up the stone, balancing the dough. **And you have a right to be mad. I hope she grovels real good. But she isn't the real enemy here and you know it.**

Into the oven the dough went, ready to rise. Rhea's chest was tight and hot, and her eyes were stinging, and she should say something, anything, but all she could think was, *What if Addien needs me and I'm not there?*

But Addien and Sylas were a unit, and Rhea couldn't do it. Couldn't face Sylas again. It was bad enough seeing him throughout the village, feeling his violent pressure on her mental walls.

I have to go, Addien said. **He's coming.**

The words knocked something loose in Rhea. What if Sylas was forcing his way into Addien's head like he'd done to Rhea? What if he listened to her thoughts and feelings and punished her for anything he didn't like? He'd already isolated her from the people who loved her. What if he'd escalated into violence?

Addien? Rhea transmitted through the broken bond. She felt the impact of the word against Addien's wall. Still, she tried again. **Addien, I need to see you. Alone.**

The barrier shifted, allowing messages inside. Rhea's heart leapt. **Our cave, tonight? Please?**

No answer, but the transmission went through. Maybe Addien couldn't answer because of Sylas.

What if Sylas had heard Rhea's transmission? Unlikely but still possible. Addien and Rhea had grown accustomed to keeping their personal transmissions secret from the rest of the world, partitioning their minds and keeping a space only for them. But Sylas had breached Rhea's mind. He might've breached Addien's too.

Alone, Rhea added. **Moonhigh.**

Addien's mind closed. Rhea tried sending a few more transmissions, but the barrier was firmly in place. Something sour twisted her stomach. She knew it was probably because of the possibility of Sylas overhearing, but something in her wondered if she'd lost the chance to reconcile with Addien.

"Well? Did you talk to her?" Granny Jestine asked.

Rhea jumped. She'd almost forgotten she was in the kitchen, drying dough crusting her hands. She met her granny's knowing blood-red eyes. "Not exactly, but we're going to later."

Granny Jestine let out a satisfied grunt. "See that you do."

Tonight, Rhea would go to their cavern and wait. Maybe for hours. Maybe for minutes. And maybe, maybe, Addien would show up.

With a sigh, Rhea stoked the fire in the oven and felt the coals in her chest die, just a little.

Apparitions of Sylas haunted the cave. Red eyes seemed to watch Rhea as she moved through the icy tunnels. His tall, lanky silhouette appeared out of the corner of her eye, but when she turned her head, it was gone, just a trick of the ice. When she finally entered the cavern, she could've sworn she saw his mocking smile reflected in the icy walls.

Rhea clutched the newly-baked loaf in her gloved hands, her head whipping around at another glimpse of tied-back white hair. He wasn't here. She knew that. But her body didn't. Her heart pounded an incessant rhythm in her chest, *tha-thump, tha-thump,* as she glanced back at the cavern entrance again, then once more. Her fur-lined hood seemed a cocoon of sorts, though she knew it wouldn't actually protect her mind.

Nothing could protect her mind, not from people who wanted to get inside it. Her efforts weren't enough. She'd thought she had the strongest mental defenses in all of Aelwyd and she'd still failed.

Light glimmered over her head, and she looked up, allowing herself to relax her watchful countenance for just a moment. Pale blues and greens and purples danced through the ice in iridescent light, courtesy of the bioluminescent creatures living inside. Addien always called it magic. Rhea's eyes welled up as she tracked the erratic movements.

He'd corrupted this place. This beautiful, beautiful place. How could she ever reclaim it as her own?

At a gentle pressure on her mental walls, Rhea whipped around. Her hand tightened around the bread before she heard Granny Jestine's voice in her head—not an actual transmission, just a specter—*Don't you dare damage that loaf, Rhea Mae!*

What if it was Sylas? What if—?

"Rhea?"

It was only Addien, testing their connection. Rhea inhaled deeply, trying to relax her shoulders. "Yes. Me." She really should've chosen another location.

A tall, slender shadow moved down the tunnel. The bioluminescence bounced off her coat, hiding her face, but Rhea recognized the way she moved—quick and purposeful. "I thought maybe you'd already left. I'm glad you're—" Addien shook her head. Her hood dislodged, falling back to reveal snow-white waves of hair.

Rhea suddenly found she couldn't speak. Months of silence, and now her best friend was in front of her and—what was supposed to do? Say? This was all wrong—they weren't supposed to be talking *aloud*. They'd always been in and out of each other's thoughts, transmitting effortlessly about anything and everything.

But Rhea didn't want to feel jabbing pain every time she tried to talk. Not when there were so many things that needed to be said.

Of course, all those things had escaped Rhea's brain.

"I brought bread," she said stupidly, holding out the loaf, which, thanks to Granny Jestine, was passable. One might even call it vaguely fluffy.

"Oh, thanks." Addien was close enough that Rhea could see her face—a faint smile, freckles dotting her pale skin, red-rimmed eyes. It was the only part of her skin Rhea could see—everything else was covered in fabric—but what if her winter gear was hiding bruises? She could picture Sylas transferring his mental violence to physical.

Addien wasn't taking the bread. Was Rhea supposed to keep holding onto it? Should she force Addien to take the bread? This was all a stupid idea. She never should've come here—

Rhea. A transmission full of pain and hope. Then Addien was throwing her arms around Rhea, crushing the loaf between them. **I missed you.**

Rhea wondered if she could easily extract her arms to hug

Addien back and how that would work with the whole bread thing. Or if she should even be hugging Addien in the first place. The whole jabbing-with-a-sharp-stick thing was still quite tempting.

Addien pulled back, her face a question. Rhea didn't let go of the bread, which was quite squished but still edible. She hoped. "Bread," she said.

Addien barked out a laugh, tears moving in a steady stream down her cheeks. "Oh, I guess I forgot it was there. Sorry. I'm just so glad to have you back."

Wait. Hold on. Addien didn't *have Rhea back*. Not yet. Not when she hadn't even really apologized, unless one counted the transmission from earlier that Rhea hadn't even acknowledged.

Suddenly wary, Rhea peered behind Addien. The cavern flickered with gentle blue-green light, not enough to banish the shadows. "Sylas isn't here, is he?"

Addien flinched, taking a step back. "Of course he isn't."

Rhea folded her arms over her chest. Her nose was starting to run, not from tears, from the cold. She waited for an explanation, an apology, *something*, but the only sound was the soft creaking of ice.

She knew this wasn't what she was here for. She was supposed to be helping Addien. But ... maybe this needed to be resolved first.

Addien's crimson eyes shimmered with unshed tears. "I'm so sorry I didn't believe you, Rhea. He broke into your mind and I sided with *him*."

Rhea's breath hitched. Memories danced through her mind like the bioluminescence dancing through the ice—a boy lit by purples and blues, his unmovable form blocking the exit, his mind bearing down upon hers. A slight chink in her walls.

Get out, she'd screamed. *Get out of my head.*

But Sylas never listened.

"I was so stupid, Rhea. I can't believe I—I'm so sorry."

Rhea's nails dug into the crushed loaf. Was it real? Was Addien actually sorry? And even if she was ... would it make up for the pain of the past few months?

She remembered inviting Addien to her hut when Granny Jestine was away, how the words had stuck in her throat as she'd told Addien what Sylas had done. She remembered Addien's disbelieving laugh, the way it had sliced through her. *"I know you're jealous of our bond, but really? Lying about Sylas so you can be my closest friend again?"*

She remembered the way the coals inside her chest had burst through her ribcage, how her bond with Addien had shuddered and cracked. A stabbing pain in her side. Addien gasping, her hand flying to her heart.

"I shouldn't have told him about this place. If I hadn't ..." Bluish green reflected off Addien's hair, forming a halo. "And then I ... I should've believed you."

Yes. You should've. Rhea didn't send the thought, but it burned inside her, pounding to the rhythm of her heartbeat.

"You tried to warn me and I just ..." Addien hugged her arms to her chest, her shoulders hunching. "I wish I'd listened."

Rhea squeezed her eyes shut, fighting tears. How was it possible to ache and rage at the same time? To need both reconciliation and retaliation?

She knew what Addien wanted—for Rhea to say it was all right and they could go back to being the way they were.

But Rhea wasn't sure she *could*. Not yet.

"He's inside my head all the time, Rhea," Addien whispered.

Rhea's blood turned as frigid as the cavern itself. She knew the feel of Sylas inside her head—the wrongness, the pain, the inevitability. And that had only been for a few minutes.

She didn't care how dangerous he was. *No one* treated her best friend like that.

"I know I have no right to ask you for help. But I have to get out." Addien's words came quicker, more frantic. "I'm going crazy, Rhea. There's nowhere I can go to get away from him. He's watching everything I do, everything I say, every *thought* I have, and I just—I can't do it anymore."

All of Rhea's senses snapped to alertness. If Sylas was constantly inside Addien's head, what if he was watching Addien right now? How far away did she have to be for his control on her to break? Or, worse, what if he'd *followed* her?

"Addien," Rhea said carefully. "Do you think he might be able to hear what you're saying right now?"

"I don't—I mean, he can't feel me this far away."

Rhea exhaled, body relaxing. So, then, what to do about getting Addien away from Sylas? She knew leaving wouldn't be simple, not when Sylas was, well, Sylas.

"What if you severed your bond?" Rhea asked. Granny Jestine had cut hers with the boy she didn't like to talk about. *"It was a knife stabbing into my torso, slicing away a part of me,"* she'd said. *"I couldn't move for what seemed like hours. But it was worth it, Rhea Mae."*

Addien shook her head vigorously. "Oh, no, I couldn't. He'd just get angrier."

"Everything makes him angry." Rhea gestured wildly at nothing. "You have to do *something*, Addie!"

Addien's shoulders shook. She wiped at her dripping nose with a gloved hand.

Everything Rhea said made it worse. But what was she supposed to do? Tell Addien to *stay* with him?

"You could tell the council," Rhea said. "What he's doing, that's a telepathic violation. They could throw him in prison."

Addien stilled, her crimson eyes wide and terrified. "I couldn't ... I mean, he's my lover. They would just say it's normal for lovers to have intimate bonds."

"Not that kind of intimate. Breaking into people's minds without their permission is illegal. You could get him locked away, Addie. ..... Then he couldn't bother you." *Or me*, Rhea thought.

"I mean ... maybe." Addien's shoulders curled in, making her tall frame appear small.

Rhea tapped her chin with a gloved hand. That could work. That is, if the council even listened to Addien.

"Maybe ... if you spoke up with me," Addien said. "Maybe they'd believe it if there was more than one person speaking up."

Rhea's limbs felt like blocks of ice. Speaking up would mean *talking* about it. Not just talking about it, but telling *strangers*. Having her every reaction, her every trauma, picked apart for flaws. Bile rose in her throat. "I ... I can't," she whispered.

"But you have to!" Addien gripped Rhea's hand, freeing it from the loaf. "They won't believe me on my own, Rhea. *Please*."

Rhea stared at the girl who was once her best friend and maybe still was. Her heart pounded in her throat. *Anything but that,* she wanted to scream. Because if the council believed Sylas ...

Addien let out a sudden cry, clutching her head. Rhea yanked her mental walls up, tightening every imagined brick, filling in every crack. Slowly, she turned.

He wasn't an apparition. He was *here.*

Sylas stepped into the cave. The bioluminescent glow illuminated his features—red eyes glittering in ghost-pale skin; straight, thin nose; hollowed out cheeks. His hood fell against his shoulders, revealing tied-back, straight white hair. He was a blizzard in human form, beautiful and dangerous and easy to get lost in.

Rhea's breaths came in short gasps. She took one step back, then another.

"I should've known you would be trouble, Rhea," Sylas said in his low, pleasant voice.

Addien whimpered, her back pressed against the wall. Tears trickled down her pale cheeks.

"Trying to convince my lover to leave me?" He shook his head. Greenish light reflected off his hair, a deep contrast to his red eyes. "She's *mine,* and nothing you do will change that."

She doesn't belong to you, Rhea thought. *She doesn't belong to anyone.* But her mouth wouldn't form the words.

Sylas gestured a gloved hand toward the twitching Addien. "Her walls are so easy to knock down," he said. "Thin as parchment. Yours, though—that was a challenge. One I relish." He grinned.

Then a thought tendril was stabbing at Rhea's walls,

pressing at their edges, searching for a crack. *Jab. Jab. Jab.*

Rhea squeezed her eyes shut, envisioning her walls, sleek and icy and unbroken. She would not break. Not again.

But that thought sent a shudder through her walls. Even ice could shatter.

"I'm—I'm not leaving you, Sylas." Addien struggled to stand upright. Her face looked haggard, her eyes haunted in the wake of his mental assault. "I love you, Sylas. I wouldn't—" She faltered.

The words nearly broke Rhea's concentration. They couldn't be true. Addien had just said she couldn't stay with Sylas anymore and she'd report him for his crimes. She had to be lying, but what if she wasn't? What if she'd decided she wanted to stay with Sylas?

"You're right," Sylas said. "You're not leaving. You and I, we belong together."

They didn't *belong together*—a ridiculous, romantic sentiment that stripped away all choice from Addien, made her the villain if she decided to separate from him. No. Addien was whole all on her own.

Rhea's mind raced. She couldn't hold up against his assault forever—she knew that painfully well. Yes, she and Addien outnumbered Sylas, but his mental forces were too strong.... He could incapacitate Addien within moments and then come back for Rhea.

They had to do something to hurt him. Truly hurt him. Give them a chance to run. They knew the tunnels better than he did; they could lose him and then report him to the council. *Both* of them.

"*I couldn't move for hours.*" Granny Jestine's words echoed in Rhea's ears. Her pulse quickened. Bond severing—that was it! If Addien severed her bond with Sylas, it might incapacitate her, but it would also incapacitate Sylas.

But if Rhea told Addien aloud, Sylas would turn his assault back to Addien, and she wouldn't get the chance to break the bond. No, Rhea had to keep his attention. But how could she communicate to Addien what she needed to do without dropping her walls? And even if she *did* open her mind for communication with Addien, Sylas might hear what she'd said.

This means he'll get inside your head.

Rhea's chest tightened, her eyes stinging. He was going to get inside anyway. This time, she would choose the situation.

"Aren't you going to beg?" Sylas grinned.

A tremor ran through her walls. Sylas' mind pressed against them harder, fiercer.

"Stop, Sylas!" Addien cried. "You're hurting her!"

The pressure eased. Sylas turned toward Addien.

Addien's scream ripped through Rhea, straight to her core. Rhea didn't think. She just threw the loaf straight at Sylas' head. It thudded against his perfect jawline, and he let out a surprised *oof*. Addien gasped, slumping against the glowing tunnel wall.

Rhea dropped her walls and sent a transmission to Addien, barely noticing the pain. *Sever the bond!*

Addien's wide eyes met Rhea's. Rhea tried to pull her walls back up, but Sylas had already slid inside. He felt like ice, cold and sharp, pricking at every exposed thought.

Go ahead, he said. **Beg me to leave.**

Rhea clutched her head, her fingers tearing through her

pale hair. She felt violated, sick, her entire being compromised by this one foul presence. It was just like before, his mind inside hers, trying to force his will upon her, to see her innermost thoughts and learn her secrets.

You know you wanted this, he said.

She slumped to the ground, convulsing. A scream split the air—hers this time, tearing from her throat without her permission.

"Rhea!" Addien cried, rushing toward her. Sylas caught Addien in his arms, locking her against his chest as she thrashed and kicked. His distraction eased the pressure enough for Rhea to form a coherent thought—*Form a shield with a word. Keep focusing on it. The unwanted person won't be able to penetrate it.*

She chose a word: *Rage. Rage. Rage.* It simmered inside her, ever-present, ever building with every violation Sylas made, every time Addien pushed her away in favor of Sylas, every way Sylas hurt her best friend. The coals inside her burned ever hotter. *Rage unending.*

She felt Sylas pushing against the word, unable to reach any other part of her mind because this was all she was thinking about, this was the only thing she would *ever* think about, so he might as well just leave—

Addien broke free from Sylas' grip and dashed into an icy crevice. Rhea's concentration slipped, and Sylas poured back inside. Not even the burning rage inside could keep his icy presence out.

"Do it, Addie!" Rhea screamed, her voice echoing through the tunnel. She tried to form the mental block again, but words and thoughts slipped away. Her eyes landed on a flash of purple sweeping across the floor.

Her mind focused enough to say, *Light. Light. Light.* She gazed at the violet trail as it changed to a deep indigo. Pure and beautiful, too pure for the likes of Sylas. She chanted the word in her head, filling her mind with the word and the concept and the radiance dancing through the ice. *Light. Light.*

Twin screams split the air—one high pitched, the other low and guttural. Sylas collapsed, his presence receding from Rhea's mind. Her walls shot back up, rigid and full of fire. *How dare you,* she wanted to scream. Not just scream—punch and kick and throttle, even though her blows would do nothing against him. Chest heaving, she tried to stand, but her legs gave out.

Addien. Was she all right? That had been *her* scream too. Grunting, Rhea crawled toward the crevice, knees and mittens scrabbling for purchase on the slick floor. Addien lay inside, prone, her face snow-pale. Rhea shook her gently. Addien let out a soft moan, her unfocused eyes on the glowing walls.

"I'm so proud of you," Rhea whispered, her breath fogging the air. "You did it. You severed the bond."

Addien just shivered.

Rhea tugged on Addien's arm, wishing she was tall and strong like her friend, but she'd gotten her granny's diminutive frame. **Get up, Addie,** she transmitted. **We need to leave before he recovers.**

Addien stirred weakly, her body trembling. Rhea hauled on Addien's arm, and finally Addien staggered to her feet, catching herself against the wall. She let out ragged, wheezing gasps.

"I know it hurts," Rhea said. "But we have to go."

Help ... me? Addien's mental voice was a croak.

Rhea squeezed Addien's elbow. "Always." She pulled Addien through the cavern and down the tunnel, leaving a groaning Sylas far behind.

"Don't you worry, Miss Addien." Granny Jestine gave Addien's shoulder a pat. "The pain will fade soon enough. Won't really go away, not fully, but you'll be able to breathe without wanting to die."

Addien was curled up in a wooden chair, huddled in one of Granny Jestine's knitted blankets. Her cheeks had regained some color, but her eyes were red-rimmed, making the bloody irises stand out.

Rhea perched on the edge of her own chair, wishing there was something she could do, but as usual, Granny Jestine had everything covered.

"Are you going to report that boy?" Granny Jestine's voice softened.

Addien looked at Rhea.

Rhea swallowed. Breathed. Then, "Yes. We are."

Fresh tears sheened Addien's eyes. She reached out and squeezed Rhea's hand hard.

"I wish I'd reported mine." Granny Jestine leaned heavily on the table, her face lined with weariness. "Understand, they might not believe you, but you might spare other girls from your fate."

Addien wiped at her nose and nodded.

Rhea stared at the crackling fire. She hadn't been strong enough to keep Sylas out. Would she be strong enough to withstand scrutiny when they reported him? Would Addien? Addien herself had pointed out that people were going to say she had asked for Sylas to be in her mind, that her consent to have a bond with him was reason enough for him to invade.

But they had to try. For those other girls Sylas would inevitably come into contact with.

"Proud of you girls." Granny Jestine sniffed loudly, then bustled back toward the stove, where a new loaf was rising.

Sorry about your bread, Addien said.

It was a good way for it to go, Rhea said.

The bond wasn't fully healed. Rhea wasn't sure it ever would be. But the pain had lessened, and that was something.

Addien squeezed Rhea's hand. **I don't know what I'd do without you, Rhea.**

Rhea swallowed the sudden lump in her throat. **Probably fall off a cliff somewhere.**

Addien's laugh filled the hut, as warm as freshly baked bread.

A LETTER FROM A BROKEN SOUL

Lorelei R. Jensen

To my best friend,
If the world asked for me to choose
Between you and I,
I would choose you every time
Because what is a world without you in it?
After all, the days are far brighter,
And life is much lighter
With you by my side.
A candle in the pitch dark of night
Can hardly compare
To the light you bring to my life.
I'm in awe that someone like you
Would be willing to pour your energy
Into someone as messed up as me.
It has been my pleasure
To see you at your best,
And it's been my honor,
To be there at your worst.

And it's been the greatest privilege
To have you at mine.
If by chance, we must go our separate ways,
My heart will always have a special place for you.
I owe you more than words can express.
You changed me into a better person.
Your love and friendship has reached
The deepest part of my soul,
And I am eternally grateful.
With every fiber of my being,
I wish you happiness,
And with every part of my soul,
I pray that you'll achieve your dreams.
So know,
That if the world asked for me to choose,
Between you and me,
I will always choose you.
Because a me without you
Is no longer me.
Love,
The broken soul you changed
Best Friends
Jenni Sauer
I've loved you my whole life...
Except we didn't meet
Until a few years ago
But loving you
Is such an integral part of my life
That I've forgotten what it feels like

To not know you
Your fingerprints on my heart
So permanent
That my mind whispers of an alternate reality
A parallel timeline
Where we were shared girlhood
Where we ran barefoot and scraped our knees
Where we braided each others hair
And played with each other's dolls
Where we swapped books
And shared inside jokes and made memories
Pinky promises and jump ropes
Dandelion puffs and mud pies and leafy brews
Where we get a little older together
And those dark years are a little less dark
We talk in hushed tones
About trauma and our moms and questions
We don't know who to ask
—or even if we should—
I've always had a vivid imagination
My favorite maladaptive daydream
Is the one
Where Little Me knew Little You

I've loved you my whole life ...
Even if I didn't know it was you
My heart was waiting to meet

WHO YOU COULD'VE BEEN
Effie Joe Stock

Fingers that trail effortlessly across strings, across keys, memorizing each note even though you've only just begun. The music springs from your soul. You see it in the way the grass moves under the summer breeze, you feel it when you canter down the stairs. It presses against you in the darkness of the night and settles in your soul like the dew of morning. When you find the time to sit at the bench, fingers trailing keys, or to hold the wood between your hands, swaying in a patch of light as fingers trail strings, it comes easily. You let go and it springs forth like a fountain.

Arms that wrap around another, holding them close, simply listening, understanding, living only in the life of the person who you hold. Your mind is clear as you nod and smile, tears glistening in your eyes because yes, you've felt that way too. You know what that pain is like. But even more, you know the light will come. And you tell them this, assure them this, that the morning will dawn again, and they will have a new beginning. And when they need a tissue, you've already got one in hand, pushing a glass of water to them, whispering to stay hydrated, to blow their nose. You wrap a blanket and your warm arms around them, and you let their sorrow cling to your heart as your hope to clings to theirs.

Smiles that shine brighter than the stars. You glow in the golden hour of the sunset—that moment of majestic honey as the light hangs just over the tree tops and everything is all honey and gold and warm. "Stand there. Touch your face like this," you say, praising the way the light hits my brown curls. "Like warm embers, burning with love in the heart of a thousand lovers." You have such a way with words. I don't believe your descriptions until I'm on the other side of the lenses, staring at the image of me you took. It doesn't look like me. It's something ... wholly other. So much more beautiful. "It's the way I see you," you say. And you smile again, and I wish I could capture the way I see you. Because the sun has hit your eyes, and I'm drowning in their icy waves, seeing the flashes of that majestic honey that now hang their blue instead of the sky's. But I haven't the way with the camera like you do. I never take the picture. The moment is lost. The sun has set. You never see yourself the way I see you.

Because I only saw the way you should have been.

But now I can't see you at all. I only see what's left—a few etches in cold stone. It's quiet here. Nothing close to what it once was like. Or rather ... what it should have been ... if only ...

A tear rolls down my cheek as I kneel in the still freshly churned dirt. A small flower has sprung up next to the still monument that bears your name. You have something to say about this flower, springing up with color, with joy in a place so forlorn, so full of sorrow.

But I can't hear you.

Because a darkness had always clouded your music, and stopped it from springing from your lips and fingers. You were bursting to create, but slowly the weight of that emotion grew too much to bear and it rotted inside of you, unable to escape, to be free. The sorrow that lived in your heart was too great to look past. You saw others hurting. You wanted to reach to them, but the only body your arms ever held was your own as you rocked back and forth, unable to stop the shaking, or the tears that burned your eyes.

My words were not enough. My pictures were not enough. You could never see what I saw in you. What I knew you were meant to be. No lens could capture it. No words could make you understand.

We had so many plans. "Let's go see this. Let's go there. Let's do that," I would say. "Yes," you would answer, "but not today. Maybe ... another day." And I would nod. "Another day," I repeated and onto its empty promise, I clung desperately.

But I knew. I'd always known your darkness was too strong to bury the light. But I had hoped ... against all, I had hoped ...

If only someone had told me how dangerous it is to love someone, not for who they are, but who you know they could be.

If only you could've seen the soul I saw hidden in you. If only you had known that the person you killed when you pulled the trigger wasn't only who you were—the version of you that you hated—but also everything you could've been ... should've been—the version of you that I loved.

And now I am left wondering what it is that *we* could've been, and who I am left now to be ... alone.

Before I can stop myself, I pluck the flower and lay it on the top of your headstone. If you couldn't finish blooming before death stole you away, then I suppose neither should this flower.

A hollow ache forms inside of me. Is this the same ache you felt all those long, slow days we spent chasing empty dreams under our shady oak? Is this the darkness that consumed your soul when the music wouldn't escape and the tears wouldn't stop? The thought drags itself through my heavy heart, and something else grows inside of me—something almost like a comfort.

Maybe now you are free. Maybe life itself is what tainted your soul. Maybe now in death you are finally at liberty to be what you were meant to. Or maybe my overwhelming love simply has nowhere else to go and is trying to romanticize this dismal reality I'm left in.

I stand from your grave and take one last look at the flower. The wind blows softly, like the way you would breathe whispers and dark secrets in my ear. The sun has begun to turn everything gold again. Blue petals, not quite yet bloomed, catch the majestic honey of the light and once more, as if you're saying goodbye. I'm drowning in your eyes.

"JUST FRIENDS"
Jenni Sauer

"**Just friends don't** look at each other that way
Like they hung the stars in the sky
Or like they're your entire world"

Do you not see your friends
As elegant ethereal beings?
With magic in their fingertips
Stardust on their tongues
Beauty etched into their features
And their souls
Hanging on their every word
Waiting breathless with anticipation
At what they will accomplish next?

"Just friends don't look at each other that way"
Maybe you deserve better friends who do

ACKNOWLEDGEMENTS

Above all else, I must thank the authors whose incredibly beautiful words have built this anthology from the ground up. It is their stories and their dreams of being published in this collection that made it possible. Unconventional Love is an incredible gathering of poetry and short stories that is both comforting and insightful because of them and I glow with pride every time I think of it. Thank you, authors, for opening your hearts and pouring them onto the page for our readers. Never could be possible without you!

Nathaniel Luscombe played a massive role in this anthology from reading and weeding out submissions to edits and marketing. It's been incredibly fun to create an anthology with the anthology king himself and I couldn't be more grateful for all of his excitement and support.

Time has since wiped the name of the author from memory, but I have a special thanks to give to an author who once submitted a beautiful short story to Aphotic Love back in 2022. Their story was about a mother and daughter (and as such didn't fit the theme of said romance anthology), but it was that story that inspired me to create this collection to explore not just romantic love, but also platonic and familial.

My mother has also played an important role in the inspiration of this anthology. She's taught me so many different ways to love and always encouraged me to find my own meaning of love outside of traditional norms. It's for her that I created this collection to showcase all the beautiful ways humans can love each other.

And thank you, reader, as always, for giving this book a chance. I hope it held your heart in soft and gentle ways and gave you the courage to find and experience your own kind of Unconventional Love.

—Effie Joe Stock

Authors

Effie Joe Stock

Effie Joe Stock is the author of The Shadows of Light series, creator of the world Rasa, and head of Dragon Bone Publishing. When she's not slaving away in front of her computer, you can find her playing music, studying psychology, theology, or philosophy, playing fantasy RPG video games, riding motorcycles, or hanging out with her farm animals. Her publishing journey only just beginning, Stock looks forward to the release of the rest of her fantasy series along with other Dragon Bone titles.

Instagram: @effie.joe.stock.author
Website: www.effiejoestock@outlook.com
YouTube: Effie Joe Stock

Nathaniel Luscombe

Nathaniel Luscombe is an author and publisher from Ontario, Canada. He's known for his existential writing, mashups of speculative genres, and making everything cozy (even horror). He has published *Moon Soul*, *Human Scars on Planet Skin*, and *When One World Ends, Another Begins*, as well as several anthologies. When he's not writing, he's busy co-running Dragon Bone Publishing and Dragon Heart Press.

Instagram: @nathaniel.luscombe

Abigail Hawthorne

Abigail Hawthorne can usually be found obsessively studying, organizing, reading, writing, cleaning, and people-watching. As a first responder, psychology geek, slight conspiracy theorist, and all-around nerd, she powers her tales with pieces pulled from the broken world around her. And the best part of all? Beneath all the brokenness is a little bit of beauty, just waiting to be revealed. Find her on

Instagram @abigail.hawthorne.author

Abrigail Julian

Abrigail Julian is an author and musician with a passion for truth and teaching. She has been writing Christian fiction and nonfiction for as long as she can remember, and enjoys writing about Christian characters with real-world struggles. When she isn't writing, Abby can typically be found playing cello, teaching music, or spending time in her garden.

Aisling Revell

Aisling Revell knew at thirteen that she would never love anything as much as telling stories. She has had work published in her college's literary journal, and hopes to publish the novels she's working on in the future. When she isn't writing she loves to read, spend time outdoors, and snuggle with her cat, Gracie.

Ava Lauren Grayson

With a background in fashion and costume design, Grayson has a youthful retro flair to her visual art, photography, and creative direction. All of her work promotes female strength, power, and boldness. Grayson is passionate about blending fantasy with historical comedy, writing kick-butt female heroines, and making you enjoy tragic romances. If she's not writing or directing, you can probably find her rewatching Lord of the Rings, getting a tattoo, or feeding her cat.

Instagram: @avalaurengrayson

Bethany H. Watson

Bethany H. Watson is a young writer and poet from Southern California. She draws poetic inspiration from song lyrics, classical mythology, and the *sehnsucht* infused in a warm breeze. You can follow her on Instagram at @bethantree_writes and find more of her poetry and musings on life at surfacingpurpose.substack.com.

Brett Salter

Hey there! My name is Brett Salter, and I write dragon novels!!! My background in writing stems mostly from the inspiration I found as a kid when I read Fantasy and Sci-Fi books. These include The Chronicles of Narnia, The Xanth Novels, The Time Quintet, The Lord of the Rings Trilogy, and everything from Shakespeare to Dr. Seuss. In my formative years, I joined several punk rock bands and wrote songs, poetry, and short stories aplenty. As an adult (?) I took on a dare and wrote the first book in my Talisman Series. I loved the feeling it gave me and the idea of inspiring others so much that I kept writing until I had an entire series.

@Talismanbrett

Cassandra Hamm

Cassandra Hamm is an art collector, jigsaw puzzler, and cat lady who spends most of her time lost in another realm. Her award-winning work appears in various anthologies such as *A Sky of Tragic Moons* and *Aphotic Love*, and she served as editor-in-chief for the charity anthology *The Sun Still Rises*. A mental health advocate with a passion for social justice, she writes about shattered girls finding their way in the world.

Charleigh Frederick

Charleigh Frederick is an author from Duluth, Minnesota, whose works blur the line between good and evil. She is known for her novels *DEMON SCOUT* and *RULE 25: DON'T FALL FOR THE TARGET*. She has a BFA from Pratt Institute. Find her online @ author_charleighfred

Darby S. Fisher

Darby S. Fisher is a passionate writer living in South-East Georgia. Growing up, her family shared their love of everything magical and fantasy driven. In her work, she often explores emotions and expectations with her other-worldly characters. With three self-published novels under her belt, she has plans for more books of varying genres in the coming years.

Honora Quinn

Honora Quinn is a student at Mount Holyoke College in Western Massachusetts where she is pursuing her B.A. in English and Classical Studies. Outside of school Quinn is the host and producer of On The Shelf with Honora Quinn, a podcast where she interviews authors every week while asking the hard-hitting questions... like what kind of plate they are.

Jacob Kelley

My name is jacob kelley, inspiring writer and poet. I seek to become a full time fantasy author and weave many tales of sword and magic and tell my bardic tales to the world.

Jenni Sauer

Jenni Sauer writes fairy tale retellings for soft, angry hearts, passionate about people seeing themselves in stories about messy, broken people who get to heal.

When not writing, she spends her time hyping up herself and everyone around her, overanalyzing her favorite stories, and drinking copious amounts of tea. If you're looking for her, she's probably bent over her laptop plotting treason—er, her latest story idea—or procrastinating on that by making another playlist or cute aesthetic.

If you'd like to connect with her, you can find her on Instagram @IvoryPalacePrincess

Jessica Erdmann

Jessica Erdmann is the real name of a German. With her master's degree in materials and nano-chemistry, she finances her book collection, her cosplays and her motorbike. In addition to her day job, she also studies literature part-time, as her hobby is collecting university degrees and she likes to never be at peace any second of her life. For a perfect time-out she likes to go mosh-pitting to emo guitar riffs on the weekend. Legend says, she is also a writer and has already published several short stories and poems in various collections. Jessica hopes to expand her lore by publishing a novel in the near future. The keeper of all updates shall be her Instagram: @book.of.jess

Jess Autiero

Jess is an Italian author situated in Sweden. When they're not working as a teacher, they're often found daydreaming, drinking an unhealthy dose of tea, and annoying their cats for some love. They've self-published a supernatural novella in May 2023, *Away from Grace*, a short story, *The Choice*, and are now working on two fantasy novels. You can follow their writing journey on Instagram @autierowrites.

Judy Liu

Inspired by her love of sci-fi, old Taiwanese dramas, and ridiculous anime, Judy scribbles mini-stories wherever she can (and subsequently forgets them!). She resides in Texas with her pup and had spent some time living in rural Japan before working in the legal and compliance sphere. With her debut novel *The Vending Portal* and her other writing, Liu hopes to meaningfully add to Asian American literature to further enrich the YA genre. You can follow her journey on Instagram @judyliu_author.

Outside of work and writing, Judy enjoys dancing with her teammates and friends, exploring unknown spots or cities, and making nonsense sounds to her sister.

June Elliott

June Elliott hails from the deep cold North. She loves breathing frost and fire into emotions with her poetry. She especially enjoys poetry and novels that are particularly atmospheric.

Kelly Hellmuth

Kelly Hellmuth loves to tell compelling stories to kids of all ages. She originally began crafting worlds for her four children and is currently working on a hopeful dystopian novel. She has been published in Havok and Twenty Hills anthologies with more to come. More of Kelly's writing can be found on Instagram at @khelmetauthor, where she regularly writes flash fiction, bookish content, and poetry with a wonderful cottage full of creative souls. When Kelly isn't writing, she teaches high school literature and Latin and dabbles in a variety of artistic pursuits.

K. R. Yauger

K. R. Yauger is a writer and reader of fantasy, sci-fi, and steampunk. She loves iced coffee, Star Wars, Star Trek, history, and mythology. She believes stories are an extension of the soul and her stories reflect hope and love amid darkness. She's an avid rocker and drummer. She lives in the rolling hills of Appalachia with her husband and stepson. Instagram: @k.r.yauger

Katie Fitzgerald

Katie Fitzgerald writes short stories in a variety of genres, from humor to mystery to contemporary to kissing-only romance. A former librarian married to a librarian, she is a voracious reader and listener of audiobooks and the careful curator of a large home library of children's books. She loves bookish tee shirts, Flannery O'Connor, song lyric jokes, and Little Free Libraries. Katie grew up in a small town in New York's Hudson Valley, but now lives in the Maryland suburbs with her husband and five kids.

Kara Siert

Kara Siert is a Chinese-American author who began crafting stories at the age of four, although they were rather nonsensical. She is passionate about using fantasy to explore themes of mental health, disabilities, and platonic relationships ... but that's assuming she's actually writing and not making mood boards, playlists or talking to her friends on Discord. Kara's work also appears in Artifice & Access, and she resides in the Appalachian mountains with her beloved husband and son.

Katherine Kempf

Katherine Kempf is a US expat with her Bachelors in Anthropology and Masters in Journalism from University, City London, both of which seep their way into her stories more than a little bit. Originally from Virginia, she now calls Germany home, which has fueled her love for multicultural stories even more. Katherine is a chronic mood reader and a hiker who always packs the most (best) snacks.

Her current project is The Mimameid Trilogy, the first of which, The Mimameid Solution, released in 2023.

Follow her on Instagram @katherinekempfwrites or sign up for her newsletter at www.katherinekempfbooks.com

Kit Aldridge

Kit Aldridge, author of *Unraveled: Book One of the Stormbringer Saga*, is currently based in Dallas, TX—though she finds her home among worlds built from restless imagination. She graduated from Texas Tech University with a Bachelor of Arts in English and Creative Writing. Inspired by a lifelong love of fantasy and characters that blur the line between good and evil, her passion for the written word only continues to grow as she does. To keep up with her writing endeavors, check out her website at www.authorkitaldridge.com or follow her Instagram @authorkitaldridge.

Lexie Kauffman

Lexie Kauffman is an undergraduate student at Susquehanna University with majors in Creative Writing and Publishing & Editing. She is the Creative Works Editor of Ginkgo Magazine and a member of Sigma Tau Delta, the international English honor society. She started reading and writing before she entered kindergarten, and she has no plans to stop. Her first stories were written on copier paper with crayons and Crayola markers. While those handwritten works are not available to the public, you can find her current work in *Rivercraft*, *Ginkgo Magazine*, *The Bluebird Word*, and more. You can follow her writing journey on Instagram @ lexie.kauffman or follow her author page on Amazon.

Lorelei R. Jensen

From a young age, Lorelei R. Jensen has adored books. It wasn't uncommon for her to read way past her bedtime with a flashlight. Her love of books has only grown since then. Currently, she lives in the hot desert of Arizona as she works hard on completing her degrees in English and East Asian Studies. Some of her other works can be found in the Aphotic Love anthology compiled by Effie Joe Stock, Here Lies Wanderland compiled by Alex Silvius, and her debut novel and the first book of the Neforian Abyss series, Deadly Trials.

Marion Cedar

Marion always wanted to be a writer. At thirteen, she decided that she wanted to be a published author. While working on her books, she got into poetry. When she isn't writing, you can find her practicing ballroom dancing, painting, or riding her dirt bike.

Michaela Bush

Michaela Bush is a Christian author, editor, and entrepreneur. She graduated Magna Cum Laude in 2019 from Clarion University of Pennsylvania, where she earned a B.A. in English and a minor in Psychology. She has enjoyed writing from an early age, and mostly writes Christian fantasy and romance. When she isn't working or creating her next story, she enjoys spending time with her family, horseback riding, playing violin, and spending time at church. Follow her @tangledupinwriting.

Michelle Bulsiewicz

Michelle Bulsiewicz has a degree in journalism and previously worked as an arts and entertainment editor for a local newspaper. She is also a certified yoga instructor, and a lover of tea, puzzles, and the beach. She lives in Southern California with her husband, two sons, and their cat and dog. Find her on Instagram at @michellebulsiebooks.

Myka Silber

Myka Silber grew up surrounded by the forests, mountains, and ocean of the Pacific Northwest. They now live in Ontario, Canada, with a mercurial cat and a bean of a dog. Myka holds both a BA and an MA in International Relations. They have previously published a short story collection and a novel, and you can follow them on Instagram @myka.silber.

R.C. Lloyd

R.C. Lloyd is the author of Chronic Defiance who writes with the hope that people will feel seen in her words. She's currently working on multiple speculative fiction books, but somehow her poetry fought its way onto the page. No small feat with all those characters battling for her attention.

Rhyker Dye

Rhyker, a queer writer from the Arkansas River Valley, began writing as an academic with a focus on historical research. Building on the technical skills honed as a non-fiction editor and researcher, he found a love for fiction and poetry writing. Most Saturday mornings, Rhyker can be found haunting the local coffee shops as he writes best alongside indie albums and whispered gossip.

Seren J.H. Wolfe

Seren J.H. Wolfe is an indie author, award-winning poet, and visual artist hailing from beautiful British Columbia, where she lives with her husband and two bunnies. A writer for over twenty years, Seren has found inspiration in music, mythology and folklore, loved ones, and her own path as a witch, all of which inspired her current books: *What The Sea Has Wrought*, *Veins of Pluto*, and *From The Throat of the Eldest Daughter*. When she isn't writing, Seren enjoys video gaming, playing D&D, creating art, curating music playlists, and enjoying the outdoors.

Follow her on Instagram and Threads @thebalefulprimal or sign up for her newsletter at https://thebalefulprimal.ca/

Tristan Durant

Tristan Durant grew up in a world where secrets were a currency he learned to earn, barter, and gamble with ease. From a young age poetry became a safe haven for the emotions he was never taught to process or express, an outlet for conversations previously had only with his bedroom ceiling or his therapist. He is the author of An Infinite Measure of Metaphors.

Continue the Experimental Exploration of Love Through Unconventional Love's Sister Anthology,

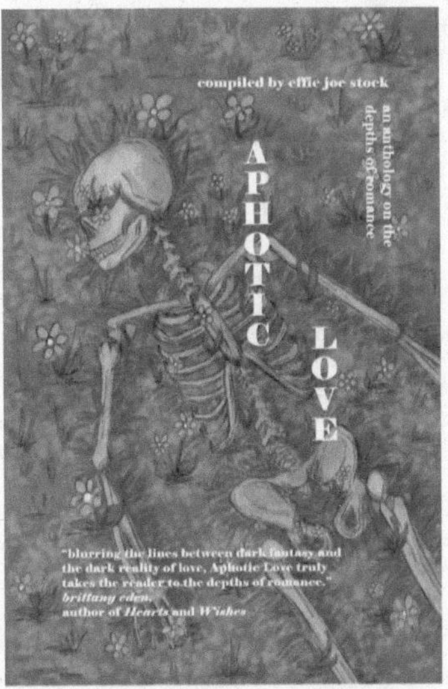

APHOTIC LOVE

An Anthology on the Depths of Romance

Love is often depicted as light, joyful, fun, exciting, or carefree. But a darker side to love lurks under the surface—a frightening, desperate, tragic side.

From the love of gods and goddesses, to mortals who fell in love with death. From pure sweet romance gone astray, to villains who loved the hero. An actress no longer acting she's in love, a phoenix whose lover gives everything to be with her reborn, a lonely queen whose touch turns loved ones to ice, a space station caught between the pain of two lovers.

Dare to dive deep into this raw, emotional collection of short stories, prose, and poems which strives to expose the lightless side of tragedy, heartbreak, desperation, and love.